PRAISE

Few stories are as fulfilling to the soul as this one. Zoey Wheeler delivers a powerful portrayal of the struggles faced by teenage athletes and the love that rises from competition. The enemies-to-lovers trope has never been more emotionally driven—or so beautifully crafted.
Kailey Holbrook | Author, *Return of the Keepers*

Told with sharp emotion and cinematically, Zoey captures the intensity of trauma, ambition, and healing with surprising maturity for a debut author. Powerful, honest, and deeply human.
MJay Ally | reviewer

The emotional intelligence in this book floored me. It's about racing, yes—but more about daring to be seen.
Josephine Hernandez | aspiring author

WHY THEY RUN

ZOEY WHEELER

DEDICATION

To my 8th-grade English teacher, Mrs. Randall,

I wouldn't have started writing without you

You gave me the confidence to find myself and my love
for storytelling

You will always be my Miss Trefusis

This book contains depictions of domestic violence and abuse. Some scenes may be distressing or triggering. Please prioritize your well-being while reading.

You are not alone. If you or someone you know is in danger or experiencing abuse, help is available:

National Domestic Violence Hotline
Call or text **988** or **1-800-799-7233**, or chat online at thehotline.org.

1

JASON

If I knew he was drunk, I would've never come home. Typical, yes, it's like a climber saying 'if that rock were loose I would've never grabbed onto it!' But in all honesty, that's what Jason thought. Yet despite that, he stood in the doorway, greeted by the familiar smell of alcohol and the eucalyptus candle his mom burned to hide it. He should've backed out of the house, hopped on his skateboard and ridden off to a friend's house to stay the night instead. Did he do any of this? No, instead, Jason gingerly closed the door behind him and crept into the kitchen. As he stepped over the bottles and cans strewn about the house, he patted himself on the back for his stealthiness. The way he tiptoed across floorboards and made his way from the kitchen to the living room made him feel like he was in *The Quiet Place* or something.

Sure, Jason thought. *I think I could make a good Lee Abbott.*

He continued his trek through the house to his room. He was feeling pretty good about himself when a particularly worn board decided to betray him and let out an eerie scream from underneath his feet. Jason froze. He stayed still, not daring to move or breathe. *5–10–15–20.* After twenty seconds, Jason allowed himself to move again, this time keeping an eye on the old wooden floors.

The entrance led straight into the kitchen. It was small, but if only one person was cooking, it was pretty sizable. Across from the kitchen sat the dining room. Not a fancy only-eat-in-on-holidays kind of space, just the simplest meaning of the area. A large rectangular wooden table surrounded by the same style of wooden chairs, lit by an old fixture in the ceiling. The same place that Jason had set the table since he could count forks. Around the corner of the dining room was a hallway. Jason felt his stomach drop at the sight. A narrow walkway with two doors on one side, and two doors on the other, which seemed to surround a final door at the end of the hall. There was no light in this hallway, but there usually wasn't a need for one, as sunlight or light from another room usually provided enough brightness to see. Jason ran his fingers down the corner of the wall, grimacing at the goosebumps on his arms. Ignoring the feeling of nausea that ate at him, Jason turned the corner and started down the hall. He passed the first door without an issue, holding his breath the whole time. The rough floor scratched at his socks and seemed to be asking him to go no further. He moved through the hall swiftly, successfully moving past the second door, and to the end of the hallway. Gripping the copper handle, Jason cautiously pushed the door open, removing the one barrier that separated him from his sanctuary. His room was the only place in Jason's house that actually meant home to him. He felt so relieved at his seemingly successful mission that he almost didn't hear it.

"Jason, get your ass in here this damn minute!" A scratchy voice slurred.

The feeling Jason got next was something that couldn't be described as anything other than pure dread. A knot instantly formed in his stomach, and his limbs felt like they'd suddenly been draped in ankle weights as he trudged towards the second door, which was opened just a crack. Light flooded through the slit, painting a thin line of light. Jason gathered his bearings and trudged in the direction of the voice, cursing himself for being too loud. He was so close. Jason peered through the crack into the room from which the voice had come. Inside sat a large, old mahogany desk, with a matching set of library shelves for storage. Storage for what, Jason didn't know, because there certainly wasn't any reading going on in there. At the desk stood a black leather swivel chair, like the kind in offices. Sprawled in it sat an older man with disgusting gray stubble, a beer belly, and a thin white scar making its way down his cheek. His face was contorted with anger and irritation. He seemed to want Jason in the room but was simultaneously disgusted by his presence.

Jason opened his mouth to speak, but cursed his scratchy voice. He cleared his throat before trying again.

"What, Dad?"

Jason's dad looked up and saw his son standing in the doorway.

"Did I say stand in the door there like an idiot? No, I said, get your ass in here!"

Jason had no choice but to comply, so he stepped into the room, and instantly the air got cooler as if a ghost had just flown by. "OK, now what?" he asked.

The man stood up from his chair angrily, but swayed a little. "Did you get my Miller Lite from the store this morning?" he asked. "I left you money on the counter and told your mom to tell you. I swear if that dingbat didn't ask you—"

Jason felt himself tense up the way he did every time his dad said something bad about his mother. *She hadn't asked me,* he realized. *Shit.*

"Er, yeah, she asked me, I just. . . forgot." The man raised an eyebrow, questioning the simplicity of his excuse, so Jason decided to add on. "Practice ran late today, so I had to come home. I didn't have time."

"And why the hell did you not buy it on the way home?" He growled.

Jason was getting irritated. "It's a two-mile walk from the school, Dad. If you wanted me to go to practice and then get your beer, I wouldn't have made curfew, and then you'd be mad anyway."

Jason hated the number of times he'd walked the far distance just to supply his dad's alcohol supply. Beer was a vile thing. Jason made a promise to himself that even after he turned 21, he would never drink it. Just the smell of it made his stomach churn with disgust. Not for the drink, but disgust for his father.

Who, it seemed, was getting pretty ticked off at Jason's argument. He stepped towards his son and, without warning, struck him across the face. Jason staggered back in shock. His heart stopped, and he froze as the memory of his strike rang against his cheek. His dad took advantage of this pause and grabbed the collar of Jason's shirt, pulling him forward. Jason had to physically stop himself from gagging at the rancid smell of alcohol and poor hygiene coming from his dad. He held his breath as his father growled in his ear.

"I don't give a damn about how far you have to walk; you don't disobey me. You don't wanna miss curfew? Walk faster. And screw practice, because the next time you don't show up here with it, you're gonna get a lot more than that. Here's what I'm gonna do. I'm gonna give you an hour to get the beer, right now, my buddy's waiting outside the store, you just give him the money and he'll buy the stuff. Do it or I will beat the shit out of you, Jason."

He let go of Jason with a shove and threw himself back down in the leather chair. Jason started back towards the doorway, hands shaking. His heart burned with hatred so strong, like a bonfire, but he couldn't do anything about it. He couldn't put it out, so it just burned inside of him for eternity. Not if he wanted to jeopardize himself and his mom, and he would never do anything to hurt his mom. Even if that meant being forced to calm the waves of anger that flared to life inside him. Even if that meant living with his dad and living with Brian. He looked up and saw that his dad was asleep now, passed out in the armchair. He stepped into the room, so he stood over Brian, facing him. Jason couldn't help the tears that filled his eyes as he stared at this man. He could live without him. He could get a second job, or live with a friend, or anything but this. Jason turned his back on Brian and walked out of the room, shutting the door behind him. As his shoes slipped on, the tears fell out of his eyes, and he numbly reached for the money left out on the counter. Above the kitchen cabinets, in a glass case, was a rifle that his dad kept for 'safety reasons.' Jason eyed it anxiously. He thought about Brian in the other room. His father. He was asleep, alone, defenseless. He turned back to the gun and stared for what he thought to be at least two minutes. It was shiny and sleek. Jason knew where he kept the bullets— in the drawer below where they kept their utensils. He also knew that Brian never had time for stupid shit like that, and so the gun was already loaded. It was loaded. Ready for use, itching to be fired. And his dad sat in the other room. What if? No. Jason snapped out of the daze, grabbed his bag, and headed out the door, typing 'BevMo' into his Google Maps.

2
SCARLETT

Scarlett Artega stood on the number 4 lane on the wide, orange track, the fastest lane for the fastest runner. She tugged her dirty blonde hair tighter in its ponytail and scanned her surroundings. She would be running with seven other people, two from her own school, New Wellis, three from the all-girls academy, St. Coleman's, and two from Camden High. Scarlett already knew she could outrun any girl from her own school, so she pushed that thought out of her head. Now it was just the private school snobs and the Camden girls. She knew Camden—had run with them and trained with them. They weren't contenders; they only had one good sprinter, Kacey Tillman. Scarlett would watch out for her. The private school girls were new to her. Scarlett didn't know how they ran. She didn't like not knowing. She wanted records, times, anything she could get from these girls, but so far, all she knew was that they were good enough to compete against her. That's all she needed to know to motivate her.

That's only four girls out of seven runners. Four girls that she could possibly be beaten by, she only needed to outrun four girls. *Hell yeah, I can do that.* A loud screech blared in the distance, and a short, chubby man blew a large silver whistle in his mouth. His face was red from blowing so hard to create this noise, but he looked satisfied with himself.

Once he had the attention o f the crowd, he took out a comically large megaphone and began speaking into it with a shrill voice.

"Girls' 200m sprint is about to begin, please find your seats and stay seated during the race. In lane 1, we have Charlotte Williams from Camden High, lane 2, Audrey Pike from St. Coleman's, lane 3, Kacey Tillman from Camden High, lane 4, Scarlett Artega from New Wellis, lane 5, Meghan Truth from New Wellis, lane 6, Peyton Randall from St. Coleman's, lane 7, Zoe Boyer from New Wellis, and lane 8, Trudy Hill from St. Coleman's. Ladies, line up in your lanes, and we will begin in just a moment." He gasped, clearly winded from listing every girl.

Scarlett brought her left arm over her shoulder and stretched, trying to appear as intimidating as possible. She turned her head and saw her parents in the bleachers, cheering with dark green face paint smeared on their cheeks. She smiled and waved. Her mother blew her a kiss, as her dad did a terrible fake running rendition with his fingers. Scarlett couldn't help but laugh, which would make her appear weaker. She couldn't have that, so she turned away from them and instead looked at her coach. He was a tall, bulky man, and almost everyone in the school was afraid of him. They nicknamed him 'Hulk' because everyone thought he looked like a more muscular Fred Tatasciore. Scarlett raised her eyebrows in a 'what's the strategy?' kind of way. He took his fingers and pointed them to his eyes, and then at the finish line.

"Run like Hell," he mouthed to her.

She chuckled at the Pink Floyd reference, but she understood what he meant. Run fast, don't think about anything else, and keep your eyes on the finish line. Scarlett took a deep breath and stared ahead into the distance. She could already see the finish; to the right stood a podium, and she thought about standing there. She wanted to stand there, taking in the world from a few feet higher. *So I will,* she thought.

"OK, girls, we're all ready here." The short referee announced. Scarlett stiffened and hardened her face to her competition expression. Determined, poker face, prepared, greedy.

"On your marks." She slid her foot back into the starting blocks. And put her fingers out in front of her on the hot, synthetic rubber.

"Set." Scarlett and the seven other girls took their final positions, which consisted of their asses sticking straight up like in downward dog. *I'll bet a man came up with that one,* Scarlett thought. The next few seconds were pure anxiousness, excitement, and agony waiting for the gunshot. The referee took out a tiny gun and fired one shot into the air.

'BANG'. Scarlett took off like a rocket. She sprinted as fast as she could, past the parents in the bleachers, past the girls from New Wellis and St. Coleman's, and past all of the Camden girls. Well, except for Kacey Tillman. She ran not more than two inches in front of Scarlett, her platinum blonde ponytail swinging back and forth rhythmically like a grandfather clock pendulum. Scarlett pushed even harder and knew that she only had a few seconds to pass her or it was all over. She pushed harder and gave everything she had into her speed. Her eyes were trained on the finish line just like the coach had told her, and she had one thing on her mind—winning. Being on that podium, but she didn't want to be on that podium unless she was first. *How do you get first, Artega?* Her coach's voice rang in her ears. *You run like hell.* Scarlett sped past Kacey like a bullet train and took a three-foot lead as she neared the finish. One last push of adrenaline sent her over the line, and a loud cheer erupted from the sidelines, where the rest of her teammates were sitting.

"And in first place, from New Wellis, Scarlett Artega with a time of 23.45 seconds!" Scarlett slowed to a stop and put her hands on her head to let more air in her lungs. She beamed with joy and saw that same joy in her father's face when she looked up into the stands. He grinned down at her, clapping his hands and shouting like a maniac. Her mother smiled and nodded at her approvingly. Someone handed her a water bottle, and Scarlett thanked them before effectively draining the entire thing. Kacey Tillman ended up taking second, followed by Audrey Pike, Meghan Truth, Peyton Randall, Zoe Boyer, Charlotte Williams, and lastly, Trudy Hill.

Scarlett pulled Meghan and Zoe into a hug and congratulated them on their race. She may have beaten them, but her team was the most important thing in the world to her, and she'd be proud of them no matter what. She walked over to coach 'Hulk' Allen and felt an elated sense of relief when he smiled at her. No matter how many races she won, having her coach's approval would always make the victory sweeter.

"Great race today, Artega. You'll make a new record if you keep this up!" This took Scarlett by surprise.

"Seriously?"

"Yup, the record in our district, and the country for girls 200m is 22.11 seconds. You could beat that, Artega."

"Wow." She thought about having a record added to her list of accomplishments. Even better, she added to her college applications. That would be something. "Thanks, coach. Do we have any more events today?" Coach Allen took a look at his clipboard, which never seemed to leave his grip.

"Nope, I think that's it for today. Now, you go on that podium and when you get on the first-place stand, give the Camden coach a stink eye for me." He winked. Scarlett smiled, deviously.

"Gladly." She loved feeding the rivalry that New Wellis and Camden had, especially between the coaches. Last year, the Camden team beat New Wellis at the finals, and Coach Allen had vowed to beat them in every race this year. So far, they had. And with every race, the victory felt just as good. Scarlett made her way to the podium, where the other two girls were standing. Kacey turned to her with a glare. She held out her hand for a shake. *Why the hell is this girl trying to shake my hand,* Scarlett thought. Then she saw the camera pointed at the two of them and realized Kacey was just 'putting on a show' for them. She hesitantly gripped Kacey's hand and repressed a wince as Kacey virtually crushed her hand in a vice grip. The second the picture was taken, Scarlett ripped her hand away and smiled sweetly at her. The blonde snapped and stormed away before even receiving her medal. The short ref announced that the school board would be handing out medals, and that they had the great honor of congratulating the students and all that. Scarlett found this funny. It was the one exciting thing board members got to do, though, so she let them feel proud of it. *'Here, you want to feel special? How about putting five-dollar medals on a bunch of sweaty teenagers?'* She thought it was ridiculous, but that didn't keep her from bowing when a random old dude placed the award over her neck, and thanking him as he turned away. Scarlett faced a camera facing towards her and smiled. She felt good, but not as good as she thought she would. Before the race, she wanted nothing more than to be in the limelight, but now, she kind of just wanted to go home. Be away from the people, the crowds. She took a few more pictures and stepped down from the podium before finding her coach.

"Coach Allen, do you need me for anything else?" That was her way of asking, 'Can I leave?'

"Nope, you're good to go, Artega. Congratulations again." She nodded her thanks and turned to the exit of the track, already picturing the warm shower waiting for her.

3
JASON

Jason blinked open his eyes and then squeezed them shut again at the brightness of the sunlight seeping in through his window. His phone alarm blared a tune that sounded cheerful to everyone who didn't have to wake up to it. He reached for his phone, which was charging next to him. It read 6:45 a.m. Jason groaned and stretched out like a cat. He swung his legs over the side of the bed before standing. He glanced around his room. It wasn't much, and wasn't very extravagant. A twin bed with blue bed sheets sat in the corner of the room under his window. Next to it was a small wooden nightstand with a lamp and a half-eaten box of M&Ms on top. On the other wall, there was a desk that he'd painted a dark gray and a matching gray chair. On the wall by the door, there was a small closet where he kept his clothes and shoes, and a round, navy blue carpet was spread in the center of the floor. Jason loved his room. He lived there, studied there, and spent most of his time there. Well, when he had to be at home. He tried to be out of the house as much as he could, but with a 10:00 curfew, he had to go home eventually. On his walls were posters. So many posters of various bands and people. He had taped pictures of himself and his friends on the wall, as well as the track team. One of his favorites was the group track photo they had taken last year. It was displayed proudly above his headboard like a valuable painting. He was the captain of the varsity track team, having won several championships and national-level competitions.

But as Jason stared at the picture, he remembered how his smile was fake. He hadn't been happy that day. No, Brian was angry that day, and he made sure no one else around him could be happy either. Jason walked to his closet and pulled out his Safeway uniform. It was Saturday, which meant it was a work day. Jason didn't have much free time, but what free time he did have, he used to 'provide for the family,' as Brian called it. But to be honest, anything Jason could do to make things easier for his mom, he would. Even if that meant helping his dad, too. He slipped on his shoes before heading to the bathroom to brush his teeth. He splashed cold water on his face and combed his hair. He stared at himself in the mirror for a while. He wouldn't say he was attractive, though he knew others thought he was. He was tall, tan, and brown-haired, and Jason supposed that's all girls needed to like someone. His eyes were a dark brown, but his mom said that they looked golden in the sunlight. Jason's hair fell down his forehead in messy curls, and his nose was sprinkled with freckles. He looked away from the mirror and took a deep breath before grabbing his things and heading out the door to work. As he drove, Jason thought about his life. He made money.

Not a lot of money, hell, he made just about minimum wage, but money is money. And he was sure he could afford a half-decent apartment for him and his mom. No one knew, but Jason had been saving up. Every week, he took part of his wage and set it aside, in hopes that he could live somewhere nicer, away from Brian. He loved his mother so very much, but Jason had no idea how she could stand to live with him. He told her to get divorced hundreds of times, but she said they just couldn't afford a place to live without his share of the money. He was a dick. But he was a dick who paid the bills. Jason just wished his mother would remarry, but Brian had promised that if she divorced him, he would sue them and do everything in his power to make sure they got nothing— which, to be honest, is probably the only smart thing he's ever done, considering he could afford an actual lawyer and not one of those public defenders you get assigned to the morning of the trial.

Jason also wondered how the hell no one from his office had reported his drinking habits to HR, but he supposed Brian must have some sense of a brain to keep his work and home life separate. But now Jason was close. He was making some money, and saving some money, and if he could do anything, he could at least get his mom an apartment before he went to college. College. That's another thing. College was expensive these days, easily costing thirty thousand. The Everetts weren't poor, but they couldn't just dish out thirty thousand dollars on college. *So, I'll just have to get a scholarship, then,* Jason thought. He'd already applied for at least ten different scholarship programs, all for track. If he could convince some college that he could improve their track team, and get a full or even half-ride scholarship, that would change his life. But the one he needed. The one that mattered was New Wellis's Harley Mavera athletics scholarship. Twenty thousand dollars is given to the most outstanding athlete in each department. This wasn't something he could pass up; this was a real, life-changing thing that no other schools in his district had. This was his way out. *And possibly my downfall.* He took a shaky breath. Set his jaw in a seal of finality. *Then that's it. I'll work hard, set aside the money, and get my scholarship.* Jason pulled into the Safeway parking lot and parked in an employee-only spot.

As he opened the car door, he realized that he was still tense from sneaking out earlier in the morning. He forced himself to relax his shoulders and take a deep breath. His job wasn't bad per se, just not exactly the most thrilling thing to do. He worked weekends 8:00 a.m.-3:00 p.m., and weekdays when he could. His boss, Pete, was kind. Jason really looked up to him in that way. He helped Jason out by giving him raises and bonuses when he could. But what Jason liked the most about him was the advice he gave. He always had something to teach Jason, and even though he scored a low-paying grocery store job, he seemed to know a lot about life, about noticing the little things and building relationships. He was the one who taught Jason to notice the little ticks about people, their tells.

"See that young girl in the flower apron?" He would say, and Jason would always crack a smile when he knew Pete was about to drop some lore, some gossip about the people in his town.

"I see her." Pete would hum, squint his eyes and smile his devious smile.

"Came in last week, bought a pregnancy test and a jar of pickles. Look what she's got now." Jason strained his eyes to see the piles of books and magazines in her cart, all with a similar theme: 'Infants, how to raise them and do a good job of it.' Jason scoffed. "Congratulations, Juno." He would mumble. He showed Jason how to see past people's eyes. How to see past what they wore and ignore how they wanted you to perceive them, instead focusing on perceiving them as you see them. Jason saved himself from a lot of bad influences that way. He headed in through the employee entrance and scanned his key card to log his hours. Pete was in there as well, giving orders to a girl who looked a couple of years older than Jason. She was gorgeous with long, red hair and dark eyes. But she looked nervous. Her hands were fidgeting, and she looked like a caged animal. Her name tag said 'Maria'. Pete finished talking to her and turned to Jason.

"Morning, Jason. We have you on restock today if that's alright."

Jason gave a tight smile.

"Sounds great, but I have to leave a little early if that's OK," Jason asked.

"Track meet?"

"Heh, yeah, it's the last chance to qualify for the quarterfinals. Not that I need it." Pete grinned, which made Jason smile in return. He always showed enthusiasm for Jason's sport, and having his support, even if small, really helped.

"No problem, and tell you what, I'll pay you for the whole day, how bout that?" Pete asked. Jason's smile widened.

"That'd be great, Pete, thank you, really."

"Ah, don't thank me, just beat those damn private school boys. They're too snobby for their own good." Jason laughed at the thought of private school kids coming into the grocery store and doing something to make Pete angry with them. People could be irritating, but rarely did anyone get on his bad side.

"I will, promise." Pete gave him a clap on the back, old-bro style.

"That's my boy. Now, get to work. I have your assignments right here." Pete handed Jason a clipboard with different shelves that needed restocking and products that had gone bad that needed to be thrown out.

"Yeah, of course. Hey. . . is that girl new? Never seen her before," Jason asked hesitantly. Pete turned to him with a smile.

"Yeah, just started this morning." Jason's smile grew the tiniest bit, but was quickly squandered.

"Don't bother, Jason, she's older than you and engaged. One of those college sweethearts. Engaged for at least a few years based on the condition of that ring," Pete inquired.

"Maybe she just got engaged and is working here to get a better ring?" Jason guessed, leaning over Pete's shoulder. Pete furrowed his brow, studying the girl further, like he hadn't even thought about that.

"I'm messing with you, Pete, you'll give the poor girl a heart attack if she catches you staring like that." Pete chuckled and gave him a wink. Jason groaned in response. He put his backpack down in the staff room and put in his AirPods, scrolling through the playlists until he found his 'Team hype' playlist from the previous season. He found that it wasn't nearly as unpleasant when you have Arctic Monkeys on in the background.

4

JASON

Jason decided never to do anyone a favor ever again. It was 1:00 p.m., which meant he only had to get through another half-hour of work before he could get off and head to the school for his meet. He'd been planning it out all day. Thinking about his victory, and the looks on those upright private-school kids' faces when he won. He was in a good mood, that wasn't a secret.

Unfortunately, good moods get passed around, and the word spreads. Before lunch, he had three co-workers ask him to help out with their shifts, hoping that his mood would somehow compromise his thinking, and maybe just work out in their favor. Jason would've thought they were delusional, but when it came down to it, doing something kind for another person really wasn't that bad, was it?

Boy was wrong. Currently, Jason sat over the sink in the Safeway bathroom, preparing to clean the toilets. When one of his favorite co-workers, Micheal, had asked him, it hadn't seemed that daunting. Just a few minutes of unsanitary work and he would be finished, and Micheal would be grateful. What he hadn't bothered to mention was the fact that a man had just eaten raw food from the buffet, and vomited all over the floor, turning the already mediocre bathroom into a hazmat zone.

So yeah, Jason's mood tanked. He finished cleaning the sick off the floor and continued his regular bathroom cleaning work with a mop and bucket. Jason nervously checked his watch every couple of minutes just to make sure he wouldn't forget to leave early. It was daunting.

He wanted nothing more than just to make this day end and go to the meet. There, he would feel better. Surrounded by his team and coaches, and doing the thing he loved most—running. Not to mention, the quarterfinals were one step closer to the championship, which is a chance at a scholarship. As the time ticked faster, so did Jason's heart. Until finally, the clock hit 2:15 p.m., Jason almost tripped over a stack of boxes as he rushed to the staff room, swiftly scanning his card, and rushing out to his car. He stepped out onto the concrete, not even bothering to look both ways. Jason was so ready to sprint, ready to beat Camden, ready to make semis.

Suddenly, a hand shot out and grabbed his shoulder, yanking him backward. Jason stumbled, breath catching, and almost tripped, but caught himself. Not a half a second later, a large white Ford sped past, the driver obviously not paying attention to the road. Jason turned to see who had grabbed him when his savior spoke. "Holy shit, Jason? What the hell are you doing, you idiot? You almost died; why would you do that?" *Cross out Savior. More like Satan.* Jason mentally face-palmed. It was Scarlett Artega, the fastest runner on girls' varsity, and the captain, too. Dirty-blonde hair she swore was more blonde than brown (it wasn't), a beauty mark above her left eye, and stormy gray eyes that pinned him with a glare. If anything could make Jason's day any worse, running into Scarlett would do it for him.

"Dunno, I just felt like walking in front of a car, what did you think?" Jason rolled his eyes and wiped the spot on his jacket that Scarlett had grabbed with much more enthusiasm than necessary.

"Don't you have a race anyway, Artega?" Scarlett reached into her bag and pulled out a medal.

First place. *Of course,* Jason thought. "Already did it, and the coach said I could head out. What about you, roadkill, don't you have a race?"

Damn, roadkill? Really? "Yeah, I was going there right now until you grabbed me," Jason retorted. "Which really messed up my *zen,* just so you know, so if I lose this race, I blame you entirely."

Scarlett gestured to the road. "If I didn't, your *'zen"* would be smeared all over the ground. I think what you're trying to say is 'you're welcome', roadkill." "Fine, thanks. Why are you here anyway? Poisoning your family with your desperate cooking again?" Scarlett smiled sweetly and then proceeded to flip him off.

"What I'm doing here is none of your business." He picked up his bag from where he dropped it and slung it over one shoulder. "What I'm doing here is none of your business." Jason mocked in a high-pitched parody of Scarlett's voice. "I really didn't care, Artega. I was just trying to be polite. But the ear plugs are in aisle three. I have a feeling that if your ego gets any bigger, it'll blow up." This earned Jason an elbow to the stomach. He doubled over and coughed, which brought a smile to Scarlett's face.

"Five bucks says you'll trip over the first hurdle," she said and started off towards the open double doors.

"What? Says who?" Jason pouted. He hated it when people bet on him, or more specifically against him.

"Coach Allen. Don't be late, roadkill." She stalked away, and Jason flipped off her back before rushing to his car. The drive from work to New Wellis only took a few minutes, thankfully, but the game day traffic made it worse. Why can't New Wellis just have football games on Fridays like every other school? Jason didn't know, but he did know that if he had to swerve past another jeep with ten drunk cheerleaders stuffed in it, he would scream. He pulled in after what seemed like an eternity and changed into his running clothes. These consisted of black shorts and a green running tank with the school logo in the corner. He also wore his favorite black Adidas trainers. He fitted them with dark green laces to match his jersey. Once changed, Jason jogged to catch up with the rest of his team, who were receiving tips from Coach Allen. A tall, somewhat skinny boy with smooth mocha skin turned to Jason and motioned for him to stand next to him.

"Jason, what the hell were you doing? You were almost late," he whispered so that the coach didn't hear.

"Hey, Marcus. I ran into Scarlett, better-than-everyone Artega at work, and the traffic was terrible," he spoke softly back.

"Really? Traffic, I thought you were a better liar, Jason. Moving on, let's just win this race today. See that kid from Camden over there? With the blonde mullet?" Marcus pointed to a strong-bodied kid with the most uneven haircut Jason had ever seen.

"Yeah, why?"

"That's the same guy from finals last year. He's back, but from what I've heard, he's hardly trained since then. This is our chance, man." The kid's name was Will, and last season he beat Jason by just under half a second. Jason had never forgiven himself, and since then, he had been itching to compete against him again just to get back at Will.

"Hell yeah, and he's in our heat?" Jason asked, the adrenaline already building in his chest. Marcus nodded. The sound of a throat being cleared startled them both. The boys turned to find Coach Allen glaring at them both.

"I sure hope whatever you boys are chatting about won't interfere with today's race. I have you up against William Kravitz." Jason shook his head aggressively.

"No coach, we were just coming up with a strategy. I'm so ready to beat that son of a—"

"He means we're prepared and excited for the win, coach," Marcus quickly interrupted and put a hand over Jason's mouth before he could get them in deeper shit.

"Good. Now get to the line, the race is about to start." The circle of boys dispersed, and Jason started off to the line.

"Hey Everett." Jason turned back around.

"Don't get it in your head like last time. You have a real chance to beat this kid now, don't waste it," Coach asserted.

"Yes, coach, I won't screw it up." Coach Allen patted him on the back and stalked back to his spot under an umbrella, clipboard still in hand. Jason took a deep breath and stretched on the number 4 lane. He brought his knees to his chest, trying to ignore the nervous feeling that ate at him like a virus. What if he was as bad as last time? He couldn't bear to see the looks on his teammates' faces if he lost to Will again. He also couldn't bear to exist knowing that Scarlett was right about the bet. The short referee made yet another appearance, and Jason wondered if he would be reffing all of their meets. He pulled out his megaphone and started announcing the names.

"In lane one from Camden, Luke Taylor, in lane two from St. Johnson Boys Academy, Kyle Turner, lane three from New Wellis, Marcus Levine, in lane four from New Wellis,

Jason Everett, in lane five from Camden, William Kravitz, in lane six from New Wellis Adam Hunt, in lane seven from St. Jonson, Zachary Royal, and in lane eight from Camden, Isaac Brown. Line up in your lanes, and we will begin shortly."

Jason shook out his hands in a nervous habit and took a deep breath. In the lane next to him, Marcus smiled and winked. Jason didn't deserve him. They'd been best friends since 8th grade, and getting to be on the same team was just a dream come true. It was a nice day out, with hardly any clouds, and by this time the sun was just setting. A golden film was painted over the bleachers. Jason looked up into the crowd, not expecting to see his parents, but still hopeful. There were adults with face paint, signs, and coolers, but no Mr. and Mrs. Everett.

"Hey," Marcus whispered. "I'm sure they'll come next time, alright? Just focus on winning, and anyway, my parents will be loud enough for the both of us." He laughed. Jason smiled at this, too. Marcus's parents had always been so caring and supportive. They sat in the same spot on the bleachers every single meet.

"Yeah, I guess you're right." The referee stood on his tiptoes in an attempt to increase his height.

"We'll be starting the boys' 400m hurdle race now. Please take your marks."

This was it. Jason slid his foot into the sensor that recorded when he took off, ensuring that a false start would be recorded. His fingertips brushed the ground, and all he could hear was his heartbeat pounding in his head.

"Set."

He arched his back and prepared to take off the second he heard the gun go off.

BANG.

His feet left the ground, and suddenly Jason was moving like a sports car going full speed. He kept his breaths even and routine, and timed his steps so that he didn't lose balance or get off beat. His eyes narrowed in on the first hurdle coming up. He sped up his pace a little bit as he neared the jump, and threw his legs over it, doing his best to regain his speed the second he hit the ground. *One down, nine to go*, Jason thought. The next four were just as successful. He sped up as he got closer to the pole and threw his legs over like he was a kid jumping over his couch. He noticed Marcus beside him, running like a jet and breathing just as hard. Will Kravitz ran fast, too, but Jason was faster. He pushed harder, jumping hurdle after hurdle. A strangled cry erupted from beside him, and suddenly, Marcus wasn't next to him anymore. He glanced back for one second and saw his best friend on the ground, hands clutching his left knee like a lifeline. He regained composure just as quickly and continued running. Will had gotten ahead of him now, and he only had two more hurdles to catch up to him. This race was on him for both of them now, not just Jason. Still, in the back of his mind, he was screaming for Marcus, wondering if he was okay. He knew he had a bad knee, but the last time he got an injury, it was minor. Still, the sound he made sounded nothing short of a bloody cry for help, so Jason was sure he'd done something. *What the hell. Jason, focus.* This was all on him now. His race, his win. He pumped his arms and legs harder, swinging them over the second-to-last hurdle. Music in Jason's head began to build, as it always did when he ran —a reminder to go faster, a sound in the background that drowned out all his other senses. The fast thrumming of oboes and loud violin screeches reverberated through his mind, and as he ran, the music built. He managed to speed up to where Will had taken first place. When he noticed Jason, he seemed almost surprised that he'd made a comeback. To be honest, Jason was surprised too. He ran faster, trying to get just a bit in front of Will to throw him off. Faster and faster, louder and louder. His brain was its own orchestra, and right now, whoever was conducting the symphony in Jason's mind must have *really* sore arms. All he needed to do was swerve in front of Will, not cutting him off just enough to show he was there. That he wasn't done yet. This seemed to work, however, because Will seemed to slow down, allowing just enough time for Jason to brush past him. The last hurdle was up ahead, and Jason sent it. He sprinted as fast as he could towards the last hurdle and cleared it by an inch. Upon landing, it all caught up to him, the true desperation of this race, how much it meant for him, for his future. He gave it his all and thought only of his future, as well as the look on Will's face as he crossed the finish line. The music stopped, and Jason panicked. He put his hands on his knees, panting, but quickly recovered, jogging to where Marcus had fallen. He was still on the ground, sitting up and being supported by Coach Allen, and a paramedic who always came to the meets just in case. Jason was glad for him now.

"Marcus, dude, what happened out there? Are you OK?" Jason asked, crouching down by Marcus's side.

"Did you win?"

"I . . . yes, but—"

"Then that's all I care about. Now I gotta know what Will's face looked like when you smoked his sorry ass."

Jason smiled, knowing that Marcus still had his sense of humor. "It was pretty incredible." He sighed. "But really, you think you'll be OK? That didn't look fun."

Marcus stretched out his knee and grimaced. "Might've sprained it again, but nothing terrible. Go let my parents know, will you?" Jason nodded and handed Marcus a water bottle, which he gratefully accepted. He grabbed his track bag and stalked over to the podium, where his medal was waiting for him. He held it in his hands and peered at the back. Engraved, it said

2024 Spring send-off meet

Boys 400m hurdle

First place: Jason Everett, New Wellis High School

Jason smiled at himself, silently congratulating his victory, when his phone buzzed. "Hello? Mom?" A shaky, whispered voice answered.

"Hey, look, I need you to get back here as soon as you can, it's almost curfew and. . . He's not in the best mood."

Brian, that's who she was talking about. Jason's throat ran dry at the news that he wouldn't have a peaceful night, but he quickly shook it off and replied, "Yeah, I'll be right there. But just tell him I'm trying to hurry. Marcus hurt his knee during the race today, and I just wanted to make sure he was alright. Has he been drinking?" He could imagine his mother's sad smile from the other end of the line. Her wrinkles slightly down turned, and a worried glint in her eyes.

"I don't know," she whispered. *That means he absolutely has*, Jason knew. "I'll tell him, but I wouldn't expect him to be very understanding right now." She paused, and Jason could hear her exhale into the receiver. "Just hurry, please? And if you won, it could make this a little better yet."

Jason felt the slightest inch of relief. At least he had some reward for being late. "Yeah, I-I did win. I'll be home soon." The phone went dead, and Jason broke into a nervous jog to his car.

5
SCARLETT

Scarlett had a mental list of things. It changed from time to time, but at the moment her top three consisted of these things:

1. *Track*
2. *Getting into college*
3. *Friendships or Family*

She still valued plenty else, but these? They sat on the highest shelf. Her main priorities. Track, she knew. After running for four years of high school, you pick up a few things, and get the hang of the rhythm, how it works, what to expect, and how to win, most importantly. She wasn't too worried about that part.

Getting into college, however, was another story. She could try for a scholarship, sure, but that wouldn't help her unless her grades were perfect. *No room for B's, no room for error.* She spent all of her extra time studying, thinking about studying, or reprimanding herself for not studying more. Currently, Scarlett is sitting cross-legged on the carpet, and the AP Bio textbook is sprawled open, prepping for tomorrow's biochemistry exam. Her hair was bound over her shoulders in a loose braid, so she had to keep blowing unwelcome bangs out of her face.

She had pencil smudges on her cheek, and some on her notebook from accidentally dozing off during a review. Scarlett couldn't tell you the time, but she knew that it was 12:30 when she finished her first practice test, which she could confidently say was *about an hour ago. . . maybe?*

Her hand slipped out from where it was positioned, holding her face up, and Scarlett slipped forward, jolting awake. A few feet away, her phone vibrated, its glow lighting up her now dark room. *I don't remember the sun setting.* She reached over her piles of blankets and binders and stretched her fingertips out to grab the device. The contact name read Milo Artega with a contact photo of an older boy with dark blonde hair and light green eyes, complementing his pale complexion.

"Hello? Milo?" There was some rustling like covers on a bed before she got a reply.

"Hey, Scar! I just finished my class, so I figured I'd call you and check in. How's everyone?" Milo questioned.

"They're good, mom and dad are still fighting sometimes, but it's gotten better." He sighed.

"If you ever need anything, call me, OK? If it ever gets to be too much."

"I know, I will. How's Oregon? Is the track team as good as they said?" Milo had gone off to college at the University of Oregon three months earlier on a full-ride track scholarship. He won the state championship his senior year and set a new record for the 400-meter steeple chase.

"It's great actually, the coach is incredible, apparently he went to the Olympics in '12, which is super helpful for me to go all the way."

He'd been trying to get to the Olympics for years now. It was his dream. Scarlett clenched her fist but kept a smile on her face and a sweetness in her voice. "So you still want to do that? The Olympics, I mean?"

Milo chuckled. "Of course I do, Scar, you know that. I just wasn't sure it could actually happen until I got here, but now it's looking good for me." He drew in a deep, sharp breath. "Things are going really great for me, Scar. I wish you could be here to see it."

Scarlett twirled her fingers around her necklace. "Yeah, me too. Hey, I won my race the other day. 200-meter sprint." She smiled, thinking back on her victory and the pride she felt in herself.

"Oh, great job, Scar! How much did you win by? Did you set a record?" Scarlett felt her face flush with embarrassment, like she always felt when she had to admit her inferiority.

"About a second, but no, no record yet."

"Ha, well, not everyone can be as cool as your big bro, huh?" Her heart dropped. *He always makes it about him.*

"Yeah, I guess not." Silence filled the receiver.

Milo cleared his throat. "Well, it's late and I have an exam tomorrow. Keep me updated, will you?"

Scarlett snapped back to reality and fought off the biting feeling of sadness at her brother's sudden need to leave. "Um, yeah, I will. It was good talking to you."

"Yeah. You know I've missed you, Scarlett. But hey, you'll be here soon after you get that scholarship, right?" *Damn, him too? How come everyone expects us to go to the same college? Track isn't just in Oregon, you know.*

"If only it were that easy. I'll talk to you later, Milo, thanks for the call. And inspiring advice as always."

Milo laughed from the other line. "Anytime. Make Mom and Dad proud, alright? Another Artega on a full ride to keep up the family legacy. How's that for inspiring?"

A knot formed in Scarlett's stomach at the mention of her future. The pressure that was put on her to keep the family in line, afloat, and to manage their reputation. "I'll try, Milo. You know I'll try." She could feel him smile from the other end. "Yeah, I do. See ya, Scar, say hi to Mom for me." "I will. Dad too." "Goodnight, Scarlett." The line went dead. Scarlett put the phone down and sat in the dark, her face reflected by the glow of her lamp. "Goodnight."

She lay her head back onto her bed frame and welcomed the salty tears that flowed down her cheeks like rivers. It was all too much. She had so many expectations and people wanting her to do better, be better. It easily got to be too much, but was never enough. Her parents didn't see the hours spent studying or the plans with friends that she refused so that she had more time to review notes. All they saw was the outcome. The grade, the race time. She had to be the best, because good wasn't good enough. She fell asleep on the floor, head on the edge of her bed, dried tear tracks paving rivers on her face.

Scarlet woke up the next morning at 5:30 a.m. like she did every single morning. She had her routine and liked to stick to it. It was something she could control, and she needed as much control as she could get. She made her bed, took a shower, changed, brushed her teeth, did her hair and makeup. All of this while listening to her special morning playlist. Mornings went by smoothly with music to calm her nerves. Scarlett reviewed her notes, had a quick breakfast, and went over her schedule for the day. Then, at 7:30, she got in her car and started for New Wellis. Scarlett hummed along to 'Champagne Problems' along the way, silently thanking God that traffic wasn't as bad as usual.

Her first class was Honors English with Mr. McApherry. The door opened, announcing her entrance. She cursed at herself as she lowered into her desk. She hated English. All the passages, writing, and poems just didn't make sense to her. They were so opinionated, so diverse. Scarlett preferred blunt, logical thinking like mathematics or biology. This was so out of her style, but still required on transcripts. Thankfully, Meghan and Zoe, two of her track teammates, were also in that class. So at least she didn't have to suffer alone.

"Morning, Meghan."

"Hey!" Meghan called as she strutted in the door and to her desk. Not even five seconds behind was Mr. McApherry. Scarlett chuckled silently to herself. Meghan always managed to get to class just a second before the professor did, always saving herself by less than an inch.

"Good morning, all. Or should I say, 'Even so my sun one early morn did shine, With all triumphant splendour on my brow; But out, alack, he was but one hour mine, The region cloud hath mask'd him from me now.'" Mr. McApherry recited in a singsong voice, which was very unnatural to his deep tone. The class grumbled in response. "Very well, I guess Shakespeare is too advanced for you this morning." This got a chorus of nods from the tired audience. "How about I introduce something a bit more exciting then. I know you all were so disappointed with the school's budget cuts creeping into our annual History-English collaboration trip. If I had my way, we'd be in Paris studying literature at the moment, and the new football field turf would only be a distant thought." A few students chuckled. The football players raised their hands in mock defense. "Now don't get on Charlie, he didn't do anything." Mr. McApherry nodded towards a large, burly boy with curly blonde hair.

"Yeah, guys, don't get on Charlie," Charlie called out. More people were smiling now. "And now there will be no more need to blame anyone, as we have found a loophole! Everyone needs to thank Coach Allen for his generosity."

"Coach Allen? Like our Coach Allen?" Meghan whispered yelled. Scarlett's eyebrows shot up. "What did he do?" She laughed. "It seems the semifinals for track have picked a location, and the dates line up, so if everyone will behave. . . He has graciously invited our classes on their trip to Washington D.C!" Excited gasps and exclamations rang from around the room.

"What?" Scarlett gasped. A smile broke out on her face. Meghan returned the expression. A small ginger-haired boy raised his hand. "Yes, Ben?"

"Is this trip counting for our applications in any way? Do we get anything out of it, besides the trip, I mean?" Mr. McApherry smiled.

"Yes, I thought you might ask that. This program is for Honors English students only, so not only does it show that you worked hard enough to be here, but you will also receive volunteer hours for a project we will be doing, as well as the opportunity to win awards and achievements that you can add to your transcripts." Scarlett's head snapped up. This was it. This was how she was going to get to college, and finally show her parents that she was more than just Milo's little sister. She raised her hand.

"Yes, Scarlett?"

"When can we fill out attendance forms? And what's the cost?"

Mr. McApherry sighed, but a small contented smile crossed his face. "Don't get ahead of yourself, Ms. Artega, but yes, I will be getting into that shortly. All of the information for this trip will be posted on our class website this afternoon, as well as the dues. I'll have you all know that my past students have all looked back on this trip as the most rewarding moment in their high school career, so I would hope you all attend." The class exchanged excited glances and murmurs.

"You're staying after the meet, right, Scarlett? We'll have about the whole week in D.C. if you do." Meghan implored.

"Of course, anything to add to my application." Meghan rolled her eyes. "Yeah, plus it's gonna be super fun! Where's your sense of adventure?"

"I have plenty of adventure, and that's going to pay off when I'm full-riding into an Ivy League." Meghan rolled her eyes. "What about you, you coming?"

She nodded. "And Zoe too, I texted her this morning." Scarlett lit up. This was going to be perfect. A fun-filled trip with two of her best friends in D.C., and it looked good for college. Finally, something other than track that sped up her heart, and got her adrenaline pumping. But that too would be a challenge. With a record to set and times to beat, Scarlett had a feeling she wouldn't be enjoying this trip until the semis were over. A loud bang echoed through the classroom, and 26 stunned students turned to see Mr. McApherry holding a mallet and standing next to a vibrating gong.

"Apologies, pupils, just had to get your attention somehow. We have to get back to our lesson, so just remember to sign up for the trip and pay our dues! But in the meantime, let's analyze some historical artwork." Almost like a trance, the entire class immediately slapped back on their bored expressions, as they sat there listening to a dude in his sixties talk about a specific ear less painter with psychosis.

Scarlett, however, was enthralled. She twirled her pencil around rhythmically and daydreamed about the experiences she would have in D.C. She'd read about it but never been there. It was a big city, with historical landmarks everywhere you turned. There were almost as many statues as there were food trucks or pigeons. And the museums. There were at least seventy museums in just the capital city alone, which meant there were so many different things to see and try. Scarlett successfully zoned out of class, thinking about all of the possibilities ranging from who she would sit next to on the flight, or how she could celebrate her birthday, which fell in the exact middle of the trip. She almost didn't notice Mr. McApherry calling on her. Almost.

"Scarlett? What do you think about that?"

Crap. Thankfully, Scarlett thought of acting as one of her many talents, so she swiftly glanced around the room and slid for clues about what the question might've been. On the whiteboard were three years, only one of which Scarlett recognized. It said 1889, which Scarlett recognized as the year Van Gogh completed his famous Starry Night painting. And in the background was a picture of the painting itself. *Oh, it must be asking what year it was finished.*

"Um, was it 1889, sir?"

Silence filled the room for a moment. Scarlett's cheeks lit up in a faint red flush as she waited to hear Mr. McApherry's response. She hated being wrong, even if it was just a simple English question. She twirled her 'S' necklace nervously and studied his face for an indication that she said the right thing.

"That is correct, Van Gogh finished one of his most famous paintings, Starry Night, in 1889. Now, Aubrey, could you tell us what this painting signifies?"

Scarlett breathed a sigh of relief and took that close call as a sign to start paying attention. The rest of the day floated by in a blur, with plenty of schoolwork all around. Her AP statistics class was as boring as ever, but at least that was numbers, which Scarlett considered herself to be good at. The third period consisted of IB Spanish, which Scarlett positively adored. The language in itself is beautiful, and it brought her closer to her heritage. If Scarlett could pick any one of her classes to keep, this would be it. Her friends hated Spanish because it was hard, and truth be told, it is hard. But every time Scarlett entered that room, her worries drifted away just a bit as she engulfed herself in the delicacy and warmth of the Spanish language. Scarlett is currently enrolled in her AP sports medicine class taught by Mrs. Basu.

She was a sweet teacher, with a thick, South Indian accent, which made Scarlett strain her ears to understand what she was talking about. That was one downside of the class, the other being that she didn't have any friends in the course either. She had acquaintances, sure, people she did group projects with. But no *friends*. She sat at one end of a rectangular-shaped table surrounded by a blonde girl called Maddy, who almost constantly talked about her Karate classes. As much as Scarlett liked Cobra Kai, she got tired of Maddy comparing herself to Torry Nichols. At the opposite end of the table was a dark-haired girl named Sammy. Scarlett liked her. She was quiet, keeping most of her thoughts to herself, but when she shared her ideas, they were almost always genius. She respected her for that. Sometimes Scarlett wished she could be mysterious like that, but she liked talking. She liked expressing her opinions. Sammy didn't even need to talk much, though, because Jason and Marcus, who sat right in front of Scarlett, did all of the talking and laughing that was needed for their group. For the whole room, probably. They could spend hours talking about music, movies, track, basically anything they could agree or debate on, they talked about. Today was different, though. Scarlett was bent over an anatomy of the forearm diagram, sketching in the labels for muscle groups and tendons, when the entrance bell rang. She glanced up at Marcus's seat, which was empty. She shot Jason a quizzical look.

"He's not here today. Hurt his knee in the race yesterday." He informed, taking the hint. Then his head went right back down to his packet.

"Oh." She paused. "Is he OK?" Jason's head snapped up, seemingly irritated.

"Fine. Just a sprain, he'll be fine. He's not weak, you know."

"Yeah, I know I was just checking in." Jason lowered his gaze even deeper into his text.

"I'm sure his knee appreciates that, thanks."

Scarlett rolled her eyes. *Why is he being such a douche today?* Like, more than usual.

"What's your problem today, Jason?" He balled up his fist on the table and peered up at Scarlett. She noticed that his left eye was tinged with purple and yellow, along with a small cut on his chin. As quickly as he tensed up, he relaxed again, recoiling into his previous position.

"Dunno, just tired and Marcus probably can't run for the rest of the season. It's a bummer."

Scarlett thought about it for a second and allowed the excuse. Of course, he was upset; his best friend just got injured, and now he couldn't run with him for his final days as a senior. She shrugged off his defensiveness, but decided that she wasn't done with the questions.

"What happened?" Her eyes filled with confusion. "To your eye, I mean. Bad fall?"

Jason paused for a second, unaware of what she was referring to, then remembered the ugly purple that painted his face. He flushed. "Just tripped." He added, "I'm fine." Once again, he buried himself back in the schoolwork.

Scarlett studied his expression for a few more seconds, not believing that he was so enthralled with arm muscles. But she didn't question that he fell, probably on his way to school. *He is an idiotically clumsy person,* she figured. Scarlett didn't give the matter any more thought, as she busied herself with structural work and was already preparing a mental packing list for D.C.

"You're going right?" she asked Maddy. "Going. . .?" "On the English-history trip to D.C."

Maddy posed her face in an exaggerated expression of recollection. "Ohhh that, yeah, no. I have a Karate tournament that week, and I would hate to lose my match because I didn't train."

Scarlett frowned. "That sucks, well, good luck anyway." She turned to Sammy. "What about you?"

Sammy looked up, blushed slightly, but smiled sweetly. Scarlett loved her smile. It was the most friendly thing she'd seen all day, and some days she needed that. "I'm gonna go, I just need to fill out the form. And ask my parents, but I'm sure they'll let me."

'Must be nice not to have to go full Shark Tank mode to get your parents to agree to something,' Scarlett thought. It would be hard for them to say no to semis, though, so she was already halfway there.

"I'll see you there then," she said, and continued with her work.

"Ahem." Scarlett looked up, and Jason was staring straight at her.

"What?" she asked, a little unfriendlier than she intended.

"You forgot to ask me if I was going." Scarlett groaned.

"I don't need to spare your feelings, you're not four." Jason continued drilling his gaze to her like a laser.

"Fine, Jason, not like I give a shit, but are you going?" Jason leaned back in his chair, satisfied.

"Yes, I am, thank you for taking an interest in that Artega." He chuckled to himself, obviously proud of the annoyance which he caused.

"I should've let the car hit you," she mumbled, but Jason only grinned back.

6

JASON

Jason sat on the floor of his bedroom, nervously fiddling with his pencil while he worked on his AP biology assignment. He loved biology, especially wildlife and marine biology.

Since he was little, Jason has been enthralled by animals. How they acted, their habits, and how they could adapt so quickly to changing environments. He wished humans were the same. *If we could adapt instead of retaliating and fighting, If we could love instead of showing anger.* Marine life moved and lived in such harmony. He glanced up at his wall, staring at the cetacean poster that was gingerly plastered on his wall.

The way their tails moved so gracefully as they glided through the water reminded him of a family vacation he took when he was younger to L.A. His father gambled their lives away, while his mother took Jason to the pool for some mother-son bonding time. He dove right into the water, allowing the cool, refreshing liquid to wash all over him. His mother watched with a yellow sun hat and brown sunglasses as her son frolicked and had the time of his life. He felt like a shark, wading through the ocean with a level of serendipity and glee that only an animal with virtually no predators could have. *I know who my predators are,* Jason thought. But his didn't have fins and pointy teeth. They had brains, hands, and hate. He tore his eyes away from the wall and slammed his binder closed, trying to focus on something else to keep him busy. He scanned the floor out of boredom when his eyes fell upon the permission slip for D.C. The trip. If he could only get permission from his parents, then he could pack, or at least do something productive. Jason snatched the paper, along with a black ink pen and darted out of his room. Down the hallway and into the living room, where his mother sat watching 'Wheel of Fortune.'

"Hey, Mom." Jason's mother turned around, her long brown hair sweeping over her shoulders.

"Hey, honey, come to watch with me?"

Jason blushed, embarrassed that he didn't have as much time to spend with his mom as he used to. "For a minute, I have some homework. But actually, I wanted to talk to you about a trip I have."

"I'm listening," she said as she leaned forward.

Jason smiled. His mother has always been attentive, but when she fixed her big green eyes on you, it was impossible not to feel heard and appreciated. Jason spent the next ten minutes diving into a five-star sales pitch of the trip. Where they were going, chaperones, costs, hotels, all of the above. The entire time, his mom eyed him like an investor, perfectly calculating which stocks to pick in order to make it big. When he'd finished, she took the paper from his hand and scanned it over.

"Why did you wait so long to give it to me? This trip is in two weeks, Jason."

"I thought you'd say no, so if I asked you later, then maybe it would be more of a high-pressure situation and—"

Mrs. Everett pursed her lips. "Three hundred dollars, huh?"

Jason gulped. "Yeah, and I know it's a lot, but I can contribute some, take on some extra shifts at Safeway, or—"

"Nu-uh, slow down, Hun."

Jason creased his eyebrows. "I want to do this for you. As a present of sorts. An expression of my pride in you."

The words rang in Jason's ears. *'Of my pride in you.'* "Really? Are you sure? Dad won't be mad?"

His mother just rolled her eyes and sighed. "I'll talk to him, don't you worry about that. I want you to go on this trip with your friends and make some good memories. Be happy, Jason, that's all I want for you." She reached up and pulled Jason into a tight hug, which he graciously accepted.

"Thank you, Mom, really thank you." He held her tight, not wanting to let go, suddenly seeing every gray strand of hair, every wrinkle. He squeezed her tighter still.

She only hummed in response and sank further into his embrace, savoring every second. As they pulled apart, both Jason's and his mother's smiles were visible. "Now, I want you to go and pack up, and don't forget anything."

Jason nodded eagerly and patted himself on the back as he unloaded his suitcase from the garage. The next few hours were spent in a packing frenzy. As Jason realized his limited time, he also realized his limited clothing supply. He looked over his options, and suddenly saw everything wrong with his wardrobe. Just looking at it all laid out made Jason cringe. There was no cohesion, just different colored shirts of the same brand, and denim jeans and khaki shorts. He glanced down at the school-issued packing list in his hands.

We will be attending a play, so dress accordingly: Men, black trousers and suits. Women, appropriate formal dresses. Jason made an internal note to update his fashion sense and pick up some 'trousers' as he shoved his belongings into the small red luggage. He tilted the bag upright onto its wheels and leaned it in a corner. That was one thing to take off his list, and one step closer to a parent-less trip. A familiar insistent knock on the door turned Jason's head. The irritating rapping continued. Jason shuffled over to the door and swung it open. Marcus let himself in the second the door was opened, limping a little on his knee brace, and shrieking.

"Why the hell do we need trousers?! We're going to a play, not a damn funeral!"

Jason chuckled. "And suits too, did you see the suits?"

Marcus stared at him and threw up his arms in protest. "What the hell?"

"So I'm guessing that's why you're here? To go suit shopping?" Marcus nodded. "Give me a second, I'll get my keys."

Less than ten minutes later, the two boys were cruising along the road, following the GPS to the closest mall and singing 'Hey Mickey' at the top of their lungs. They pulled up to a stop, still howling like they were on top of the world and switching off lines, like they'd rehearsed.

"*Oh, Mickey, what a pity, you don't understand?*" Jason sung.

"*You take me by the heart when you take me by the hand,*" Marcus finished.

A black jeep pulled up beside them as they finished the next few verses. Meghan Truth pulled up blasting her own music, but quickly turned it off as she noticed the two boys singing like idiots next to her. Jason noticed and shot Meghan a smile. She grinned back and made a gesture towards Marcus, who didn't seem to notice a thing, and was still in his own world.

"Oh Mickey, you're so fine, you're so fine you blow my mind, hey Mickey," Marcus continued singing, so Jason elbowed him hard in the shoulder.

"What the hell, Jason I—" He made eye contact with Meghan, who was cackling in her seat like a madman.

"Oh shit," he mumbled.

"Ahem, hey Meghan, how're you doing on this fine evening?"

She laughed again and drove off, leaving the boys behind in their own embarrassment. Jason turned to face Marcus, who looked positively terrified. Jason's face twisted up as he exploded with laughter.

"Shut the hell up, Jason, or I'll never sing Toni Basil with you again, "Marcus threatened.

Jason quickly wiped the smirk off his face and quieted as they pulled into the mall parking lot. "I'm sure she'll still like you, man," Jason offered as they stepped into a Nordstrom on the first floor.

"I hope so, but if you were her and you saw the guy you liked singing 90s classics, wouldn't that interfere with feelings?" Marcus countered.

"It's not like you said she looks like Toni Basil, or like you would rather date her or something. She probably thinks it's like endearing and shit."

Marcus shrugged. "You'd better be right because I think she watched us for at least half a minute before we noticed anything."

"Forty-five seconds. I counted the light."

"Oh, screw you, Jason. That's not helpful," Marcus said, but broke out into laughter.

They left the subject up in the air and continued through the aisles to find their suits. After a brief browsing, Jason picked out a striking navy blue sports coat and black trousers. He also bought a sleek navy blue belt to tie it together. Marcus went for a dark crimson suit with matching trousers and a tan belt. They headed for the changing rooms, only being stopped by an old store clerk who gave the boys so many compliments, you would've thought they were on a reality show or something, though Jason wasn't sure if they were taking the compliments the right way. "Now you two boys look just like Leo DiCaprio!"

"Young DiCaprio or old?" Jason asked.

The old lady just smirked, which didn't instill any confidence in Jason. Marcus blushed a deep red. "Are you sure she knows what Leonardo DiCaprio looks like?" He laughed, and shrank into his dressing room. Jason threw the coat on in his own room, smoothing the creases with his fingers. He stood in front of the mirror, analyzing himself like a spectator, suddenly aware of his flaws. He looked like his father. Same dark brown hair as his mother's, same warm smile — but everything else was Brian. His eyes were brown, and every time he stared at himself, he remembered looking into the same brown eyes as the person who they belonged to hurt him and his mother. His nose was slanted and round. As he breathed in and out, he could almost see his father's nostrils flaring in his anger. But when it all became too much, smiling brought him back to his innocence, reminding him that Jason is not his father. Father's looks, mother's heart. He could live with that.

Jason stepped out of the room. From around the corner, Marcus appeared, red suit on. He looked clean-cut and dashing. The red shade complemented him perfectly, and the light tan he chose for his belt contrasted with his skin with elegance. Jason looked at Marcus's expression, which was zoned in right on him with fiery eyes.

"What?" Jason asked.

"Jason, you look so damn sexy!"

Jason laughed, hard. He decided to play along. "Marcus, marry me, you dashing boy!" Marcus snorted. "Oh, fetch me some water, I'm getting dizzy!" Jason doubled over, clutching his chest while he wheezed.

From behind them, the store clerk cleared her throat. The boys caught each other's eyes, and they simultaneously widened as they turned to the woman. "You two don't have anything going on after this, do you?" she drawled, pursing her lips.

Jason wanted to throw up, but Marcus beat him to it, gagging obnoxiously before yelling. "Run, Jason!" They paid for their suits, then dashed out of the store, laughing and glancing back to make sure they wouldn't be followed. They ran right through a PacSun, where something caught Marcus's eye, and he stopped abruptly enough that Jason smashed into his back. "Holy shit, Marcus, you're gonna wrinkle our suits—what?"

"She's right fucking there, man."

Jason turned. Meghan stood by the jewelry rack, holding up two pairs of earrings, seemingly deciding between the two. "OK, so are you gonna do anything about that, or just stand here?"

"What the hell do you think?" Marcus grumbled.

"She'll like you, Marcus. She likes you, and you talk like every practice. Why is this any different?" Marcus scoffed.

"Does this look like practice to you? I'm completely out of my element." Jason sighed, running out of ideas.

"Just go, and if you do, and she says she hates you, or humiliates you in front of the whole store, then I'll do like a dare or something to make up for it."

A small smile made its way across Marcus's face. "If this goes wrong, in any way, you're gonna show up to practice tomorrow in your dance clothes, tell the entire team you're taking dance, and then perform your routine for them."

Jason frowned. "What the hell, no!"

"Too late," he said, as he spun around and confidently strutted towards Meghan, who was still buried in her earring choices.

Jason strained his ears to hear as much as he could, but he could only make out a few sentences.

"I know we hang out a lot at practice, I just thought—"

"You're a really nice guy, Marcus. I just. . ." He stopped trying to half ass listen to their conversation and instead looked at the racks of men's clothes they had in the corner of the store. There wasn't any use in paying attention anymore anyway, as the pair moved off into a quiet corner and were whispering and laughing about. . . something. Jason found a couple of band shirts that he liked, as well as a pair of sweatpants that he thought were suitable for the flight and decided to splurge a little on himself. As he waited in line for the checkout, Marcus shuffled towards him, a twinge of sadness etched on his face. Jason's stomach dropped. "So. . . I almost don't want to ask. How'd it go?"

Marcus's sad face turned into a slight smile. "Start dancing, Shirley."

7
MARCUS

Marcus had never been so excited to go to practice. He woke up a couple of extra hours early, just to be able to make it on time to record the priceless moment when Jason would perform like a princess in front of his team. He loved poking fun at Jason for his dance class, especially because he knew he didn't want to be taking it. But then again, everything for the college of your dreams.

Marcus couldn't argue about that, though. He was stressing himself about getting into Johns Hopkins for pediatric nursing. But his applications were in, and now all he could do was wait. Wait, and record videos of Jason doing a pirouette. Marcus slipped on a pair of dark blue Jordans and slung his track bag over his shoulder before piling into his dad's old Toyota. A part of him felt a little bad for lying to Jason. So yeah, Meghan hadn't flipped him off and told him he looked like Shrek and a buffalo had a baby. She actually smiled ear to ear when Marcus said he liked her, and gladly accepted his offer of a date in D.C. in a few weeks.

But to Marcus, *a prank opportunity is a golden opportunity.* And to Meghan, too, it seemed. So when he suggested pretending like she rejected him in order to get Jason to perform, she quickly agreed. So now, Marcus had to pretend to be heartbroken while secretly enjoying every second of Jason's embarrassment. He pulled up to the school and practically skipped into the track area, but was stopped by Jason.

"Morning, Jace."

"Oh shut the hell up, you're really making me do this?"

"You know, that was the deal." Jason groaned and threw his head back.

"I'm the best friend in the entire goddamn world, you know that, right?" Jason asked.

"And the best dancer. And I assume that would make me the second-best friend in the entire world?" Marcus asked, with pleading eyes.

"You're a piece of shit, that's what you are. Now go warm up while I put this piece of string-on." He opened his bag to reveal a shrunken black pantyhose-looking thing with black straps and legs.

"What the hell is that?" Marcus gasped, cackling as hard as he could, and taking the outfit in his hands. "It looks like a baby outfit."

Jason snatched it back and wiped it off. "It's a leotard, you idiot. Now go," he said and stormed off toward the bathrooms to change.

Marcus started to feel a little bit bad that the whole team would have to see him like that. But it was just *so* funny. Marcus figured Jason would forgive him eventually and decided just to enjoy the moment. At practice, he warmed up with the rest of the team, but shot Meghan knowing glances. She broke down in laughter every time, which caught Scarlett's attention. "Should I tell her?" Meghan asked.

"Not yet, I want that to be a surprise," Marcus replied, through his own tears of laughter. Meghan turned to Scarlett.

"Sorry, girl, no can do."

Scarlett threw her arms up in frustration. "What the hell? So I'm just chopped liver?"

Marcus put a reassuring hand on her shoulder and tried to contain his laughter. "Don't worry, I'm sure it'll happen soon." He managed, and then fell into hysterics once again, Meghan following close behind.

"Weirdos," Scarlett mumbled.

Meghan flipped her off from where she was kneeling on the floor. Then, it was time. All heads turned as a speaker suddenly started playing a smooth symphony, and Jason, dressed in his black leotard, strutted out. Marcus lost his shit. He laughed so hard he thought he might be dying, and then he laughed some more. There were almost as many heads turned on him as on Jason because he was acting so crazy. Marcus willed himself to keep composure. He couldn't watch the show very well if he had tears in his eyes, could he? Jason brought a megaphone up to his mouth and spoke roughly, laughing in between as well.

"I'm here today, looking like a sexy black swan because I lost a bet with Marcus." Catcalls and cheers were erupting from the girls' side of the track field, with eyes staring at Jason's exposed muscles. He did look quite muscular. The tights brought out the tightness in his thighs, and his arms looked strong wrapped in black fabric. "Many of you don't know this, but you need to take an art in order to graduate. And I like forgot that you had to do that." Scarlett facepalmed, which brought a chuckle to Marcus's lips. "So when I tried to apply for an art, they said dance was the only one with spots left, so I kind of had to." He shook his head, obviously disappointed that he ever let this happen. "I'm doing this because Marcus got rejected, and I told him if anything went wrong, I would do a dare to make up for it. So, thanks a lot, Marcus." The crowd now turned to Marcus and cheered for him. Marcus raised a fist and pumped it in the air, grinning. "Glad I could be of service, Jace."

Jason smiled cockily. "So I now present to you a shitty rendition of Swan Lake in less than two minutes." Jason set the megaphone down and pressed play on the speaker. The song started out slowly, then turned into a fast-paced fight scene type rendezvous. Jason lazily threw his arms up and leaped from side to side, turning a brilliant red shade, but laughing when he saw Marcus's amused face. He jumped in place a few times, switching his feet as he did so, and keeping his toes pointed. Marcus watched in awe and turned to Meghan. "You're getting this right?" he asked. "I'm kind of living in the moment."

Meghan turned her phone camera to him. "Bitch I've been recording since he first got out here, don't you worry," she replied.

So Marcus didn't worry. Instead, he just sat back and absorbed the sight of Jason struggling to leap and spin like Anna Pavlova. But as soon as it had started, the song slowed to a stop, and Jason ended with a dramatic low bow before stalking over to Marcus and holding out a hand.

"OK, we're good now?" he asked.

Marcus grinned and took his hand, performing their seven-step handshake that they'd known since fifth grade. "Yes, sir. In fact, your movements were so beautiful that it convinced Meghan to go out with me."

He said, draping an arm around Meghan, who stood next to him.

Jason paled. *"No damn way."*

"Yes way. I guess you were just like too majestic and shit." Jason shook his head violently.

"I call bull, she said yes in the first place, didn't she?" From a few feet away, Scarlett cackled for the first time that morning.

"Ha! Meghan, did you really? Oh, that's funny!" She sank to the floor, laughing and rolling around. Jason turned back, not finding it amusing. Marcus shrugged.

"Maybe. But if you think about it, I did you a favor. Now you don't have to hide your dance bag in the office, you can just bring it to practice."

Jason elbowed him playfully. "Not worth it." He groaned.

The crowd settled down after Jason changed, and they resumed their usual warm-ups and exercises. Jason came up to Marcus during their mile run and ran with him. Marcus limped along the way, so Jason slowed down to match his pace, helping him when needed. He couldn't race for the team anymore, but Marcus still vowed to come to the practices as a support system. "So, she said yes, huh?"

"Yeah, I'm taking her out in D.C. I think she matches my energy, like, perfectly," he admitted, and for once, that seemed true for someone other than Jason. For his whole life, Jason had been the only person Marcus could count on to relate to, but now it seemed like that might change. *And she was a girl, how great was that?* Jason grinned.

"But you know that to get revenge, now I have to show her all the bad pictures of you, right?"

Marcus gasped and feigned hurt. "You actually wouldn't, Jason!"

"Oh yes, I would." He laughed, and his grin slowly disappeared as they finished up their warm-up mile. "I'm the third wheel now," he said to himself.

Scarlett came up from behind him and patted him on the shoulder. "We both lost good ones today." She sympathized and then stalked away.

Jason brushed off his jacket where she'd touched, and sent a quizzical look to her back. Marcus, meanwhile, planned out where they could go in D.C., the things they could do, and all the different restaurants there were. Jason suddenly wished he'd danced for the intended reason, because Marcus got denied. But he had to admit, seeing Marcus act all excited, and truly being happy, made it worth all the embarrassment. Marcus went back home after the halfway point of practice. His knee was killing him, and he didn't technically have to stay the entire time. He pulled out of the parking lot and headed out of the school. His phone buzzed. Marcus checked it at the stop light, sighing when he read it. It was from his younger sister, Cora. She was eight years old, a great speller, and had Marcus in the palm of her hand from the second she was born. Marcus loved her, truly loved her. They fought, like all siblings, but it was always Marcus who caved and gave her what she wanted. He couldn't help it, he was her older brother and he had to protect her, and keep her happy. If he had to pick up McDonald's in order to do that sometimes, then that's what he'll do.

Hi! Lina and Samantha are coming over for a sleepover tonight, just syk. Can you please get out of the house for the night? It read. Marcus groaned. He really didn't want to be away from home, especially with the trip coming up, and Marcus still needed to pack. But Cora would enjoy it, and Marcus remembered the nights when he would have sleepovers, and they were definitely better when his parents were out for the night. He caved, like always. *Fine, I'll pick up some snacks for you guys on the way home. Any requests?* Five minutes later, Marcus stood in the middle of Raley's with a cart full of junk food and snacks, along with some things he needed for D.C. Something about those mini toothpastes and tiny deodorants always tied a vacation together. He paid for his things, but glanced across the store. There was a tiny jewelry stand, like the one in PacSun. And they had the earrings Meghan had put back. She was deciding between a pair of golden hoops or little golden teddy bears holding a bow. She'd decided on the golden hoops, but Marcus could see how much she liked the other pair. "Um, one more thing, I'll be right back," he told the cashier, who nodded. He quickly grabbed the bear earrings and added them to his basket.

"For someone special?" he asked.

Marcus flushed. "Yeah." Marcus couldn't help but see her everywhere. Acts of service and receiving gifts were his love languages. They were how he expressed his gratitude and affection for another person, and always had been. He truly enjoyed buying gifts for people he loved. Marcus froze in place. *Did I just think that? That I love her?* He paled. *But I do love her, right? I mean, just as any person loves their. . . wait, what are we? Is she my girlfriend? Do I have to ask for her to be my girlfriend, or does she already assume?* Marcus's thoughts were racing. Why didn't he ask her sooner? Marcus gathered up his groceries and piled them into the cart, racing back out of the parking lot and to his car. How would he ask her? And what if she decides she doesn't like him anymore?

Meghan was the first person that Marcus really felt like he clicked with. She was funny, hell, she thought he was funny! And she was beautiful, like, *really beautiful.* Marcus could play with her smooth brown hair for days. And her smile lit up each room like the sun crash-landed in the middle of it. As he drove, he thought about all the times they'd shared, and all of the feelings that Marcus got when she looked in his direction. He couldn't take it anymore. He pulled out his phone and carefully clicked in Jason's contact while making sure to pay attention to the road. He was pinned, of course, so it was easy to find. He put the phone on speaker and set the phone back down with trembling hands as he re-focused on the road. It rang twice before Jason picked up.

"Hey, Marcus, what's up?" Marcus stayed silent, unsure about how to approach the topic. "Marcus? You alright, bro?" he asked, chuckling a little bit.

"Um, yes? Maybe?"

"I'm not sure I'm following." He sighed.

"I was at the store, and I saw a pair of earrings that Meghan wanted, but she didn't get them. So, I got them for her." Marcus confessed.

"Uh-huh," Jason mumbled to show that he was listening.

"So I was checking out, and I just thought about how I loved buying gifts for people that I loved." He went quiet, but from the other end of the line, he felt a moment of realization.

"So now you're freaking out because you were thinking that you love her?"

"Yeah."

Jason laughed. "Of course you love her, man. You guys have known each other for years, and you always knew you had a thing for her. "

Marcus groaned. "Yeah, but are we even technically dating? Hell, I haven't even asked her to be my girlfriend. Does she already assume she is? Or is it like a whole other thing?" He sighed.

"Look. You got her a gift because you care about her. Labels don't matter when you care about someone so much that you randomly get things you think they'd like at the store," Jason explained. "Oh, I got you a blue Celsius by the way, too," Marcus remembered.

"Thanks, man," Jason breathed. "My point is, you can worry about her not being your girlfriend, and all this shit about labels, or you can go out there and ask her. You know she likes you. I know she likes you. I see the way she looks at you."

"Like, I'm someone she likes spending time with?" Marcus guessed.

"Like someone she *loves* spending time with. I guarantee you, just go for it."

Marcus sighed heavily as he pulled into his own driveway. "Thanks. It feels good to tell someone, even if I still have no idea about how to ask her."

"You'll figure it out. You always do," Jason reassured.

Marcus perked up. "Jason?"

"Yeah?"

"I wouldn't happen to be able to spend the night at your place, would I? Cora's having a sleepover, and she kicked me out," Marcus asked.

"Sorry, man, my dad's home tonight, and you know how he is about that stuff." Marcus was disappointed, but he brushed it off. Jason's dad was not one to be messed with, and he knew that Jason would be in big trouble if he even asked to have a sleepover. Jason didn't openly talk about his dad much, but Marcus knew enough to respect his decisions.

"All good, but where should I go? Usually, I could go to my cousin's place, but they're out of town." An idea formed in Jason's head.

"Why don't you ask Meghan if you can crash at her place?"

"What? Are you insane? Why on earth would she agree to that?"

"You've stayed over at her house before, it's not like you're having sex with her or anything." Marcus gritted his teeth.

"That was different. You were there, and Scarlett, and Zoe, and Adam. It wasn't just me." Marcus thought about it. It would work out nicely, and it would be the perfect opportunity to give her the earrings. "Do you really think I should ask her?"

Jason grinned. "Why the hell not? Just stop worrying so much and go for it."

Marcus sighed. "Fine. But if this backfires..."

"I am done doing your bullshit dares. You are not getting anything out of me if this goes badly."

Marcus laughed, throwing his head back. "Yeah, fine, alright. I'll text you later. See ya, Jace."

"Bye, Marcus," Jason drawled and hung up. Marcus unlocked his door and started unloading groceries in the kitchen. He pulled out his phone.

Hey Meghan. Look, I'm in deep shit, my sisters are having a sleepover and kicked me out of the house. Jason's not free, so I'm out of options. Could I crash at ur place? Just as a friend in need of a place to stay, nothing more.

He finished putting away the groceries and was about to get a head start on his packing when his phone buzzed.

Hi Marcus! Yeah that works u can come over whenever, my mom's out and my dad doesn't really care who comes over. Bring ur computer too, my parents deleted my Netflix account after I dyed my dog's fur pink a while back and it hasn't come out.

A grin quickly reached Marcus's face, and he laughed at the thought of Meghan being scolded for turning her Labrador into Pinkie Pie. Marcus breathed a sigh of relief, which was quickly replaced by a tightness in his stomach and a newfound nervousness as he read the next line.

Just as friends, huh? We'll see how long that lasts.

MEGHAN

What. The. Hell. Marcus is coming here? Like now? Meghan struggled to get her thoughts together. *It's OK.*

She can do this. After all, he was the one who asked, and if he wasn't comfortable with it, why would he have asked in the first place? Meghan paced back and forth in her room, her pink lab Lily pacing around with her. Meghan made her way out to her living room, where her dad sat reading. "Hey, Dad, Marcus is coming to stay the night. He doesn't have anywhere to stay tonight, so I told him it was fine to come here."

He didn't even spare a glance up from his book before replying. "That's fine, you know the rules."

"Yup. Thanks, Dad!" She grinned and scurried back to her room.

Lily followed. It was unusually pretty clean, save for some schoolwork laid out on her desk, and her collection of drawings scattered about the floor. She tidied up the schoolwork but left the drawings in a pile on the desk. Her room was sizable, with a walk-in closet, desk on one wall, and a queen-size bed; she knew she had it better off than most. Her bed sheets were white with light blue stripes, and a puffy white comforter. She had oak wooden floors, and on one wall were hundreds of paintings, sketches, and drawings pinned up on a light string. There were sticky notes with random doodles from class mixed in with detailed artworks that took her weeks. Meghan couldn't be more proud of her creations. Each one held a memory, an experience, even a random afterthought. But each one meant something to her. She finished cleaning up the mess scattered around her room and instead focused on herself. She wore a blue, cropped baby tee with black leggings and her hair tied back in a loose braid around her shoulders.

She redid the braid, carefully tucking in each strand of hair to ensure that there were no flyaway hairs. Her makeup was already done, but Meghan touched it up, adding one more layer of mascara and reapplying her lip gloss. All the while, she could hardly think. She liked Marcus, maybe even loved him. But she didn't want to take anything too quickly. If she acted too quickly and scared him out of it, she could never forgive herself.

But hell, he's so perfect. When she saw him singing Toni Basil at the stoplight, she laughed. But inside, she thought it was just about the cutest thing he's ever done. He was so carefree, and seeing him not worry, or overthink like he usually does, and just be *Marcus*. Meghan couldn't think of a more heartwarming thing. The doorbell rang. Meghan's heart just about stopped. *Shit. What do I do?*

"Meghan, your friend's at the door." Her dad called out from the other room.

That's right, go answer the door, and then just take it from there. She made her way to the door and peeked through the peephole to make sure it was him.

He stood on the porch, a small duffel bag in one hand and a plastic bag in the other. He wore a muted green camouflage hoodie with a white button-up layered underneath that poked out at the bottom, gray sweatpants, and *God, his hair.* It was parted perfectly, and the curls folded down over his forehead like they were placed there by an angel. She loved its color and how it smelled distinctly like his conditioner every time. She loved how it felt in between her fingers. Silky smooth, but also thick and strong. And his smile. He was almost always smiling, and Meghan would never get used to the way it made her feel. Her stomach filled with butterflies every time. *I would love to get used to it, though,* she thought. She pulled open the door to reveal him smiling down at her, of course.

"Hey! Thanks so much for letting me stay here. I was not about to have Cora give me a makeover like last time." He shuddered, and Meghan laughed.

"I would pay to see a picture of that." They stepped inside, and Marcus kicked off his shoes.

Lily immediately ran up to him and jumped up on his leg, wagging her tail like a crazy person. Marcus doubled over in laughter at the sight of Meghan's pink dog.

"Hey girl!" he cooed, stroking her lovingly. Lily beamed.

"Is your dad here? I should probably say hi, right?" Marcus asked, attention still on Lily, who was soaking it all up.

Meghan rolled her eyes. "Don't bother, he's reading. Besides, he's met you before. You're not a stranger around here, you know." She motioned for him to follow, and then started for her room.

She was nervous to see his reaction. Not that it was a big deal, just her room. But she craved approval almost as much as she craved seeing him. "This is my room. Um, you've been here before, so you know what it looks like."

Marcus stepped in and set his bag down on the floor, glancing around the room as if taking it all in. He stepped over to the desk and looked at the artworks fastened to the walls. "Some of these are new. This wasn't there last time," he said, pointing to a collection of cat charcoal sketches.

"Yeah, I've added a lot lately. That's my neighbor's cat, she came by sometimes, so I like to draw her," she explained.

He smiled brightly, and Meghan's heart fluttered. "These are really damn good. I mean, like, professional good." He laughed, staring at the works. "I'll never understand how you do this, it's amazing, you're amazing." He flushed, and Meghan caught her breath.

"Well, all in a day's work, you know." She chuckled and moved past him to his duffel bag. She carefully unzipped the pocket that she knew his computer would be in and pulled it out. "Now please, can we order some pizza and binge-watch *something?* I'm screen-starved."

Marcus laughed, and less than half-hour later, the two were completely settled. They had pizza and pajamas and had set up a spot for Marcus to sleep on the floor. Currently, Meghan was leaning against her headboard, sitting awkwardly as Marcus sat stiffly next to her. There was a tension in the air that bit, that was certain, but Meghan was just glad to have the chance to be this close to him at all.

"Alright, so what'll it be?" Marcus asked, scrolling through the various shows and movies.

Meghan noticed how his mouse lingered on a specific show more than the others and laughed to herself. "Let's watch Grey's Anatomy," she suggested. Marcus lit up.

Oh, how she would love to see him smile like that all day, every day. "I love that show! What season are you on?" Truth be told, Meghan really liked the show. She made it to the end of the fifth season before taking a break to watch the new season of Bridgerton. Now seemed like the perfect, meant-to-be time to watch some of the rest.

"I just finished season five. What about you? Jason told me you've seen every season at least ten fricking times, don't you get bored?"

Marcus smirked. "You kidding? I could never get bored with this, it's my comfort series."

Meghan thought about what her comfort series was. Gilmore Girls was always a great option. But the Office was a stand out for a feel-good comedy. Right now, with Marcus, Grey's Anatomy seemed like a good option too.

"Right then, let's start!" She clicked play and felt Marcus's eyes flick from the screen to her, though she didn't know why. He was watching her, waiting for a reaction to. . .something.

Less than twenty minutes later, she had the answer, as she felt tears pooling in her eyes. "He's dead?! He can't be dead, this has to be fake!" she cried, staring in disbelief at the computer.

"All good things come to an end." Marcus sympathized, tucking her hair behind her ear. Meghan hoped he didn't see her blushing, but at this point, she didn't care. How could he just die like that? With no warning? Meghan felt an ache from her childhood creeping up on her like a ghost of Christmas past. She felt tears streaming down her face, though she wasn't sure if it was from the show or her own experience. Marcus noticed and pulled her in for a hug.

"Hey, Meghan, what's wrong? You know they have to kill off some of the characters, right? Otherwise, people would stop watching after the second season." Meghan turned and buried her head in Marcus's shoulder, not caring that just ten minutes ago, there was an awkward tension in the air. Now all she wanted was someone to hold her.

"I'm s-sorry, I don't know why I'm so upset. He just d-died like that? With no warning?" she mumbled into his hoodie.

"Unfortunately, that's usually how it happens." He spoke softly, his voice full of care and a twinge of sadness.

Meghan gripped him tighter and cried into him. He just held her, stroking her long brown hair, and breathing softly and evenly. After a few minutes, Meghan pulled herself together, wiping her eyes to remove the tears. Her hands came away smeared with black.

"Shit," she muttered, wiping away the mascara that had dripped down her face. Marcus reached out and wiped away the smudges on her cheek with his thumb. He stared into her eyes, and Meghan saw a longing, a want in his dark brown irises that wasn't there before. Meghan smiled at his gentle demeanor.

"Why do you think you reacted like that? I'll admit I almost cried when he died too, but that. . . " Marcus trailed off.

Meghan looked away, embarrassed. "That's a story for another night. Sorry."

"No, don't be. We all have our moments," he assured.

"And I think I have something to cheer you up," he said.

Meghan perked up. She knew Marcus was noted for giving gifts, but the thought that he would do something for her out of his free time made her heart hammer like a gong. He took out the plastic grocery store bag from earlier and set it on the bed. "Open it," he instructed.

Meghan took the bag in her hands gently and opened it, revealing a small black box. "Marcus."

"Just open it."

She did so, and inside on a small cushion lay two tiny golden bear earrings, each one holding a little bow. The same earrings that she'd put back just the other day. She hadn't stopped thinking about them, wishing she had gotten those instead of the hoops. Now, thanks to Marcus, she had both. She felt the butterflies returning to her stomach again, stronger. "Oh, I love them! How did you even remember?"

Marcus winked. "I always know," he joked, and Meghan nudged him playfully before putting the earrings in.

"What do you think?" she asked, turning right and then left to show off her new jewelry.

"I think you look beautiful," Marcus stated.

Meghan stopped. He said it, and she could tell he meant it. There was no hesitation in his voice. Just pure. . . love? Meghan stared into his eyes. *God, she could swim in them. Drown in them.* She would let them pull her under, deprive her of oxygen, and she would probably thank them.

"What?" she asked.

"You heard me." She gaped at him and his perfect curls.

"Meghan Truth, you are beautiful," he said again, probably just to mess with her.

Meghan's stomach was doing back flips. "You wanna elaborate on that, Marcus?" she said breathlessly, grinning.

"Your hair is so good damn perfect all the time, and your smile is like someone bottled up the sun and put it in your toothpaste. I want you so bad, Meghan. I want your green eyes and how they always make me second-guess myself. I want your hands, and how they always make me want to hold them. I want your laugh, and how it fills every room like liquid gold. I want you, Meghan, and I don't deserve you, I know that. But this whole time I've been so fricking scared to screw this up that I forgot how much I just want *you.*" He spoke, like honey dripping off his tongue, gripping Meghan's focus like a vise. Meghan tried to think and reason. But there was nothing. Nothing except him.

"Then come get me," she whispered.

Before she knew what she was doing, Meghan took Marcus's face in her hands, wrapping her fingers behind his neck and kissed him. The second their lips met, it was electric. She could feel him everywhere, taste him everywhere. She moved her hands up into his hair, and ran her fingers through it while he slowly undid her braid and did the same. His lips were soft, inviting. Meghan's heart was racing like a horse at the Kentucky Derby. She never wanted it to end. She wanted to feel this, feel him forever. He moved from her lips to her jawline and traced kisses down her neck. Meghan fought the urge just to let him kiss her forever. To just live like this, with Marcus's sweet taste lingering on her always. But already, she missed those eyes. Meghan grabbed Marcus's face again and turned it up to face her. She held him like that, staring into his eyes like they held the whole universe in their onyx depths.

"Damn, you're perfect," she breathed, taking it all in.

Marcus smiled again, and her whole world collapsed. This was it. She was his. "So, would now be an appropriate time to ask you to be my girlfriend?" Marcus asked, breathlessly, savoring the feeling.

"That would be a yes, you perfect idiot. How could you not tell I liked you before?" she asked, raising an eyebrow.

Marcus relished the relief that she said yes, before realizing that he was being asked a question. "I just wanted to be sure. Getting rejected by someone as insanely amazing as you might just kill me." He smirked, and Meghan fell apart. "I wanted to be sure." Meghan reached up and drew her fingers through his curls again.

"Then let me ease your nerves," she said. "I want you, Marcus. I've wanted you since junior year, and I haven't stopped wanting you. And the scary thing is I'm not sure that I ever will," she said, locking eyes with him the whole time.

Marcus drew her in for a hug, and Meghan couldn't help but feel warmth at how Marcus showed his affection. A kiss like lightning followed by the world's warmest hug. She leaned her head on his shoulder and drank in every second. She squeezed one final time before pulling away and standing up. Marcus followed in suite, and the pair got ready for bed. Brushing their teeth, which regretfully removed the taste of him on Meghan's tongue. And crawling into their respective beds. Once the lights were off, Meghan felt a gap next to her.

Loneliness. *Screw it.* "Marcus, are you awake?" She heard a low groan, and a sleepy voice replied.

"Yeah, why?"

"Come here with me," she said quickly.

"What?" Marcus asked, seemingly awake now.

"You heard me." Meghan grinned, stealing his line, which made her heart twirl earlier. She heard Marcus chuckle before also hearing the swish of a sleeping bag and the sound of Marcus moving across the room.

"And your father is OK with this?" he asked, arranging himself on the bed next to her.

"Well, we aren't doing anything, are we?" Meghan asked, breathing in his distinct bergamot and lemon scent.

"Just sleeping," he replied, fiddling with her hair in between his fingers.

"Then I don't see why it's a problem." She decided, snuggling up against him a little closer. They stayed like that the rest of the night. Marcus wouldn't admit it, but once he was sure Meghan was asleep, he planted a gentle kiss on her forehead.

"Goodnight, Meghan." He paused, uncertainly, and then spoke again, this time quietly and quickly. "I love you."

Meghan wouldn't admit it, but she was too nervous to fall asleep at all that night.

9
JASON

Jason was glad to finally get a good amount of sleep, and on the night before D.C., too. His mind had other plans as he tossed and turned despite getting into bed at a reasonable hour. He was beyond excited.

And he knew it would hurt him later, but Jason spent the majority of the night thinking about the semis. About the trip. About. . . anything. But just as quickly as he finally drifted off, his alarm clock blared once again, and he was forced to get up. He checked his phone, scrolling through messages as he always did first thing in the morning. Doing that first probably wasn't very healthy, but old habits die hard. He was surprised when he had about a million texts from Marcus. He called him immediately, fumbling with his phone as he listened to the line ring. Once. Twice. Three times. "Crap," Jason cursed. His phone buzzed.

At Meghan's pls pick me up don't ask questions. I'll explain later.

Jason laughed. He figured Marcus had gotten up to something last night, though he wasn't sure if that was a good thing or not.

Be right there. I'll grab your suitcase. Be ready in ten, he shot back.

Jason climbed out of his bed, straightening the sheets as best he could before making his way to the bathroom and quickly straightening up. His curly brown hair looked messy and unkempt after a night of sleep, but he didn't mind. He knew enough to figure that it usually straightened itself out after a while. He brushed his teeth and put on a pair of gray sweatpants and a loose-fitting tan Hollister hoodie. He slipped on his white Air Forces, and double checked his suitcase to make sure everything was there. It was only a four-day trip, but he liked to be prepared. He grabbed a few extra things and crept down the hallway to the door.

"Hey, Honey."

Jason jumped up. "Mom, what the hell? It's like 5:00 a.m.," he asked, pulling his mom into a farewell hug. She raised one eyebrow in a way that suggested she didn't agree with Jason's language, but she didn't push it.

"I needed to say bye before my baby goes off. This is like a preview of college." Jason's heart stung.

What was he gonna do, not knowing if his mom was being treated ok? What was she gonna do if he wasn't there to protect her?

"I'll call every night, promise. But I do have to go, Marcus needs a ride." Mrs. Everett smiled and handed Jason a small fold of cash.

"What's this?" Jason asked, meeting his mother's eyes.

"Just in case you need to get food, or a souvenir or something," she explained. "I want to know you'll have something with you if you need it."

Jason took it gratefully and put his hand on his mother's shoulder. "I'll be alright, you know that, right?"

Mrs. Everett sighed. "I know. Just be careful. And make sure Marcus stays out of trouble. I don't wanna know what shit that kid's gonna pull if he's unsupervised."

Jason laughed. "I will, don't worry. Take care of yourself, Mom. I don't want you to worry about me; I can hold my own," Jason stated.

Mrs. Everett wrapped her arms around Jason, her head now only reaching his shoulders. "You're getting tall, you know that?"

Jason grinned. "I know it. I love you, Mom."

Mrs. Everett breathed in sharply. "I love you too. Now go get Marcus before he blows your phone up," she said, chuckling, and Jason noticed that his ringer had been going off almost nonstop for their whole conversation.

"I will," he said. He stepped out of the house and grabbed his keys on the way out. "Call me if anything comes up, OK?" he said to her. She just nodded, and he stepped outside, closing the door behind him.

It was still pitch black outside, with the tiniest sliver of sunlight threatening to peek out from behind the trees. Jason yawned, as if suddenly aware that it was only a couple of hours ago that he had gone to bed. He hopped in his car and started to Marcus's house to grab his things. He lived only five minutes away, but when they were younger, they joked about moving in next to each other. Sleepovers every night, and Nintendo every morning. *Now he's having sleepovers with his girlfriend,* Jason thought. He smiled at the thought of Marcus finding the one, even if this wasn't the case. He loved seeing his best friend happy like this, even if he was the third wheel for a while.

It was all worth it to see the glow coming from Marcus whenever he talked about Meghan. He pulled up to

Marcus's driveway, slamming the door shut behind the parked car. He took the key from under the doormat, where it always was and unlocked the door. As he pushed the tall oak doors open, a voice called out from the kitchen. "Marcus? Is that you?"

It was Mrs. Levine, Marcus's mom. "No, Mrs. Levine, it's Jason. I'm just picking up his stuff before we head to the airport," he explained, stepping into the kitchen to greet her. She was short, about 5'2" and was sporting a floral bathrobe, with a matching bonnet tied around her head. She was holding a coffee pot in one hand, and as she strode toward Jason, he could see the bubbling anger in her eyes. "Where the hell did Marcus go last night? I swear if he was out with that girl, I'll—"

"No, no, he stayed at my place last night, he just wanted to sleep in, so I told him I'd get his bag for him," Jason quickly lied, already preparing to scold Marcus about not telling his mom earlier.

"Oh, well, good. His stuff is in his room, sorry about how dirty it is, but you know him." She laughed and pulled Jason in for a hug. "It's good to see you, Jason. You keep my boy outta trouble, you hear?"

Jason reciprocated the hug and laughed. "I will, don't worry. But we gotta let him have a little fun sometimes, right?"

Mrs. Levine laughed. "Right, because that's how teenage boys get into medical school. Fun," she reasoned and moved to the counter to pour a cup of coffee.

Jason headed to the back of the hall, where Marcus's room was. It had navy blue walls, with a twin bed in the middle. There was a white desk to one side, and on the other wall was a collection of shelves, each holding trophies and medals from his track career. Jason felt a twinge of sadness. Marcus had worked so hard all these years to get to varsity track, and now that he was here, he went and sprained his knee. He picked up one of the silver trophies, turning it over. On the back, it read, *2019 men's 400-meter champion, Marcus Levine.* Jason reminisced. He remembered that meet, Jason himself won second, but he couldn't care less. Not when his best friend just won his heat and qualified for finals. Jason himself had qualified the previous week, but he had silently prayed every night that Marcus would, too. It wouldn't have been the same without him. Now he would have to finish the season without his best friend by his side. That stung.

However, Jason knew that Marcus would still support him. He reached for the small black suitcase on the floor, as well as a small black fanny pack.

"The hell is this?" Jason laughed to himself. He grabbed it anyway and started out the door, but was quickly stopped by Mrs. Levine.

"Heading out, Jason?" she asked sweetly.

"Yes, ma'am, I've got all his stuff. I'll tell him to call you once we land."

Mrs. Levine smiled. "You're too sweet. And thank you for keeping him in line. He wouldn't be where he is now without your influence. You're good for him, Jason." She smiled and squeezed his shoulder.

"I'm not sure I'd be either," Jason chuckled lightly.

"Now you go have a good time," she instructed.

"We will, thanks again, Mrs. Levine!" Jason called out, already walking out to his car.

"I've told you, boy, just call me Jane," she replied.

"Sure, Mrs. Levine." Jason stepped into his car and slowly pulled out of the driveway. Jane rolled her eyes and waved from the doorway, before turning and shutting the door behind her, her floral robe swirled behind her as she did.

"God damn it, Marcus." He groaned, driving to Meghan's house to pick him up. It's bad enough that he had to lie to Jane, but having to pick him up from her house? Jason just hoped it didn't get awkward. The drive was short, only a couple of miles away from where Marcus lived, but with how slow the sun was rising, it felt like years before he pulled up at the familiar orange -tinted driveway. He didn't even have to get out of the car, before Marcus stepped out of the door, followed by Meghan, who. . . *What? Gave him a kiss?* She stepped back inside, and Marcus started for the car, grinning at Jason like a madman the entire time.

"Meghan doesn't need a ride?" he asked, raising his brows and tilting his head a little in a look that said *'I refuse to be your personal taxi.'*

"Nah, her mom wanted to take her to say goodbye," Marcus explained. Then he gave Jason a nudge at the look on his face.

"Oh, shove off," he said, waving his hand.

Jason put the car in reverse, backing out of the driveway, and entered directions to the airport in his Google Maps. "So...anything I should know about?" Jason asked, and he could hardly hold in his laughter.

"Yeah, um, we watched Netflix, and I gave her the earrings, which she loved, and we just sort of...clicked," he explained, folding his arms behind his head and kicking his feet up on the dashboard.

"Get your nasty ass feet off the dashboard, and give me more details. I did not just lie to your mom about you staying at Meghan's just for you to tell me it was 'good,'" Jason lectured, giving Marcus a glare.

"Fine, we kissed. And it was. . . intense," Marcus admitted, flushing deeply.

"Oh." That was all Jason could think to say. He knew they had gotten closer, and especially after sleeping over, they were bound to kiss eventually. Jason just wasn't expecting it. "That's amazing, man. I mean, was it amazing? Or am I getting the wrong message here?"

"No, it was pretty damn amazing. Everything about her is just perfect. And she knows it too." Marcus laughed.

"She's hot, that's for sure. You scored on that, Marcus," Jason admitted.

"She's beautiful," Marcus corrected.

"I'm happy for you, really. You found your other half," Jason said, smiling. He remembered learning about Greek mythology in history class. About the Myth of the missing half. It was believed that humans were first created with four arms, four legs, and a head with two faces. The humans were then divided in half, and it is said that they would spend the rest of their lives searching for their other half. Their soulmate.

Jason thought about what Meghan and Marcus would look like as an Androgynous. Then he cursed himself mentally for ever daring to think about that. But if Marcus did just find his second half, Jason couldn't help but be a little jealous. He thought about his second half, if it was out there somewhere. What was she doing right now? Painting? Writing? Playing a sport, or maybe she's in a different time zone and is still asleep. Jason lost himself in the idea that his second half was out there somewhere, trying to find him, too. Instead, he decided to let the light shine on Marcus, who was currently trying to find himself in the mix of friendship and love.

"It's all gonna work out. You'll take her out to dinner or something in D.C., treat her right, and she's gonna love you. You're more lovable than you think you are," Jason insisted, and he smiled when he saw a flash of confidence across Marcus's face.

"Thanks, man. Now we just gotta get you a girlfriend," he joked.

Jason sighed. "It'll happen when the time is right," Jason philosophized.

"Or in other words, 'I can't get a girlfriend.'" Marcus nudged his shoulder. "I'm kidding. It'll happen. Just give it time, and while you wait, enjoy life."

Jason sighed, turning his head. "Your lip OK?" Marcus asked, noticing a small red cut on Jason's lip from earlier.

"Fine," he replied, a little more snappily than he intended.

Marcus smiled sadly and put a hand on his shoulder. Jason leaned into the touch. It was a touch he trusted. Warm and welcoming. He smiled softly, then yawned.

"Why does our flight have to be so damn *early?*" Jason groaned.

"Not a morning person, huh?" Marcus laughed.

"You know I'm not." Instead of putting in the effort to stay awake through conversation, he turned on the radio and cranked the volume high. He loved music. It didn't matter what genre or what time of day. The beats and the lyrics always managed to bring Jason to another world. Jason queued something he thought fit the mood, figuring Marcus wouldn't notice. Marcus noticed and immediately shot him a lazy glance.

"Now you're just patronizing me." 'Brown Eyed Girl' by Van Morrison blared from the car's stereo as Marcus rolled down his window, allowing air to flow in the car like a tornado. It was like a dream. Jason was sure the minimal time he'd spent on his hair that morning was all for nothing now, with the way the wind was blowing it around, but he didn't care. Right now, there was just him and Marcus, the wind, and the music. His father, miles and miles behind him. His future is miles ahead. They cranked it up louder as they pulled into the airport's parking lot, and continued singing in the car even after they parked, making sure they had time to finish the song.

"And you're my brown-eyed girl." Jason leaned back in the seat, plopping his feet up on the dashboard and squeezing his eyes shut as he mouthed every word.

Marcus let out an exasperated laugh, folding over until his head hit the dash. He was positively glowing. Jason smiled. "Always the right song for the right time. You might be like a DJ reincarnate," Marcus mused.

"Or a Bach or a Mozart, or a Beethoven or something, right?" Jason prompted.

"You think you could be a Beethoven? What makes you even remotely close to Beethoven? He composed symphonies *without being able to hear*," Marcus argued, his brows drawing together as he no doubt pictured a younger Beethoven plinking away at keys that produced no noise.

"I feel like I could do it."

"How could you even say that?"

"Well, for starters, I *can* hear. So one step ahead."

"He was an icon, Jason, a historical figure!"

"The only reason I'm not a historical figure is because I'm not dead yet. Quit giving Beethoven a lead." Jason smiled to himself at Marcus's discomfort. He knew he could never be a Beethoven; hell, he listened to his music while he studied. But he loved to make Marcus squirm.

He laughed, pushing up out of his seat. The pair made their way to the security check-in to find the rest of their group. It wasn't a huge margin outside of the track team, but enough —about 20 people, including Jason and Marcus. Meghan, Zoe, Scarlett, Adam, Ben, Logan, Beau, and the rest of the others that Jason recognized from their history and English classes, but never bothered getting to know.

"Settle down, everyone. I know we're all excited, but let's keep composed, shall we?" Mr. McApherry instructed. "Now let's get into pairs of three, who you'll sit with on the plane. Every seat will be full, so please don't argue too much about where you end up," he addressed. People shuffled their feet. "That means move, people!" Coach Allen bellowed from where he stood behind them. Students began shuffling into pairs. The track kids laughed a little at the other kids' terrified faces. The only Coach Allen they knew was a strict, demanding teacher who didn't give second chances. Jason wondered how they would've reacted if they knew that the whole track team had set up a Tinder account for him, and were currently trying to help him find love. He didn't protest, which made it even funnier.

"Where do you wanna sit?" Jason asked Marcus, who was eyeing Meghan out of his peripheral vision. "I'm with Zoe; she's scared of flying," Meghan explained. Marcus leaned over to Jason's ear. But he didn't have to say anything. Jason knew.

"It's OK, you go with her," he said. Marcus looked at him gratefully and moved to where Zoe and Meghan were talking. From the looks of it, Meghan was thrilled when he asked, based on the way she threw her arms around him. Jason was less than thrilled, however, as pairs moved to their respective areas, slowly draining out.

"Hey Jason, wanna go with me?" Logan asked, stepping forward. Jason was a good friend of Logan. Not like Marcus, but still, they'd known each other for a good few years. He had ginger hair, but he dyed it brown once, so it was more of a muted strawberry brown. His eyes were so blue that it was almost scary when he looked at you. He wasn't pudgy, but his frame was less defined and more muted. He wore a black athletic tee that hugged his form and black sweatpants. He stifled a yawn.

"Sounds great. Who else do we need three to a row?" Jason asked, openly. From across the airport, he spotted Meghan and Zoe, linking arms with Marcus, and arguing with Scarlett about something. Jason could tell by her body language that Scarlett was not happy about what they were telling her. She threw her arms up in the air in protest before dramatically stalking away, and turning towards.

Oh no. Hell to the no.

"Hey, Logan, is it cool if I sit with you guys? My friend wants to sit with her boyfriend, and I'm officially the third wheel now, so. . . " Scarlett trailed off, staring at the floor.

Oh, knock it off, Jason thought. It was all an act, he could tell. Logan, however, was not the brightest and obviously wasn't picking up on the social cues because he seemed ecstatic at the idea. "Yeah, sure. We needed one more person anyway, so that checks out," he agreed.

"No, actually, I was about to ask um. . . Ben if he wanted to sit with us. He doesn't have a group, so I think that would be better," Jason quickly interjected, hoping he could save the situation.

"That's nice of you, Jason, but I actually do have a group," Ben called out from a few groups over. Jason palmed his face and groaned.

"Thanks, Ben," he grumbled sarcastically.

"No problem," Ben jived cheerfully. Jason lifted his head to reveal Scarlett glaring down at him.

"Listen, I'm just as upset about this as you are, but I'm fine with choosing Meghan's happiness over my own. So please just pull yourself together, stop acting like a little bitch and sit on the stupid plane," Scarlett hissed through gritted teeth.

"Rude, but fine. At least you said please," Jason relented, slightly shocked at her forwardness. Logan slithered in between the two and draped an arm around either of them.

"This is gonna be great," he cheered, like a positive ray of sun.

Scarlett scoffed and pushed his hand off of her shoulder, but Jason couldn't help but smile a little.

10

SCARLETT

An hour later, Scarlett sat in the window seat of a freezing plane. *Seriously, I couldn't have remembered to bring a jacket?* At least she got the seat she wanted. Looking out the window always eased a little bit of the anxiety she felt when flying. She couldn't help it. Zoe was scared of flying too, but it was worse for Zoe, so Scarlett took the knife's sharp end and sat with someone she hated, just to make her happy. But that wouldn't stop her from doing it again. Even if she had to endure something that wasn't great, she would do it if it meant her friends wouldn't have to. So she sat next to one person she truly hated, so her best friend could sit by someone she truly loved.

Sometimes she just wished someone would think about her needs like that, too. That someone would willingly prioritize her. It wasn't all bad, though. Logan was there, too, but he'd never been much of a conversation starter; instead lingering on the aisle seat, his nose already buried in his computer.

"Just catching up on homework," he'd say, though Scarlett wasn't sure what classes he was taking, to constantly have that much missing work.

Jason sat in the middle, sandwiched between them, and while they each had a good amount of room, Scarlett couldn't help but feel a little bit bad for his unfortunate seating. At least she had the pretty view of the ocean beneath her as they flew from the California coast to the capital of the world. She decided that between reading and watching movies, she could pass the time fairly well. The plane jolted and Scarlett tightened her grip on the arm rest without realizing. The pilot announced takeoff, and as the plane sped up on the runway, so did Scarlett's heart. Her knees bounced up and down rapidly as she tried to calm the panic that squeezed her heart. Her hands hurt from how hard she gripped the arm rests, but she didn't care. Not at a time like this. Jason seemed to be watching the takeoff happen with a pleased expression, but that quickly turned to confusion, and then concern as he noticed Scarlett visibly picking at her nails, and shaking like a newborn lamb.

"Are you dying or something?" he mumbled lazily.

Scarlett didn't reply, shutting her eyes as hard as they would go. Jason sighed.

"Don't make me regret this," he complained before placing one hand on Scarlett's thigh to slow the shaking and lacing her fingers through his with the other. Her breath quickened as she looked over at Jason, who wasn't even looking at her, but was now stroking her hand with his thumb in an act of comfort. Scarlett would usually fling him off, but now she knew she needed this. No one else would help her, so why not him? She squeezed his hand harder as they gained altitude and soared into the air. She kept her eyes fixed on the horizon the entire time, glad for Jason's presence, but also hardly aware of it. She was too nervous about the fact that they were literally in the air to pay attention to the way Jason squeezed her thigh, gently, comfortingly. She tried to let herself be grounded by his touch, an ever-present warmth on her thigh. She took some deep breaths once their altitude evened out and turned her head. Jason was still there, scrolling through something on his phone, the other hand still gripping hers. She swiftly let go of his hand, completely aware of the imprints she made in his palm with her nails.

"Sorry," she breathed.

Jason didn't even look up. "Don't be, my mom is scared of flying too." He shrugged, and that was that. "But don't go telling everyone about that either," he requested.

Scarlett nodded. "What happens in the air, stays in the air," she joked and scrolled through movies on Netflix before settling on some romcom she'd definitely seen before. She could've sworn she saw the ghost of a smile lingering on Jason's lips for a second before he quickly replaced it with his usual solemn expression. Hours passed, and Scarlett seriously thought she might die on this plane; she was so bored. Logan and Jason had taken to playing Mario Kart on Logan's Nintendo Switch, which left Scarlett alone with her thoughts. She decided to take out a book she'd brought and read for a while instead. They were close, less than two hours away from D.C. She grabbed 'If Cats Disappeared From The World' by Genki Kawamura, and flipped to the first page. This wasn't the first time she'd read it, but Scarlett could never get bored with stories that made her think. And how she would spend her last days was definitely something to ponder over. She felt Jason's gaze over her shoulder, and she turned her shoulders a little, blocking the book from his vision.

"Is that Genki Kawamura? The cat one?" he asked, still eyeing the cover.

"Yeah, you read it?" she asked.

"About a hundred times," he stated, then went right back to his Mario Kart game.

A hundred times. Damn. Scarlett read for a while, then simply stared out the window. The sun was fully raised now, with the time difference, it was around 3:00 p.m. D.C. time. She looked over at Logan and Jason, hoping for some entertainment, but the pair were both asleep, Logan leaning on his tray table, and Jason stretched out against his headrest. Scarlett rolled her eyes at them and turned to the window again, squinting out into the clouds rolling over the sky.

Whump!

What the hell was that? Scarlett tried to turn, but felt something soft and heavy on her shoulder, which prevented her from doing so. Jason's head lolled against her shoulder, his curly brown hair covering her neck like a blanket. His breathing was slow and even, and his shut eyes revealed long dark lashes protruding from his eyelids. Scarlett stiffened. *What could she do?* If she moved him, she could risk waking him up, and she saw how tired he was earlier. He shuffled a bit, a low groan escaping his lips before going still again. Scarlett watched his face with fascination. All the anger and resentment he sent towards her melted when he was asleep. His face was so calm, not twisted up in a grin or scrunched up in disgust. Just calm.

Scarlett shoved down the feeling of warmth that threatened to show and decided to just let him sleep. She turned towards her window and let the view of Washington, D.C. slowly come into view.

When they landed, roughly a half-hour later, Scarlett gently nudged Jason off her shoulder and prayed that he didn't notice. *This whole situation would be much easier if he didn't know he practically drooled all over me.* Jason stirred and slowly opened his eyes, drinking in the lights through squinted eyes. He blinked away the confusion as he realized where they were. Scarlett pretended not to watch his sleepy glances around the plane from the corner of her eyes. He sent a suspicious glare her direction before shaking his head slightly to himself. Then he turned to Logan and nudged him awake.

"Get the hell up, man, we're here," he growled, his voice low from rest.

"Go away," Logan mumbled, eyes still shut.

Jason rolled his eyes before shoving Logan off of his tray table and clipping it up, removing any possibility of Logan finding a comfortable position. He fell forward, but woke up enough to sit back up before he embarrassed himself and sprawled out into the aisle.

"Damn it, Jason, you suck," Logan snapped, rubbing his eyes.

Luckily, they were in the first half of the plane, so they would get to unload quicker than most. The trio stood up, gathering their belongings from the floor and their suitcases from the overhead bins.

"Need some help, Artega?" Jason asked, laughing as he watched Scarlett struggle to grab her suitcase from the bins.

Scarlett grunted in frustration. "Honestly, yeah, that'd be great, Jason," she admitted.

"Thought so." He turned and started off the airplane, not even sparing a glance back at Scarlett, who stood there, mouth gaping.

"I'm gonna kill that kid," she cursed, still struggling to pull the suitcase out from above.

"Want me to do it?" Someone asked.

Scarlett turned. Beau Singh stood behind her, smiling with a mouth of white teeth. He had blonde hair, with brown roots, which made it obvious that he dyed it. His eyes were a honey amber, and when he smiled, his full pink lips upturned a little more on one side than the other.

"That would be great, thanks." Beau nodded, and swiftly grabbed the suitcase out of its compartment like it weighed nothing.

"Not a problem. Scarlett, right? It's been a while."

"Yeah, hi, Beau." That earned her a nod.

"Our parents are friends, right? I swear I've seen you at parties before."

Scarlett scoffed. "If you did, I was probably the one on the couch with my phone. I'm not really a party person."

He laughed, the noise echoing through the plane. "Well, it was good to see you, but I think I'm holding up the line."

Scarlett blushed as she realized she'd been holding up the whole plane from unloading. "Right, we'd better get off." Beau agreed.

They made their way off the plane and rejoined the rest of the group. Scarlett moved to stand by Zoe and Meghan, who were now joined by Marcus and. . . Jason. Scarlett sent Meghan a glance, which she meant as *'Why the hell does he come with the package?'* Meghan replied with a pitiful puppy-eyed look, as if saying, *'I know you hate him, but he comes with Marcus, so please understand.'* Scarlett rolled her eyes in defeat, deciding to try to ignore Jason's lingering presence as best she could. Instead, she listened to Mr. McApherry giving out handbooks of D.C., as well as rooming assignments and maps. Zoe stared at her rooming arrangement and squealed.

"Scarlett, Meghan! We're all in a room together!" Scarlett sighed, relieved. She hoped she'd get put in a room with someone she knew, but it seemed like God was on her side today, because she got put with two of her best friends.

"Wait, there are two beds and only three of us." Scarlett reasoned.

"Someone is gonna bet a full bed while the others share." Zoe raised an eyebrow and smirked at Meghan.

"Maybe Meg should get the full bed. You know, in case Marcus wants to come over--" She was cut off by Meghan slapping a hand over her mouth and flushing a deep crimson. Scarlett laughed at Meghan's embarrassment.

"You don't have to be embarrassed, Meg, Zoe's just jealous that she can't get a boyfriend." Scarlett shot back, jabbing Zoe in the ribs with her elbow. Zoe rolled her eyes.

"Like you have one either."

"True," Meghan piped.

"Oh shut up. Both of you," Scarlett grumbled, not finding the situation amusing. Meghan and Zoe just looked at each other and burst into laughter, tears filling their eyes as they clutched their stomachs.

"Something funny, girls?" Mr. McApherry asked, raising an eyebrow at the two girls cackling on the airport tarmac. Now it was Scarlett's turn to laugh. She chuckled at herself as they immediately flushed and straightened up.

"No, sorry, Zoe just said something stupid," Meghan stuttered. Zoe glared while Scarlett fought back a smile.

"I see. Now I want you kids to have fun, but there needs to be some rules." And with that, he jumped into a long list of rules and expectations for the trip.

Some were simple enough, like no going out after 11:00, always staying with a buddy, etc. But Scarlett thought some rules were unfair, like how their phones had to be taken away when in museums, or that AirPods were banned on the buses. Mr. McApherry explained that these have been the rules since the trip started, and that it helped keep the students in touch with reality and their own friendships. Scarlett thought that was bull. Just because she wants to listen to music to make time pass doesn't mean she's out of touch with reality.

Nevertheless, she made an effort to put them to memory. If she broke the rules and got in trouble, she definitely wouldn't be winning any awards for her application, now would she? The group finished with their brief rules lesson and boarded the chauffeur bus to the hotel. It wasn't the fanciest hotel in the world, just a local Hilton, but it was nicer than where Scarlett had ever stayed before. Her family was more into camping, or backpacking through Europe and staying in hostel-type accommodations rather than the clean, white sheet hotel room type. Scarlett remembered a time when they stayed in a hostel on the coast of Sweden, and an older man cat-called her the entire night. She had to sleep on an itchy cot less than ten feet away from him, and she couldn't sleep the entire night. After that, she decided to let her family take trips without her.

She smiled, hoping that this would be a new and exhilarating experience. The second they made it to their hotel room, Scarlett flopped on the bed, exhausted.

"Long day, huh?" Zoe smirked, staring down at her.

"Mhmm." Scarlett groaned from the mattress.

"You probably have time to take a nap before dinner. We're going to get sushi!" Zoe grinned. Scarlett smiled. Zoe loved sushi. Scarlett wasn't a fan, but she did like teriyaki chicken, so it worked out.

The schedule that Mr. McApherry had given them said that they would attend dinner and then the play, so they should dress formally. Scarlett had brought an old dress of her mom's that she loved. It was long and silver with a slit going up to her thigh. The straps were flowy and fell off her shoulders, revealing her collarbone. Scarlett hardly ever felt pretty, but in that dress she felt beautiful and confident. She made herself comfortable on the bed and slowly drifted off, comforted by the thoughts of her gorgeous dress waiting for her and the memorable experiences that were destined to come.

11
JASON

Jason sat cross-legged in a swivel chair, AirPods in, and mind elsewhere. The minute they'd gotten to the room, he'd unpacked, tucking everything away neatly, and making sure he was all settled before curling up and taking some time to relax before dinner.

He pulled up the search bar and typed in aquariums in the area. There was one, the National Aquarium in Baltimore, that Jason had been dying to go to. His heart raced at the thought of being able to observe the marine life, maybe even sketch some anatomy. There was one problem, though. It was roughly an hour away, so unless he could convince Mr. McApherry to let him stray from the group for a couple of hours, he was screwed. He fingered the tiny black tip reef shark necklace, which was always strung around his neck. His mother had gifted it to him three Christmases ago, and he hadn't taken it off since. It served as a reminder of why he wanted what he did, and that no matter how chaotic life got, at least he had ambitions.

"Thinking about something?" Jason turned to see Marcus peeking up at him from his phone.

"Nothing."

"Say it," Marcus prompted.

"Fine, the National Aquarium is less than an hour from us, and I've been fricking dying to go since I was like twelve," he admitted.

"Good thing we have some free time, then." Marcus grinned, tossing him a folded-up brochure.

Jason unfolded the paper. It read, 2024 English-History D.C. trip agenda. "Look at the highlighted part."

Jason peered down at the Tuesday schedule. 1:00-4:00 p.m. recreation before the National Museum of Art, and grinned. Marcus smiled at seeing Jason happy like this. Marine life had always been a hobby of his, but Marcus was starting to think it was more than that. Jason tilted his head back onto the edge of the chair, swiveling around in circles with his feet. D.C. was beautiful. The bustle of the city, accompanied by the delicacy of the art and the integrity of the monuments. Each building had a purpose, a story. There was hardly a single store in the city that didn't have some historical background to it. Except maybe the Starbucks, but even those seemed to feel more important. The boys' phone dinged at the same time.

This is a group chat for every student participating in this trip. Please meet at the lobby in half an hour.

There was a pause, and then another ding. *If you're late, I will leave without you; you're old enough to be punctual.*

"Guess we'd better get ready then," Marcus proposed.

The two made eye contact before both rushing to the bathroom door, shoving each other out of the way, and fighting to get to the area first. Jason stubbed his toe on the edge of the dresser. "Ah God damn it!" he cursed, gripping his foot like a lifeline. Marcus let out a shrill laugh and turned the knob of the bathroom door.

"It's locked!" Marcus put an ear to the door.

"The shower's on." Jason raised his eyebrows before coming to a realization.

"Beau, you in there?" he called out.

"Yeah," a low voice called back. Jason laughed.

"Hurry the hell up, we're leaving in thirty." Beau cursed and turned the water off.

"Be out in a minute, patience, Jason."

"Patience, my ass. My hair is a mess," Marcus complained, scrunching his curls in the mirror.

"It looks fine, trust me." Marcus looked skeptical, so he added, "Meghan would think so too." That seemed to do the trick, because when Beau finally got out of the shower, he let Jason change first. He grabbed the blue coat and belt, along with the black trousers. He pulled them on carefully, smoothing out his coat and tucking his necklace into the collar, so it wasn't visible. He parted his hair and moved it to one side, combing it out with his fingers. The dark blue of his jacket reflected the coolness in his eyes and the sharpness of his features. Once satisfied enough with his appearance, he sprayed some cologne and gave the bathroom to Marcus, who ran right in, shutting the door loudly behind him.

"Someone's gotta tell that kid there's a closet to change in, too," Beau joked, smoothing his hair with a comb.

"You did kind of take forever in there, to be fair, man." Jason chuckled dryly, but he didn't find it funny. Beau had been on his nerves ever since his last track meet. He never even reached out to Marcus to make sure he was alright after his accident. That didn't sit right with him, especially because he was sitting right in the bleachers. Beau just shrugged it off and went right back to touching up his hair, stroking it with such delicacy you would've thought it was spun gold.

Jason turned away, not being able to bear Beau gawking at himself for a minute longer, and instead grabbed his shoes from the drawer. He needed black dress shoes for the occasion, but since he didn't have any, and the cost of a suit was already high enough, he wore Brian's. They were almost too big, with a bit of wiggle room at the toe, but they worked. Jason slipped them on, stoking the sleek leather with his thumb, and staring at them like a foreign object. But they weren't a poisonous apple or a UFO, just his dad's shoes. Jason shook off the gnawing feeling he got when he wore anything of his father's and stood in front of the mirror. He was Jason, captain of the varsity track team, an all-A's student, reliable friend, and hopefully someday, to someone, loving boyfriend.

But when he looked in the mirror, he didn't see himself. He saw Brian. The suit and dress shoes made that resemblance stand out even more, in a way Jason was not ready for. His fingers closed around the shark on his necklace as he twisted it around in an attempt to calm the waves that churned in his mind. The person looking back at him could be him. Or it could be a monster, someone who'd promised to take care of them, but took advantage instead, the second he had their trust. To be honest, sometimes it was hard for Jason to tell the difference between the two. Marcus stepped out of the bathroom, dressed, and ready.

"Stop admiring yourself, Jason, you look fine," Beau smirked, tying his own dress shoes on the foot of the bed. Marcus looked at Jason and recognized the self-conscious glare that Jason gave himself in the mirror. When he struggled to tell himself apart from his father. Marcus planted a hand on his shoulder.

"You're not him, remember?" he assured, loud enough so only Jason could hear. He took a deep breath, only somewhat shaky.

"Yeah, I know." He exhaled and stepped away from the mirror. He did a once-over of Marcus. The blood red of his suit and trousers looked like rich dark roses against his molten chocolate skin. The belt tied it all together, bringing out the warmth in his eyes and the sweetness in his smile. Jason stared at him and understood why Meghan liked him so much. The two were made for each other.

"Marcus, you look great! I mean, really, great! Shit, I'd better start unpacking my things into your side of the bed, because no way is Meghan letting you sleep alone tonight." Jason absolutely grinned, clapping Marcus on the shoulder and giving him a brotherly hug.

"Thanks, man, but no way am I sleeping in a room with Scarlett and Zoe, too," he poked.

"Yeah, Artega seemed so fed up with you being around Meghan today, she might just off you in the middle of the night."

"Zoe would probably help too," Marcus added, and shuddered.

"You shouldn't say things about them like that," Beau piped, standing from where he'd been scrolling in his phone.

"You have to admit, being the third wheel is rough, but Scarlett's being a little dramatic. I mean, I'm technically the third wheel too, but I'm not acting like *that*," Jason explained. He saw her send a couple of good death glares in Marcus's direction before they'd even gotten through customs. If that wasn't best friend jealousy, Jason didn't know what was.

"Maybe she's just pissed about having to sit with you," Beau smirked. "I mean, she does hate you, right? Can't really blame her, I wouldn't be chipped either," he remarked, then stalked out of the room to meet with the group.

"'You shouldn't say things about them like that,'" Marcus mocked, balling up his fists and uncurling them repeatedly.

"Since when is he such a shit sack?" Jason had to admit, he felt a little betrayed. Beau used to be so nice, always coming to sleepovers and birthdays; he was the life of the party. Now, it seemed like he had something against Jason, but he couldn't figure out why.

The two headed down into the lobby, where the group was already waiting for them. "Where's Scarlett?" Zoe asked from a few feet in front.

"Not sure, she said she was just grabbing her purse," Meghan said, checking her lip gloss application with her phone camera.

Jason thought it was weird for Scarlett to be running late. She was usually pretty on time, except for History class, though Jason figured that might be on purpose. He figured she probably got lost in the elevator or forgot what floor she was on. Scarlett was smart, but her sense of direction was nonexistent.

"Alright, children, gather round Mr. McApherry, there you go," Mr. McApherry announced, waving kids in like a shepherd.Jason rolled his eyes and moved closer. "The bus is leaving in two minutes, it doesn't wait for you, so don't wait for it, get your butts on, that's it," he instructed, guiding the crowd of kids up the steps and into the bus. It was more of a large van than a bus, though. There were no sticky bench seats or windows that were stuck shut, but rather actual seats and cup holders. *They really spoiled us this time.* The bus doors closed, a signal that every student who was going to be here was here. Jason turned his head around, scanning the bus.

"Marcus, Scarlett's not here yet."

"Well, she'd better put being a runner to use because I don't think Mr. McApherry will wait for anyone," Marcus quipped.

"Should I tell him?" Marcus shrugged, and before Jason could think, he called out.

"Wait, I don't think Scarlett's here yet. We can't just leave her." This earned him a glance from Mr. McApherry and a nod of approval from Meghan.

"That's what I've been trying to tell you! Just wait like two more damn minutes, *please*."

"Language, Meghan," Mr. McApherry said sternly, raising an eyebrow.

"I was very clear on the time of departure, but since you two seem so insistent, we will all wait for Miss Artega," he concluded.

Meghan smiled and went right back to watching out the bus window, waiting. Thirty seconds later, Scarlett came running out, her hair tied up in a braided bun updo, golden curls spilling out all over her head, framing her face. She wore a shimmery silver gown, with a slit up the side that made Jason second-guess his morals for a moment. Her collarbone was draped in a silver cross that she always wore, as well as a silver and navy blue heart gem, on a silver chain.

Her eyes were painted in a gorgeous brown eye shadow, with a sharp black eyeliner wing to tie it all together. On her face was a look of relief as she hurried to the bus, grateful that it hadn't pulled out minutes ago.

"Look who finally showed," Mr. McApherry jeered, sending her a curious look.

"Crap, I'm so sorry, I know you said west exit, but I couldn't find it on a map, so I had to ask an employee, and then the elevator got stopped like *fifteen fricking times*, but—"

"Save it, I really don't care, just please don't be late next time? I know you love the museums; it would be a shame if you missed out." Scarlett nodded in appreciation and sat with Meghan, who gaped at her dress for at least ten minutes.

Jason rubbed his forehead in annoyance and watched out the window as they made their way through the bustling city.

They stopped for dinner at a sushi place on a corner, filling up on sashimi and bento boxes before making their way to the theater. It was large, with extravagant fixtures lining the ceiling, and illuminating the neat white tile floors that led to a wide entrance with double doors. The entire senior class lined up for a group picture outside the elegant building. Jason thought it just looked like an old. . . well, theater. But he noticed that Meghan seemed to be gushing to Scarlett about the architecture, the art that lined the walls, and anything you could see, she could talk about. Scarlett listened with the same amount of reciprocation, nodding and smiling at Meghan's enthusiasm.

"She loves this, the art, the structure, theater, all of it." Marcus admired from next to Jason. He spoke to him, yet his eyes were fixed on her the entire time. She wore a black bow in her hair that matched her black dress, and it swayed a little as she glided along the hallway. His eyes trailed from Meghan to Scarlett, who walked beside her, her silver dress trailing ever so slightly behind her, and the bounce of her curls only reflected the gold streaks in her hair. But this was Scarlett Artega; she wasn't anything but competition, Jason reminded himself. Nothing but an object blocking Jason from his scholarship, an object that had to be moved aside in order to reach his goal.

The group filed into the theater, taking their seats in the marked rows. Jason and Marcus sat with Adam, Ben, and a couple of other boys on the trip, as well as Beau, who very obviously tried to sit as far from Jason as he could. In the row behind him sat Scarlett, Meghan, Zoe, and the rest of the group. The play was *Hamlet* by Shakespeare, and while it was a tragic play, it was Mr. McApherry's favorite, so naturally, he dragged the whole class along with him.

"Hey." A voice called from behind him.

Jason swiveled his head around to see Scarlett leaning forward in her chair to reach his ear. "Can't you duck or something? Your big head is blocking my view." Jason snorted.

"Is it that I'm too tall for you? Or you're just too short? What are you, 5 feet?" Scarlett rolled her eyes and gave him a cold glare.

"5'2", and I already told you it's not your height, just your head." Jason raised an eyebrow.

"So I'm too smart and I have more brains? My intelligence is blocking your view?" he jeered, knowing it would annoy her. "Or your ego."

She sank back in her seat, seemingly giving up on the hopes of ever being able to see. Jason turned back around to face the stage, but quietly attempted to sink a little lower in his seat. The play went well, with the backstory being laid out, and Hamlet's need for revenge being displayed in the first half. During intermission, the lights came on, and Jason decided to head to the lobby and check it out while they had some extra time.

"Skittles, Jason," Marcus called when he spotted Jason leaving the row. Jason nodded at him and continued out of the theater. He wandered for a bit, admiring the beautiful interior of the building and eyeing anything that seemed interesting before locating the snack booth and stepping in line. He'd almost made it to the front of the line when he spotted a familiar head of dirty blonde waves in the crowd. Scarlett made her way towards the booth while Jason was eager to get away from it.

"What can I do for you?" the concessions clerk asked, tearing Jason's focus off the stormy-eyed girl.

"I'll take a Skittles, and M&Ms, please." He pulled out a couple of dollars from his wallet and handed them over as he received his candies.

"Thanks, have a nice night." The clerk nodded. "Enjoy the show."

Jason turned and walked quickly back to the theater, desperately trying to avoid his enemy's glance. The last thing he wanted was to converse with the one person who could take away something he desperately needed for his future. But fate had other plans as Scarlett ran straight into his chest, her play program and phone flying out of her hands. Jason's candy dropped from his own grasp as well, and he smirked as she picked up her things.

"Just can't stay away from me, huh?" Scarlett elbowed him, and he grunted.

"On the contrary, I was just getting a soda, but you seem to be everywhere tonight, so this is just my luck." She scowled, and her brow creased in frustration. She reached her arm out to him, holding the two boxes of sweets.

"Yours?" Jason snatched them from her and walked past Scarlett, brushing her shoulder as he moved around her.

"I never would've thought you to be a Skittles guy." She mumbled, already heading for the line. "You're not very. . . " She trailed off.

"Vibrant? Sweet?" Jason guessed.

"Not very personable," she finished, satisfied with her insult. Jason swiveled around, still moving backwards.

"I'm not, that's Marcus. I'm more of an M&M guy myself."

12
JASON

All throughout the hotel, kids on every floor, in every other room, were greeted at 4:30 a.m. with a phone call.

"Good morning to you, too, Scarlett. Now get to the bus."

"No, I don't have your charger, Meghan. Bus. Now."

"Adam, what did you think would happen if you drank at 1:00 a.m.?"

Coach Allen spared no runner from his drowsy early morning phone call, not after a kid didn't show up at last year's quarterfinals. Now everyone got a personal invitation to get their ass to the bus or else. Jason had his bag packed from the night before, his running shoes, protein bars, and athletic tape all tucked away in their respective pockets. He was used to the early morning track meets, the way his eyes stung for the first five minutes after dragging himself out of bed. But what was new today was the aching panic swimming in his chest.

The kind that lingered in your body like his heart knew he had something on the line today that his brain didn't. Semifinals weren't just an opportunity; this year, they were the only escape. Win finals, and scouts see you. Don't place, and Jason knew he would have to spend at least another year or so at home before he could scrounge up enough to get to college. *But if he won. If he only won.* Earbuds went in both ears, volume cranked up as loud as he could have it without the music leaking out the sides. His music wasn't for other people to hear. It was just for him. The bus wasn't fancy, but it was a hell of a lot better than the school buses. This one was a sleek black chauffeur bus, the kind with velvety seats, and plastic footrests at the bottom. Jason even noted outlets in every other row as he strode down the aisle. What he also noticed was his competition, Scarlett, struggling to stay awake in her seat. Her knees were drawn up to her chest, head leaning against the cool glass window. Her eyelids would flutter open every few seconds before seemingly deciding she liked how the world looked with them closed better. *I thought I wasn't a morning person, but she looks like she didn't sleep for shit.*

Jason felt a pang of worry; he didn't want Scarlett to win, oh no. That would interfere with the scouts, and New Wellis's athletics scholarship only had one spot. He needed eyes on him, attention on the gold he had to win. But seeing Scarlett fighting sleep like a gnat trying to escape a Venus flytrap, he knew that if Scarlett didn't snap out of it, if she didn't give it everything she had today, she wouldn't make finals. And not making finals might just be the equivalent of burning the last three years of work in one great big bonfire of failure. And walking out of this meeting without a medal? That would be handing Scarlett the matchstick.

The D.C. quarterfinals were the biggest track event Jason had ever seen, which briefly intimidated him for what semis and finals would be like, if he qualified. Who was he kidding? Of course, he would qualify. Schools from all over the country, all in his division, gathered here, in the center of the nation. And somehow, Jason had to beat all of them. He sat under a fold-up tent, one of dozens splayed across the grass in the middle of the track. It was adorned with New Wellis's logo and the black and dark green colors that made up almost every surface in that school.

This not only meant free school advertisement, but it also meant he had to share the space with all the other New Wellis runners. Not a problem for anyone else. But he and Scarlett had seemed to form a mutual agreement, each squeezed in the farthest corner away from one another. Still, Jason didn't miss the occasional glances (glares) Scarlett spared him, and he was sure she caught his. He knew his race was up soon, but the nerves squirming inside him stopped him from doing what he usually did before a race. Stretch, drink plenty of water, and pray to God that he didn't somehow forget how to run in the last 24 hours. Despite his worry, he got to his feet, lacing up his shoes and working the strain out of his arms.

"Nervous yet?" Marcus mumbled from where he lay on a spread of towels on the grass. "Remember, it's only quarterfinals, only your qualifier for the rest of your life, really. Unless you don't make it, then it's just another race, really." Marcus raised his hands in front of his face in a spreading motion. Like he could see Jason's future, and wasn't quite sure if it was good or not.

"You really are starting to be something of a motivational speaker, Marcus. I feel so much better," Jason lied through his teeth.

Marcus chuckled, sitting up and stretching out his back. His face fell into a more serious expression.

"Seriously, Jace, don't be nervous. If there were one person here that I knew could qualify, it would be you. Track captain. Running enthusiast. What's one quarterfinal? It's the same as last year, and the year before that, and—"

"But it is different this year. Because I can't just run to win anymore. I need to run to win and to be *seen*. I need to perform. To be the best one here, and beyond that."

Jason ran shaking fingers through his hair. He took a deep breath.

"I know I'll probably do fine, and all this stressing is for nothing. But all that's going through my mind is every possible way this could go wrong." Jason dropped his hands to his sides, looking to Marcus for support, for comfort, for *something*. Even if it were just lies to make him feel better, he would take them.

"Which is exactly why you need my positivity. Stop thinking. Let me do it for you. And I'm thinking it's just a race. Nothing different from before." From across the field, over megaphones stuck high on poles surrounding the track, an announcer called out Jason's first event. The only one that mattered, the only one that could qualify him for the semifinals. It was one he'd done dozens of times before, the men's 400m sprint. He ran it every day at practice, like clockwork. He would be fine. *More than fine. I would be more than fine.* Still, his blood ran cold.

"And now you don't have any more time to worry about this anyway." Marcus stood, clapping Jason on the shoulders and grinning like Jason had won already. "So seriously, just chill, and go win this thing."

"You'll be watching?"

"And praying." Jason's head snapped back at him. "Just a joke, promise." Marcus raised his arms in innocence. Jason brushed it off; he had to. There wasn't time to pore over the little, minuscule apprehensions that stuck to him like glue. There was only time to send up a prayer of his own, put on a mask of indifference, and get to that line.

As Jason took his place on the marker, settling his foot into the trigger, he looked over for only a moment at the spot next to him. The spot where a guy named Shiloh from a school Jason didn't care about enough to remember was crouched. The spot that should've been Marcus's. But Marcus was in the crowd, and he was cheering, and he cared. Jason told himself that that was enough. He left behind his longing for his best friend to be running his last quarterfinals of high school with him, and just ran for him. *Devoid of guilt.*

A crack snapped through the air, and as fast as Jason's brain comprehended what was happening, he was running. Like never before, he strained every muscle, burned through every scrap of energy he had left to accomplish this. He felt himself passing the others, but didn't see it. He didn't hear the crowds cheering; his heart filled all the room in his ears. It was as if his senses were tired of sticking around. . . like the adrenaline drowned them out. As he ran, it was like classical music building up inside him; he could hear the violin chords, sharp and chaotic. He could hear the piano, fingers slamming against the keys in a frenzy of movement. Every note was one step faster; he had to move. Every drop is a reminder. He pumped his legs faster, his breath came faster, the tension built. A crescendo fuming higher and higher as drums banged, trumpets flared, stringed quartets threw their most outrageous, beautiful, and violent symphonies at him.

Faster, and faster, and faster. The tension eased —an elation like no other. Jason crossed the line a full second in front of his competitors. The music slowed, a melody like warm blankets, like flying through the air, into the clouds. Like *relief.*

"Jason!" His head turned to the voice he would know, stripped of all senses. Marcus ran as fast as his legs would allow towards Jason, initiating their handshake. It was familiar. It was a comfort, and now? Jason could be relieved forever as soon as he heard that announcement.

"Oh my god, that was incredible! You beat them by like a full second; that shit stain Shiloh had *zero* chance. I told you, Jason, you just gotta *believe*." Marcus rattled off, never stopping to take a breath.

"Fuck you guys." A low male voice snapped from the side. Jason bit his cheek to keep from laughing.

"Sorry, Shiloh, he didn't mean it. Great race today." He extended his hand in a peace offering, but wasn't surprised when the brunette looked at him like he was crazy and stormed off. The glare he sent to Marcus only made him laugh harder.

"My bad," he managed.

"Yeah, whatever, we'll never see him again. But thank you. And thank you for staying. I get that shit probably wasn't easy." Jason saw for a moment that look in Marcus's eye. Not sadness, but not joy either. The silent mourning for the future you could've had. It disappeared as quickly as it came.

"You thought a bad knee would stop me from seeing your race? Just because I can't run?"

"I thought it might contribute." Marcus held up a hand.

"Never doubt me. And even though it sucks that I can't run, that doesn't change the fact that I've run with you these past three years. This doesn't change anything except for the fact that now I'm on the bleachers." Jason smiled gratefully at him. They didn't always need words; the time spent together was enough. Still, the reassurance helped. He fingered his necklace absentmindedly. *Where was this announcement?* Did he somehow not make it? Did they already have too many runners for semis? Or maybe he had a false start, and his win didn't even count.

"I know that look. What is it?" Marcus asked. Jason dropped his hand from his necklace, faking nonchalance as best he could. It would be fine. It *was* fine.

"Don't they make an announcement after each race? I mean, if I qualified, shouldn't they say something? They did for the other races." He was interrupted by the telltale crackle of the megaphones as the track team's favorite short announcer piped into the mic.

"A wonderful race from these boys, and a wonderful race for Jason Everett with a time of 46.34 seconds. Congratulations on the following for the semifinals qualifications: Shiloh Parks, Jason Everett, and Theo Dentry. Next is the girls' 200m sprint in just a few minutes." Jason could have sunk to his knees in relief at how good he felt. One step closer, and now he could just enjoy his trip. Not white knuckle his necklace or turn his music as high as it could go without causing permanent ear damage. Of which his mother was genuinely concerned.

"Ok, now I can have fun," Jason breathed, slumping a little deeper as all tension eased from his body. The music was only a trickle now, a slowly dying close of high piano keys and soft violin strums.

"Let's watch the other races, my knee wants to sit down."

"If you're out of shape, just say that," Jason joked. He staggered back as Marcus shoved him, a look of genuine betrayal written on his face.

"How dare you use my affliction against me. I'm wounded, Jason, truly."

"Oh, save it for Meghan, come on." And they sat, Jason's worry for Marcus hiding, at least for now. At least he felt comfortable enough telling Jason when too much was too much. Jason didn't do a great job of that himself. But the part of Jason that denied it. The part that was terrified of giving Marcus any indication of his home life screamed that this was for the best. That he was sparing Marcus the responsibility of worrying over him. Of pitying him. He was sure Marcus worried over him plenty anyway, but there was no need to deepen that fact. So, he cared for Marcus, listened to him, and waited on him like he wasn't dying for someone to clear the fog off the windows and see just how much he was struggling.

Like he didn't feel the music getting slower.

13
SCARLETT

The fear was no more real than the facts. Facts were what Scarlett relied on. There were seven other girls she would be racing against. She'd run against two of them before. Five were new, unpredictable; they were risks. Another fact was this: she would either qualify for quarterfinals today, or she wouldn't. What she knew, if only in the back of her mind, was that fact number three was clear and set in stone.

She couldn't not make quarterfinals, and she might stay stuck in Milo's shadow for the rest of her life. Hidden behind her golden brother, the holy Trinity of the Artega family. So, she braced to shatter that feeling and embedded her own fact into the mix. She wouldn't let him dictate her future any more than Scarlett did. She would qualify, and she would win, and then she wouldn't call Milo. Wouldn't tell him. Scarlett needed a victory of her own, something for herself to enjoy, empty of criticism. She lined up at the track with pounding in her ears and fire in her heart. If Meghan were here, Scarlett knew she'd be more relieved. Running with one of her best friends did that. It was warmth, even if it was competition. Some good things happen in bad scenarios. Some brilliant memories are kindled in the dark. A diamond can come from ruins, and a golden light can glow in the darkest town.

But Meghan was not here; she was in the stands, racing against time and her sore legs to get from her race to watch Scarlett's. Zoe, too. *Doesn't change anything; just pretend they're not even there.* She said this to herself in a mantra, and yet she could feel every eye piercing her. She could hear Zoe playfully joke with Meghan. Something like *She's got this, don't even worry.* Or, *ten bucks that she'll get a record right now.* Scarlett shivered and bounced on the balls of her feet to let some of her nerves fall. *What if I don't got this, Zoe? What then?* The world seemed to zoom in, everything focused, and Scarlett felt like a superhuman. Her nerves were frying, her heart pounding, and every breath she took was like a wave crashing in her ears. Shake it off again, and again. Shakily, she settled into her position, back arched, foot in the trigger. Her fingertips brushed the ground, and it was like she could feel every rumble of the earth. She wasn't focused. Her senses were on fire.

"Shit," she whispered. She blinked rapidly, clearing her senses. She flexed her fingers.

Nothing could clear that fog of panic smothering her like a net. Scarlett didn't pay attention to it, though; she told herself it was just nerves. Said that it would go away when she started running. So, she waited. And when the crack sounded through the air and the announcers started yelling, people started cheering, and she ran. And nothing changed. She strained her muscles, taking long, broad strides, unceasing, unrelenting. The crowd was a cacophony of voices, an arena of onlookers into what could be Scarlett's death. They jeered and pointed at her. She ran faster; she really tried.

Every step, she was aware of everyone around her. The eyes of her friends, which she tried to ignore, burned into her. Her parents, watching the live stream on YouTube, saw her too. All around her, voices, pressures, and volumes. She heard cheers from her friends. She heard the commands from her coach, critiques and comments. She felt her mother's rage from behind the television. It was a heat she couldn't explain. It burned behind her eyes, in her stomach, hot on her hands. She just wanted it to stop. So, she ran from them. She ran from them like they were right on her tail, and if she could only outrun the noises, outrun the pressures and responsibilities, they would all vanish. One million years passed in roughly 25 seconds; it should take Scarlett to run 200m. She flew past the line, her senses coming back to her, her brain catching up with the way her thoughts flew. She had no idea how fast she went, no idea if she placed, or who was in front of or behind her. What usually felt like control, like grabbing the reins and running this whole event, was gone for those 25 seconds. She felt like a puppet in someone else's show. And then the scoreboard flashed their places, and she was. Fourth place. *Fourth*. Fourth place out of eight girls. Scarlett ground her teeth to keep from crying.

"No, *no*." She gripped her elbows and squeezed until her knuckles went white. She tried to focus on her breathing. In for three, out for three. Place your feet on the ground, feel your surroundings—no spiraling, not today.

But when she breathed, it was shallow, and when she rubbed her arms for circulation, they shook because in the back of her mind a voice pounded through her ears—another fact. One Scarlett didn't even consider because she didn't think she had to.

Only the top three runners qualify for the quarterfinals. And Scarlett had been a moment too late.

"It's alright, it's going to be ok. I didn't qualify either," Zoe soothed from where they stood in the bleachers. Scarlett was sandwiched between Zoe and Meghan, as she had been since the moment she made it to them after the race.

She felt like she was wading through thick mud, like what was happening wasn't really happening.

"It's not alright, I'm not getting a scholarship. Jason wins, and I—" her voice broke. "I'll just be another burden, another half success riding Milo's tail." She slumped down onto the bleachers, the girls following suit.

"You could still get the scholarship, I mean, you've been the most dedicated runner I've seen on this team for three straight years," Meghan supplied.

"No one else would meet five weeks ahead of the season to talk strategy with Coach Allen. That's straight suck up shit, but it's dedication," Zoe admitted. Scarlett prayed they were right, but she knew inside that it wouldn't be enough. It wasn't a scholarship for those who *tried*. It was for the record breakers, the risk takers, the people who went all the way. Some things were for Milo's, and some lesser things were for Scarlett's. But Scarlett faked her most realistic smile like she wasn't actively dying inside. Like her last hopes weren't just crushed. The motion hurt, pretending everything she'd worked for wasn't for nothing. A sport she loved but didn't adore. A future she wanted but didn't pine for. She shrugged her shaking shoulders.

"You guys are probably right. It's fine. And I'm sorry you didn't qualify either, Zoe." *Either. As well as. Because I didn't qualify either. Because I was too slow.*

"I don't mind, this season has been too stressful anyway with applications and everything. I honestly don't know how you juggle it all." Zoe shrugged, and Scarlett, at that moment, would give anything for her relaxed posture. For genuine relief at losing something like this. How could someone be relieved for failing?

"Lots of sleepless nights, I guess," Scarlett said, and they laughed. And she tried her best to laugh, too. They watched the rest of the meet in a blur, cheering, watching other students who Scarlett had beaten before advance farther than she had.

"This is dehumanizing. I literally smoked her two weeks ago!" She threw up her arms in frustration.

"I remember her; she won't make it very far, don't worry."

"Still made it further than me. I fucked up, Meghan." Meghan set her phone down and looked at Scarlett, really looked at her.

"To be so honest, I cannot imagine how hard this must be for you. I know how hard you've worked, and I don't think there's anything I can say to you to convince you it's going to all work out. I don't know if it will. But the world is still spinning, and we're still in D.C., and you're still here with me. I know that's enough for now, and it's all I can do not to grab your shoulders and shake you until you realize that. You can't win every time, Scarlett. But it's over now, so please don't compare yourself to every other runner out there because it hurts me to know that you beat yourself up so much." She leaned her head on Scarlett's shoulder. "I love you, Scarlett, I really do. You are my *best friend*. And I just want you to be able to see how amazing, and funny, and incredible you are through my eyes."

"That's impossible," she mumbled, but a smile upturned the corner of her mouth.

"*You're* impossible. Just let me compliment you." So, Meghan did, and by the end of it, Scarlett did feel a little better. She hasn't seen Coach Allen yet, and he hasn't come to see her. She didn't know if that was a good thing or not. And by some miracle, when Jason caught her eye, he avoided her for once. Though the anger in his eyes wasn't hidden, Scarlett was sure he wouldn't spare her feelings for long. Another megaphone announcement made Scarlett jump.

"Apologies, everyone, but we have just reviewed the camera footage from the girls' 200m sprint occurring a little over half-hour ago and Kacey Tillman in second place has now been disqualified for running outside of her designated lane, and excessive taunting. Again, I would like to apologize for the delay with the camera footage, but our second-place finisher has been disqualified from the girls' 200m and for her qualification in the quarterfinals. Refs, please adjust your qualifications accordingly." And silence. Meghan didn't say anything for at least fifteen seconds. Scarlett didn't either. She didn't know if it was shock or if she was dreaming. Had the meet even started? Was this all a wild dream, and she'd wake up to Coach Allen's phone call in a few moments? Finally, though soft, Meghan spoke.

"Oh."

"No shit *'Oh'*," Zoe breathed. Scarlett sat still. Stiff. Wasn't this what she wanted? Yes, yes, it was. *So why do I feel so burdened?* Relieved, yes. But the blanket that eased off her shoulders for the last half-hour just flopped back onto her with full force. Full expectation. She had to do better this time around, and this race made her see that.

"Ok. Ok, we're good. I'm good. I think." Scarlett turned to see her friends' faces, written with the same shock, confusion and relief as Scarlett herself felt. It all felt like a fever dream. Her phone rang. Coach Allen confirmed what she'd already heard.

"You're in, kid."

"You're not messing with me?"

"Why would I mess with you about this? This is your second chance to do better, Artega. So *do better*."

"*Thank you*," she breathed. Meghan and Zoe were looking at her like a messenger waiting to be handed a scroll. Scarlett pocketed her phone and took a deep inhale.

"It's not a joke." They were silent for one more second. One more moment of letting this weight in the air, one more instant to let Scarlett breathe. Then Zoe squealed.

"Scarlett! Oh my God, thank God. I was seriously scared because I knew how competitive you were and how much this meant to you. This is seriously the best-case scenario, I mean, unless I qualified, but I was honestly getting tired anyway, and—"

"Breathe, Zo." Meghan chuckled. "But yeah, thank God Kacey's a bitch. How did she manage to get disqualified for 'excessive taunting'?"

"And running out of her lane. You didn't notice Scarlett?" Zoe sat again, turning off her endless energy supply for the sake of the conversation. Scarlett's palms grew sweaty. She didn't know how to explain what had just happened out there. How it was like the world was caving in. Like all eight billion people in the world had something to say about her, and she could hear all of it. So, she didn't.

"Not really, no. I think I was so nervous I just blocked them all out." She cracked a smile, and it worked. They collectively breathed out in relief, flinging their concerns into the open air. Scarlett tried.

And joy did form a warm sunny coin in her chest, but not as big as the tightness that remained. The panic she'd felt when she didn't place had been monumental, and part of her almost didn't believe she deserved to qualify anymore. It wasn't genuine, was it? It wasn't fair. But Milo wouldn't place his bets on fairness. He would say a win is a win, even though none of her wins could ever live up to his. He would tell her to act like she belonged. The only outsiders at the semifinals are the ones who don't think they belong. "I belong. I belong. I belong," Scarlett whispered under her breath.

14
SCARLETT

Scarlett was so kindly awoken by Zoe flicking the light switch on and off and shouting, "Get up, Scarlett, you're eighteen!"

Scarlett cracked her eyes open and peered out from under the covers at the pale girl with short black hair that curled around her face in rivulets. She was bouncing up and down like a maniac and grinning ear to ear, showcasing her bright dimples.

"Good morning, Zoe," Scarlett mumbled, smiling as she swung her legs over the bed and sank out from under the covers. Today was her eighteenth birthday, and while Scarlett was nervous, she was also thrilled. She could now officially do whatever she wanted, with no strict rules from parents and no limits. Except for the law, of course, but Scarlett knew better than to do something to get her in jail. "Where's Meghan?"

"You'll see," Zoe squealed, still shaking with excitement, a fire in her light honey eyes. "So..." Zoe began. "How does it feel to be eighteen?"

"You realize asking that has no point? We both know I feel the same as I did yesterday." Zoe raised an eyebrow. "Fine. It feels like I can be arrested, I can live on my own, and I have to get a job because I've got to pay for all my shit now," she said cooly, laughing a little at the tremendous number of responsibilities that came with her birthday. Her joints ached, reminding her of her close call the night before. "And it feels like I really, *really* have to step up my game at the semis."

Zoe laughed too, but hers was free and not tight and fake. Zoe stopped her feud with the light switch and bounded over to Scarlett, crushing her in a tight hug. Scarlett leaned into the embrace, grateful for her friend. They'd known each other for less time than Meghan, but the two clicked. Zoe had all the energy and excitement that Scarlett sometimes struggled to find, and Scarlett had the calmness and responsibility that Zoe needed to keep her out of trouble.

"Happy birthday, Scar." Scarlett smiled at the nickname. When anyone else called her that, it felt wrong, but something about the warm way it slid off Zoe's tongue made it alright, welcome even. Only her father had called her that before, so to Scarlett it was a sort of signal. If she was okay with the nickname, then it probably meant she liked you.

"Thank you, Zo," Scarlett breathed on her neck, squeezing her tight, which Zoe returned. She pulled out of the hug when a phone buzzed on the nightstand.

"Mine?" Zoe asked.

"Nah, mine," Scarlett said, reaching for the device. "Hello?"

"Happy birthday, Scar, I can't believe you're eighteen now! How's my girl?"

Scarlett lit up at her father's voice. "Hey, Dad, I know I can hardly believe it. I'm good, we're going to the National Museum of Art today, but we have some free time before, so I'm sure we'll think of something to do." Her father hummed.

"Just stay safe, I miss you back here, Scar. I wish I could be there."

"I know, me too." Scarlett sighed, missing her father, but glad he even called. "How's Mom?"

"She's getting Milo from the airport right now; he got the week off for Thanksgiving," Mr. Artega said, and Scarlett swore she could hear a hint of worry in his voice over the coming holiday.

"Well, I'll be back by then, so you won't have to suffer Milo's fruitless cooking alone." He laughed, a sound low and rumbling that Scarlett adored. He was pushing the topic away. As much as she wanted to, Scarlett couldn't do it. Not anymore. " So, you heard then? And mom and Milo? That's why they're not calling, right?" The line went quiet. There wasn't much to say, she knew that. She screwed up.

"I can't tell you if the qualifier is why she hasn't called, I mean, you still have time. But I honestly wouldn't be surprised." He sighed, and Scarlett dropped like a wilted flower.

"If they can't call, at least tell them to text me. Gotta make sure mom's not disowning me behind your back." He breathed a laugh which lightened the air a little.

"Don't let the race plague your whole day. I'll tell her, and you just enjoy the day. You qualified already, so I don't see what the big deal is."

"The big deal is that I almost didn't."

"Almost. I hate that word."

"It could be nice."

"Yeah." He spoke. Then, as if considering. "I *almost* dropped out of college."

"You didn't."

"And now I have a job I love. I *almost* pulled Milo out of track."

"Also didn't."

"And I have a clone of your mom."

Scarlett smiled real for the first time that morning. Her father wanted the best for her, wanted the opportunities, the contracts, the successes. But it became their little running joke how absurd the pressure got from her mom and brother.

"Pretty soon you'll have another. Though I'm sure Milo will have ascended to godhood by then."

"The God of running and arrogance." Scarlett laughed, a strand of her hair falling in her face. She flicked it away. "I gotta go, Dad, Zoe is practically lasering me with her eyes right now." Zoe blushed.

"Hi, Mr. Artega!" she called into the speaker.

"Hello, Zoe. Keep my daughter out of trouble today."

"I always do." Scarlett and her father simultaneously rolled their eyes. She did not. "Last thing—if they can't call or even text, tell mom I said hi. I miss her."

Mr. Artega promised he would, and the two said their goodbyes, followed with many 'I'll call you tomorrow's' and 'I'll believe that when I see it.' Scarlett imagined her father after she hung up. Sitting by the phone for a moment, reliving their conversations, and noting down the important things.

Then, she reached for her iced coffee to watch the week's Survivor episodes. The hotel room door creaked open, and Meghan stepped in, holding a Starbucks coffee tray loaded with drinks in one hand, and a large bag with tissue protruding from it in the other.

"I come bearing gifts!" she called, closing the door with her foot.

"Yes, coffee!" Zoe rushed to help her carry the goods, and the trio sat on Scarlett's bed, taking in the morning like fresh air. Scarlett was stunned and touched by her friend's acts of kindness. They'd done all this, whereas her brother and mother hadn't even called, and she was sure they weren't going to. Not after her near disqualification. She was speechless.

"Thank you, guys. Really, thank you."

Meghan and Zoe exchanged smiles and went back to sipping their mochas. "So, what's in the bag?" Scarlett questioned, peering into the tissue paper forest.

"Nope! Not yet, Miss Eighteen. This is for later."

"Alright. I guess I'll have to be patient then." Zoe snorted.

"Right, like there's a patient bone in your body."

Scarlett rolled her eyes and reluctantly handed the bag back over to Meghan's outstretched hand.

A few hours later, the girls met up with the rest of the group in the hotel lobby, where Mr. McApherry stood on a chair, counting heads. "Good morrow, my children, today is another beautiful day in Washington, D.C., and I hope the city life is faring ye well thus far?" he asked, clearly happy with his Shakespearean tongue. Scarlett cheered with the rest of the group. Mr. McApherry was a weirdo, but he was a weirdo who cared about his students, and everyone on this trip saw that. He explained the schedule and the gap in time that allowed the students to roam about for a couple of hours, and kids from all around the lobby smiled a little brighter at the thought of being able to sneak around the city alone.

In no time at all, kids were booking Ubers to cafés, and going on walks around the city. Couples snuck around corners to no doubt smother each other's faces, and some just went back to their room to nap. "We should do something with the guys," Meghan suggested, batting her eyelashes at Zoe.

"Fine with me, Scarlett?" To be honest, the last thing she wanted was to hang out with Jason, but she wanted to be with her friends, so she figured she could put up with it for a couple of hours if it meant they could all do something fun together.

"And purposefully submit myself to Jason's company? Sure, that sounds good." The girls didn't say anything.

"I'm kidding." She blinked.

"Not really. But it's fine, that sounds fine." They met up with the guys and formed their own mini-trip group. This consisted of Zoe, Meghan, Scarlett, Marcus, Jason, Beau, and Adam. Scarlett didn't know Adam all that well, apart from the fact that he was on the track team. He seemed nice enough, however, so she didn't have a problem with him. He had shaggy blonde hair and blue-green eyes that complemented his dark lashes and brows. He was shorter than Jason and Marcus, but still quite tall. The way that Scarlett was able to recognize him, however, was the freckles that spotted only the left side of his nose. He was attractive to say the least, but Scarlett had never felt attracted to him. They discussed where in this huge city they could go, and Scarlett saw Jason fidgeting with his shark necklace.

"We could go to the National Aquarium? It's not very far, and indoors if it starts raining," he suggested, smiling as he thought about it. Marcus made eye contact with him and quickly jumped in.

"Hell yeah, I wanna see some turtles, man."

"An aquarium? I want to go, I love those little sea squirrel things," Adam quipped.

"Otters?" Scarlett asked, her chest erupting with laughter.

"Yeah, otters," Adam corrected, rubbing the back of his neck. Jason looked at them gratefully and turned to the rest of the group. Scarlett had never been to this aquarium before, but she loved jellyfish, and the ocean had always been too beautiful to her, so why not?

"I like that idea," Beau agreed immediately after, making eye contact with Scarlett and smiling. Slowly, after the rest of the group agreed, they split up into different cars to travel. It was only about an hour away with all the traffic, but Scarlett was restless. She didn't expect her mom to call, but Milo? She couldn't help the growing knot in her stomach, making her feel uneasy. Were they really that mad? Her brow creased as she stared at the passing buildings and structures.

Soon enough, the aquarium came into view, and Scarlett was awestruck. It was huge, with rooftops and rooms protruding from the outside at awkward angles. Giant posters of whale sharks, turtles, and every sea animal you could imagine lined the front entrance, framing a large blue sign that read 'National Aquarium.' The knot in Scarlett's stomach transformed from sadness to excitement as she stared at the looming structure before her. They paid their driver, thanking him for the ride, and stepped into the ticket line.

Hundreds of people waited in line for the chance to experience the ocean's life, and Scarlett could already see dozens wandering around through the glass panels in the building. They made it to the front of the line, purchased their tickets and met the others at the front entrance. Jason, Marcus, Beau, and Adam stepped out of the ticket line, joining them. Jason was looking around him like this was a whole new world, and grinning ear to ear. But when his eyes fell to Scarlett, the grin was replaced with a cold glare. Scarlett rolled her eyes, not caring about being bothered by Jason's jerky personality, instead focusing on her friends. Zoe was taking a picture of Meghan and Marcus, arms wrapped around each other's shoulders in front of the entrance sign, both smiling at each other. Love was written all over their faces, and Scarlett gave Meghan an enthusiastic thumbs up when her eyes fell on her.

They filed into the entrance. *Wow.* If the outside was considered remarkable, then the inside was purely magical. Dozens of different rooms, all filled with tanks and exhibits of different creatures, littered the entrance, which stretched out farther than Scarlett could see. They scanned their tickets and picked up some maps from the holster by the door. They spent a few minutes pointing and exclaiming over the many exhibits and reefs that lived here, and Scarlett noticed Jason gasp and light up when he caught sight of the Blacktip reef exhibit.

"Where first?" Beau asked, leaning on a marble pole, coolness etched on his face. "Turtles?" Marcus suggested, shrugging.

Beau rolled his eyes and turned back to Scarlett. "That's fine with you?"

"Yeah, why wouldn't it be?" she questioned, scrunching her brow.

"Dunno, just doesn't seem fair that they pick everything that's all." Scarlett rolled her eyes.

"We're gonna go everywhere in here eventually; it really doesn't matter to me," she clarified, annoyed with Beau's childish attitude. "I don't know why you're so concerned with what I want now anyway."

"Alright. Sorry," he drawled out, shuffling with the rest of the group towards the turtle tank.

Marcus smiled when they reached them, Meghan squeezing his arm and staring into his wonder-like eyes. Scarlett smiled to herself, watching Meghan with so much happiness, and she noticed Jason smiling the same at Marcus. It was at times like these when she remembered it wasn't just Marcus taking her best friend; Meghan was also taking Jason's.

In the jellyfish exhibit, Scarlett lit up, enthralled with the species' elegance and poise, drifting through the water with movements that seemed so graceful, yet so calculated. She stared at the creatures, long stinging tentacles swirling around the clear water like deadly curtains. She admired their ability to be so beautiful but so vicious, so enthralling yet so deterring. A click of a camera turned Scarlett's head, and she found herself in the lens of Meghan's Polaroid.

"Sorry! It was a cute moment, I had to," Meghan apologized.

Scarlett smiled. "Well, did it at least turn out good?"

"Yeah, you look gorgeous. I love that little freckle above your eye, it's like your signature thing."

"It's a mole. I don't like it."

"Be positive. It's a freckle, and it's cute, and so are you. Deal with it," Zoe stated, staring at the slowly forming image of Scarlett admiring the crystal tank. Scarlett caught Jason's eye, and he quickly looked away, instead focusing on his notebook in a feeble attempt to sketch a crab resting on the sandbar.

"What's his deal? I mean, he looks at me and then just turns away, like if you're going to glare at the back of my head, just do it when I'm not looking." She groaned, tearing her eyes from him and back to Meghan, who was smiling.

"What the hell is that look?"

"Oh, nothing. You haven't ever thought you two would get along? If you could get past whatever it is that has you at each other's throats all the time?" Scarlett snorted.

"Wait about four years until I get a scholarship, go to Oregon State and get my master's, then we'll see about a truce." Meghan whacked her arm lightly.

"You stubborn bitch." She laughed, ripping the developed photo from the camera and stashing it in her pocket. Scarlett just shrugged, feeling her point was valid. The reason she despised him so much was that he could stop her from doing the one thing that could make her family see her and be proud of her. Aside from her father, of course, everyone else just saw her as an undermined version of Milo, who hadn't completed anything important because it wasn't as important as the things he'd done. Sometimes she just wanted to knock a reminder into them that she isn't Milo's copy and paste, but that didn't seem to be an option. The only other solution was to be exactly what they wanted her to be and do it how they wanted her to. And if that killed her in the process. . . well it might. But Scarlett was sure they wouldn't approve of that, so she put the thought away.

"Hey, guys," Jason called out, in as high-pitched a voice as she'd ever heard. She stifled a laugh, reminding herself that Jason was anything but funny. "The Blacktip exhibit is right here!" He pointed to the entrance to another large room with ominous black lighting lining the ceiling. His excitement made Scarlett's heart skip a beat.

All his anxiety seemed to melt away when he got excited, in a way that Scarlett couldn't help but be jealous of. She caught the tug of a smile piercing her lips and quickly ripped it off. *Stop it. Stop it. Stop it. What the hell is wrong with you?*

She squeezed her fists so hard she was sure the crescent of her nail was embedded in her palm. Gritting her teeth, she followed the group into the narrow entrance of the exhibit.

15
SCARLETT

Scarlett thought Jason was going to explode. He bounded right up to the glass, eyes wide as he gawked at the different species of sharks. His hands shook with excitement, and Scarlett was almost worried about his well-being. "OK, what the hell is wrong with him, because no way that's normal," she muttered to Marcus, pointing to a grinning Jason with his nose pressed against the glass.

"You don't know?" Marcus raised an eyebrow.

"Know what?"

"He lives for this stuff. He wants to be a marine biologist, but blacktip sharks are his favorite. There's not really aquariums where we are, so. . ." He gestured to Jason, brighter than the sun, breathing in everything around him.

Scarlett thought back to the necklace that Jason was constantly seen fidgeting with, and the blacktip reef shark charm that constantly found its way into his fingers when he was feeling anxious. "I didn't know that," Scarlett mumbled, and suddenly his behavior kind of made sense, if for a moment. If this was the closest he could get to living his dream before actually getting to do it, Scarlett could see why that would make him ecstatic.

Still, it was foreign to her to see him so brilliant and carefree, so unlike the solemn expressions he wore during practice or in class. Before she could tell what she was doing, she walked over to Jason, standing beside him at the tank. She didn't know why; it was just that one second her feet were still, and the next, they were moving towards him. She stood a few feet away from him, shoulders stiff and silent. Jason hardly noticed, still captivated by the various sharks swimming before his eyes.

"What can I do for you?" Jason asked in a low tone, not taking his eyes off the sharks. But when he did, his expression fell. "Oh, sorry, Artega, if I knew it was you, I would've just left already." He rolled his eyes

"Would've saved you some embarrassment, roadkill. Why are you so obsessed with sharks anyway? Are you some kind of nerd?" she inquired, cocking her head to one side and smirking.

"Yup."

Scarlett paused. "What?"

"I'm a nerd, not what you were expecting?" He laughed at Scarlett's bewildered expression. "You can't study sharks and marine biology for eight years and not be considered a nerd, Artega. Just like you're a nerd for Spanish," Jason reasoned, poking her shoulder.

Scarlett swatted at him. "I am not a nerd for Spanish; it's a beautiful language, that's all."

"Says the girl who's literally in IB Spanish as we speak." He shook his head and turned back to the glass separating them from the sea life.

Scarlett flipped him off. "That doesn't make me a nerd just because you can't get into IB classes."

He feigned hurt against his chest. "My IB biology course is in deep pain right now. I hope you know that. It's ok to be a nerd, Artega, you've worked enough to earn it."

"Don't act like you can stand the fact that I've earned anything."

"Yes, your biliteracy makes me feel inferior every day." He rolled his eyes. "So, say something then."

"*Eres un gi lipolas*," she growled, the words rolling off her tongue like English.

"The hell does that mean?" Jason asked, looking somewhat impressed.

"It means you're an asshole." Scarlett shrugged, not caring enough to sugar coat it for him. But still, his comment from earlier still weighed on her chest. *How does he know I'm in IB Spanish? How does he even know my classes?*

"Maybe I'm an asshole, but at least I'm an asshole with ambitions," he retorted.

Scarlett felt the insult sting. She had ambitions; she just didn't know if they were really hers or her family's. "I have plenty of ambitions. I'm going to Oregon State on a scholarship."

"And?"

Scarlett eyed him warily. "And I'm going to run track and get my degree." She raised her eyebrow.

"Alright, so you have some idea of college life, but what about after that?"

Scarlett stiffened. She didn't really know what to do after that. Her whole life had been one big book that was hers to write until her family stole the pen. She knew she had passions, but where would those take her? "I-I'm not really sure."

She looked back at the sharks, fins grazing the glass closest to her. Then, at the flick of a light switch, her mood changed. "You know, you don't get to do that."

"And what exactly is it that I'm doing?"

"You don't get to interrogate me like we're in prison about a future that we both know I have years to figure out. But instead, it's like you're *trying* to psych me out about it."

"Competitors have been intimidating each other for centuries. It's called strategy." Jason's eyes were still fixed on the glass, but he spared her the slightest side glance.

"Now you."

"What?"

"Your turn. If you know so much about your life plan, then I want to hear it. Tell me exactly what you're doing after college." Scarlett stuck her nose up, certain that he would be unsure of something. Still, Jason managed to surprise her even then. "A selachimorphologist. I'll graduate from Florida University with a bachelor's in marine biology and animal sciences. Then, I'll contact animal research facilities and become an intern for about a year before hopefully starting my own research center for endangered sharks and rays on the Red L list," he said coolly, eyes fixed on the sea life all the while.

Scarlett's mouth hung open, and Jason chuckled when he saw it. A warm rumbling laughter that Scarlett had to force herself not to like. "OK, what the hell? What even is a selacamorp—whatever?" she asked, sounding out the name.

Jason smiled, revealing white teeth and the ghost of a dimple. When he smiled, his nose scrunched up, moving his freckles around, creating gorgeous constellations across his tanned face. *Stop it, you idiot.* "A selachimorphologist, sweetie, is a shark biologist," he explained.

Scarlett cringed at the nickname. "Don't call me that unless you want a punch to the gut. I hate pet names," Scarlett threatened, balling up her fist.

"Call you what, sweetie?" He smirked, lips upturning for a second before changing into a grimace at Scarlett's strike to his ribs.

"Damn Artega!" Now it was Scarlett's turn to smile.

"I warned you." She hummed, stalking off to where Meghan stood, ruffling Marcus's hair. She stopped for only a moment, swiveling back to Jason with a gleam in her eye and a smirk on her lips. "You know, Jason," she said sweetly. "You can't be a selacamorphologist at Florida University if you can't pay. You don't get a Florida education if you don't have Florida money." She saw his finger twitch. She was getting to him. And Scarlett knew it. She blew him a fake kiss.

"You're only qualified because D.C.'s cameras are shit and Kacey Tillman is a well-known pain in the ass. Don't get all cocky now, you shouldn't have even made it," Jason snarled.

Scarlett's smirk faltered for only a moment. She tried to block it out for so long, to convince herself it wasn't true, but it was. She shouldn't have made it. And yet, for some reason, it took Jason saying it for her to truly believe it. She lowered her voice.

"Well, I'm here now, aren't I? And I can guarantee you that I will train myself to the bone, until I am *barely breathing* if that's what it takes to beat you," she breathed.

Jason held her gaze for a second more, eyebrows drawn up into a look like fear but not quite. Like watching the zebra for once kill the crocodile. Admiration, terror, worry. Then he turned back to the tank slowly, his posture stiff.

Scarlett took that he was done with this conversation and walked away.

"Having fun over there?" Scarlett interrupted, stepping between Meghan and her boyfriend. "I need some Meghan time, sorry, Marcus."

"What's mine is yours." He smiled.

Scarlett yanked Meghan's wrist and stalked over to a tank with penguins jumping in and out onto rocks. "Have her back by 10:00!" Marcus called from where he stood. Meghan smiled, and Scarlett could hardly hold back a laugh herself. Marcus was perfect for her; she needed that.

"So why exactly did you kidnap me?" Meghan asked, reapplying her lip gloss.

"'Kidnap' is a loose term; I merely borrowed your company."

"OK, why did you 'borrow my company'?" Scarlett put her arm around her friend and leaned her head on her shoulder.

"Is it so bad that I miss you?" She batted her lashes, which got a snort out of Meghan.

"Alright, so do I. I'm not used to this boyfriend thing. I really, really like him, but I need to have time for you guys, I know." Meghan sighed, and Scarlett could see the guilt in her eyes.

"It's alright, I want you to be happy, and if that means you can't be with us all the time, then that's fine." Scarlett wrapped her arms around Meghan, squeezing her tight. "Just don't forget about me, alright?"

Meghan set down her purse and returned the hug. "I couldn't forget about you if I got amnesia, even like a thousand times." She smiled, pulling back and looking Scarlett in the eyes.

"Something's wrong, tell me." Scarlett felt warm at how Meghan was always able to sense when something was off. She didn't say it like a question, but rather a statement—a fact she knew to be true.

"I'm fi— "

"None of that, you're a terrible liar," Meghan cut in.

Scarlett heaved a sigh. "Fine, I know I'm going to college and getting my degree, but what about after that? Like, I'm supposed to have all these responsibilities, but my whole life, my parents dictated what I did. So how am I supposed to know what I want to do?"

Meghan smiled at her, though it was filled with sadness. "Sometimes you don't know, and that's just life. Trust me, once you're at college and your parents aren't forcing their dreams onto you, you'll realize what's important to you," she promised, grasping Scarlett's elbows with her hands and staring at her with honey eyes.

"And besides," she continued. "Don't worry about that today.Just enjoy the freedom for a minute. It all works out in the end."

"And if it doesn't work out?" Scarlett asked, daring to wonder.

"Then it's not the end," Meghan stated simply.

Scarlett wasn't so sure about that, but she decided to listen to Meghan against her better judgment. They fell into a comfortable silence, admiring the views around them. A particularly skinny penguin jumped off a rock and into the clear water, gliding peacefully. Another sat perched in a groove of rock, protecting a mother who sat hunched on her eggs. Her gaze slowly drifted from the penguin exhibit back to the shark exhibit, where Jason was now sitting criss-crossed on the floor. He was holding a small notepad and pencil, seemingly attempting to sketch the great beasts. The smile on his face was visible even from where they stood, and his eyes shone with love for these creatures.

A soft chuckle got Scarlett's attention. "He looks like a little kid," Meghan admired, smiling sweetly.

"Who?" Scarlett knew damn well she was talking about Jason, but she didn't want her to think she was looking at him.

"Jason. He must really love this, he's positively glowing." Scarlett didn't reply but allowed herself to watch him for a moment. There was a serene air around him, and as his breath rose and fell in even yet exciting rhythms, Scarlett knew he felt right at home here. His breath caught, and he smiled even bigger every time the black tip swam by. He would reach for his necklace, comparing it to the shark before him, no doubt. Scarlett let her eyes trail over him. The rustle of his hair when he turned his head, or the delicate sprinkle of freckles over his cheeks. His eyes were a deep, dark brown, and when Scarlett was caught in the onyx depths, she felt like a black hole was pulling her in. Everything about him was stupid and predictable, yet Scarlett felt every encounter she had with him was like a new adventure.

He knows what he wants; I don't. So, don't let him take what future we could have by distraction, Scarlett reminded herself. The very last thing she needed was a distraction, something to tear her away from her goals.

Still, when the light reflected in his eyes, sparkling with enthusiasm and glazed with his calm demeanor, she could swear there was a small ring of green around his iris.

16
JASON

"Damn it!" Jason cursed, frantically rubbing at his notebook paper with his eraser, which was now a stub from how many times he had to use it. No matter what he did, he couldn't seem to get the lemon shark's tail right; every time he drew the line, it just didn't seem right and for a reason Jason couldn't place. So much for trying to sketch anatomy. Now, he just had a smudged paper, ripped in the middle from his hard erasing. So much about this day was perfect, and yet the thing that was frustrating him was a stupid drawing. He set the sketchpad down, turned up his AirPods, and looked at Scarlett instead.

Ever since their conversation earlier, he'd been wondering about her. He knew she was smart, borderline genius, and she knew it too. So why did she seem so clueless when it came to her profession? She was headstrong, always speaking her mind, so why was it such a struggle to know what your passion was? Jason knew he wanted to be a marine biologist since he was around nine, watching Shark Week with his mother. Something in him just clicked, and ever since then, that's been his goal, no doubt about it. He knew she had passions; he saw how much she loved Spanish, so why not just do something with that? His eyes flickered up and down her body, pausing at her hair. It was long and wavy, half of the dirty blonde mass tied up in a black ribbon, which flowed down her shoulders. A single strand strayed from the updo, curling around her forehead, and Jason had to resist the urge to walk over and tuck it behind her ear. Then, her shoulders started shaking in response to something Zoe had just said. She was laughing. *She's laughing*. Jason wouldn't admit it. *Couldn't* admit it, but the sound of Scarlett's laugh might just be the best thing he's ever heard. And that said a lot, coming from a music buff. He smiled and turned back to his notepad, deciding to give the lemon shark another chance.

"Watcha doing there?" Jason flinched, hard. *Scarlett?* "Sorry, did I scare you?"

No, this voice was too high to be Scarlett's. Jason turned to face the brown-haired girl. "Hey Meghan, yeah, you walk so quietly I didn't hear you coming," he joked, laughing, but inside, she really had given him a scare. He liked knowing what was behind him, what was coming. Being snuck up on was an experience he would be glad to avoid indefinitely. "I'm just trying to sketch some anatomies, but this lemon shark won't stop *moving*."

"Here, I'll help," Meghan supplied, and before Jason could react, she was criss-crossed next to him, tracing the sharks' curves with his pencil. "The trick is to sketch it lightly and then fill the shaded parts in later," she explained, eyes switching from the shark to the paper and back to the shark. "Which can be difficult if they're moving, so I don't blame you."

Jason rolled his eyes. "I appreciate you coming up with a sorry excuse for my artistic abilities, but I know I'm terrible at drawing." Meghan smiled at him, but all he saw in her eyes was friendship. He longed for that kind of relationship. He wanted someone to look at him the way Meghan looks at Marcus. She doesn't give that look to anyone else. It's reserved, just for him. *It must be really nice.*

"Marcus said you were applying for Rhode Island, right?" Jason asked. "Yeah."

"How are you feeling about that?"

Meghan paused, eyeing him before responding slowly in an unsure tone. "Scared out of my mind, but why do you ask?"

Jason shrugged nonchalantly. "Dunno, just seems like it's a lot of pressure right now, I want to make sure my friends are doing alright."

"Friends? Since when were we friends? You hate my best friend's guts," Meghan argued, crossing her arms.

"Since you started dating *my* best friend. And for the record, no one said this means I have to like Scarlett, too. It's weird enough to get used to you being glued to him all the time." Meghan flushed, and Jason regretted letting the words slip from his mouth.

"Is it really that weird? I feel so bad, I really don't want to intrude, I just —" Jason let out a sound in between a groan and a sigh.

"That's not what I meant, I'm glad you two are finally together; he's only talked about you for like months. It's just different. But that's OK, different doesn't mean bad," he assured, staring at her honey eyes.

"Jason."

"Yeah?"

"He talks about you, y'know, like a lot. Marcus, I mean."

Jason perked up. He figured he'd be brought up a bit, but not a lot necessarily. "All good things, I hope?" He smiled, flashing his white teeth.

Meghan rolled her eyes. "Yes, all good things. You just mean a lot to him, and I think someone should tell you that. You make him a better person." Jason was caught off guard by Meghan's sudden gush of Marcus's appreciation. He knew Marcus thought of Jason like a brother, and with all the times he stayed at the Levine house, they pretty much were just that. Still, it made him feel nice to know that he was making a difference in the kid's life, like Marcus had done to him. Always leaving his door open when his dad was in a mood, helping when he could and just talking when he couldn't. Jason owed him more than he had, that's for sure.

"It's not all me, though. He's helped me in more ways than one," Jason confessed, not wishing to go into detail. "Nice to know I rubbed off on him, though."

"And a good thing too, he's like the biggest gentleman. Are you sure you're alright with us being . . . us?" Jason gave her his signature smirk.

"Positively. You guys are seriously an amazing match." Meghan's smile only widened as she scribbled along a few more lines and added shading to the completed shark sketch.

"All done, now all you have to do is label it, but I'm not into that stuff, so I'll leave the nerdy part for you." Meghan handed over the pad of paper.

Jason gaped down at the drawing. It was perfect, with the fins jutting out at just the right angle and shading on the lower part of the tail that directly matched the specimen before them. "Wow, this is amazing, really, thanks," Jason pressed, rushing to add labels and facts to his now perfect replica.

Meghan watched over his shoulder as he labeled the pelvic and pectoral fins, snout, spiracle, and gill ridges all from memory. It was impressive how sure he was of himself and his abilities. His handwriting flowed in neat cursive, flowing almost as fast as his mind was racing with each part of the body and external structure. "Impressive. If I didn't know you've been studying this stuff, I would just think you're a mermaid." Meghan laughed, and although Jason didn't find the joke particularly funny, Meghan's laugh was contagious, and soon the two were giggling like children on the floor of an aquarium.

"Thanks, although unfortunately for you, I'm no mermaid, just a humble biologist." He smiled, winking before turning back to his work. Meghan stood up, brushing dust from the floor off the long black skirt that she wore, which fell down to her ankles. "Alright, humble biologist, we're gonna head to the gift shop. Coming?"

"Yeah, um, real quick, do you still have the Polaroid you took of the jellyfish?" Jason's heart raced.

"Yeah, why do you want it? Scarlett's in it, though I suppose you can still see the jellyfish well from there." Meghan reached into her purse and pulled out the photo, handing it to him.

"I'll white her out; I just didn't have the time to get a picture of those ones." He laughed, fidgeting with his necklace. *Liar.* Meghan grunted in response and made her way to the gift shop.

Jason let her leave, returning to his work, buried deep in his sketchpad again, and he could swear he heard Meghan mutter something about a 'petty fish nerd whiting out my best friend,' but he pretended not to notice as he finished his labeling. He also pretended not to wait until Meghan was gone before slipping the Polaroid into his phone case.

The labeling finished up later than he thought because by the time he got to the gift shop, Beau, Marcus, Zoe, and

Meghan were sitting on a bench, sharing jellyfish gummies and bottled waters as they waited for the rest of the group. Jason headed into the gift shop, browsing over the various magnets, hoodies, and souvenirs that made a good chunk of the museum's profits. He turned into a stuffed animal aisle, littered with plushies and turtle Beanie Babies when he heard a groan from behind him.

"Excuse me." The voice demanded, attempting to squeeze past Jason to get through the aisle.

Jason would recognize that annoying pitch anywhere. "I think you forgot your 'please,' Artega. Do I have to teach you some manners?"

Scarlett rolled her eyes. "If I say, please, will you move? You're blocking the whole aisle."

"Someone's feisty today. Are you upset that Adam bought the last turtle candies? I'm sure he would share if you used your pleases and thank yous," he teased, knowing it would get on her nerves.

"The only thing I'll be thanking is my own self-control if I don't punch you in the nose right now," she growled, pushing past him and further into the aisle. Jason followed.

"Don't you know walking out on a conversation is rude, Artega? The least you could do i look me in the eyes when I'm talking to you." Jason grabbed Scarlett's wrist and turned her toward him, finally locking his gaze with the calming gray of her stare that he'd been waiting for. He felt her breath hitch at the contact, but she quickly calmed herself, sending a scowl in his direction. Jason was expecting a knee to the stomach, or something or other, but Scarlett didn't seem in the mood for physical violence today.

"Let me go, Everett." Jason's heart ached at the nickname. Not his favorite, considering he couldn't be sure who it was directed towards. Although his father was hundreds of miles away, he still plagued his thoughts.

"Everett, huh, that's a new one." He thought it over.

"What would you prefer? Roadkill? Or just aisle-blocking-asshole?"

"Jason would do; that's kind of the point of first names."

Scarlett huffed, and Jason smirked in victory. They glared at each other for a moment, taking each other in like animals sizing themselves up before mauling each other to death. But this was no fight for survival, just a fight for college. But to two seniors, getting into a good college might just be their final battle. Scarlett heaved a sigh and dropped her glare, resigning. Jason was preparing more insults as they stood, but decided to drop them, seeing that this friendly run-in was just about over.

"I can't do this today. Can we just have a truce? Just for today? It is my birthday after all." *Shit, was it?*

"Your birthday?"

"Yup, big eighteen. I can get arrested now, you know." Jason tried to act cool, playing the role of tricking her into believing that he hadn't completely forgotten about her birthday. They learned each other's birthdays in track last year, celebrating each one as the season went on, and yet Scarlett's never stuck. And now he was paying for it.

"You did know it was my birthday, right?" She was studying him.

"Yeah, I knew. From practice, remember?"

" You're lying."

"Am not." Jason spat back, annoyed now.

"You're playing with that stupid necklace again, you do that when you lie." Jason looked at his check and realized that he was, in fact, fidgeting with the shark around his neck. *Damn it, Jason, you couldn't hide it any better than that?* Still, his ego got the better of him, and he kept playing along, despite how she very clearly just called him out on the lie.

"I just do that . . . sometimes. I know today's your birthday; the whole team knows."

"What did you get me then?" she asked, raising an eyebrow at him and scrunching her remaining brow into a quizzical yet expectant stare.

Jason froze. He didn't think about that. "Bold of you to assume I'd get you anything, but for you, Artega, it's something really special," he enticed, looking around for something, anything he could pass off as a gift. He spotted a medium-sized grey shark plush lying on the racks piled up against one another. He spun around, making a show out of it and grabbed the shark, swiveling back and handing it to Scarlett with a mocking bow. "Here."

Scarlett plucked the animal from his hand, inspecting it. "Really special, huh?"

Jason spluttered. "Yes, well, you see this specific kind of shark is a grey reef shark."

"Uh-huh." Scarlett hummed, clearly not interested.

Jason ignored and continued anyway, making it up as he went. "The grey reef shark is hunted commercially, even though it's illegal for soup and shit. It's also a very aggressive species, known for its many attacks on divers and fishermen. Even though they're constantly hunted, it doesn't dwindle their fiery spirit," he explained, quite proud of himself for the analogy.

"And this is supposed to mean exactly what to me?" Scarlett inquired, one hand holding the shark, the other resting on her hip.

"It means don't let anyone extinguish your spirit, your drive. You might not know what you want out of life yet, but when you do, don't let anyone take that passion away from you. Be like the reef shark, and if someone wants to hunt you for their soup."

"Bite their fricking hands off," Scarlett finished, a smile tugging at her lips. Oh, how he wanted to see that smile more often.

"Metaphorically, yes. These species are dangerous, but they can teach us about human morals more than you think. Sometimes it wouldn't hurt to be a little more like these guys."

Scarlett held the shark out in front of her, as if trying to see it in a new light. She gave up, dropping her arms to her side. "Very inspiring, Jason, it almost makes me want to forgive you for forgetting about my birthday."

Jason's face dropped into his hands. Of course, she wouldn't believe it. "If you don't get the deeper meaning, it's alright, Artega, I wouldn't expect everyone to understand." The corner of his mouth upturned.

"I'll be sure to come to you when I need help decoding mediocre metaphors," she said flatly.

"Whatever, just give me the shark so I can pay for it." He groaned, giving up.

"Taking back my gift already? Some gentleman you are."

" Oh, shut it, you wanna see jail for stealing the day you turn eighteen? Wouldn't be a very fun present, but alright."

He grabbed the shark and paid for it at the register, Scarlett waiting behind him.

He saw Beau approach her out of the corner of his eye, but he didn't assume anything of it. Still, he felt a teeny tiny pang in his chest that resembled jealousy. But that couldn't be it. You couldn't be jealous of something you don't have, something you don't *want* to have, could you? He finished up paying and started back to them, Beau standing with his hands in his pockets, blonde hair swept to one side. Scarlett clutched her arms tightly, replying sweetly to his questions with short appreciative answers, but Jason saw the way she inched tentatively away from him, while he only moved closer.

"Here. *Feliz cumpleanos*," Jason grumbled, handing the shark over to Scarlett, who stuck her tongue out at his comment.

"Well, I'm gonna head back with the group, but it was nice talking to you, Scarlett," Beau said, sending a cold glare in Jason's direction.

"You too, Beau," she replied, though it didn't sound entirely wholehearted.

"So, he's like what, your boyfriend now?" Jason asked, trying to keep the jealousy out that desperately begged to seep into his voice.

Scarlett wrinkled her nose. "Hell no. Our parents are friends, so he suddenly thinks he's entitled to me or something. He's a sweet guy, but it would be like dating a piece of whole wheat bread," she complained, grimacing at the thought.

Jason suppressed a chuckle. "I'm guessing he's not very exciting then?"

"Incredible guess, no idea where you got that from." Scarlett crossed her arms, letting the sarcasm that dripped from her words seep in.

"Just trying to help, don't get your panties in a twist."

"Why? You don't wanna untangle them?" She groaned, stalking off to Meghan and Zoe, the stuffed shark still held limply in her grasp. And Jason just about died.

17

SCARLETT

The stale bagel that Scarlett had been chewing on for the past five minutes didn't make her stomach nearly as queasy as the thought of competing for an award to add to her application. She and Zoe sat side by side on the school's charter bus and veering off towards the Smithsonian National Museum of Natural History. It was the last stop on their trip, and the only chance to compete for New Wellis's English-history scholars award. The tradition started on the first English-history class trip, and ever since, it's been a standing chance and a prestigious award to give anyone a boost over their peers during application review. Scarlett remembered when Milo won and how proud her parents were of him. That wasn't the only thing that got him his scholarship, but it sure did help. She leaned her head against the cold glass of the bus window and let it bounce on the glass as they rolled through the streets. She glanced around the bus at the other passengers. No, they're competitors now. However, they didn't seem too anxious about the day's events. She watched Jason pulling a pack of peanut M&Ms from his backpack and popped a few in his mouth. He had his AirPods in and was leaning on the headrest, enjoying the view. Her gaze flickered across the rows of students, all minding their own business. Zoe was napping beside her while her friends and classmates buzzed with activity. She could hear Adam doing karaoke on the back of the bus to annoy some girls sitting back there, including Sammy. She was glad Sammy was able to join the trip. Although they weren't best friends, it was good to see her have fun. Her gaze shifted to Ben, nose in an anatomy book, and then to Beau, who was scrolling on his phone but also seemed to be eyeing Scarlett from time to time. She found him peculiar. Was he kind? Yes. Did he seem to like her for who she was —also yes. But something in Scarlett's gut felt off whenever she was around him that she couldn't quite place, but it was enough to convince her to keep her distance from the bleached blonde. She sighed as her head tilted to the window once more, and the outline of the museum slowly came into view.

"If you children don't settle down right now, I will literally leave you all in D.C.," Mr. McApherry threatened, standing on a small bench in the museum's lobby for height.

"Works for me, some homeless guy tried to give me a beer on the way in here, I could take him up on the offer if I'm staying," Adam quipped.

Meghan laughed through the caring concern in her voice. "I do not think that's a good idea, Adam." Adam just shrugged, unbothered.

"No, she has a point, please don't drink beer from a homeless man, Adam. I'm technically still responsible for you. Your parents would kill me." Mr. McApherry shook his head, presumably wondering what other kind of stuff his students got into while they were on their own.

"Then leaving us in D.C. wouldn't be a great start." Scarlett's head turned to Jason, who leaned back against a column, fingering his necklace.

"Precisely my point, so can we please pay attention?" A couple of heads turned in his direction, but some just continued their conversations. "Good enough, now the reason you aren't currently enthralled in historical artifacts yet is because this, as you know, is the exciting time of the trip where you each have the chance to earn New Wellis's English-History scholars award." Mr. McApherry enunciated each syllable with great gusto, framing its importance.

"While some of you aren't interested." He gestured towards a small group of kids laughing in a corner, faces turning red when they noticed the spot on them. The rest of the students chuckled. "Those who are will be pleased to know that this award has always been beneficial when applying for colleges and jobs. Basically, it just sets you apart from your peers. And for those of you in sports, the Harley Mavera scholarship likes to see more than athletics on your transcripts. This would aid you magnificently. It is not an easy win though. You must put your mind to it, or as Shakespeare would say —"

"Get on with it!" Someone shouted from the back of the group.

Scarlett ignored the burning desire to win for a moment to laugh along with the others, although she somewhat enjoyed her history teacher's sudden poetic outbreaks.

"Fine, fine. Quite the patient and conversationalist lot you are." A scratchy grunt escaped his throat as he cleared it. "The instructions to compete in for this award are simple. I will choose your partners, and you will compete together, no questions asked. There will be no arguing about who you are assigned to."

Meghan made eye contact with Scarlett, her expression said, *'I'd better not get assigned to some rando.'* Scarlett wasn't hyped about that either. Not being able to choose a partner just meant one more thing to worry about.

"Once you are assigned, you will receive a three-page packet complete with difficult trivia, questions, and writing prompts that are to be filled out and answered correctly. Some of these answers are found around the museum, some rely on your own personal knowledge from my teachings this semester."

Scarlett picked at her nails. Meghan didn't fare much better, twisting her hair like Scarlett knew she did when she was nervous. Meghan, however, had already been accepted into some smaller colleges, which would take at least a bit of the pressure off. Still, it was the big arts and literature schools that really piqued her interest in attending.

"I want to make it clear that this isn't about who turns it in to me first that matters, although if multiple groups get all the answers correct, then I will be taking the first one handed in to me. More than speed, I care about accuracy and effort of your answers, and the effort of your work. With that, those of you competing stand to the right of me, and the rest of you enjoy your visit to the Smithsonian." Mr. McApherry smiled and clapped with excitement, directing those who were not competing through the doors and into the museum.

That just left Scarlett, her friends, and a good other handful of students to compete for the prestigious award.

"Alright, with that, I'll start listing off groups. Remember, no bitching and whining." Adam burst out laughing. "Yes, Adam, teachers can curse too; you're not completely children anymore." He eyed Adam up and down before muttering, "Well, perhaps some of us aren't." Scarlett cracked a smirk that Meghan mirrored. As names were read, Scarlett felt increasingly unsettled at her potential pairing. So far, Meghan and Sammy have been matched, along with Adam and Beau and Ben and Marcus. "We have Maddie and Logan. And Jason and Scarlett. Happy hunting, and don't get lost. This museum is huge."

Scarlett could swear his eyes lingered on her after that last line, which she took great offense to. She didn't get lost *that* often. But wait, did he say Jason and Scarlett? "Mr. McApherry, what did you say my group was again?" Maybe this was a mistake.

"Ahh Ms. Artega, let's see. . . you are with Jason Everett." Scarlett froze. *So, it wasn't a mistake.*

"Hey partner." She recognized that voice; the smell of caramel and eucalyptus only confirmed her suspicions.

"Jason," she greeted.

"Looks like we're in this together then."

"Yes, but I—"

"I just thought you should know before we start, I'm in this thing to win it. Getting on board with that wouldn't be a bad idea," Jason stated flatly. Scarlett was speechless.

"I —yeah, same. I need this— for college, I mean."

Jason opened his mouth to speak, determination in his dark eyes, but was interrupted by Mr. McApherry. "A quick tip to anyone still listening, try to see into each other's minds. Get into their perspective, walk in their shoes, whatever you must do because it helps, trust me." Jason closed his mouth, a smirk lighting up his stupidly freckled face instead.

"I'd try to get into your mental space, but I just can't seem to get my head that far up my ass," Scarlett replied by jabbing his shoulder with her elbow.

"Ow, what the hell, your elbows are so pointy." He groaned, rubbing his shoulder.

"You think my elbows are pointy? Wait until you see my knuckles flying towards your face."

"Testy today, are we, Scar?" Scarlett stiffened.

"Don't call me that."

"Scar?"

"I'm serious, Everett. Call me Scarlett, Artega, *sweetie,* if you have to, anything but Scar. Don't piss me off." Jason made a face akin to regret before bouncing back like always.

"Fine with me *sweetie.*" Scarlett cringed.

"Forget what I just said, don't call me that either." Jason smiled, his nose crinkling.

"Nope, too late. Sorry *sweetie.*" He shrugged, as if there was nothing more he could do on the matter.

Ripping the packet from Jason's hands, Scarlett scanned over the questions, already analyzing her answers. "If you could control your name-calling, we could actually start on this. It seems simple enough, the hard part is trying to remember whatever the hell he taught in that class."

Jason snatched the paper back from Scarlett, looking over it himself. "Sure, let's find somewhere to sit and do the ones we know before the museum questions," he proposed, and soon enough they found a corner with two bean bags to do their work.

Scarlett sat cross-legged, while Jason stretched one leg out, the other crossed underneath, balancing the packet on his knee. They wrote for a couple of minutes in silence, only spoke to compare notes or confirm guesses, to check answers or provide input. Scarlett let out an exasperated noise, annoyed with the deafening absence of sound.

"Something up, Artega?" Jason asked, head still buried in the packet.

"Just too quiet is all. Hey, why were you so serious about this earlier?" Scarlett remembered how eager he'd been when letting her know that he was 'in this thing to win it.'

Jason sighed, the kind of sigh that was sad, embarrassed, cautious. "We can't afford college. I need a track scholarship if I want to get in anywhere, let alone somewhere good," he admitted, shoulders sinking the tiniest bit.

Scarlett creased her brow. "Oh."

"But you knew that, didn't you? Or just a lucky guess?" Jason narrowed his eyes at her.

Scarlett remembered their argument at the aquarium. *You can't get a Florida education if you don't have Florida money.* The insult now burned like salt on a scrape in her mouth.

"Not everyone's as well off as you, Artega. It's not tragic, just how the world is." He shrugged, and just like that, the pair were swallowed up by silence once more. They were almost finished with the questions they could answer without help from the museum when Mr. McApherry approached.

"Ms. Artega, Mr. Everett," he greeted, peering at their work before catching sight of the white earpiece worn by Jason. "Mr. Everett, please do take out your AirPods when working with a partner, it's extremely discourteous." Scarlett felt Jason stiffen from the beanbag beside her, and she wondered why an AirPod would mean so much to him.

"It's alright, Mr. McApherry, really. I don't particularly care." She shrugged, and it was true. If anything, his blasting music would hopefully deter him from making as much contact with her. She was genuinely surprised when Jason returned her comment with a glance that could only be read as a grateful thank you.

"You're sure?"

"Absolutely."

Mr. McApherry didn't look convinced, straightening his burgundy tie, but allowed it anyway. "Very well then, you may carry on." He padded away, stopping in on other groups to check on their progress as well.

"Thanks." Scarlett turned, hearing his voice, but his head was already buried in the packet once more.

"If it means you talk less? You are so welcome. Why do you wear it anyway?"

"I just love being discourteous."

"*Jason.*"

"What is this, a Q &A?"

"You know it's not, I'm just curious." Scarlett hated being so curious, so eager for answers about this boy, but she found herself wondering despite convincing herself not to. There was so much about the track captain that she'd yet to learn.

"I don't know what you want to hear. My life is complicated and weird, but the music just makes it better."

Scarlett took this in and thought about it, attempting to draw a conclusion. "So, it's a coping mechanism?"

"Coping mechanism for what?"

"For whatever it is that makes you constantly fidget, I'm assuming." Jason looked up from the packet, meeting her gaze and the second his dark onyx eyes met her gray ones, she felt his vulnerability. "Sorry, that's not my place to know."

"You're right, it's not," Jason agreed, still digging into her with his night-like irises. "But you're probably right, as much as I hate that." Scarlett's breath hitched, and it was as if she saw him in a new way. The way his hands shook slightly when holding the pen, or how he always seemed to be zoned out. She wanted to push it, wanted to ask more, to get to know this boy who was as much a mystery to her as anyone. But mysteries can be solved. And with time, Scarlett intended to do just that.

"Where the hell does this museum end?" Scarlett groaned, dragging her feet along the corridors. They'd been walking for two hours, attempting to collect as much as they could for their final question. *What is the most important piece of history in this museum, and why?* So far, they had a good list of options, but they had yet to come across something Scarlett deemed worthy enough of an answer. Something told Scarlett that this was deeper than the original star-spangled banner, or Dorothy's ruby slippers.

"You know, if you just chose something for us to use, we wouldn't have to keep walking." Scarlett rolled her eyes at him.

"If I just *chose something* like you suggest, we might not get the scholars' award. It has to be perfect."

Jason narrowed his eyes at the dirty blonde, as if calculating her opinion about the project. "What about you? Why are you so . . . *passionate* about this award?"

"Passionate?"

"It was the best I could come up with without saying bitchy."

"Fine." Scarlett slowed her pace and breathed in and out once slowly. "I need the award because I need a scholarship. Not because I can't pay for college, but because my older brother got into Oregon State on a full ride, and now that's all my parents expect of me." She picked at her nails, still not looking at Jason. "He won this award when he was here, and it seemed to help him a lot with scholarships, so that's why I need it." Scarlett was about to say *'want it'* but deemed that too unprofessional. This was something she had to do, had to have. It was non-negotiable.

"I heard about Milo. He's going for the Olympics, right?" Scarlett nodded, feeling slightly nauseous as she always did when her future, and moreover her brother's future, was discussed.

"Always five steps ahead of me. My mom was, too; they have that in common."

"So, what about the qualifier?" A crawling sense of irritation spread across Scarlett's skin at the mention of it.

"What about it?"

"Like, did they say anything about it? I know if it were my dad, he'd be pissed. Same?"

She breathed out. "Yeah. My dad said it didn't matter; I was qualified now at least."

"And your mom?"

"She texted, finally. I've been too nervous to check it." It felt nice to admit her fears. To put something on someone else for once and admit that someone she was supposed to love unconditionally can frighten her with just a text message. Jason cracked his knuckles to break the silence and shrugged.

"I could read it."

"What?"

"If you want. Might help." The first thing that crossed her mind was yes. Then *why on earth would I say yes?* She wanted to read it forever, but for some reason, staring at the words bright on the screen, which was so *real,* made it scarier. If someone can tell her themselves, she could turn it into a joke if it was bad. Pretend it was fake.

"Why not?" She handed her phone over, scrolling to her mom's profile. She tried not to peek at the beginning of the paragraph, but she caught the words 'embarrassed' and 'ungrateful' which pretty much told her all she needed to know.

"Before you read it, let me guess." Jason nodded to her. She pitched her voice in what she hoped was an accurate to her mother's tone. "You have just come within an inch of throwing away everything we've worked for your entire life. I hope you're happy about that. Milo is disappointed, we all are. It's a disgrace to his reputation, and selfish of you to do so. I will see improvement, or I will see a disinheritance." She cleared her throat. "Maybe that last part was too dramatic."

Jason scanned the message, eyes widening and shrinking as he swept over certain parts. "Honestly? Pretty spot on." He scoffed like the text personally insulted him. Like it was about him. "Listen to this: as of now, it seems the only thing you and Milo have in common is a last name. I'd like you to change that.' Did she by chance escape from Dance Moms or something? Want me to take her back?" He handed the phone back, but Scarlett shoved it in her pocket before she could read it herself.

"No, but I'd check in with the anger management class on Heugh Street. Maybe they have a spot available."

"And what does Milo have to say?"

"I'm done giving shits about what he has to say. Everything that comes out of his mouth is either a symphony or a haiku. I can't win with him." The silence stretched like a plastic sheet being tugged over a surface, its corners slowly spreading, filling in the void. She didn't want to make Jason any more uncomfortable than her judgmental ass family probably already made him, but she didn't have anything else to say. She tried to form an explanation. "Sorry. I'm sure they mean well, they just want me to succeed and —"

"It's okay, we don't have to talk about it anymore. I get it." Scarlett turned her head and looked at Jason for the first time in that conversation. His dark eyes were full of emotions, like he was reading her thoughts, reading how uncomfortable she was with the topic she was on. He also looked like he was gorgeous, with dark waves curling around his forehead, mirrored by the freckles scattered about his cheeks and nose. But that wasn't the important topic right now. Not when something better caught Scarlett's eye.

"C'mere."

"Artega, I just said we don't have to talk about it. What are you doing?" Scarlett, without thinking, grabbed Jason's hand to drag him across the museum. She stopped abruptly, realizing what she was doing, although the look on Jason's face was anything but hesitant. He smirked at her, nose crinkling. *Stupid nose crinkle.* "Sorry, you were just walking slowly."

"Don't be. It's always nice to have someone dragging you across the floor." He leaned into her ear, lips almost brushing her helix. "But maybe next time it'll be the bedroom floor and not the museum." Scarlett flushed a deep . . . Scarlett and wished the hotness to leave her face immediately. He was doing this to get on her nerves, she knew that. And yet it was working brilliantly well anyway.

"Keep your big boy pants on, Jason. I think I found something." Now it was Jason's turn to blush, but Scarlett was already striding to the opposite wall in the room, eagerly taking in everything she could about the exhibit.

"You know who this is?" Jason asked, eyebrows raised. Scarlett took that as he knows who this is, but just wanted to test her. Works for her; scholars especially like to surprise people with their knowledge.

"Yes, I know who this is. Duke Ellington, born in 1899, was basically a staple in music production for all of America. His music inspired generations of pop, jazz and changed the minds of millions of musicians and composers."

"Liar, you literally just read that off of the plaque."

"That a challenge?"

"Only if you know what you're getting into."

"I did a report on him. Fifth grade, and I have an amazing memory. Do *you* know what you're getting into?"

Scarlett cleared her throat and stepped away from the plaque, closing her eyes. "Another thing about Duke Ellington is that--" She stopped at a warm touch on her face. Gentle fingers brushed her eyelids and settled on her.

"Just covering your eyes, Artega, we don't tolerate cheating around here," Jason murmured.

Scarlett was tempted to remove the contact but found the touch somewhat comforting. "As I was saying, he shaped the culture and influence of society with his teachings and music. His work was described by Winton Marsalis as 'sounding like America.' Which is supposed to be affirming, and I guess in a way it is. But I also only picture eagle sound effects when I hear that. He died in 1974, but his music is still influential even now, and shaped the American sound." Scarlett reached her own hand up and removed Jason's from her eyes, holding it while lowering it back to him. She opened her eyes. "That good enough for you?"

Jason grinned, revealing his white teeth. His nose scrunched, freckles dancing across his face and bringing a glow to his eyes that she'd only seen a few times. "You never cease to surprise me, Artega."

"I guess we found our long answer topic then." Jason nodded, not taking his eyes off her stormy gray ones.

"But you knew all that first, didn't you?"

Jason chuckled lightly, shaking his head. "You notice more about people than most."

"I have more interest in noticing than most." She crossed her arms.

"And you still didn't answer my question."

"Yes, I already knew all of that. Music is one of my passions, so don't expect me not to know about one of the biggest influences on it.

"Your passion?"

"You could call it a hobby, but I listen constantly."

"Why? I get it —coping mechanism. But why?"

Jason leaned in closer. "It's comforting. You're never truly alone if you have music. All the artists, their words will keep you company." He straightened back up, eyes burrowing into Scarlett's face, her hair, her everything. "When I find someone whose voice I enjoy hearing more than music, I'll take them out, how 'bout that?" Scarlett scoffed and couldn't help but laugh.

"Like you don't get annoyed by the tiniest things, let alone someone's voice." Jason cracked a smile. "That's the best I can do for you. Now let's finish this thing up, and we might even be first to turn it in."

18
JASON

They were not, in fact, the first to turn it in. After about half-hour of frantic writing, editing, and erasing, they'd finally finished, only to be beaten by Adam and Beau.

"Yes! Haha, now I finally have something to brag to Jay about!" Adam squealed, positively glowing. He taunted Jason with fake ballerina twirls and laughed maniacally.

"Looks like you were a bit too slow this time, *Jay*." Beau spat, giving Jason an obvious cold glare.

He turned to Scarlett, and Jason saw his entire demeanor shift. "Don't worry, Scarlett, you're smart enough to get into a great college even without this stupid award."

"Thanks, Beau, you're probably right." Scarlett smiled sweetly, despite gritting her teeth and pressing her nails into her palms.

Beau nodded and stalked off, still celebrating obnoxiously with Adam. Scarlett visibly relaxed once they were gone, making her way to Jason.

"What is the likelihood that Adam and Beau got everything correct?" she whispered.

"What are the odds that we're gonna get struck by lightning right now?"

"Less than one in a million." Jason's lips twitched.

"Then probably about that much. I wouldn't worry, Mr. McApherry said it was about skill, not speed." Still, Jason couldn't help but feel a sense of nervousness himself, even though he knew there was still a definite chance of success. Now all he could do was wait.

"Alright, children, gather round the historical bean bags." Mr. McApherry's voice boomed throughout the museum lobby, gaining the attention of most of the students.

Jason quickly moved to the wall, leaning against it and fidgeting with his necklace. He hated feeling like this; he was nervous and anxious, and not in control of his feelings. At least he wasn't alone. He glanced at his partner, picking her nails and quietly conversing with Meghan and Zoe. Her long, dirty blonde hair was half tied up in a braid, surrounding the top of her head like a crown, the rest of her hair flowing down like a golden cascade waterfall. Her hair seemed so relaxed with the way it flowed, but her expression told a different story. Those stormy gray irises looked worried, panicked even. Her hands shook slightly, a sign of anxiety that Jason dared not miss. She was saying something to Meghan, but her words were tumbling out quickly and unorganized. Jason hated how his heart panged at the sight of her so worried. He wanted to help her, to tell her that what's done is done, and they could only do so much. But when he looked at her, he still saw a competitor rather than a friend. And competitors don't comfort one another. He set his jaw and turned to give his attention to his teacher.

"I know you all have so patiently waited for this, so let's get on with it." He pulled out a stack of papers, along with the group's place on the top of the page. "I will hand back your packets to you and your partner. The number on top is what rank you were. Only first place wins the Scholar's

Award, but I think I have a box of Tic Tacs if the second-place team would like them."

Jason cracked a smile. History might not be his favorite class, but great teachers bring up the mood. With that, he began distributing the packets to their respective groups. Jason watched groups' faces fall, and others nodded with approval. Jason's gut twisted at every reaction. *They could have won. Or them.* He watched as Adam and Beau received their papers. Their faces rose for a moment, then fell with disappointment.

"Mr. McApherry, are you sure you graded this correctly? I'm sure we had them all right!" Beau complained, clutching his packet against his chest.

"Sorry, boys, but I'm afraid your long answer on the last page was not incredibly convincing. But hey, the Tic Tacs are multicolored, so that's fun, right?" Adam shook it off and quietly tried to ask for the Tic Tacs without pissing off Beau, who was running his hands through his hair and kicking the ground. *Some good sport he is.* Mr. McApherry turned to Jason and Scarlett and started towards them, flipping through the packets as he went.

"I would like to be the first to congratulate you two," he said, smile seeping into his voice as he overturned their packet. There, on the top right corner, was a big red one circled in red Sharpie. *We did it.*

"Are you serious?" Scarlett asked, eyes wide with surprise.

"Completely and fervently serious. Your long answer on Duke Ellington was inspiring, and a nice break from the typical 'original American flag' answer that I see year after year. I liked your creativity, along with your other answers, which were all correct and accurate. You two deserved this. Your awards and certificates will be sent to your homes, along with a note from me for any colleges you are applying to."

He released the packet into Jason's frozen grip and turned away; a final congratulations being said over his shoulder. Scarlett turned to face Jason, her face saying that she still wasn't completely sure what was happening. Then, it was all smiles. Her face broke out in a giant grin, dimples exposed, and gray eyes glistening with pride. Jason was sure he looked about the same. He could feel his cheeks burning from how hard he was smiling, but he didn't care. It was all worth it, all the hard work, because now they get to reap the rewards. His track reputation, along with this, could be his ticket to a track scholarship. A thousand thoughts must've been spinning in her head—and it showed. It felt so surreal. Jason realized how excited he was acting and decided to tone it down in respect to the students who didn't win. Scarlett did the same, taking a deep breath and switching her beaming grin for a solemn smile.

"Well, Artega, seems like you did know what you were talking about." Scarlett laughed. That sound that squeezed Jason's heart and made him crave the noise again.

"And it seems like I was wrong about your selfish tendencies. We made a pretty good team." Jason raised an eyebrow.

"I wouldn't say good, maybe acceptable, or decent, or —"

"Just take the compliment, Everett." Scarlett took out her phone, snapping a picture of the packet for proof before walking back towards her friends, a jump in her step.

"I guess we do make a good team," Jason whispered, sure that Scarlett didn't hear. But if this was true, if they could find a way to work together . . . *no*. This was just a way to get ahead of the rest of them. Everything else is still a competition. Yet all that night, Jason couldn't get that thought out of his head.

And while he wouldn't admit it, he knew. They made an amazing pair.

19

MEGHAN

The rest of the trip went by in a blur, which Meghan thought was much too quick. She gaped and was overjoyed at the National Gallery of Art, taking photos of art pieces from all over the world. She was sure Marcus had been eyeing her, happy to see his girlfriend in such high spirits, but she couldn't even focus on that when there was so much art, so much *life* in the room. The days that followed were of a similar routine, with certain museums and monuments being attended to by the whole group, and others a special chance to go off on their own and see things for themselves. Meghan was in heaven with all the statues and architecture. The whole place was just so creative. Still, all good things had to come to an end, which is why Meghan sat shyly on an airport chair, waiting for her boarding number to be called. She scrolled through her photos, reliving the memories. One showed Adam with his mouth stuffed with exactly twelve turtle gummies—yes, he counted. Another was Scarlett and Zoe making a heart with their two hands in on the bank of the Potomac River during sunset.

Her favorite, though, was a candid shot of Marcus reading the directions pamphlet at the Museum of Natural Sciences. He didn't even know she took it, yet it quickly became her favorite, seeing his face relaxed and calm, yet also intrigued by whatever he was reading, evident in the way his eyes creased with interest. He wore a red sweater with a white collar poking up from underneath. He always dressed a tad bit over the top, but Meghan adored it. She put her phone away to conserve battery and instead took out a small sketchpad and pencil. She scanned her eyes among the crowded airport to find the perfect target. There, sitting in front and on the far left was an older man holding his granddaughter in his lap. She was reaching up to tug at his graying beard, and he was trying to stop her, while also balancing a book in the other hand. Perfect. She began her sketch, drawing the frames of both figures before going in with the dark shading and working her way up to the highlights. She loved people watching and creating works from around her. It made her work seem more personal, like she was living through the experience.

"What are you doing?" Meghan spared a glance from her sketchpad. Jason stood above her, peering down at her work. He wore dark wash jeans, red Adidas, and a Conan Gray Bourgeoisies tank showcasing his arms.

"Just sketching."

"Sketching what?" Jason pushed. Meghan tilted the pad to Jason while subtly pointing to the grandfather and child.

"Oh, a creep I see."

Meghan rolled her eyes. "I'm not a creep; I'm just people watching."

Jason smiled and let out a chuckle, though Meghan wasn't sure why. "I find inspiration in crowds. If I can capture their lives, I can capture the moment." Jason nodded, looking from the sketch to the people, then back to the sketch.

"It's good."

"Thanks."

"I have something to ask you," Jason started taking the seat next to her. *Sure, that seat's free.*

"Shoot."

"I think Scarlett should sit with you and Zoe this time." Meghan's eyes widened.

"Why?

Jason groaned. "I dunno, she didn't have any of her friends with her, and she's scared of flying."

"What? She told me she got over that. Was she okay?" Meghan felt terrible. All this time, and she thought Scarlett had gotten over her fear of flight, but in reality, she'd just left her to be scared with someone she hates and someone she barely knows.

"She was fine, but I think she'd feel safer with you guys this time. I have a feeling you'd handle it better than I did." Meghan wondered what he could mean by that but fervently agreed.

"Yeah, of course. Damn, I completely didn't realize. Do you think Marcus will be fine with that?"

"Yup, I already talked to him." *Wow, he really took care of everything already.* Jason was surprising her in more ways than one, making her wonder if he was as bad as they thought he was.

"Then that's alright with me. Are you gonna tell her?"

Jason shook his head. "Um, I was hoping you would, you know, with her hating my guts and whatnot."

Meghan laughed. " You know I don't think she hates you nearly as much as you think she does."

Jason paused and turned from where he'd been walking away, a quizzical look on his face. "Really, what makes you say that? Because so far, every encounter I have had with her has involved her being physically violent towards me."

He turned his body to the side, facing Meghan, showcasing his shoulder, which had a small bruise forming on it.

"She elbowed you?"

"Only like twenty times." Meghan's hand flew to her mouth to stifle the erupting laughter.

"Sure, laugh, it's really funny anyway ." Jason quipped, yet his solemn expression said the opposite.

"Sorry, and sorry for her um 'violence', but I really think you guys should chill out a little when it comes to your . . . interactions." Meghan wasn't quite sure what she was saying; she just wanted to de-escalate their feud a bit, but the confused look Jason gave her didn't reassure her.

"You know what? I'll just tell her, forget it."

"No, you're right." Now it was Meghan's confused look that bore into Jason's dark eyes.

"We should chill out, but we can't help that there's something we both want and she's in my way of getting it."

"And you're in her way."

"Exactly." Jason sighed, and Meghan saw a glimpse of him for a second. Not the track captain or the grumpy competitor, but just him. He was just a boy after all, trying to get into college like so many others. Meghan couldn't help but feel a little sorry for him, but still, she had to support Scarlett more. She was her friend, and if she had to be cold towards Jason to help her, she would without a second thought.

"It makes sense, just . . . weird, I guess. But alright, no judgment, just don't kill each other, and I'll let her know."

Jason thanked her and abandoned his seat, finding his group.

"He really said that?" Scarlett asked, surprise etched on her face. They had just started boarding, and Meghan needed to let her know before getting in their seats.

"I know, I was just as surprised as you. And why didn't you tell me you still don't like flying?" Meghan had to admit that she felt a little betrayed that her own friend would hide something like this from her. Something she could help with.

"I dunno, I guess Zoe already doesn't like flying and I just didn't want to add any burden, so I just . . ." she trailed off, but Meghan knew. She pretended not to be scared anymore because she didn't want to be a burden, an extra thing to add to the list. It killed Meghan that she could ever think that.

"Listen to me. You are not a burden; you are not fricking cargo. You're our friend, and if something's bothering you and I can help, I want to know. OK?"

"OK," Scarlett quietly agreed, thankful she didn't have to hide her fear anymore. Unbeknownst to Meghan, Scarlett took out her phone, creating a private chat with Jason from their track group chat.

Meghan told me what you did. Can't believe I'm saying this but thanks.

He responded within seconds.

Please Artega, it was more for me than for you. The last thing I need is for you to go all psycho again on takeoff and cut off my hand's circulation.

Once in the air, it all settled down. Meghan gripped both Scarlett's and Zoe's hands during takeoff, taking the middle seat. Scarlett wanted a window so she could see if they were about to crash, whereas Zoe didn't want to know what was happening so long as they were safe. It was exhausting, comforting one, then turning to the other, but she was glad to do it. The fasten seatbelt sign turned off, letting the girls know that they were in the clear, and were not plummeting to the ground. Once comfortable, Zoe took out her headphones and turned on the monitor, settling into her chair. *Grey's Anatomy* caught her eye while she was scrolling, which reminded Meghan of that night. Oh God, she'd completely freaked out and probably freaked Marcus out, too. She wasn't sure Zoe would understand—that girl hardly cared what people thought about her and would probably say just 'let it go' and that 'he probably doesn't even remember'. So, she turned to Scarlett, who was rummaging through her bag for advice.

"Hey, Scarlett?"

"Shit, I can't find my book . Did you or Zoe read it?"

"Um, no, I don't think so. Can I talk to you about something?" Scarlett immediately set down the bag and turned to face her.

"Go ahead, but crap, I really loved that book."

Meghan smiled. "Something happened the night Marcus slept over."

Scarlett's jaw dropped. "Something like.... . . *something*?"

"No! What? No, not *that* something."

Scarlett visibly relaxed, knowing she didn't have to be concerned about her friend becoming a teen mom. "Okay, so what does 'something' mean? That's very vague, Meghan."

Meghan sighed, speaking a little quieter than usual. "We were watching *Grey's Anatomy*, and a certain episode came on. It. . . it reminded me of my grandpa and like that whole night."

Scarlett kept eye contact, nodding along and actively listening the entire time despite Meghan getting more teary-eyed through the explanation.

"And I just flipped out. He didn't ask questions, thank God, but I'm worried I made him uncomfortable, or like irked him, or something."

Scarlett took her hands in her own. "How did he react to that?" Meghan thought back on it. He was sweet, actually, keeping his cool and attempting to distract Meghan from her grief.

"He was good, great actually. He made me feel better."

"Then that's amazing!" Scarlett stated, tucking her hair behind her ear.

"He knows how to help you, and it worked. I see the way he looks at you, Meghan; he's in love. And if he really does love you, then he'll want to love all of you. Even the bad." Meghan was skeptical, but Scarlett looked at her with such seriousness and complete conviction that she couldn't help but believe her.

"Even the bad?"

"Even the weird Meghan who takes pictures of him when he's not looking." Scarlett laughed lightly.

"You saw that?"

"Of course, I saw that. And it's adorable, so don't stop. He wants to know you, so let him." Meghan looked over her shoulder at the seats three rows behind them. Marcus was typing something on his computer, with his reading glasses on. Those were her favorites. Marcus thought they were nerdy, but to Meghan, they just made him seem more distinguished.

"Do you think I should explain what happened to him?" Scarlett gave her hand a gentle squeeze.

"I think you should do whatever Meghan wants to do, because she's the girl who Marcus loves, not me."

"I'm gonna tell him then," she decided. It might not go exactly as planned, but it was something she needed to do. Besides, she couldn't just break down every time something like that came on without some explanation, could she?

"Good. I'll be there when you're done." And just like that, it was decided. But for now, at least, she wasn't nervous. Instead, she felt ready and excited. Excited to share more of her life with him, to give him more of her. And if that could hurt, it could hurt. But it still needed to be done.

20

MEGHAN

The phone rang four times before he picked up. Meghan sat alone in her room, cross-legged on the very bed they'd shared just a week before. The plane ride home was exhausting, along with the welcome home greetings and necessary chat about her trip. It was late, about 1:00 a.m., so thankfully they didn't have school the next day. Coach Allen didn't seem to care; still scheduling early morning practice, so that was for nothing. She itched to call him from the second she got home, restraining herself so she didn't arouse suspicion. Around 1:30, she couldn't stand it anymore and picked up the phone.

Ring. Rin Ring. Ring. Ring.

Meghan was growing impatient when a familiar voice at the end of the line spoke to her.

"Hey Meg! What's up? Holy, Meghan, it's like 1:00 a.m. You need to sleep." Meghan rolled her eyes.

"OK, I need to sleep. What's new? And so do you, why are you up?"

"Studying."

Meghan internally slapped herself. She should've known Marcus would resume his erratic medical studies the second he got back from what was supposed to be his vacation. She decided not to tell him that she noticed he had packed his textbooks with him.

"Why are you actually up?"

"I need to talk to you."

"Everything alright?"

"It will be."

Meghan formed her words in her head, planning out how she was going to tell him. This wasn't something she told just anyone, making it even more important that he listened. "Meg, you're scaring me a little bit."

"Don't be scared, just listen closely, okay?"

Marcus agreed, and before she knew it, she'd dove off the deep end. "I know you remember last week. How I flipped out at George dying?" A sharp intake of breath sounded from the other line.

"Meghan, I already told you it's alright —"

"I owe you an explanation," she insisted. "If we're gonna be together, and you're gonna want to get to know me. Well, this is part of me."

"Then tell me." Meghan took a deep breath, ashamed of how shaky it was.

"I lost my grandfather last summer. We were, um, driving back from the beach. He had a spot that he loved to bring me to, not many people knew about it, so that became our thing. "

Marcus hummed along in response, a reminder he was still listening.

"One day we were driving back, and a van cut across the lanes in front of us. The car swerved and hit us right in the front. I was sitting in the back. He always insisted I sit in the back in case . . ."

"It's alright. Keep going."

Meghan sniffed and gathered her courage. "He died at the scene. I— I watched them try to save him; they did CPR, but um, the glass punctured a vein or something, there was *so much blood*. There really was nothing they could do; he took most of the impact."

"Sounds like an arterial puncture," Marcus mumbled, probably to himself. Though strangely enough, this little quirk was slightly comforting to Meghan. He didn't rush to drown her in pity and clichés as if that would fix anything. He just sat there whispering his medical jargon. Something inside Meghan snapped, probably she was hysterical, but she couldn't help but laugh. She giggled loudly at the ridiculousness of the situation. Here she was, talking about her dead grandpa, and he talks about 'arterial punctures'? The whole thing was too funny.

"Meg? You alright over there? I can't tell if you're laughing or crying."

Meghan snorted, laughing even harder. She was unable to control herself, shrill noises erupting from her chest. Her shoulders shook with laughter; her stomach hurt with it. "I'm sorry, sorry," she apologized, doubling over again.

Marcus caught her hysterical bug and began laughing along with her. "You're something else, Meghan, you know that?" he said between breaths.

Meghan pulled herself together, reapplying her lip gloss and taking deep inhales. "Wow, I'm really losing it, huh?"

"Well, if you're losing it, so am I because you make me laugh so hard it doesn't matter the situation," Marcus breathed, still gathering himself.

"Hold up, don't give me that power, it's a dangerous thing. You never know when I'll make you laugh now."

"If we're talking about dangerous things now, you have me outnumbered."

"You're gonna be performing life-altering surgeries on people, and *I'm* more dangerous? What about me is so dangerous?"

"Your eyes." Meghan's breath hitched.

"Are they now?"

"Yup. You could ruin my life, and all it would take for me to forgive you is to be looked at with those eyes again." Meghan wiped away a tear she didn't realize had fallen and broke out in a grin.

"You make me happy, Marcus."

"You make me feel alive, Meghan." No matter what else happened in that moment, if a hurricane washed them away, or a tornado swept up their houses, she couldn't care less. Right now, in the whole universe, it was just the two of them. Marcus and Meghan.

"Now, my little bee, you didn't finish your story." *Crap.* Meghan was half hoping he wouldn't bring it up again.

"Did you just call me 'little bee'?" Meghan asked, trying not to cringe.

"Yes."

"*Why?*"

"You're little, I can pick you up, and your eyes are like honey. So, bee." Meghan had to give him points for creativity. Though it wasn't her favorite, she could hear the smile in his voice, so she decided to let it slide. She spent another good half-hour talking about that night. The ambulance ride to the hospital, where she knew he was already gone, but still refused to let go, how she hated ambulances every day after because of it. And how ever, since then, when she sees a car wreck out her window, or in Marcus's case, sees a car accident episode on TV, she can't help but cry. She cried for herself and for her grandfather, whom she still should have. All the while, Marcus listened intently. When it was all over, Marcus knew of her past, of the girl he now knew a little better. And Meghan felt better knowing Marcus could be told these things and would quietly listen to what she had to say.

"Thank you for telling me. You didn't owe it to me or anything, but . . . it's nice to know that you trust me enough to talk to me about the big stuff."

Meghan shrugged. "You're one of the only people I do trust. You were going to find out eventually. But still, it's hard to talk about."

"I can see why." They fell into a comfortable silence, Meghan absentmindedly braiding her hair while Marcus sat at his desk, simply thinking about what he'd just been told.

"Tell me something, Marcus."

"Tell you what?"

"Tell me something I want to hear."

"Oh, so like how beautiful I think you are? Or how I forget what I was saying every time you walk into a room?" Marcus supplied.

"No, not like that. Although you're free to compliment me whenever you feel the need." A deep chuckle rumbled from the other line.

"I meant something about you. Something I don't know yet." Marcus thought about it for a second before replying.

"Let's see . . . um, I have a sister, Cora. She's eight."

Meghan smiled. "Aww, I've always wanted a sister. What does she like to do?"

"Spell. She's an amazing speller, I swear she's gonna be a writer someday or like a poet or something."

Meghan imagined Marcus growing up with a younger sister. She didn't have to ask; she already knew he'd be an amazing older brother. "Why didn't I know you had a sister before?"

"You never asked."

Meghan let that thought sit. She knew Marcus, knew his hobbies and tastes, and yet she didn't really know him as well as she thought she did.

"I have an idea."

"Oh yeah? What's that?" A smile worked its way up the brunette's face.

"I'm gonna ask you a question every day. Something new, something that I don't know about you." She smiled at the thought. Was there anything more romantic than slowly getting to know your boyfriend better each day? Meghan already had a list of questions in her mind. There was so much about this boy that she wanted to know, so much of *him* that she wanted to know.

"Sounds fun, but only if I get a question too."

"It's only fair." Meghan agreed.

"Meghan?"

"Mm?"

"I know this is probably the last thing you want to hear, but I am sorry that happened to you. No one should have to go through that, and you're really brave for sharing that with me." Marcus spoke firmly. There wasn't pity in his voice but rather understanding. A kind of tone that tells you you're not alone —a tone Meghan wanted to get used to.

"Thank you, really thank you." They talked for a few more hours, and neither was able to sleep. Eventually, though, Meghan could hear the yawning and tiredness in her boyfriend's voice.

"Go to bed, Marcus. I'll be all right, really."

"You're sure?"

"Positive." Meghan hadn't felt better in a while. She had a loving boyfriend, who cared enough about her to call her in the late hours of the night. Who cared about her well-being and interests. That was all she needed right now to be all right.

"If you say so. Goodnight Meghan. I . . ." The words trailed off on his tongue. Meghan swore she stopped breathing for a second. He was going to say it, wasn't he? Still, if it was coming, she wasn't going to rush it. "Goodnight, Marcus."

The sun came way too soon. Meghan fell asleep around 3:00 a.m. the night before after her loving chat with Marcus, and now she was paying the price. She stumbled out of bed, accidentally stepping on a collection of charcoal sketches strewn about the floor. No matter how much she cleaned it, her room always seemed to get messy again. She changed into her practice clothes, which consisted of leggings, her running shoes, and a black sports bra with New Wellis's logo on the back. She made a disgusted face at the open arm structure of the outfit, thankful for the leg coverage but still feeling the sting of cold on her upper half. She shrugged on a track team hoodie to cover her arms, now dotted with goosebumps. Makeup was hardly a priority, not when she was already running behind, but she still took a minute to add a dab of concealer, curl her lashes, and apply her favorite lip gloss before stepping out the door. The drive to New Wellis was cold and lonely. Hardly anyone else was on the streets at this hour, making the journey peaceful yet eerie. Hot air blasted her face, warming her frozen fingers as she cranked the temp up. *Ring. Ring.* Meghan glared over at her phone. Perfectly positioned on the passenger seat, just out of her grasp. She willed her fingers to grow, but they didn't.

Ring. Ring.

She leaned over in her seat, stretching the seat belt to its maximum before just barely wrapping her grasp around the phone without veering into the next lane.

"Hello?"

"Good morning, my bee." Of course, it was Marcus, who else besides Scarlett and Zoe would call her at 6:00 in the morning?

"The nickname?"

"Just let me have this."

"Fine. Morning. Are you coming to practice?" Meghan's gut wrenched. She loved track, but she knew Marcus loved it too. She couldn't help but feel guilty when talking to him about it.

"Of course I'm coming, moral support, remember? And I have a surprise for you."

"Oh, really?" Meghan's heart fluttered in her chest.

"Meet me outside the locker room before practice."

"Marcus, I'm already running late, I really shouldn't." Marcus sighed, no doubt running his hand through his gorgeous curls.

"It'll be quick, promise." Meghan hesitantly agreed, so great! She gets to see her boyfriend now, but that means even less time to warm up. She shook the feeling out of her system and parked in her usual spot. It was painted elegantly, with beautiful roses, lilies, daisies, and tulips wrapping around Meghan's name. She wanted it to be perfect for her senior year, so she spent hours painting each flower meticulously. Stepping out of her car, her eyes flickered around the parking lot. No sight of Marcus. She headed towards the locker room, where he said he'd be waiting. Nothing. *Maybe this was a bad idea. I should go.* She stalked off towards the track, but only made it three steps before strong hands covered her face.

"Guess who?"

"Don't play with me." Meghan took his arms off and turned to greet her boyfriend. A gasp took her breath. There Marcus stood, knee brace covered in winter pajama pants with a cozy white knit sweater on top. He was clinging to a bouquet of roses and daisies with one hand and a piping hot coffee in the other. Meghan melted, flinging her arms around his neck and jumping up into his arms. Not caring if she looked like an idiot, she squeezed him, taking in his scent of roses and honey, which perfectly mirrored the ones held in his grasp.

"Surprise," Marcus whispered, his lips near Meghan's ear. She smiled brightly.

"You really are the best damn boyfriend in the world, you know that?"

"All in a day's work." He winked. *How dare he use my own lines against me? And how dare they work?* She reached over to his head, covered in a gray beanie and gently tugged it off, revealing his jungle of perfect black curls. She took one in her hand and fingered it, staring at it like a foreign object. But it wasn't foreign. No, he was hers, and that's how she wanted it always.

"You have really nice hair."

"Yeah, but you know what? I'm thinking about dying it brown," he said, staring straight into Meghan's eyes, still holding her around him. Her heart pounded and she cursed it for being so loud.

"I think." She cupped his face in her hands.

"That your hair is so perfectly incredible just how it is." She tilted her head in a way she knew he loved, and pulled him in. Sparks flew, and all the cold that seeped into Meghan's bones before was suddenly replaced by scalding heat at his touch. It was so refreshing, so astounding, so right. His hold on her tightened, and he explored her mouth with his own.

He tasted like coffee and toothpaste, and it was something she didn't ever want to forget. They pulled apart for a brief second to meet each other's gaze. Their lips crashed again, and this time, Meghan felt completely and utterly free. She kissed him greedily, eagerly. Her fingers glided through his curls as she found herself getting increasingly lost in his taste, his touch, him. She smiled against his lips, letting herself fall into his dark eyes. "C'mere," he whispered, lips kissing her temple. She obliged and leaned into him, resting her head on his shoulder. They stayed like that for a few moments. Just the two of them and the bitter wind. It was at that moment that Meghan decided she wanted more times like these. Life was too short to die waiting for them to come. She was going to find them herself, or better yet, make them. She knew life was fleeting; hell, her grandfather taught her that. But right then, she was sure that if she had him, and they had this love, passion, whatever it was, her life wouldn't be fleeting; it would be fulfilling. She uncurled her legs from around his waist and allowed him to lower her back to the ground, where she engulfed him in a hold again, wrapping her arms around his waist. He stroked her back lovingly, still clutching her coffee and flowers.

"Yo, lovebirds!"

Meghan shrieked, jumping out of his hold, whipping around. The second she caught his eye, she relaxed.

"Hey, Adam."

"Morning, Adam," Marcus shouted, a flush creeping up his face.

"So glad you two are going steady, but Coach *will* kill you two if you don't get to practice." He chuckled, pedaling backwards, track bag fastened in his grasp. A sharp eye roll is exchanged between the two, pointed at the blonde. Still, a sigh escaped Meghan's lips, the tingle of a lost kiss lingering.

"Never thought I'd say this about Adam, but he's right, we should go."

"No fair! I'm right about plenty of stuff," Adam protested. Marcus's lips curled into a grin.

"Yeah, like when you said chocolate cupcakes took longer to cook than confetti ones and we burned half the batch."

"It's *Funfetti*, and yeah, so much for a track fundraiser," Meghan added.

"In my defense, you two didn't say anything about it either. And neither did Jason, or Logan, or —"

"Alright, so maybe that was a group effort. Jeez, you're stubborn," Marcus cut off, playfully shoving him once the pair had caught up.

Adam raised his hands in surrender, his signature sly smirk spreading across his face, upturned slightly more on one side. The trio started off towards the track together, the sun just beginning to rise, painting the sky a glorious pink. Meghan wondered if she could conjure up such shades from her own paint palette. Then again, maybe some moments weren't meant to be captured.

Only to be lived in once and appreciated for all they were worth.

Meghan would be more than glad to spend her moments and her life like this.

21

MARCUS

"Took you long enough." Jason's deep voice called out from across the track. He jogged up to meet them, sporting a loose gray tank and school- issued exercise shorts.

"Sorry, Jason, someone kept me busy," Meghan's sweet yet dangerous voice taunted.

"Kept you busy, huh?" Jason shot daggers at Marcus, questioning him with only his eyes.

Just what did you get into?

"Someone's grateful for her coffee, then." He met Jason's gaze, hoping that answered his question.

"Most grateful, thank you, Marcus." She fluttered her lashes at him, and it took all he had not to wrap her in his arms again. To feel her warmth against him was like feeling his very heart melt. A gruff grunt boomed over the track, telltale sign of their stern coach.

"Let's go, let's go! Get your privileged butts over here before you're all running 800s," he threatened, successfully quickening their paces.

"Sorry, coach!" They called out in unison.

"Now, today's practice is going to be a bit different. The tracks are having some renovations, so this is the perfect time to brush up on some *cross country.*" He waved his hands next to his face, mocking jazz hands. A grumbling Logan raised his hand.

"Yes, Logan?"

"Sorry, coach, but if we wanted to run cross country, wouldn't we join cross country? And like . . . not track?" Marcus stifled a smile, knowing that laughing would probably make Coach Allen more pissed.

"Well, *Logan,* not everyone can have their track redone. Look at Camden—they've had the same track surface for like twenty years. Be thankful for what you got and just act like this is a free chance. Cross country is . . . fun!"

"Right, running through the damn forest is *fun,*" Jason quipped.

Marcus laughed, hands flying to his mouth. Coach turned to them, eyebrow raised in suspicion.

"I expect you to treat this like you would every practice. With seriousness, endurance, and passion. You will run three miles in the forest surrounding the school." He swiveled on one foot to the girls.

"And for those of us who have trouble with directions, not to worry, there is already a path." He glared at Scarlett, who only laughed. Marcus wondered about their relationship.

No matter how many snarky comments the coach made about Scarlett, she never seemed upset or hardly affected by them; she just laughed it off. Marcus suspected there was more between them than just Coach and athlete. Marcus had to admit, while Coach Allen wasn't the kindest, if he got to know you, he could be a real friend. He had a feeling Scarlett knew something about that.

Before long, the group had set off on their run, and Marcus had taken his respective seat on the benches surrounding the forest. He grimaced, glaring down at his knee, no longer strapped to a brace, but still wrapped. Still unable to run for at least four more months. Lucky for him, track was over in two, so there really was no use. To Marcus, though, it wasn't the scholarship he was after, so track didn't matter for school as much as it did for him. Still, it stung badly when his sport was taken from him. Something inside him knew this was the way it was going to be. Another part of him felt resistant, eager to push against the injuries and run despite them. But the sane part of him knew that wasn't an option, and so he resided on the cold metal bleachers, watching his friends and lover embrace the sport he wished he could be a part of.

"Enjoying your morning, or just jealous of the runners who can . . . run?" Anger bubbled underneath Marcus's surface, yet he forced himself to smile at the sight of his former friend.

"I don't know Beau. Enjoying your morning, or just watching them compete in the sport you couldn't make the team for?" He turned back, ignoring the egotistical brute behind him. Beau, however, made no move to leave, instead plopping down a few feet away from Marcus.

"You know I could've made it. But I have more important ways to occupy my time."

"Like what? Watching runners sprint cross country at seven in the morning?"

"Like getting into MIT."

Marcus couldn't help but feel the shock that must have been written all over his face. "Didn't think I could do it, did you?" Beau taunted, fixing his gaze on the forest surrounding them. You could barely make out the sight of stomping feet and the sound of shoes crunching on dried pine.

"No, I just . . . you really did it, huh?"

"I did." Uncomfortable silence swallowed them. Marcus tried to feel happy for him; he really did. Beau had been working as far as they knew him to get into MIT. Back when he didn't hate them, they would plan out each other's college essays and imitate fake acceptance reactions. A little part of Marcus felt warm at the thought that his dreams had come true even if he wasn't there to see it happen.

"How long ago?" Beau turned his gaze towards Marcus, honey eyes meeting onyx ones.

"Last night. Found out after the trip." Marcus ran his hands through curly black waves.

"That's. . . wow." Beau nodded, boastfulness settling down to reveal a true feeling of relief. "I'm glad you got what you wanted. Really." Beau stiffened, apparently taken aback by Marcus's act of a truce rather than teasing him.

"T-thanks. How's medical school going?"

"Still haven't heard." Marcus had been dying to get into Johns Hopkins medical school, and while not hearing back doesn't mean a no, he was still struck with the application anxiety.

"What about them?" Beau asked, nodding in the direction of Jason and the others, still running through the forest. "I heard a rumor that Jason's shooting for a track scholarship."

"Yeah, he just applied for it a few days ago. So did she, now all our applications are in and all we can do is wait. Patience is key."

"Wait, *she*?" Beau's lips pursed with interest.

"Scarlett. She's been trying to get the same track scholarship, that's why they're at each other's throats so much. I'm surprised you didn't know with all the *rumors* you hear."

Beau laughed, though the sound was anything but joyful.

"Guess I've been busy with other things."

"Guess so." Marcus couldn't stand it anymore. The tension, the weird, awkward encounters, and he didn't even know what it was he did wrong. He hated not getting along with people to begin with, but when that person was someone you used to see every day, it hurt worse.

"Beau, what happened, man?" Beau turned to face him, expression suddenly laced with seriousness.

"I'm not sure what you mean."

"Weird, because I think you know exactly what I mean. You went from seeing us all the time to ignoring us, ignoring *me* like we've never met." He sighed, running fingers through inky curls. He wasn't sure what answer he was looking for, just something he could hold onto. Something to explain the strangeness now between them.

"Life happened. You really didn't expect us to stay friends forever, did you? Things change sometimes, Marcus." He didn't know what, but something in Marcus broke at that. The truth. That sometimes there wasn't a reason, just the course of life.

"It's fine to move on, Beau. Fine to meet new people and be further away from your old friends, but why do you have to hate us so much? I mean, what did we ever do to you?"

"It's not you! And I don't know how to explain that to you, I don't know how you would understand because you wouldn't understand. Is that what you want, Marcus? Is that what you want to hear?" Marcus stiffened, clenching his jaw.

"It's not your fault, so you can just stop caring because it's not. *Your. Fault.* I know that's all that matters to you. So, relax, because this isn't on you." An exasperated noise slipped past Beau's lips, and he ran his hands through bleached blonde hair. Marcus didn't know what to do. He had a million questions racing around his mind. *If it wasn't my fault, then why does he still hate me? What could have happened that made him hate us so much so quickly?* "Sometimes you don't get an answer, Marcus. And you just have to live with that."

Marcus opened his mouth to speak, interrupted by a shrill, blood-curdling scream echoing through the forest.

22
JASON

Jason really hated cross country. They had just passed the two-mile mark, and he was already sick of the trees. It was hard enough keeping your pace when running long distances, but to keep your pace *while* steering away from branches and roots was much harder. He took a moment to mentally show some respect to the cross-country runners. If they had to do this every day, they deserved some kudos.

A high-pitched scream pierced the air in front of him. The hair on his neck stuck straight up.

It wasn't just a scream; it was a voice he recognized.

It's her scream.

Before Jason even knew he was moving, he was tearing through the woods, narrowly avoiding branches and stumbling over roots. He needed to get to her fast.

Why do I care so much? Why am I doing this for her? He pushed away the questions swimming around his mind and focused on his goal. Get to Scarlett. He forced his legs to move faster, pumping his arms like a machine, and through the trees, he saw her. Breaking through the foliage, he rushed into the opening of the dirt path. There, Scarlett sat, shivering and shaking.

"Scarlett? Artega, look at me, what's wrong?" he pleaded, and Jason Everett didn't plead.

But for her, it seemed he would do many things he wouldn't usually. Scarlett didn't reply, eyes trained on something in the distance. She slowly inched back on her hands, trying to get away from . . . what? Jason followed her gaze to a slithering red snake with yellow and black bands. *A kingsnake.* Jason almost laughed, but figured Scarlett probably wouldn't appreciate that.

"Damn, Artega, you had me scared for a second. It's just a kingsnake; they're harmless," he explained, reaching for a nearby stick. Scarlett didn't seem convinced, still shaking, terrified whimpers slipping past her pink lips. Jason took a deep breath, sinking knees beside the horrified girl.

"Scarlett, I know you're scared right now, but you have to trust me, it's not going to hurt you. I won't let it." For the first time since finding her, Scarlett's eyes tore from the reptile ahead of her, stormy gray eyes crashing with onyx ones. They were wide with fear, perfectly matching the scared expression on her pale face.

"Look away."

"What?" she mumbled, barely a whisper.

Jason pretended not to notice the way her voice shook. "I said, look away. Trust, right?"

Scarlett hesitantly ducked her head, turning away from Jason and the snake. "Trust," she mimicked.

Jason took that opportunity to scoop up the snake with the stick, coiling it around the wood and promptly flinging it into the surrounding bushes.

"There," he announced, wiping off his hands like a job well done. "You can turn around now, sweetie." He flashed her a grin.

Scarlett flipped him off with a shaky hand but obliged. Her breath was still coming in short rasps, too short for Jason's liking. He offered a hand up, which Scarlett deliberately avoided.

"Too brave to need my help? Or just too stubborn to admit you need it?"

"Take . . . a wild . . . guess," she hissed, pulling herself up with the help of a tree. She was still hyperventilating, struggling for balance. The root of a tree caught the back of her foot, sending her sprawling onto the mossy ground.

"Careful, Scar, you're going to hurt yourself. You need to calm down." Jason held out a hand again, and this time Scarlett took it.

"Don't . . . call me . . . Scar," she breathed shakily. ". . . Asshole."

Jason cracked a smile, freckles spreading. He pulled her up halfway, leaning her against a tree, and stretching out his legs beside her.

"Not. A. Word." She growled, and to be honest, Jason wasn't going to tease her for needing help. But now she mentioned it, what a golden opportunity.

"A word about what? Needing my help, or being scared of snakes?" At the mention of snakes, Scarlett stiffened again, her breath speeding up slightly. Jason's nose crinkled, his mouth lined with concern. "Alright, I'm sorry, but you really should calm down, Artega. You're breathing too fast." He took her hand in his own, pressing it against her chest.

Scarlett's breath hitched. He savored the feeling of her cold fingers in his grasp.

"Do you feel that?" Scarlett nodded.

"That's what you don't want. You need to breathe deeply and slowly." He then removed her hand and placed it on his own chest.

"Feel my heart. Slowly, like this." He made a big show of breathing in and out. Scarlett's lips upturned in a smile. *God, her smile.* "In. And out. In. And out."

Scarlett began to follow in suit, breathing in and out shakily. It wasn't the best, but it was better than whatever wheezing and gasping for air she'd been doing earlier.

"Good." Jason winked, earning an eye roll from the dirty blonde. She continued those deep breaths until her shaking had all but stopped. She opened her eyes, lashes fluttering. Her gray eyes stared at Jason with a preoccupied look, as if she were trying to say something but couldn't.

"I think you're trying to say thank you, Artega." A cold glare was his only reply.

"I —I can't believe I'm saying this." She took a deep breath, shaking out her hands. ". . . Thank you." Jason grinned, nose crinkling. He poked her shoulder lightly.

"There you go! See that wasn't so bad, was it?"

"No, it was. I'm planning my transfer of schools already." Jason laughed lightly but watched her with careful care. Her eyes narrowed.

"You alright there, Everett?" Scarlett waved a hand in front of his face, attempting to bring him back to reality. Jason flinched, and Scarlett quickly moved back.

"Yeah, sorry. I just —are you sure you're good? No post snake trauma or something like that?" Scarlett snorted.

"I'm fine. No post snake trauma." She reached up, brushing pine leaves off Jason's shoulder.

"If I didn't know any better, I'd think you were worried about me, Everett."

"And what if I were, Artega?" Jason fixed her with a serious stare again, the air suddenly colder, tighter. Scarlett looked bemused and utterly surprised that Jason would give a damn about her. Still, she forced her playful smirk back onto her face.

"Then I would be grateful for you not leaving me with the snake."

"And are you? Grateful?"

"I don't know. Were you worried?"

Jason leaned back, deep chuckles rumbling through his chest and into the open air. "You are ridiculous." He laughed, but the question weighed on him.

"That's not an answer." Scarlett's brow creased, accusation written all over her. Jason played with his necklace, avoiding her gaze.

"I think I'm more worried about the snake. Did you see how far I flung that thing?"

"Must've missed it, especially when you told me to turn around." Scarlett let out a breathy laugh.

"Forgot about that part." Jason pulled himself up, cracking his back and knuckles. He noticed Scarlett cringe at the popping noise, only encouraging him to crack the other hand as well.

"So, Artega, that's planes and snakes now. Any other phobias I should know about?"

Scarlett huffed, but she shook her head. "Nope, that's all I have for irrational fears. What about you?"

"What about me?"

"What scares you?"

Jason thought about it for a second before shuddering. "Needles."

"Pffthaha." Scarlett's hands flew to her mouth, cheeks burning.

"Sorry, sorry. That's not funny, it's just . . . needles?" A shudder ran through Jason's body at the thought.

"Don't be judgmental—and yes, needles are completely terrifying. I don't tolerate sharp things being stabbed into me." Jason remembered when he went with Marcus to get vaccines one year ago. He tried to convince Jason that they were for the better, using fancy medical jargon to explain how they worked, but Jason didn't want to hear it. Getting a cold was well worth not having a piece of metal stuck in you. There were other things he could say, too, other fears that protruded deeper than any needle could. But those weren't to be shared. Not with Scarlett, not with Marcus, only to exist within Jason and the Everett household.

"Well, alright then. I'll be sure to teach you deep breathing next time a *needle* shows up in the middle of the path." She gestured to the dirt trail in front of her.

The sound of scattering foliage and shouts erupted from behind Jason.

"Hey! What the hell is going on? I heard a scream!" Marcus shouted, frantically glancing around in search of a threat that wasn't there. He stepped over the bushes, finally reaching Jason while only having a slight limp to show for it.

"Chill out, everything's fine. Scarlett here got spooked by a kingsnake."

"A what? Aren't those things like not poisonous?"

Scarlett rolled her eyes, not amused. "They can still bite."

Marcus laughed, patting Jason on the shoulder.

"She's got a point. But wow, you scared the shit out of me, Scarlett. I swear I thought Michael Myers was hiding around here somewhere." Another breakthrough in bushes startled Jason, but at the sight of the visitor, he wished he hadn't even looked.

Beau tore through the bushes, rushing up to Scarlett and grabbing her by the shoulders. "What happened? Jason, what the hell did you do?" he demanded, glaring at the dark-haired boy.

"Beau, get off me!" Scarlett shrugged out of his grasp. "And he didn't *do* anything. It was a snake." Jason noticed her flush a little at the mention of her encounter. It wasn't something to be embarrassed about, but he had a feeling Scarlett thought differently.

"Oh. Well, alright then." He awkwardly stepped away from the group.

"And why the hell did you think it was me?" Jason accused, sending a pointed glare in Beau's direction.

"Well, you two aren't exactly the friendliest pair now, are you? I know you hate her. What better way to remove the competition?" Jason scoffed, utterly bewildered.

"*Remove the competition*, what are you talking about, man? It's a damn scholarship, not a ' Drop Dead Gorgeous' sequel, are you insane?" Marcus stepped in between the two, hands out before him like a mother separating her quarreling children.

"Not to ruin the mood, but Coach will kill you both if you don't finish this run." He turned to Beau, prodding his finger at his chest.

"So, I suggest you sit back down. And you two enjoy the rest of your run." He smiled at Scarlett, relief in his tone.

"And Scarlett, glad you're not dead. That would've really darkened the mood."

"And screwed us up for finals, not to mention," Jason added.

"That too. Now have fun, you two, Uncle Marcus is gonna go if no one's dying." Jason smiled and reached for Marcus's hand with his fist. Marcus grinned, piling his fist on top, and they exploded into a well-memorized handshake.

"Ahem."

They ended with a double fist bump, expanding into an arm slide, hooking each other's fingers at the end and bringing down their arms.

"Patient, are we Artega?"

"You know I'm not, and if you two could finish your . . . ritual, we could actually finish this death race." Marcus took this as his signal and silently backed down the path, gesturing a two-fingered salute to Jason.

"You know you didn't have to wait," Jason said, and noticed Scarlett blinking like she hadn't even considered that.

"I know."

"Oh. Well, alright Artega, you ready?"

"Ladies first, Everett." Scarlett smiled sweetly, her words dripping off her tongue like sugary honey. The third mile wasn't as bad after all, and while they didn't complete it first, they completed it with purpose. And to Jason, it was worth it. Scarlett had opened up to him, and while it wasn't a lot, it was something. It was something Jason could hold onto. And when you're falling, something to hold onto is all you need to survive.

23

SCARLETT

Running had never felt so good. After training in the woods for the past couple of days, a meet at another school meant only one thing. A real track. Their team had driven to Camden for the semifinals. Only a few more meets until the end of the season, until their fate is sealed, and there isn't anything else to show for their scholarship. These would just have to be the best meets she'd run then. Scarlett was breezing through her first race, girls' 200-meter sprint. Giving it her all, her arms and legs pumped in unison, hot breath exhaling rapidly. Her long ponytail swayed as she ran, tilting left then right along with her steps. Her muscles burned, and it was a feeling like no other. She ran with herself, Meghan, three Camden girls, two from St. Coleman's, and two from a school she'd never heard of. That worried her, not knowing how they ran, how they strategized. But it proved to be no issue, as Scarlett was currently sprinting in first place with a good length in front. She panted, calves burning, head reeling. It was when she was running that she felt most alive. Her eyes narrowed in on the finish line up ahead. Giving it one last push, she ducked into the finish, slowing to a stop, and admiring her handiwork.

22.35 seconds—just shy of the record. She was close, Scarlett could feel it. Just not close enough. A cold water bottle found its way into her grasp, and the gray-eyed girl drained it, savoring every drop of cool liquid. She spotted Meghan, heaving with exhaustion, her hair sticking to her forehead.

"Meghan!" The brown-haired girl turned, bounding over. "Hey! You were so amazing, you were so close to the record."

"I know, I just can't seem to get there."

Meghan placed a hand on her shoulder in an act of comfort. "You will, I know you will. Just give it time, don't think about it too much."

A warm smile split Scarlett's lips. "And second place, that's amazing! If Zoe were in this race, New Wellis would've taken all three podium spots." Meghan scoffed, eyeing two blondes breathing quickly in the corner.

"I don't even know them, and I hate them already."

"Good Meg, that's the energy we need for finals." Scarlett made eye contact, and the two fell into laughter.

"But really, though, I don't even know what school they go to." Meghan nodded, and the two stepped onto the podium, graciously accepting their medals from the school board leaders.

Scarlett couldn't help feeling guilty at the quick ease in which she claimed she won. In truth, she was terrified the entire time. And still, even after winning, even after qualifying for finals. After her nearly damning mistake at quarterfinals, every success after that didn't feel earned. It didn't feel right. Scarlett could only hope that by winning more, doing better, *being* better would eventually blur it out —at least to the point where it wasn't at the forefront of her mind anymore.

"Boys 800 meter, boys 800 meter starting soon." The short announcer huffed, megaphone pressed against his flushed face. Meghan grabbed her arm, squeezing tightly.

"Oh, we're watching. C'mon." She dragged Scarlett to the bleachers, sitting in the front row. Scarlett cringed at the cold metal on her thighs.

"Who's in this one?" She recognized a couple of people from varying schools, but not many.

"Three from Camden, three from St. Johnson, and two from here. I think it's Jason and Logan." *Damn, he's everywhere.*

"What was that?" *Shit.*

"Did I say that out loud? Sorry, it just seems like he's a shadow or something. Everywhere I go, it's like he's right there."

Meghan raised an eyebrow. "And . . . that annoys you?"

"Like hell it annoys me, you know he does." Scarlett's eyes flickered across the tarmac before she saw him. Slick with sweat, hair falling over his face in messy waves. A dark green tank with New Wellis's logo clung to him, embellishing his figure, along with matching black shorts. And of course, a shark chain draped around his neck. Annoying, maybe, but he sure knew how to pull off emerald. Scarlett's nails found their way into her palms, squeezing out her feelings. No, there aren't any feelings to squeeze out because there aren't any feelings for him. None besides loathing and hatred, at least.

But, oh God, now he's jogging to the start, brushing strands of perfect waves out of his freckled, dotted face. From where Scarlett sat, his eyes almost looked black. Like the whole universe could fit inside them, like she could fit inside them. And then, she really *was* inside them as Jason made eye contact with her. His frown was cold; however, his eyes displayed a smooth, almost warm expression. Then those black orbs drifted, no longer trained on Scarlett. She must admit, she didn't like the lingering look of his gaze. She either wanted it on her always or never at all. She watched him for a moment longer, eyes sweeping across the bleachers looking for something, no, someone. She watched as his shoulders fell, expression falling with it. But as quickly as he slumped, he picked himself up, carrying himself with fake confidence and false pride.

"Come on, Logan! Jason! Whoop Camden's assess for me, huh?" Scarlett rolled her eyes, scooting to make room for a certain raven-haired girl.

"Glad you could make it, Zoe."

"Like I'd miss this. I just had to win the 400-meter real quick before I got here, sorry for being late," she boasted, showing off the gold medal draped around her fair neck. Both girls congratulated her, leaving Zoe beaming with pride and smiling even more. The trio watched as all eight boys lined up in their respective lanes, Logan in lane 3, and Jason in lane 4. The ref made the final call as a couple of passing watchers took their seats.

And then it was time. Eyes tracking her target, Scarlett looked on as Jason stretched his muscles. Not missing the gentle kiss he gave the charm on his necklace before getting in his place.

"Gentlemen, please take your marks." Jason crouched, fingertips brushing the rough tarmac beneath him.

"Get set." He thrust his body upward, keeping his upper body low to the ground while his legs stretched out higher. *No.* The crack of the gun sounded, booming loudly over the courtyard, but not after Jason had slipped from his position, launching just before it sounded —*a false start.* Jason realized what he'd done almost immediately, harshly running his fingers through his hair and fingering his necklace now more than ever.

'Damn it,' she saw him mouth, though she wasn't sure if he'd said it.

"And a false start from Jason Everett will put him back a bit, disappointing for this young athlete, especially with the fruitful season he's managed to complete so far."

Scarlett thought Jason might strangle the commentator with the icy glare in his eyes, but he kept his onyx scowl pinned to the track, quickly returning to his position.

"Let's try this again. On your marks. Get set." This time, the gun rang out, and Jason didn't miss a beat. He lunged forward, legs carrying him quickly and effortlessly. His arms pumped in rhythm with his strides, quickly gaining speed. He was third, Logan in second, and William Kravitz in first. Scarlett despised William almost as much as she despised Jason. He was arrogant, selfish, and snobby, all things she couldn't stand. Maybe that's why she stood up and shouted.

"C'mon, Jason, faster!" she cheered, almost surprising herself.

"Scarlett, what? We're cheering for him now?" Zoe asked, perplexed.

"Would you guys rather have *Prince William Kravitz* win?" The same disgusted expression crossed their faces.

"That's what I thought, now cheer." As they shouted, Jason sped up. It was almost as if he were in a dream, a dream that he'd just woken up from. He snapped into action, legs carrying him faster with each breath. He sped in front of Logan, although that wasn't the real competition. William was up ahead, still looking poised and cocky. Scarlett thought he resembled something of a horse when he ran, feet clopping along the tarmac like a royal equestrian. Still, it seemed to be working because Jason couldn't seem to push in front.

"You got it, Jason, run man!" Marcus shouted, cupping his hands around his mouth. The jealousy in his eyes was undeniable, though Scarlett didn't mention it. As they drew closer to the finish line, Scarlett's heart squeezed. *He has to do it; he can do it.* Just as they neared the finish, Jason pulled through. Giving it his all, he increased his pacing, letting go of his rhythm and just ran. She barely had time to blink before he was suddenly ahead of Kravitz, leaping through the finish with a final bound.

"Yes!" Marcus cheered, already limping down to congratulate him. *Not a bad rebound, Everett.* The relief in his victory was undeniable, but not as much as the shock that came with a false start.

"The last time he had a false start was sophomore year. What do you think happened?"

Meghan pressed, looking to both Zoe and Scarlett for answers. "Dunno, he just seemed distracted. At practice, too." Scarlett remembered her snake encounter and how Jason seemed so out of range, like something was on his mind.

"Don't harp on him about it, I'll bet he's chewing himself out already," Zoe added, prodding Scarlett with an acrylic nail.

"I wasn't going to harp." She thought about it for a second. "Tease maybe but not harp." The girls laughed as Scarlett excused herself for water.

Scarlett stared at her empty water bottle, willing it to fill. When it inevitably wasn't, the water fountain was the only place left to go. She waited for it to fill, staring at the clear trickling stream flowing from the machine and into her bottle.

"I know, coach, I know I really didn't mean to." She knew that voice. Jason's voice.

She peeked around the corner, where Jason stood with Coach Allen. "I know you didn't, Jason, but this kind of thing can't happen." Jason nodded, and Scarlett could tell his spirit was drained.

"Coach, I don't expect you to understand, but please don't tell my father. *Please*." Scarlett drew in a sharp breath. His father, why? She knew Coach Allen had a policy: anytime someone was hurt, made a noticeable mistake, or won their race, he contacted the parents to congratulate them. In this case, it is to mention a noticeable mistake. But why would telling him be a big deal? Scarlett remembered when she tripped during her hurdle race once; she completely ate shit. Coach Allen contacted her; they talked about being careful, and that was that. Still, she couldn't help but be curious about his insistence. Coach Allen drew a deep breath.

"Your father isn't the best man, is he?" To Scarlett's surprise, Jason stiffened, a silent tear forming in the corner of his eye, though he quickly blinked it away. He shook his head, still fixed on the ground.

"You can't tell him. I know you have a policy, but you just can't," Jason begged, and Scarlett knew Jason didn't beg. Coach Allen drew him in, providing a comforting embrace. He clapped him on the back, exhaling loudly.

"The things I do for you kids." He smiled sweetly at the boy. "I won't tell him. And you listen to me, if that man isn't being good to you, you let me know, alright? That's the deal." He held out a wrinkled hand, kindness reflected in his eyes. Jason visibly relaxed, wiping away a second tear that made its way down his freckled face. He took the coach's hand, shaking it lightly.

"Thank you, coach, really. And I promise that it won't happen again. I was just . . . out of it today."

"It's alright, I get it. You still have finals." Jason's eyes lit up.

"You mean we made it?" Coach Allen laughed, adjusting his New Wellis hat.

"You dare doubt my coaching abilities, Jason? Of course, we made it. Now go get some water, kid." Jason turned to leave, wiping the remnants of salty tear tracks from his face. Gray and black eyes met, and Scarlett froze for a moment, gaze lingering. She broke out of contact first, grabbing her now full bottle, and quickly striding away, leaving Jason stunned and flushed behind her.

24

JASON

She knows. She knows. She knows. She knows. She knows. She knows. Jason stood pacing fervently around his room, fingering his necklace and clawing at his own thoughts. All this time he'd kept it a secret, the hurt his father had put him through, the pain his mother endured just for bearing his son. Jason knew he'd never loved him, though sometimes his mind would toggle with him. Sometimes he thought Brian might care about his only son. Through drinking and gambling addictions, he saw glimpses of his father every once in a while. Things like watching cooking shows in the living room or helping out with Jason's applications. They were few and far apart, but it was just enough to convince Jason that maybe the next time would be different. The strings to which he clung to would snap, convincing him that he was nothing to be loved. Then, just as quickly as he shut down, another string would wrap around him, giving him just enough hope to still stand his father. He knew every single time that Brian had let him down. Jason could remember all of it, everything. And now, Scarlett knew too. Maybe not, maybe she wasn't even listening, ignoring him with cold glares like she did everything else. Still, he felt like throwing up. Marcus was the only one who even slightly knew what really went on in the Everett household. And even then, Jason didn't share much. He let out a frustrated groan, sinking to his rough carpet, bed frame supporting his back.

I'm a fool for telling Coach, because now she knows, and everyone else will too. Jason tugged at his shirt, overwhelmed with pounding feelings and reeling thoughts. His breath caught in ragged inhales, which he forced back into his throat. The climbing feeling reappeared, this time stronger. He pressed his heels into the ground, grounding himself.

She knows. Stop it, please stop it. She knows. They'll all know.

His head felt dizzy, overcome by the thousands of thoughts swerving around his brain. It was as if his body wasn't his own. He was alone in his room—but he felt anywhere but. . . He was at the Dollar Tree, reaching for a candy with young hands, his father striking him for 'stealing.' Then he was on his kitchen floor, quietly cleaning up spilled beer cans on his hands and knees while Brian snored on the couch.

Stop it, stop it.

At fifteen, he got the courage to fight back, resulting in a broken nose. Flashes of him and his mother sneaking out of the house and to the urgent care danced in his mind.

Go away— dammit, stop!

Anger, and yelling, and this man, this angry man with violence. So much hate, so much violence, so much hurt. Eight years old, a young boy sat on the stairwell, watching through the wooden bars as a man he thought to be his father hit his mother for the first time. He didn't believe it. *'It's just a game your daddy likes to play,'* she said. It was never a game.

Jason felt his heart pound. He fumbled with his hands, attempting to place them on his palpitating chest like he'd done with Scarlett.

Scarlett.

He forced a shaky breath into his lungs and closed his eyes. He was at the aquarium, admiring the beautiful beings swimming before his eyes. Turning around, he saw her. Long, dirty blonde hair flowed down her tanned shoulders. She flashed a smile at him, big and bright and so *real*. Jason wanted to reach out and grab it, pocketing it with him forever.

"You're alright, Everett," she said. "In and out. Just like you said." She took a step towards him, feet padding gently on the marble floors.

He squeezed his eyes shut, almost expecting pain, almost expecting to be hurt again. A warm hand was placed on his shoulder, and Jason flinched.

"Open your eyes, Jason. *Trust, right?*" One beat, two. He forced his eyes open, nerves panging in his chest over what he would see.

But when black smoky eyes opened, lashes fluttering, it was just her. Smiling at him and holding his life with the hand still placed on his shoulder. "I don't know what to do anymore." In his mind, Scarlett was now stroking his hair, lightly scratching his head with freshly done nails. She laughed lightly, confusing Jason.

"You sound like me now. I'll tell you what to do." She knelt beside him, gripping his hands in hers. "Live your life like he's not in it. Be bold, make mistakes, be a damn teenager." She stood up, tucking her golden waves behind her shoulder.

"What if I don't know how anymore?" Scarlett backed away, moving further from Jason.

"You know." She smiled, and then the stormy-eyed girl was gone. *Don't leave, please.*

"But I'm right here, Jason. You see me every day." The voice echoes in his mind —her voice.

Jason opened his eyes, suddenly aware of his breathing, which was much less ragged and now more serene, calm. *She helped me.* How was that possible? That she wasn't even there, and yet the thought of her alone tamed the raging fire that constantly burned in Jason's mind? A gentle knock on his door startled him, tearing him from his thoughts — more like delusions.

"C-come in." The door swung open, revealing his mother, draped in an apron, hair tied up in a bun.

"It's just me, baby." She moved swiftly through his room, kneeling beside him. "Are you alright? You look clammy." She smiled sweetly, tucking his hair out of his eyes.

"It um, happened again," he admitted, feeling like a turtle sinking into its shell. "Oh, Jason." She pulled him in for a hug, and Jason sank into her smell, the smell of a mother. And her touch, something only your creator can manage. A single touch to heal any wound or fix any hurt. She stroked his hair, and while it didn't feel as warm as when Scarlett did, Jason still melted at the contact.

"Why didn't you get me? I was right in the kitchen, honey. I want to know if things are difficult," she soothed, speaking in a light tone, though Jason could tell the regret that tinged her voice.

"I know, I'm sorry. I didn't know if he was home, so . . . . I worked it out. Calmed myself down." He didn't have to say who the 'him' was. There was only one 'him' that would leave Jason cowering in his room, afraid to even step outside his corner of the house.

"Well, I'll be here, and I want you to get me next time." Jason cringed at 'next time.' This was not something he wanted to ever happen again, though he feared it would.

"And your coach said you won the 200 today! I'm so sorry I couldn't be there, but I am so proud of you." She grinned, the bun on her head flopping down slightly.

Twisting anxiety pushed on Jason's stomach, then came relief. *So he didn't tell them.* "Thanks. You can go back to what you were doing. I'm fine, really." She just smiled, lightly kissing Jason's forehead in affection.

"You're doing great, hun, really you are." A piece of a smile found its way to Jason's lips.

"I love you."

"Love you, too." Mrs. Everett stepped out of the room, her echoing footsteps padding back down the hallway. Jason let his head fall back onto the mattress with a thump. All through the rest of the day, through his shift at Raley's, confrontations with his father, even his deep-felt conversations with Pete, a certain girl lingered in his mind.

Like the plague, Scarlett Artega haunted his thoughts and filled his head, getting him drunk with her glance, poisoning him with her voice. Worst of all, he smiled at the thought. Jason was falling for her. And he hated himself because of it.

25
SCARLETT

"So, what are you doing to celebrate?"

"Celebrate what?" Scarlett asked as they trudged down the halls of the biology building.

"Your birthday. Don't just skip around it like you always do. Let's do something fun! You only turn eighteen once, you know." Scarlett shrugged.

"You know I'm not the biggest party person, Meg. That's you… and definitely Zoe."

"Uh-huh, yeah sure, but like it could be you. You're so busy with college stuff and getting your holy grades, so just be a teenager for a night!" Rolling her eyes, Scarlett brushed off the thought, yet the idea stuck in her brain.

It would work out perfectly. Her parents would be gone for Milo's parents' day the following weekend. If that wasn't a golden opportunity, Scarlett didn't know what was. "I'll think about it."

Meghan jumped, grabbing her arm and shrieking. "Really? You will?" She peeled out of her grasp.

"Slow down, Meg, that's not a yes."

"From you? Totally is." She grinned, completely convinced that Scarlett's shy 'maybe' was a definite 'absolutely.' "Whatever, see you at practice, weirdo."

"Bye, Meghan," she teased, pushing the brunette off her and stepping into AP biology. They were testing genetics today, comparing themselves to their parents and analyzing which traits they received from each other. Scarlett set her bag down, carefully opening her computer and setting up her station.

"Morning." Scarlett huffed, recognizing Jason's husky voice immediately. She decided not to reply, sealing her mouth shut and going about her business like she didn't even hear him. He raised an eyebrow, nose crinkling.

"Did you hear me, Artega? Or is your hearing as bad as your starting position?" Scarlett smiled sweetly, fluttering her lashes.

"Oh, I heard you, Everett. And to be frank, I think my starting position is incredible compared to your false start." Scarlett bit back a laugh at Jason's shock, then embarrassed expression. "Yeah, I saw that. Well, we kind of all did. But not to worry, Everett, I'm sure there's another scholarship somewhere. Maybe even one for shark biology!" She wasn't sure why she was being so rude. Maybe she just woke up in a bad mood. Or perhaps it was her parents leaving her all alone on the week of her eighteenth birthday to attend yet another one of Milo's events.

She ignored Jason's gaping expression or the intense look of hatred etched in his face and instead focused on her project. Her eyes, she got from her mother. Smoky gray with swirls of almost blue and tinges of yellow. Lips, from her father. She was blessed with full pink lips and a perfect cupid's bow. Her hair was a mix of both. The waves were from her father, but the dirty blonde color was from her mother. Her nose was straight and slightly pointed, though Scarlett resented how it looked, convincing herself it was too big. She had her mother to thank for that. She peered over the table, glancing over each of her partner's work. Maddy wasn't even working on hers, instead practicing chopping maneuvers into the metal table legs. Sammy was working intently, quietly filling out her form in peace. Marcus looked confused, his expression full of unspoken questions.

"How am I supposed to know where I got my nose from? I never asked them this, and like my ears? I don't pay attention to that kind of thing." Jason scoffed at his paper, looking visibly tired.

"Your big ass nose is definitely your dad's, sorry, Marcus." He laughed a little, chuckling lightly.

"And ears? I dunno man, pull up a picture or something," he suggested, going back to his own project. He fidgeted with his necklace and didn't even attempt to hide the AirPod that always sat in his ear.

"Unsure of your answers over there, Everett?" She raised a brow, the space between her brows creasing. He looked up, slightly startled, but almost glad for a distraction.

"No, I'm fine. I know who I look like," he insisted, though his constant fidgeting and erasing aided otherwise. She decided to let it drop, however, and finish her project. While working, she could only think of her house. Big, and soon to be empty, and so perfect for a party. She could do it. Have the big celebration she'd always wanted, and not be afraid to actually have fun.

There were no more SATs to study for, and now that her applications were in, she could finally take a bit of a break. "Marcus, do you think I should have a party this weekend?" Marcus looked up from his paper, eyebrows relaxing.

"Sure, why not? You'd better have the good snacks, though, because when Adam had his party, there were like two bags of chips." Scarlett sighed, preparing a mental list.

"Noted, thanks."

"A party? Why, I wanna come," Maddy said, words dripping out seductively.

"My birthday was last week, and don't you have kung fu or whatever?" Maddy rolled her eyes, inspecting her freshly done manicure.

"It's karate, and for a party? I'll totally make an exception."

"Guess it's official then." She slumped back in her chair, picking at her nails. Great, the decision was made. Now all that was left to do was plan it. *How the hell do you plan a party?*

Have your parents left yet? I'm getting snacks rn.

About an hour ago. Bring Zoe too, I need help with decorations.

Scarlett dug through her desk drawers, frantically searching for tape. She found two boxes of streamers to use, but that wasn't nearly enough. With Meghan getting snacks, and Zoe handling the music, all that was left to do was send invites out and get the house ready. However, Scarlett guessed that people would probably show up, invited or not. She hung up more streamers, fingering the velvety paper in her hands before sticking it to the ceiling. The living room was cleared of all valuables, stored away in her parents' room. She wanted to have fun, yes, but also be responsible. If her parents are out, there goes the Milo replica daughter already.

The sound of a door creaking open startled her, causing her to drop the roll of streamers. It rolled across the floor, stopping and tilting sideways at Zoe's feet.

"Sorry, did I scare you?"

"Just a little, Zoe." She laughed and moved to greet her, peering around the corner to her driveway. The driveway hosted many more people than just Zoe and Meghan.

"We brought help!" Meghan chirped, popping out from around the doorway.

"I can see that. Is there gonna be anyone showing up when it actually starts?" she asked, half joking, half serious. From the crowd, she recognized Meghan and Zoe, obviously, but also Maddy, Ben, Sammy, Marcus, Logan, Jason, Adam, and pretty much the whole track team.

"You have to have some people there before it starts; that way, you're not alone. It's like you've never hosted a party before." Scarlett scoffed.

"Maybe because I *haven't!*" Meghan laughed, and she guided the dirty blonde towards the kitchen.

"Just chill, we know how to do this. We'll divide into groups. Marcus, Ben, and Maddy will do snacks. Jason, Beau, and Logan will do decorations. Um . . . Sammy, Adam and Zoe will do music. And the rest can be the . . . welcoming committee!"

"Welcoming committee?" Scarlett questioned, eyebrows raised.

"*Welcoming committee,*" Meghan mocked, feigning a high-pitched voice.

"Yes, welcoming committee, oh, you have so much to learn." Scarlett jabbed her lightly in the arm, offended yet intrigued. Marcus raised a tentative hand.

"Yes, Marcus."

"Why did you split up Jason and me?" Jason nodded, looking equally hurt.

"Yeah, we work amazingly together." Scarlett snorted, and Jason gave her a glare.

"If it's anything as amazing as what you get done in biology, then it's a good thing she split you up." Meghan nodded, smiling sadly.

"Sorry, Marcus, Scarlett's right, we can't have you slacking." The two boys grumbled, yet didn't make any further arrangements. In no time at all, the music was set up, blasting all of Scarlett's favorites from Eminem to Noah Khan. She truly enjoyed calmer, more soothing music, but figured that wouldn't do for a party. Who wants to jump and dance to Adrienne Lenker?

The decorations were incredible, colorful streamers and draping banners strung across the walls, and balloons hung from the ceiling. In the kitchen, various chips and foods were displayed across the counter as well as Zoe's personal contribution—a ridiculous amount of alcohol.

"How are we gonna drink all that?" Scarlett asked, gaping at the dozens of glass bottles and cans in coolers.

"They all say that, and then they all complain when there isn't enough," Zoe explained, cracking open a Coors Light. The sun was almost gone in the sky now, painting the room a dark ambiance. They turned on LED lights as well as some light projectors Logan had, reflecting purples and blues across the ceiling. She took a moment to admire her handiwork, and in all honesty, she felt pretty proud. Maybe she was more cut out for parties than she thought.

Ding. Ding.

The ring of the doorbell brought Scarlett back to reality, and the nerves all came flooding back.

Shit. Here we go, I guess.

26
SCARLETT

Scarlett felt the buzz in no time.

The crowd grew very large very quickly, dozens of people arriving at a time. They came in droves, which Scarlett found interesting. Everyone wanted to come, yet no one wanted to be seen coming alone. Already, she'd tried dancing, but it didn't seem to be for her. Every time a good song came on, she would chicken out, backing off the dance floor, which was her living room. She tried karaoke, but realized incredibly quickly that she was completely tone deaf. So, she resorted to glumly wandering the house, sipping on a lemonade as she went.

Meghan and Zoe had disappeared hours ago, blending into the sea of people. Scarlett caught sight of a familiar mop of dark waves and cursed when her heart pounded. Probably, she was just glad to see someone she recognized, that's all. She made her way towards him, bumping people as she went.

"Sorry. Excuse me. My bad." She shoved through the final wave of people, finally making it to him.

"I never thought you'd voluntarily walk up to me," he grumbled, eyes focused on anything other than her.

"I never thought I'd be hosting a party. Guess tonight's full of surprises."

Jason faced her, eyes boring into hers. He cocked his head sideways, in a way that made Scarlett's heart flutter. "Not really a party person, are you?"

"What gave you that idea?" He scoffed, yet the hint of a smile appeared on his lips.

"Why are you here anyway? I know for a fact you hate parties," Scarlett stated, reaching back into her memory. A look of shock crossed Jason's face for a moment before returning to its usual stony expression.

"I was told to just be a teenager. Figured this was about as good as I could do." He shifted on his feet, hands in his pockets.

"Wise advice."

"It was a wise person. What about you? You don't seem like the 'dance the night away' kind of person." Scarlett creased her brow.

"Is that your way of saying I'm not social?" Scarlett could swear he laughed for a second, but it was all too quick.

"Well, you'd be right, I'm not. Meghan actually told me to 'just be a teenager' too," she admitted.

"Then I guess we've both accomplished something tonight." Scarlett nodded in agreement. She took another long sip from her drink, simultaneously analyzing Jason's outfit. He wore black, baggy denim jeans, a white long-sleeved shirt and a gray shirt over top. His hair was tossed in messy waves, yet it flowed down his forehead perfectly. On his feet, he wore his signature white Adidas, and of course, the blacktip necklace which dangled above his chest. She couldn't lie, he looked . . . good. Hell, he looked amazing. But Scarlett would die before she admitted that.

"Thinking about something, Artega? Or has the two sips of beer finally caught up to you?" She cracked a smile.

"Believe it or not, this isn't my first time drinking."

"Of course not." He winked, cracking open a sparkling water rather than a beer.

"Not a heavy drinker?"

"Not a drinker at all, actually." Scarlett couldn't help but laugh, brushing her hair out of her eyes.

"What? Surprised?" She took another sip, stepping impossibly closer.

"Surprised that the captain of the track team, and a definitely popular boy, doesn't drink? Not at all," she claimed, sarcasm dripping from her tongue.

"I just don't like it. Not much else to say." He leaned in closer, caramel and eucalyptus traveling from his clothes to her nose.

"You, however, I never would've thought you drank." Scarlett quirked her brow, itching for a challenge. She tilted the can upwards, chugging the remaining half of her drink to prove her point.

"There. Believe me now?" A smile tugged the corner of his mouth, eyes trained on her. She set the can down on the counter, already reaching for the next.

"Don't go too crazy, Artega. We have practice tomorrow, you know that, right?"

Crap, I didn't.

Well, there was bound to be a time when she eventually had a hangover, right? Why not now? "I know Everett, I'm completely capable of taking care of myself, you know that, right?" He grinned, twirling his necklace in his palm.

"Oh, I know. Just don't come complaining when you have a pounding headache tomorrow." She ignored him and shifted off to the scene around her. People drank, danced, and all around seemed to be enjoying themselves. Maybe she just wasn't trying hard enough. She moved through the house, dodging people and ignoring comments from sweaty dudes she'd never seen before. By the next hour, she'd finished off another beer, and two shots, and she felt it.

Scarlett was shocking herself. She'd never been interested in drinking, never wanted to be a reckless teen, but now it seemed she was finally letting go and getting the high school experience all her friends already had. It was fun. The alcohol twisted her mind in a way she didn't expect, making everything seem more enjoyable, more doable. Suddenly, the karaoke machine didn't seem to mind if she was out of tune. And the dance floor seemed wide open with opportunity. Her head was spinning, and she stumbled through the crowd to the dance floor. The radio blared *Dancing Queen*, and Scarlett jumped. She turned quickly, eager to find someone, anyone.

Jason.

He leaned back against the table, watching everyone else cooly, pretending not to care. Or he didn't, but Scarlett was too careless to notice. She stumbled towards him, grabbing his hand in hers.

"What the hell are you doing, Artega?" he asked, his voice rumbling in his deep tone.

"This is my favorite song! I'm dancing, you idiot!" She pulled him away, and to her surprise, Jason didn't resist. He followed her to the floor, and when Scarlett flung her hands around his neck, he hesitantly placed his on her waist. It wasn't a slow song; in fact, it was far from it. But the way this song made her feel, Scarlett didn't care if it was conventional or not. She just wanted to live it in the moment. So that's what she did, twirling around the floor with her enemy in her arms. Scarlett lived.

"Spin me."

Jason laughed, reaching his hand above her head and twirling her around the floor. She spun, her floral baby doll shirt swirling with her. She wore light-washed jean shorts and New Balance shoes, making for not the most ideal dancing attire, but she worked with what she had.

"Having fun, Everett?" she asked, giggling as she spun and moved.

"You have no idea," he mumbled, guiding her through the motion. Their eyes met, and Scarlett's laughter died down a little at the fiery look in Jason's eyes. *Longing.* Then, those eyes tracked to her forehead, locking on the small freckle above her left eyebrow. She smiled up at him goofily.

"You look like something's on your mind."

"And what if it is?" he asked, leaning closer still. The smell of eucalyptus was stronger now, their faces barely an inch apart. She exhaled, forcing herself not to laugh but rather, look deeply into this man's dark eyes. Even in her drunken state, she couldn't admit that he was handsome. Although in her heart she knew that this boy was gorgeous. She leaned in a little closer, desperately wanting to close the gap between them and find out what Jason Everett tasted like. His brows drew together, suspicion etched on his features. *His perfect, gorgeous features.*

"How much have you drunk? You smell like tequila," he said, eyes not to tear away from hers.

"Dunno, I don't really care at the moment," she whispered, drawing closer still. She sagged when Jason pulled away quickly, distancing himself from the swaying girl.

"What's the matter? Don't want to kiss me?" She slurred her sentences slightly, unaware of the sound.

"I don't kiss drunk girls."

"Not even me?" He reached out with a hand, gently tucking a stray piece of hair behind Scarlett's ear.

"Especially you." And then he was gone, swiftly darting back through the crowd like a ghost. Leaving Scarlett, dancing alone, at her own party.

An hour later, Scarlett had gotten impossibly worse. The pounding in her head had only gotten more intense, and she was struggling to even see straight. She spent her time stumbling through the house, partaking in various activities that she didn't even know existed before and others that she would've liked to keep that way. She'd run into Jason a few more times, catching his dark eyes staring at her, but she pretended not to notice. If he doesn't want me, that's his loss. She wasn't sure where this newfound confidence had come from. That, and her loss in inhibitions, but she didn't completely mind.

She moved back to the kitchen, clutching her head in one hand. The pounding was getting worse, and she felt even dizzier if that was possible. She pulled herself onto the cool countertop, trying to ground herself by pressing her palms against the marble. She closed her eyes, breathing deeply, disappointed when the world was spinning just as much afterwards.

"Hey, Scarlett." She turned, seeing a blurry figure stepping towards her.

"Jason?" The figure cringed slightly, but continued advancing.

"No, it's Beau actually. How's your night going? I haven't gotten to see you much, but —wow, you look incredible!" He trailed off, eyes glued to Scarlett's body. His eyes flickered up and down her form like he was trying to memorize her every curve.

"Thanks, wish I could say the same about how I feel." A rush of dizziness overtook her, and she slumped forward onto Beau's shoulder.

" Whoa, you all right, Scarlett? How much have you drunk?"

"Too much," she admitted, pulling back and staring into his honey eyes.

"You look good tonight, Beau." He blushed, and she smiled genuinely. Except it wasn't genuine, she was fueled by alcohol, and some part of her brain knew that. Yet the parts that didn't continued to act as if she wasn't herself anymore.

"Thanks, and when I say you look good, Scarlett, I mean *really* beautiful." His hands move from her shoulders to her thighs, leaning her back up, and pressing himself closer to her. A knot formed in her throat, and her gut wanted to scream, yet she did nothing. "You know, I always thought you were a gorgeous girl. Our parents thought so too. They always said we'd be a great couple when we were younger. You remember that, right, Scarlett?"

Scarlett mumbled, half-heartedly paying attention. All she wanted now was some water and her bed. His hands inched up higher, and Scarlett's breath hitched. Something told her she shouldn't allow this, that she wanted it to stop. But once again, the alcohol drowned out her ability to think straight, and she found herself at his mercy.

"I think it's only fair that we give it a shot. For our parents, don't you think?"

"I need to make my parents proud," Scarlett whispered, suddenly hooked by his proposal. If they got together, would it really make her family think better of her?

"Yes, you do, Scarlett, and this would do the trick. You trust me, right?" he asked, sincerity in his voice. *No, no, I don't.*

"Yes."

"Good, then let's make them proud." He grabbed her hips fiercely, pulling him into her and smashing his lips against hers. She struggled against his grasp, itching to get away but finding herself too disoriented to do so. His lips traveled from her mouth down to her neck, biting it harshly. Scarlett gasped at the pain, itching to get away from him. His grip slid up and down her torso as he pushed himself up closer to her on the countertop. She gasped and spluttered, needing to get away from this, from him. He finally pulled away, a look of mischievousness no doubt playing on his features.

"Damn, Scarlett, you sure know how to kiss. I wonder what else you could do."

"I don't know, Beau," she mumbled, hoping he would take the hint. She doesn't want this, she never did. But he just smirked, grinning with bright teeth.

"Let's find out then. I took a look upstairs a while ago. Your parents' room is big, but I think I like yours the best." He grabbed the back of her thighs, hoisting her up off the counter and down to the floor. Scarlett stumble and would've fallen if it weren't for Beau grabbing her. "Come on, Scarlett, I know you want this."

He pulled her out of the room, towards the door that led to her own. She shook her head, unable to form the words. As he pulled harder, she found the strength to fight harder. "Beau, no! I don't." She yanked away from him, yet the second she got out of his hold, he grabbed her again.

"Don't lie, Scarlett, I know you do. I see the way you look at me." She wiggled from his wrist, taking a step back, and slipping slightly.

"I don't, I won't, please don't do this. When have I looked at you?" Beau grabbed her again, this time with a grip far tighter than Scarlett could worm out of. A look of shock passed over his features for a second. Like he knew Scarlett had never thought of him like that. It only made him try harder.

"You might not know it now, but you want this, Scarlett. And when you come to your senses, you'll realize that." He grabbed her by her hair, yanking roughly. A shrill shriek slipped past her lips, and she couldn't help but kick and tug as she was dragged to her door. Beau yanked her up by her hair, forcing her to stand despite her wobbly knees. She looked at him, eyes full of hatred and fear. Yet he held only pleasure and desire.

"Hey!" A deep voice boomed out. Beau looked up for a moment, distracted, and Scarlett took the opportunity to grab his arm and sink her teeth into it, *hard*.

"Ow, Dammit!" he cursed, flinging his arm out of her reach, and pushing her aside.

Someone grabbed her by her shoulders, gently guiding her up and to a nearby chair. But this person wasn't rough and didn't want something from her. No, he was gentle and kind, and there to protect her.

Scarlett watched in blurry confusion as Jason made his way over to Beau.

27

JASON

The intense buzz of the party was starting to wear off for Jason. He'd been ignoring everyone as much as he could, trying to survive the next few hours. Which was hard, when the smell of alcohol was pungent in the air, and dozens of buzzed teens swarmed around you. He tried to distract himself by glancing around him once again, taking in the scenery, switching the songs in his AirPods. No matter how hard he tried, his gaze always seemed to fall back to her.

He saw her, sitting on the counter, hand on her head. *He had wanted to kiss her, truly, he did.* But he knew it wasn't what she wanted, not really. Besides, he had a policy, and Jason stuck by what he said. He took notice of how she was, clutching her head and swaying slightly on the countertop. He wanted to help, to offer her water or something, but after their little run-in earlier, he figured it would be best not to intrude. Beau walked up to her, hands in his pockets.

See, Jason? She doesn't need you anyway.

His heart sank a little, but he continued watching out of pure curiosity. They talked for a bit, and he cringed slightly at the way Beau's hands slowly inched further up her thighs. Scarlett shrank away from him, laughing uncomfortably, which the bleached blonde didn't seem to notice. He leaned in closer, smiling and smirking while Scarlett smiled too. While Beau's was bright and toothy, Scarlett's was more polite and gentle. More fake. A shock was sent down Jason's system when their lips connected, and Beau led her in a passionate kiss. His stomach dropped. Jason wanted to scream, yet he didn't know why. This girl was nothing to her, except for an adversary, yet the sight of her kissing another man made Jason's blood boil. Even more than that was the fact that she was drunk and clearly not thinking straight. He couldn't help but wonder if this was really what she wanted, or if it was the alcohol talking. The two finally broke apart, saying things he couldn't quite hear. He looked away, unable to bear the sight of Beau drooling over a girl he didn't want yet couldn't stand not to have. He inspected his sparkling water, suddenly very interested in it, yet when he looked up, the two were gone. He would've just left it at that. If it were anyone else, he probably would go about his business pretending he didn't see anything.

But this wasn't anyone else; this was Scarlett.

And the tug in his gut told him something was very wrong. He moved through the house, searching room after room before hearing a shrill shriek. He followed the sound, growing more frantic by the second. There, in front of a large white door, was Beau, dragging a screaming Scarlett by her hair. She was crying, clawing at him to let go, begging him to not to do this to her. Beau was unmoving, yanking harder and gritting his teeth while sputtering nonsense about 'not knowing what you want' and 'trust me, I know this is the best thing for you.' The second Jason saw him, red flooded Jason's vision. His hands shook, not from anxiety but from rage. This person, whom he thought to be his friend, betrayed him and then took advantage of someone he's known his whole life. Took advantage of Scarlett. Beau just stood there, desire consuming him while Scarlett begged for him to stop. The sight churned his stomach, making him sick with disgust. He had to do something because Scarlett couldn't do it.

"Hey!" he called, pure hatred lacing his voice.

Beau made eye contact with him, fear etched in his face. *This jerk knows I've caught him.*

The next second, Beau called out in agony, clutching his bleeding forearm. "Ow, dammit!"

Jason glanced to Scarlett, confused. The dizzied girl tugged away from him, wiping her mouth with the back of her hand. She bit him. While Beau was whimpering over his wound, Jason made a move to Scarlett, shaking on the floor. He gently lifted her up, guiding her with strong arms back through the hallway and onto a chair in the kitchen.

"I'll be back, I promise. Stay here, Scarlett." And he was gone, shock churning into loathing as he turned his focus back on Beau Singh. He was in the same spot Jason had left him, too afraid to move, and too guilty to even attempt an excuse.

"Jason, I— "

"Oh fuck off," he cursed, shoving Beau in the chest. "Don't try to explain, Beau, I know what you were doing, and you do too. How could you be so sick? Scarlett is drunk out of her mind right now, and the only thing you think of is sex?" He raised his voice, confusion lapping in with the rage now filling his mouth.

"Jason, she wanted to kiss me; she didn't pull away. I know she wants me; she just needed a little encouragement."

The way Beau spoke, as if truly believing himself, genuinely believing that Scarlett could want any of this, flipped a switch in Jason's mind that he didn't know he had.

"You absolute fucking piece of trash! She's sitting in the kitchen, shaking and crying because of your 'encouragement'!" He stepped forward, shoving Beau back further. Then Beau was shoving at him, growling and shoving. Jason barely had time to blink before a fist was hurdling towards his face, sending a sharp pain across his cheek. Flashes of his father threatened to show, but Jason pushed them aside. He couldn't have an attack, not right now. Not at something as important as this. He fired back, sending a clean jab right at Beau's jaw. He stumbled back and charged at Jason, fire in his amber eyes. Jason saw his maneuver before it happened. At the next fly of his fists, he grabbed his wrist, bringing it up to the wall and grabbing the collar of his shirt.

"You listen to me, you disgusting bastard. I don't want to see you again. I don't want to hear your bullshit stories or see you at my practices." Beau struggled against his grasp, teeth bared and breath ragged. A horrifying sense of realization crashed over him.

"This is how she felt. Isn't it? You're grabbing her like she's nothing but an object. How does it feel, Beau? Tell me how the fuck does it feel?" He shoved him up against the wall, grabbing him harder and rejecting any of his futile attempts at escape. He gave up trying to teach him a lesson, instead dragging him by his collar through the house. He squirmed and pried out of his grasp, but Jason kept a firm hold, hauling him down the halls like a cop guiding his criminal. Beau was a criminal, just not one who was caught. Not yet, at least. They reached the door, and Jason flung it open, sending Beau outside the house with a final push and a kick to his back.

"I am ashamed to have ever called you my friend. Now get the hell out, and if you ever do so much as touch her again, I will rip you limb from fucking limb." He slammed the door in his face, rubbing his temples and sighing. Looking up, dozens of students looked back at him, having heard the ruckus.

"Enough is enough," he mumbled, clearing his throat. "Alright, the party's over. I'm sorry, but you all need to get out!" he yelled over the crowd, motioning everyone out the door.

"Why? It's not even that late?" Someone called out.

"Don't be a dick, Jason, let us stay." Anger pulsed in him again, and it took everything he had not to go feral.

"You heard what I said. Get out now before I call the police," he stated. If this were any other time, the guilt for threatening his friends, people he knew, would be crushing him. This was not one of those times, however, because as he stood there, watching dozens of kids file out the door, eager to escape trouble, he felt nothing but fury and anger. Anger for these kids, and their constant need to be muddled by drugs and alcohol. Anger for Scarlett's parents for not caring enough to see that their family friend was a pervert. And anger toward the pervert himself. Jason felt a shame pressing down on him, a side effect from once being this man's best friend. It was all gone now; every time they'd ever spent together was nothing to him in a matter of seconds. The second the last kid filed out the door, he was running back to her.

She was slumped on the counter, lashes fluttered closed, yet her body was still shaking. Her hair was matted and tangled, a side effect of being tugged and twirled around her. Jason could see bruises forming on her arms from where Beau had gripped her, as well as a dark hickey on her neck, a thin line of crimson dripping from it.

"Scarlett," he whispered, not wanting to startle her.

She didn't move. Jason lightly tapped her shoulder and watched as she slowly sat up, rubbing the blurriness out of her eyes. He saw the moment when it clicked for her. Saw the fear in her eyes as she suddenly jolted, and whipping around to see Jason, and . . . no one else. Tears welled up in her eyes, threatening to join the salty tracks already running down her face.

"Hey, it's alright, you're safe," he assured. Jason reached his hand out, hovering it above her shoulder. He wanted to comfort her, to make her feel safe. But after something like that, would someone want to be touched?

"I just— never thought that would happen to me. I hear about it and stuff . . . but never to me. And Beau?!" She sobbed, hands still shaking. A small hiccup escaped her mouth as she struggled to calm herself.

"Can I touch you? Are you OK with that?" Scarlett nodded, instantly burrowing her head into his shoulder. He could still smell the alcohol on her, but it was masked by the vanilla scent that always surrounded her like a thick cloud. "It's all going to be alright, I promise you." He rubbed circles on her back, not quite sure if he was doing it right.

She pulled out of the contact first, staring at him with broken gray orbs. Her eyes narrowed at the forming yellow bruise on Jason's temple. "Did— did he do that?" She reached up, stroking the area lightly.

"Yeah, but I'm fine, no biggie." He smiled as best he could, but the sadness that seeped into his features couldn't be missed.

"You fought him, didn't you?"

"Maybe, but it seemed like you beat me to it. You really bit him?" She smiled at him sadly, nostalgia etched into her face.

"You told me to bite their hands off, didn't you? He was trying to get in the way of my dreams." Jason almost chuckled, remembering their day at the aquarium and his feeble attempt at a meaningful gift.

"I did. Good memory." He placed his hand atop hers, still resting on his face. "Hey, I'm proud of you."

Scarlett yawned, hunching over slightly, and Jason took this as a signal. He wrapped his arms around her, hooking one behind her knees and the other supporting her back and lifting her up off the chair.

"What are you doing?" She mumbled sleepily.

"Don't worry, I'm just bringing you to your room," he assured, making his way to the room where he saw his former friend and enemy moments earlier. He opened the doorknob while struggling to keep his hold on Scarlett, her head now leaning against his neck. He stepped into the room, flicking on the light switch, and he was instantly greeted with the sight of binders and workbooks strewn across desks. Oregon University banners pinned up on the wall, over a dresser with perfumes and jewelry stands atop it. His eyes trailed to the bed, and he swallowed the bile that rose in his throat at what could've happened in this very room—had he not been there. Good thing he would always be there. A gray object caught his attention. Sitting atop the blankets and pillows of Scarlett's bed was an old Gray Reef Shark plush, gently laid out on the bed with love. Jason set her down gently on the bed, pulling out a blanket and laying it carefully on top of her.

"Thank you, Jason. . . I don't know where I'd be right now if you didn't help." She spoke sincerely, yet sleep was hard on her voice. God knows she needs rest. She reached for the stuffed animal, tucking it under her arms.

"You kept it?" Jason asked, surprised to see the plush still in her possession.

"Of course I did. It was a present, and a present I quite like." Jason scoffed.

"I kind of thought you'd thrown it out the second I was out of earshot." Scarlett hugged the plush closer, breathing softly.

"Nope. He's mine now." She snuggled deeper into the covers, and Jason smiled at the sight. He tucked another strand of hair out of her eyes, savoring the feeling of this touch, this time spent with her. He flicked off the light, slowly moving out of the room.

"Wait." *Flick.*

He moved back to her bedside, where she lay with wide, afraid eyes. "What?"

"I don't want to be alone. Just . . . sit here, please?" Jason looked around awkwardly, not sure what to do. It felt out of place, but he refused to leave her. He wouldn't be able to sleep if he knew Scarlett was cowering in her bed, alone and afraid. Spotting a light blue beanbag, Jason picked it up, dragging it to the space beside her bed.

"Yeah, of course." He smiled, exhaling deeply.

"You'll stay until I fall asleep?"

"I'll stay until you get so sick of me you're begging me to leave."

Scarlett laughed, intoxicated and riding off adrenaline, yet the sound was as sweet as honey.

"Good." She winked at him from her alcohol induced stupor, flashing another round of her award-winning smile. The smile that could melt Jason's heart like ice. "You want to know the real reason I like this thing so much?" she mumbled, eyes falling half closed.

He glanced down at the shark in her grasp. "Why, sweetie?"

"It reminds me of you. Kind of smells like you, too," she hummed, lashes fluttering shut once more. "Sweet dreams, Jason."

He watched in shock as her breaths evened out, grip loosening on the shark clutched close to her chest. Her face looked so peaceful, yet there were still dried tear tracks on her face and scary bruises on her arms and neck. Still, he smiled a little. Knowing that he would now be there. To stop anything like this from happening again. To stop anyone who dared mess with the stormy-eyed girl.

"Sweet dreams, Scarlett," he whispered, planting a light kiss on her forehead.

28

SCARLETT

Scarlett shivered, cold air seeping through the end of her blanket. She was vaguely aware of the world around her, feeling drowsy and alert at the same time, yet she couldn't bring herself to open her eyes. *God, it's so cold.* Her head pounded slightly, the pain feeling unwelcome and fervent. She tried to grasp onto something, anything from this night, but each time she tried to think, the tiredness took over once more. She heard breathing to her left side, and her heart stopped.

Who is in my room? And was she even in her room, or was this someone else's house? Scarlett hoped that this was all a dream. Maybe she was just having a sleepover at a friend's house and had a nightmare, though the abnormal feeling in her gut as well as the aching in her arms told her it wasn't so. Scarlett's body trembled, shaking from the cold. Weird, she didn't remember feeling like this earlier. Someone inhaled sharply from beside her, and she listened as soft footsteps passed across the floor. A heavy weight was put on Scarlett, instantly warming her. The weight was spread out, becoming even on all sides as the figure gently tucked it in around her. Scarlett wished she knew who it was, but her brain felt like it was melting. If she couldn't even remember where she was, then she sure as hell wouldn't know who was draping a blanket around her.

"Can't have you being cold now, can we, sweetie?" the person whispered.

Familiarity tugged at Scarlett's mind as she rapidly tried to remember who this was. The voice was rugged, deep yet tinged with tiredness like he'd been sleeping. She felt a hand squeeze her shoulder, while the other tucked a piece of hair behind her ear. The voice spoke again, and Scarlett could hear the frown in his voice.

"You didn't deserve this. No one does. It's not going to happen again, Scarlett, I won't let it." Yup, definitely a him. A him that knows her name, puzzling her. "You know you're so easy to hate but so stunning that I can't help but want to love you." Someone he hates? Scarlett racked her brain, but came up with nothing. "I guess it's a good thing I'm down for a challenge then," he whispered, pulling away from her, fingertips running across the fabric to smooth it out one last time.

Scarlett grasped onto anything she could hear, his voice, the way it shook, and the tenderness in his tone. She thought about where she could have recognized it, who it belonged to and briefly why on earth she cared so much about it. Throughout the whole night, she couldn't place it. And Scarlett fell back asleep thinking about a boy whom she couldn't remember, but who she felt like she knew her whole life.

"Auggghhhhhhhh," Scarlett groaned loudly, sitting up in bed. A pounding wave of nausea and headache overtook her, and she flopped back onto her pillows. Sunlight was streaming in through her windows, and she could feel the warmth on her face without having to open her eyes. Though she did anyway, peeling open her eyes to reveal a somewhat messy room and an extra blanket lying on top of her. She looked around, not sure if it was the drowsiness or just her pure confusion, but something felt off here.

Her gaze fell onto a light blue beanbag, which sat empty yet held in it the indent of a person. Next to it lay a black track bag, one she'd seen before. Ignoring the aching in her body, Scarlett slumped out of bed, tiptoeing to the bag. She searched the pockets, finding shoes, some protein bars, and athletic tape, but she found nothing with a name on it. She opened the last pocket, fishing out a dark green New Wellis jersey. Unfolding it, she read out the name.

"Jason." Her eyes widened, and she dropped the jersey, scooting back on her hands. Why him? They hadn't done anything last night, had they? She didn't remember much, but drunkenly dancing with Jason definitely stuck out in her memory. Did she actually kiss him? Or maybe she had and had somehow convinced him to sleep with her? A part of her knew that was not true, but the sinking feeling in her stomach remained. She shuffled out of her room, unplugging her phone as she went.

Beau Singh - 23 messages, three missed calls, one voicemail.

"What?" She thumbed through the texts, piecing them together as she went. Like an avalanche, the pieces were put together. The bruises on her arms, the hickey on her neck, and why her gut felt like someone was twisting a knife into it. Beau tried to take advantage of her. She remembered it vaguely: someone pulling her hair, yelling, and kicking. She remembered biting someone, presumably him and another person breaking up their struggle. Jason. Scarlett hurried to the other rooms, downstairs, the living room, and everywhere else, looking for him. He stayed the night, she remembered that much, yet there was nothing to show for it except for his old track bag. She entered the kitchen, where a yellow sticky note was laid out on the counter along with a tube of buprofen, and a packet of M&Ms. She ripped it off the counter, reading it slowly.

Hey Artega,

I couldn't stay the whole night, we still had practice. Don't worry I told Coach your rat dog was sick so you couldn't come. Just act sad next time you see him. I'm really sorry about everything last night, talk to me about it if u need to.

Underneath was his phone number, scrawled in messy cursive. She fumbled with her phone, adding him to her contacts as 'roadkill Everett'.

Hey I got your note, ur a saint for the ibuprofen seriously my head is killing me.

She paused, debating whether she should accept his offer of confiding. As much as she wanted to talk about it and understand why he did what he did, the thought of reliving that night made her sick.

I'll tell you if I need someone to talk to, thx for the offer though. Honestly, it's a little fuzzy.

She put the phone down, pouring herself a tall glass of water, then draining it. She popped open the bottle of ibuprofen and swallowed one, rubbing her throat. She felt ashamed for missing practice, although she knew for a fact that if she ran like she was right now, she'd either faint or throw up. So, she took the time to go over some homework because nothing says 'just got abused by my childhood friend' like Spanish and AP Biology! She painstakingly opened her binder, sorting through various assignments and projects.

Ding.

She glanced at her phone, heart quickening. Then she slapped herself for caring that maybe he texted her back.

Sweetie, the ibuprofen was for me, not you. You really think I want to hear you complain all day? And you're welcome by the way.

Scarlett laughed lightly, feeling like she should hate the smile that grew on her face. But she didn't; instead, it just made her happier.

You sure seem concerned about my safety lately.

Three dots appeared on her screen, indicating that Jason was typing. They went away after a second, and Scarlett's breath hitched. When will she learn to stop patronizing people and just thank them rather than teasing them? And now it was costing her a conversation with him. The dots appeared again, blinking quickly.

Well I am a saint aren't I?

Scarlett sighed in relief, lips parting for a smile.

Tell anyone I said that and I'll tell them you slept over last night.

He didn't reply right away, and Scarlett almost regretted that. It was really sweet of him to have stayed, especially after everything that happened.

I think you're forgetting you asked me to stay.

What? Scarlett turned off her phone, sliding it across the counter in an attempt to get away from this information. She couldn't do this, no, not after the dancing, and now begging him to stay the night? The space between hate and love seemed to be shrinking by the day, and Scarlett couldn't have that. She yanked open a trash can, thrusting the M&Ms inside before turning back to her living room. She had to take her mind off the raven-haired boy in any way she could. So, she turned to cleaning. It was a mess, with trash everywhere, empty liquor bottles and chip bag wrappers strewn about. Scarlett counted three jackets that were left on the couch, as well as a couple of lost earrings and one pearl necklace, which she identified as Zoe's. *She must've had fun last night then.* She dialed the girl's number, waiting for the pale girl to pick up.

Ring. Ring. Ring.

Nothing. She checked the clock; it was 8:00. Practice wasn't even over yet. She decided to leave a message, apologizing for the night and explaining why she went missing. The dial beeped, and Scarlett cleared her throat.

"Hey Zoe, this is Scarlett. Um, I just figured I should let you know why I'm not at practice. It's not because of my dog." Her lungs filled shakily, and she let out the breath slowly. "Beau kind of . . . *attacked* me last night. I don't really want to elaborate, but he came at me, and Jason showed up, and they got into a fight. I don't remember a ton, but I think he shut down the party so… sorry for cutting your night short. Please don't freak out, and please don't let Meg freak out. I just wanted to let you know. So . . . bye." She hit the end dial and wiped at her face. Her hand came away wet, with tears she didn't even realize she had shed.

It was strange; she didn't even remember the whole story, yet she felt so utterly violated. The story was blurry, she couldn't recall half of what he said or why that night even happened. Yet the terrifying details stood out. The feeling of his stern grip on her, or the iciness in Beau's voice. He wanted her, wanted to love her, to have her. But Scarlett wouldn't give that to him. So, he took it. And now, Scarlett would have to go through the rest of her life knowing that for that night, for that moment, she wasn't a person to him but an object. She was a piece of stolen jewelry, an extinguished flame. Scarlett just hoped he hadn't taken her whole spark. That there would still be room for someone else to kindle her flame back to life. She sank down to the floor, hugging her knees and finally letting herself break down. Finally, she let herself be immersed in the fear of the situation. She wasn't sure how long she stayed that way, hugging her knees, and praying it was just a dream. Her phone dinged, and Scarlett's immediate reaction was to stiffen. What if this were Beau harassing her with more insults and begging her to come to him?

Open the door. I'm here.

It was just Zoe. Wait, here? Scarlett rushed to the door, with relief and joy filling her. She flung it open, and before she could breathe, arms flung around her, squeezing her tightly as if she could just disappear if they let go. Like they were afraid she wouldn't be the same if they ever stopped. Scarlett for one thought she wasn't.

"Oh, Scar," Zoe cried, burying her face in her shoulder. Zoe pulled away, cupping Scarlett's face in her hands.

"What happened to you?" she asked, insistence in her voice.

"Zoe I —"

"Scarlett? Are you safe?" a high-pitched voice called out, and Scarlett had a face to match it when Meghan rushed through the doorway, engulfing her in yet another embrace. A salty tear flowed down her cheek, and Meghan wiped it away gently with her thumb. "Please talk to us. You know you can."

Scarlett gave in to the sadness, a choking sob escaping her mouth. The two girls waited patiently, holding her hands and stroking her back until the dirty blonde had gathered herself. She forced deep breaths into her throat like Jason had taught her until the crying stopped. Until the feelings were buried.

"OK." She joined hands with Meghan on one side and Zoe on the other. "It's not super clear, but he came up to me last night, Beau did, and he was just . . . different. Like he was nice and all, but. . . desperate for something. We started talking, and I remember he just kissed me." Zoe gasped quietly while Meghan's eyes were fuming.

"I tried to pull away, but he wouldn't let me. He said he wanted to see what else I could do." She sniffed, remembering the horrifying events of that night. As she spoke, it seemed she remembered more than she thought. "He pulled me towards my room, and when I tried to get away, he grabbed my hair. He said I was drunk and therefore didn't know what I wanted. Said he'd do the deciding for me."

Meghan smiled down at her sadly, anger in her eyes, but a clear streak moving swiftly down her face. "Pay my bail, Zoe, because I am actually going to kill Beau," she growled, voice trembling.

"That's on Scarlett because I'm gonna be right next to you."

Scarlett tried to laugh, but it came out as a breathy hitch. "Thank you, guys, but Jason already beat the crap out of him. He found me by the door and brought me to the kitchen. I didn't see what happened after that, but when he found me after, he had a bruise on his jaw. Said he handled it."

"Did you try to fight? You know, to get away from him?" Zoe asked, emotion bleeding into her voice.

"Of course she fought, I know you wouldn't let him leave clean, right Scar?" Meghan stated, convinced of herself.

"No, I um, tried to get away. Probably scratched him plenty of times. And I also think I bit him." Meghan smiled, pride evident on her face.

"That's my girl." Zoe still looked shocked, as was Scarlett. That someone they'd known for so long would treat her like this.

"I can't believe we weren't even there. I feel horrible." Scarlett hadn't even thought about that.

"Don't. You guys were having your own fun; I don't blame you for just being in the wrong place. Besides, I would rather have kept you out of danger."

Meghan sighed, twirling a piece of hair in her fingers. "And Jason really fought him? For you?"

"I know, I was surprised too. Though I think he would've fought him if it were anyone."

"I think he would've yelled if it were anyone, but not beaten them up. He was protecting you, Scarlett," Zoe explained with a mischievous look in her eye.

"Please, I don't like him. And I don't think I'll be ready for anything for a while anyway, thanks to Beau." She shuddered, and gentle arms were wrapped around her.

"You're so brave, Scar. Don't let him ruin you." Scarlett felt their warmth in her arms. Safe, loving, and kind. She wouldn't let him ruin her life. But that doesn't mean he didn't leave his mark. She fingered the bruise on her neck and the ache in her arms. Reminders, souvenirs of his actions. Those would fade; the marks that dotted her body would go away throughout the days. But her heart? Her trust? Scarlett didn't know if that could be fixed. Not all walls can be rebuilt. Some have to be left to nature, and over time, vines would crawl their way up it, blocking it from view. But cut down the vines and the wall will always be there, cracking and crumbling.

29
BEAU

I'm the villain now.

Beau fidgeted with the hem of his shirt, pacing around his room. His dresser was littered with bandages and paper towels, in an effort to clean the bite mark on his arm, and the swelling purple bruises painting his face.

There was no stopping the rumors; half the school saw what he'd done. Saw the hurt he inflicted. But there was nothing else he could do, not without letting go of Scarlett. And Beau would not let go. It was this way ever since he was little, with the two families merging in friendships. Scarlett was pure blonde then, as many young girls are. Beau was only a few months older, yet he took full responsibility for 'teaching' his friend the ways of life. The laugh and calm demeanor of Scarlett were around Beau constantly, and slowly, he developed a love for the girl. At first, he denied it, convinced it was just a fling. Then, one summer, that all changed. They were riding roller coasters at the boardwalk, as they'd done year after year before. But this time felt different, and when they got in their cart on the Big Dipper, Beau felt a knot in his stomach that wasn't there before. And when Scarlett gripped his arm at the drop to ease her nerves, he realized that it wasn't a fling, it was *love*. Ever since, he'd been desperately trying to get her attention, calling her name, talking to her whenever he could. But something happened in the following years that he couldn't place.

Scarlett grew more distant from him. The young girl who obliged to everything he said wasn't there anymore; instead, this Scarlett was opinionated, stubborn, and unwilling to do anything she wasn't interested in. That was not what Beau wanted. Still, the thought of being without her tore him apart. He tried, really tried, but it seemed the longer he went without interacting with her, the more intense the feeling grew. Then track started, and Beau finally had an excuse to hang out again.

He sat in at their practices, watching her run and cheering her on at meets. The others thought he was there for Jason and Marcus, so he let them believe that. He got closer to them, really, he did, and the feelings of friendship grew between them. The trio became inseparable, doing literally virtually everything together. Any secret that was had by one of them was had by the three of them. They were like brothers, a bond that was stronger than any other friendship, and Beau wanted to keep it that way— until senior year, that is when Beau wanted to get as far away from Jason as he could.

Scarlett was his, and if anyone would mess with that, he wouldn't hesitate to get away from them and take Scarlett with him. No one else saw it. As far as they all knew, Scarlett and Jason were mortal enemies, but Beau saw their lingering glances. In fact, he was sure he was the only one who did. The light jabs to the arm that lasted a little too long, or the snarky comments with a note of flirting. Beau wanted to deny it, and he really wanted to be wrong, but he knew he was right.

Jason was in love with Scarlett. And Scarlett, *his* Scarlett, was in love with him too.

There was nothing that drove Beau crazier than to see his childhood best friend and love of seventeen years start to fall for someone else. Beau was angry. He'd done nothing but be a supportive older brother figure, especially since Milo was too busy being valedictorian to care about such things as being a role model. He'd taken her to her mother-daughter dance when her mother was out for the night, tied her hair in a bun for her first dance recital, and even gotten her the shoes she wanted for her tenth birthday. The ones her own parents didn't bother getting.

Yet she fell for someone else. The dark-haired boy who didn't seem to give a damn about her personal well-being. He teased her, poking fun at her insecurities, joking about her faults. If it were Beau, she would be pissed, probably ignoring him for the week. But when it was Jason, it was funny. Jason could make her laugh, and for one, Beau just wanted to be that person. The one who could make her laugh, make her smile. Now that had all gone to shit. She hated him now, no doubt, and probably would never forget the night. Beau knew he would. Still, seeing them together made his gut twist.

Attempting to push it aside, he continued hanging out with them as usual. But the side glances and constant interactions made it impossible to stay in the same room as Jason. So, he didn't. It hurt him to leave the group, hurt him to leave his two best friends and start over again, but he had to do it. He couldn't stand to live life so close to the love of his life, and so close to the boy he knew would be hers. So, he left with no explanation and no looking back. Any interactions with either boy he had now would be stiff, short, and wildly rude, for it was the only way Beau knew to handle it. He could tell it drove them crazy, not knowing what they did or what they could do to get him back, but Beau would die before he told them what they could do. If Jason could just stop looking at her, talking to her, breathing the same air as her, he would be perfectly content. With Jason out of the way, Beau thought he might actually have a chance at his love.

You should have known.

His own stupidity and blindness for Scarlett took away the fact that she didn't want him. Just because Jason was out of the picture for him, he was still very much in frame for Scarlett. This meant that, unfortunately for Beau, there was no chance he could be with her. Beau spent his nights pacing back and forth, unable to tear his mind from the stormy-eyed girl and everything perfect about her. He could go on for days listing every tiny detail about her face, how many freckles she had, and where her birthmarks were. He knew her star sign, favorite fruit, and her fears. He knew her goals and what she dreaded the most. He knew why she was reserved in love sometimes and how to heal her. He knew all these things, loving each and every one of them. But Scarlett still didn't love him. The madness that tore into Beau's mind eventually turned to anger. Why did she not love him? He was everything good for her and nothing bad. But still, friend-zoned and rejected again. It was a sort of rhythm that Beau was bored with.

He was going to get her. He wanted her, needed her, and if she didn't want him back . . . well, there doesn't have to be two sides to everything. That was when he decided to kiss her. When she was alone, the buzz of alcohol definitely helped. He wasn't planning on hurting her, just claiming her as his own. He only wanted to show her what good he could do, what good things he would do for her. But things escalated, and Beau quickly discovered he had no self-control whatsoever. The second their lips brushed, he was electric, wanting more of her, needing all of her. But all of her wasn't something she wanted to share. So, instead of accepting that and walking away like any other,

Beau fought for it. He had lost too much of her to Jason already to give up on this chance. *Maybe that's why he did it* —knowing that there was most likely no other chance to have her than now. Or maybe he was drunk, perhaps the two beers he'd had proved to be more effective than previously thought. Though Beau suspected it might've been pure jealousy that fueled his outburst. Either way, he knew what he wanted, and he intended to get it. So, he fought, pulled, and dragged the love of his life across the floor in hopes that she would take him. He was a fool. A fool for not listening, a fool for thinking that anyone crazy enough to drag a crying girl by her hair deserves any love. But above all, crazy for thinking that this beautiful girl, smart, kind, and in love with someone else, would even look in his direction long enough to see the signs.

He went through the motions for the following days, attending school with his head down, keeping himself as far away from Jason and the whole track group as possible. Currently, he stalked the halls of school, grabbing books from his locker while pushing people aside in the crowded hallway.

He spotted them, Jason jokingly holding Scarlett's beanie high above her head while Scarlett, scowling from below, cursed at him. He smiled, genuinely. Even as she stomped on his toes, causing him to crouch down and allow her to snag the cap back, he smiled. Scarlett didn't see it. Or maybe she did, and chose to ignore it. The others didn't notice either, always choosing to focus on themselves. But Beau knew. He had to walk through his school every day, seeing them teasing each other, with playful hate. Sometimes the hate seemed real, and in those moments, Beau felt joyful in knowing that maybe he'd have a chance. Then the next day, they'd be back to the insults laced with interest. Curses poisoned with care. It was like a dagger into Beau's heart.

He couldn't have her. He couldn't have her. He couldn't have her.

Some part of him knew that and knew he could never have her. But he needed her so desperately, so intensely that knowing he couldn't have her was merely a suggestion. So, he did something he'd promised himself never to do. He hurt Scarlett. On purpose, too, which made it even worse. He knew he wanted her, but at that moment he knew nothing else. He couldn't see, couldn't hear, couldn't think of anything that wasn't her. She told him no, told him she didn't want it, but his ears just wouldn't allow him to hear it. She scratched and kicked, yet his grip wouldn't allow him to let go. He wanted to let go, wanted to stop hurting her, but he couldn't. Because letting go of her meant he would never touch her again, feel the warmth of her smile or the friendliness in her voice.

So, he didn't let go. Then Jason showed up, and it all went to crap. Beau wasn't sure what would've happened had he actually gotten Scarlett into her room. Would he have gone through with it, or would the love he held for her overpower the thought of hurting her more? Now he would never know, because now she was Jason's property. He said it himself: Beau would be ripped limb from limb if he ever touched Scarlett Artega again. He claimed her. And no one else seemed to notice. Beau wasn't even sure if they saw it. Jason and Scarlett saw that their tension was tender. That their hate for one another was slowly being consumed by love. No, they didn't see it, or else they wouldn't claim to hate one another. In a way, it just made it worse that Beau could see something no one else could. Something that would keep him from the love of his life forever. But it wasn't the love of his life. She was the love of Jason's life. She was the love that he couldn't have. She was the love that would slip through his fingers like sand. It was like Oobleck — the more he gripped, the faster she slipped away. Beau squeezed her tight, keeping her with him, and she didn't leave. But the second he opened his fist, letting go of his grip, control, and power, she slipped through.

He knew she would; he understood how it worked. Understood that she was gone, slipped through his fingers and wasn't ever coming back. However, Beau knew that he would spend the rest of his life desperately trying to get her to come back. Searching for the piece of his heart that fell out the day she denied him. He wouldn't get it back. But he would keep searching, searching until the sun dipped below the horizon and until his eyes grew dry and red. Searching because there would always be a sliver of hope, no matter how small. Searching, because Beau still loves her. He always would. But he couldn't stay. Beau knew he would go mad if he ever saw them together. He knew he wouldn't be able to handle it. He'd already done so much damage, and Beau was scared. Scared of what he could be capable of if his heart broke the way it did again.

He didn't want to know, didn't want to see it. So, he would go. Leave and continue his life as normal. He was eighteen, he'd done all his credits required to graduate, and he could get out. Get his diploma early, go to MIT, and continue living his life as if that night had never happened. It would be for the best of everyone, himself included. He would leave. Quitting his past life and moving forward. But Beau knew that even though the dreams of being with her might subside, the nightmare of losing her would plague him forever. It was something he had to live with. Because that's life. There isn't always a happy ending.

30
MARCUS

"So, what do you think of her?" Marcus asked, leaning down to match his younger sister's height.

Cora grabbed his arm, leaning on him with her delicate body. "I like her," she hummed, nodding in agreement.

"Me too, girl." Marcus smiled, pinching Cora's cheek.

She was only eight, but Marcus wanted to hold onto her innocence as long as he could. She giggled, shimmying out of his grip and onto the kitchen floor, running around squealing.

"Marcus is in looove."

Marcus blushed, laughing tightly. "Cora, stop it."

Meghan came from around the corner, holding something behind her back. "What was that, Cora?" she asked, fluttering her lashes at Marcus.

"I said, Marcus is in LOO —" Marcus scooped her up, hauling the girl over his shoulder.

"That's enough from you, potato sack." He tossed her head upside down over his shoulder like a burlap bag. He's been trying to introduce the two girls, hoping Cora would take a liking to Meghan. He's right, of course. Cora adored her. He just didn't realize that would mean Cora was so chatty. He was planning on saying it eventually, just that it still felt too soon. Marcus set down the worming girl, and she ran over to Meghan, who was giggling wildly.

"You've got an attitude, don't you, Cora?" She smiled, tucking the little girl's hair behind her ears. She leaned in closer, whispering in her ear. "Don't lose it, you have a spark that will do amazing things one day." Cora smiled brightly, her missing tooth evident in her grin.

"Marcus doesn't call it a spark. He says I talk so much because my prefrontal complex isn't done growing." She smirked. Marcus's face burned.

"Prefrontal *cortex*, and mine's not done growing either, Cora. It's mid-20s, remember?" he mumbled, swinging his legs off the counter like he was an eight-year-old.

"Speaking of great things, I have a present for you!" Meghan chided. Marcus hopped down from the counter, reaching Meghan and wrapping his arm around her waist.

"You didn't have to, you know."

"No, she totally did, it's a right of passage. You wouldn't understand because you're a boy," Cora announced, holding out her hands in expectancy.

"Yeah, Marcus," Meghan teased, kissing him lightly on the cheek. "Alright, close your eyes."

Cora did as asked, and Meghan placed the object in her hands. Cora's eyes opened, widening instantly. It was a small bee plush, embezzled with a honeycomb logo.

"It's the spelling bee! From my competitions!" she squealed, hugging the plush close to her chest. Marcus was shocked. He'd mentioned she loved spelling, maybe once. And that was all it took for Meghan to come up with such a caring gift? He smiled at Cora, now examining every inch of her new toy.

"You like it?" he asked, widening his smile.

"I love it! Thank you, Meghan!" She ran towards her, wrapping her arms around Meghan's legs. Meghan bent down, returning the gesture.

"You're so welcome, Cora. I'm glad you like it." She turned to Marcus, her honey eyes looking longingly into his dark ones. Marcus chuckled, pulling Meghan closer.

"I thought you were my little bee?" he whispered, lips grazing her ear.

"You have two women in your life now. Two bees." She smiled, draping her arms around his neck. "But for you, Marcus, I will always be your little bee. Your bee, your girlfriend, anything as long as I'm *yours*." His heart pounded. It had already been upwards of eight weeks, yet he still felt the same panging in his heart, the same crush as puppy love that he felt since they first kissed.

"Good thing I don't plan on losing you." They kissed lightly, saving their electric love for when the children were gone. Still, Marcus almost likes this better. It wasn't needy or full of greed. It was soft, gentle kissing full of sweetness. It was light, yet swarming with emotion. Like having full conversations without having to say a word. Like knowing each other's favorite color. Like baking cookies and wiping frosting on each other's noses. Like a best friend.

"Ew!" Marcus slowly broke apart, wanting to make a show out of it. Meghan seemed to think so too, because they both turned directly to Cora, smiling brightly, cocking their heads before kissing again, quick and smooth. "Now you're just doing it on purpose!"

She whined, stepping in between the two. "You know you love each other, so you don't have to be kissing all the time," Cora explained, having successfully parted the two. Marcus was speechless.

"Cora."

"She's not wrong. Is she?"

Marcus looked at her, brown waves flowing down her shoulders, honey eyes feeding his desires, his dreams. Her smile was welcoming and warm. She was always right, always.

"No, she's not wrong."

They exchanged smiles, unaware of the feelings they just admitted to one another, and continued keeping Cora occupied. Which wasn't all too difficult if you had a spelling book, Cheez-Its, and *Tangled*. The evening went smoothly, with Cora eventually leaving with Mrs. Levine to go grocery shopping. She'd gotten used to Meghan being around, although when Marcus introduced the two, he did specifically leave out all mentions of making out. Other than the slight white lie, they got along quite well. She of course bombarded Meghan with all questions about her future, ambitions, and what she wanted out of life and Mrs. Levine seemed altogether thrilled with her responses.

"She seems like a darling girl to me. Don't go screwing this up now, baby," she'd told him.

"Not planning on it," he said. Meghan sighed, gathering up her stuff and looking at Marcus with a look that said, 'I love you, but I have to go.'

"Where do you need to go?"

"The movies, the girls and I are gonna go."

Marcus felt a little pang in his heart, but let it go just as quickly as it came. He didn't own her, and had no control over whether she wanted to do something fun with her friends. Her friends, not his. Meaning, he wasn't invited. Which was fine.

"What movie?"

"'My Girl!' They're having an anniversary watch party, and I needed to see it." Marcus smiled . He could hear the happiness in her voice. She loved that movie, going on about it for hours. It was something Marcus drank in like music, hearing her rant about the things she loved.

"Have fun. Want me to drop you off?"

"Why don't you just come with us? Bring Jason, or someone else, we'll make it a group thing." Marcus raised an eyebrow.

"You sure? I thought it was like a 'girls' night' thing." Meghan scoffed, bumping hips with Marcus.

"Please, 'My Girl' is for everyone. You'll like it." Marcus texted Jason, letting him know.

Sounds good, meet you in ten.

"Alright, I told him. I would invite Beau, but he's been off. I haven't heard from him since the party." Meghan's eyes widened slightly.

"No. Not Beau, don't tell him." Marcus stepped back. Since when was Meghan so defensive about Beau?

" Whoa, why? I know he's not like the best but —"

"You didn't hear, did you?"

"Hear what?"

"Hear about the attack."

"Wh —attack?"

Meghan spent the next ten minutes going over that night, the things they'd missed while dancing the night away and the terrors that Scarlett went through right under their feet. He didn't know what to say. Nothing felt right. Sorry seemed too common, yet nothing else would be appropriate.

"I know, I was speechless too," Meghan said, fire in her eyes.

"I just can't believe he was my friend. I mean, I really trusted him." Marcus's mind was reeling, struggling to comprehend. He was such a good guy, wasn't he?

"We all did. Someone like that just doesn't do . . . stuff like that. It's all weird," Meghan concluded, marching Marcus out the door.

"Alright, so definitely not inviting Beau. I'll just have Jason then, he loves romance films."

So, it was settled. They drove to the theater, Meghan telling Marcus all about her day and everything that was new with her on the way there. Marcus loved these conversations; just talking with Meghan was like entering a whole other world.

"Favorite book. Go." Meghan said, feet propped up on the dashboard.

"Is this my question of the day?" Meghan winked.

"You bet it is." Marcus hummed in thought, looking out the window like inspiration would come to him.

"Um . . . definitely *Crazy Rich Asians*," he said, leaning his head back on the rest.

"Really? Henry Golding?" Meghan asked, laughing a little.

"Is it the love or the fact that they're too rich for their own good?" Marcus smiled, keeping his eyes on the road.

"Maybe the love. But I do aspire to be like Peik Lin someday." Meghan let out a loud laugh, and Marcus grinned.

"You know, if I could make you laugh, just like this, for the rest of my life, I don't need to be rich," he said, gaze falling to Meghan's lips.

"If I could see that adorable sweater vest every day of my life, I think I'd be pretty happy," she said, leaning in. Marcus, focused on the road, but felt Meghan's glances at him, the way she was looking at him.

"God, you're beautiful." He leaned over in his seat, turning his head and kissing Meghan lightly, slowly. She grabbed his face, losing themselves in the contact.

"Whoa, can't kiss if we crash, Marcus," she said, pulling out of touch and turning Marcus back into his seat.

"Sorry, someone has the power to distract me, that's all." He veered back into his lane, and the two continued their drive to the theater in loving silence.

"Sorry, Jason, out of M&Ms," Zoe announced, carrying three bags of popcorn, Skittles, and a pouch of raisinets.

"Got the last ones, roadkill, sorry," Scarlett said, taking her seat by Zoe, and waving the pack of candies in Jason's face. Marcus chuckled.

"You know sharing is caring, right, Artega?" Jason asked, grabbing the box with quick reflexes. He laughed as Scarlett fought to get them back. Scarlett lunged for the box, successfully grabbing it from the boy's grasp, though Marcus notices Jason flinching slightly at the sudden movement. They took their seats, lights dimming and the trailers started. Marcus's phone went off, and he fumbled to open it.

"No phones in the theater, Marcus, don't make me come over there." Jason threatened from where he was, reaching over Zoe to snag Scarlett's food.

"What is it?" Meghan asked from beside him, peering over his shoulder at the text.

"It's Beau." At the mention of his name, Scarlett's head snapped up, followed by Jason, breaking his attention away from food to dissect Marcus's expression. "It's long too," he added, hesitant to open the message.

"Read it," Scarlett prompted. Marcus inhaled deeply, opening his contact.

Hey Marcus,

I know I'm the last person you want to hear from. I'm not surprised if you all hate me by now, trust me so do I. But good news you don't have to hear from me anyways because I'm leaving. I got into MIT early admission, so I'm already accepted. I figured it was for the best that I just go. This wasn't your fault Marcus, and you really have been a good friend to me. You're a good person, you're genuine. Some things I wish I could be. I'm sorry it has to be like this, really I am, but I just can't handle it anymore. I won't explain it, I don't expect you to get it. So please just try to not be too pissed at me for leaving. Hopefully we see each other again someday, though not likely. I need to move forward, not dwell on the past all that crap. So I guess for now this is goodbye. I've always hated goodbyes, but there you have it. Thank you for showing me kindness, Marcus. Do better things in life than I did.

"What?" Marcus's hands shook, setting his phone down clumsily. "He's leaving? Just . . . gone?" The others looked similarly shocked, Zoe's face displaying a look of shock, while Jason's held a sense of betrayal.

"He's been our best friend for so long, makes one shitty mistake and just leaves?" he breathed, fingering his necklace. Marcus didn't know what to do. Everyone expects him to hate Beau because of what he did, and yes, part of him did. But the other part of him was still his best friend. Part of him still cared about him.

"It's alright not to want him to go, Marcus. You two have known each other a long time," Meghan said, laying a comforting hand on his arm.

"Yeah, I guess you're right. It just doesn't make sense." He rubbed his temples.

"Of course, it makes sense. He was a good guy for a while, did something terrible that he knows we all won't forget, so instead of apologizing, he just decided to leave all the destruction he caused behind him. Like the coward he is." Scarlett fumed a few seats down from him, gray eyes lit like a flame.

"I've known him since we were little. Even then, he ran from his problems." She picked at her nails, eyes to the floor. "I just never thought I would be one of them." Jason stood up stiffly from his chair, gathering his things and stalking out of the theater, face unreadable.

"Jason," Marcus called out, but the boy didn't respond.

"Sorry, guys," Marcus said, standing up, kissing Meghan on the forehead. "And sorry, I really did want to see this with you. I promise it wasn't some grand ploy to leave."

"I know, Marcus, just go." Meghan smiled, pushing him gently off her. Marcus smiled, yet the second he turned around, he broke into a nervous jog to find his best friend.

31
MARCUS

It wasn't long until he found him. He was sitting on a bench, right outside the theater, knees brought up to his chest, where his head was resting on them. He fidgeted with his necklace rapidly, spinning the shark in his fingers and prodding its sharp fins into his palm. A white AirPod sat in his ear, where it practically always was, playing some mix of music to calm Jason, depending on his mood. His hands shook slightly, his shoulders rising and falling in quick rhythms. Jason's hair fell into his face, blocking Marcus from seeing him at all. He started towards him, taking a seat beside Jason on the bench.

"He's really leaving?" Jason asked, the sound muffled by his sweatshirt sleeve.

"Sounds like it." Marcus put an arm around his friend, pulling him in closer. "He didn't tell you goodbye, did he?" Jason shook his head slightly.

"It's not like I expected he would, not after what I did. But after what he did, I wouldn't expect him to even want to show his face here again. And I wouldn't expect a text."

"But you did," Marcus stated, flipping through all his messages with Beau before that night. Before a friend became someone to be feared. "And the fact that you didn't hurts you."

Jason lifted his head up, slightly red eyes meeting Marcus's. "It shouldn't hurt me. I don't even know how to describe what I felt when I found him hurting her. I was just . . . so *angry.* I said things that I never would've if it hadn't been *that exact* situation. If it wasn't her."

OK, not what I was expecting.

"Her?"

"Scarlett."

Marcus thought hard, trying to recall their past encounters. He had seemed slightly less anti-Artega lately, though Marcus just assumed it was because finals were coming up. He took Jason's hand in his, a gesture made purely of the kind of friendships that last you years. "You like her?" A long pause, and then a sigh.

"I don't know. Sometimes, I feel like I could like her. I feel like I want to, but then just as quickly, I remember my goals. Why I even joined track . . . and I realize I can't like her. Not when it could cost me my future," he explained, running a free hand through his hair. "I guess I don't know is my answer. I want to, but I can't. It just doesn't work."

Marcus nodded, taking it all in. He couldn't try to pretend he understood because he completely and utterly didn't. His girlfriend was perfect for him; they had their own hobbies and interests, which made for two completely different careers.

"It's just easier to hate her. For both our futures," Jason said bitterly. Marcus couldn't relate; Jason and Scarlett, though, were fighting for the same scholarship, under the same circumstances.

"She kept it."

"Kept what?"

"The gift I got her. I thought she'd just tossed it out. But it was there, on her bed. Like it was something she actually cared about. Like I was something she cared about," Jason admitted, head falling back onto his knees.

"Maybe you're something she cared about, just not in the way you think. What about after graduation, huh? After the scholarship stuff is over, your futures are your futures. Not even then?" Marcus asked, wondering what would happen then? When it was done and there were no more grades to be fought over or track meets to be won.

"I don't know. But if she takes my scholarship and I have to stay at home with my dad while she goes to Oregon State, I think that would be just enough to murder anything I felt for her," Jason said, eyes boring into a spot on the wall.

"And she doesn't know about this?"

Jason scoffed, rolling his eyes. "Hell no, besides, you really think she'd want me too? She verbally assaults me practically every time we talk."

"Maybe that's just how she flirts," Marcus suggested, shrugging. Jason elbowed him lightly.

"Don't play with me right now. I'm delusional enough as it is, and I don't need you to make it worse." He smiled a little, and to Marcus, that felt like a win. Then, just as quickly, it was gone.

"You think he'll be alright? Beau?" Jason didn't look at him, but Marcus could imagine the concern on his face. He didn't know, truly, for once he didn't know. But that wasn't what Jason wanted to hear. He probably knew himself that Marcus had no idea whatsoever if Beau was going to be alright. But he asked him not because he knew the answer, but because he needed reassurance.

"I think he'll be alright. Before he was bad, he did a lot of good. I think he'll find his place and his people."

"Those people just aren't us," Jason supplied. Marcus nodded, ruffling Jason's hair.

"They're just not us." The two sat in silence, echoes of people chatting and the buzz of the popcorn machine filling the void of quiet.

"I think I'll be OK with that. In time," Jason decided, standing up and brushing off his clothes. He reached a hand to pull up Marcus, who reached out.

"You don't agree?" Jason asked, pressing the subject. Marcus shook his head, smiling sadly.

"No, you're probably right. Just . . . it needs time." They started back towards the theater, both pausing at the entrance. Marcus and Jason exchanged a glance.

"You wanna go back in?" Jason raised an eyebrow, expecting an answer.

"Meghan's seen me enough this week. Let's do something... just us. Like it used to be," Marcus answered, leaving his other friends and girlfriend behind. But sometimes that's what was needed to happen. And it was worth it to see Jason grin, flashing white teeth that reminded him painstakingly of Beau's. But they weren't Beau's. They were Jason's. Jason, who was hilarious, and perfectly sinister at the right moments. Jason, who had always been there, even when Beau hadn't. Jason, who would still be here, now that Beau wasn't. Marcus needed time to think about his leaving, why he did it and how he could move on without dwelling on it constantly. But right now, that wasn't the issue. Because right now, he had a person whom he could confide in above all others, someone with whom he shared things no one else in the universe knew. That was a big job, and a big title to give to a person.

Because above president, king, ruler, and all other names of power and prowess were the simple, honorable title of being someone's best friend.

32
JASON

A night out with his best friend was just what Jason needed. The stress of track and college, everything he'd worked so hard for in life, melted away for just a moment when he was with Marcus. They hadn't done much; they had just gone to their favorite coffee shop and the gas station they used to go to after school as boys. A simple small building with a bright orange roof filled with your typical road trip snacks and amenities. He reached for the M&Ms, upon instinct, but paused. Instead, he took a box of Junior Mints. He might never see Beau again, but that didn't mean he could n't think of him.

"You hate Junior Mints. They taste like straight toothpaste," Marcus said, examining his selection.

"Yeah, they do." He opened the box, sliding his thumb underneath the tab to rip it open. Popping a candy in his mouth, he made a disgusted face, drawing a laugh out of Marcus.

"His favorite, though," Marcus supplied, taking one of his own. He scrunched up his nose, shaking his head violently, dark curls swirling around him.

"You know what? Beau can keep them. I'm not eating those." Jason laughed, and the boys paid for their items. Marcus had gotten Skittles, as assumed, and for a moment, it felt normal. Like a typical day after school, buying their three favorite candies and sharing, trading off their favorite colors and teasing each other for the ones they disliked. But today had been anything but normal. The one who always had something funny to say and someone to say it to was gone. It almost hurt more than him being dead. Because Jason knew Beau could come back. It could all be normal again, but it never could be. As much as Jason wanted Beau to come home, he knew that wasn't going to happen.

"You wanna do something else? The gym? Bookstore?" Marcus asked, grabbing his things from the cashier and veering them back outside to the car. Jason shrugged, a familiar weight pressing down on him.

"I kind of just want to head home if that's alright." Marcus raised an eyebrow. "Big test tomorrow?"

"Something like that, you need a ride back?" The cocoa-skinned boy shook his head, gesturing to his phone.

"Nah, Meghan just got out, so she's gonna pick me up. Said she wanted to show me a new painting," he said, looking like a man in love. A slight smile parted Jason's lip as he nodded. He held out his hand, offering it to Marcus, who grinned, took it and fell into their familiar rhythm. A handshake that had been there for years was now embedded in both their brains. Like muscle memory, they fist bumped and slid their arms along the other, locking fingers at the end and pushing down in a team cheer type fashion.

"See you later. Hey, don't think about today too hard, alright? No one knows what he was thinking." Marcus sent him a reassuring smile, backing away to the coffee shop around the corner. *Easier said than done.* Because until Jason knew exactly what Beau was thinking, why he thought it, and what was going through his mind at that moment, he knew he wouldn't be able to think about anything else. Well, maybe not *anything* else.

He stepped up onto his porch — one he'd known all his life. It was tan cement, with cracks in it from years of weather. There were small blades of grass poking out of the front walkway, as well as a baseball bat and glove thrown onto the lawn. It looked like any normal house would, felt like a normal home for a normal family. When he opened the door and stepped into his house, however, Jason felt nothing at home. Nothing normal. He crept through the doorway, turning right into the kitchen, with a distinct view of the living room —the living room, where Mrs. Everett sat on the floor.

Something was dripping down her forehead. Blood. "Mom! What happened?" Jason ran across the room to her, crouching down onto the floor beside her.

"H-he's just playing with me, it's alright. Maybe you should um, stay at a friend's tonight," she said, smiling at him with whatever strength she had left. Jason reached up to her forehead, gently wiping away the crimson that stained her skin.

"Please, tell me what happened." Jason's tone was gentle, yet demanding. He already knew the truth, knew this was his dad's doing. Brian's doing. Still, he needed to hear it from her.

"He's just . . . not in his own head right now. It's nothing, seriously." Not in his own head?

"You mean he's drunk." Jason's brow tensed, a frown splaying his freckled face. Footsteps echoed down the stairs, a loud voice calling down from above them.

"Jamie, is someone in here?" he yelled, anger evident in his voice. "I knew you were cheating on me, you *slut!*"

"Don't you call my mother that, don't say another word!" Jason retorted before he could even think. Brian appeared, stumbling down the stairs, still half buckling his belt.

"I will call my wife whatever I want, and you." He stepped towards Jason, swaying yet danger swimming in his eyes. "Stay the hell away until I'm finished with her."

"You mean until you're done beating her? Until you're done taking whatever you want from her and then leaving her here?" He felt a tug on his arm.

"Jason, please, don't do this right now. I'll be alright, just go," his mother begged, tears in her eyes.

He was tempted to leave, to get out of this situation, but his eyes flickered back to the blood seeping down her hairline. The same blood tucked underneath the crevices of Brian's nails. And suddenly all his cares for his own safety were cast out, replaced only by rage and fury for his father.

"Do you want him tonight? Want this?" Jason asked, eyes focused on the woman who raised him.

"She doesn't know what she wants, so I decide for her," Brian shouted, curling his fists.

Jason was brought back to Scarlett's house, where she told him how Beau wanted total control of her. How he told her she couldn't make these types of decisions on her own.

"I asked *her.*" He sent a pointed glare at Brian. Mrs. Everett didn't speak, but the slight shake of her head told Jason all he needed to know. He winked at his mother; a small gesture meant for comfort in a situation where comfort was a far-fetched thing.

"Alright, I'll leave. Just gimme a second," he said, trying to kill Brian with only a stare. Jason engulfed his mom in a gentle hug, brushing the hair out of her face and behind her ear. She shakily wrapped her arms around him, exhaling unevenly. Jason hugged her truly, yet amid their embrace, brought his lips to her ear.

"Mom, listen to me. I want you to go. Please, for me, I'll be eighteen in a week, and I'll meet you somewhere, I'll find you," he whispered, quiet yet strong.

"No baby, I can't —"

"No, you don't have much time, you don't deserve this, don't deserve to live like this. I can handle him, and I will, but please, for the love of God, get in your car right now and *go*," he demanded, gritting his teeth.

He loathed speaking to her like that, hated the bitterness coming from his tongue, but Jason knew that if he wanted to keep his mother safe, this was what had to be done. Her gaze fell on him, scared, defeated eyes meeting angry revenge-thirsty ones. Then that gaze shifted, her eyes tracking something in the distance. Jason followed where her eyes trailed. The gun was still sitting above the cabinets.

Still loaded. "G-goodbye baby. Be safe, promise me." Jason smiled, wiping the blood from her forehead one last time.

"It's not goodbye, Mom. I'll find you after, alright? Don't say goodbye unless you mean it." He squeezed her hand, watching a clear river flow down his mother's face as she nodded lightly. He pulled out of the embrace, where Brian was nowhere to be seen.

Phsst. The familiar sound of a bottle being opened rang from a room down the hall. One Jason knew all too well. "He's in his office; you need to go now." He helped her up gently, rushing to the counter where she kept her keys in a wooden bowl. He also grabbed a band-aid, unwrapping it and laying it with care over the cut on her forehead.

"I want you to get somewhere safe, and then get to an urgent care, alright? If you can't drive, call an Uber." He fumbled in his pockets for his wallet, removing a fifty-dollar bill from inside. "Here, take my car, but it needs gas."

"Jason, this was your trip money!" She fussed, pointing to the bill in his hand.

"Then you'll pay me back when I find you, OK?" He shoved the money into her hand along with the keys.

"Go!" He opened the door, ushering the shaking woman outside into the cool autumn night. She ran to the car, throwing her things inside and stepping in. She might've waved goodbye or blown him a kiss, but Jason would never know. He shut the door, locking it. It felt wrong to lock your own mother out of her house, and funnily enough, Jason felt a pang of guilt at the small action. Not the place nor the time yet still. Footsteps again. The pounding of feet and the pounding of a heart. Brian entered the room again, except this time Mrs. Everett was gone, and so was his old car.

"Well, where is she?" he demanded while crossing the room. He searched behind curtains, and in the kitchen, as if she were hiding somewhere. Jason didn't say a word, standing in the middle of the living room, poker face played across his expression. He flung open the curtain by the window, revealing nothing. Nothing, because she was already gone. Jason could see through the window the absence of his car. It seemed Brian did too.

"Where is the car?" he seethed, a small vein protruding from his bald forehead.

"It's not here." Jason feigned calm, keeping his voice leveled and willing the tremors in it to subside. Inside, he was a storm.

"What the hell do you mean it's not here?" He raised his voice, tone slurring in the slightest. Jason kept quiet. Brian grunted, pounding on the door which he flung open. There was no car. Jason heard his father become angrier; it was clear in his tone, the growls of frustration he made as he walked around the driveway. Once he was sure there was no car, he walked around the house, searching for something else. Someone else. But she was not there either. The front door swung open, and in the blink of an eye, Brian was an inch away from Jason, grabbing the collar of his shirt in his fist.

"Where the fuck is she?"

Jason's hand trembled, but he knew he had to stay strong. Showing weakness wasn't an option. You don't get revenge by being weak.

"She's not here anymore. She left." Brian shoved him against the counter, the pointy edge of the table digging into the small of Jason's back. He grimaced but refused to fight back. "She left because she's had enough of you. How disgusting you treat her. She is gone," he growled, gritting his teeth while his voice cracked partly from anger and partly from fear.

"This is your fault, you little bitch," Brian spat, tightening his hold. "You told her to leave, didn't you? You told her to leave and to take the car, too?" Brian raised his hand, striking Jason across the face. It wasn't like he didn't expect it, yet the blow still stung.

"Yes, I told her to leave so she didn't have to live with you, you bastard! So, you wouldn't treat us like shit!" Brian's face snapped sideways as Jason bashed his fist into his temple.

Mr. Everett stumbled at the blow, struggling to regain his balance.

"You are the most ungrateful, disrespectful kid, who the hell taught you to talk to me like that because I sure as hell didn't!" He grabbed Jason, shoving him hard across the room. Jason moved to stand behind the table, now separated from Brian by only four feet of wooden tabletop.

"She left because of you, and you know it, so don't pin this on me. You treat us like we're nothing, and I finally woke up and realized that it's not us, it's you. You're the one who needs to change, but it's too late for that." Jason leaned across the table, teeth bared and anger bubbling from behind his eyes. "Because we're not going to be here when you do change. She is already gone. Your wife, the one who you beat and hurt, is finally gone." Brian slammed his fist against the table, buzz ing with emotions in his eyes. "You don't care about her, and you sure don't care about me, so why even pretend? Let me leave and go back to your office. Sit on your ass and gamble everything you own."

"You don't know half of what I do for this family, but if you leave, you'll find out what. You ruined this family, Jason; we could've worked it out."

Jason laughed bitterly; he wanted to scream. To say something, to let out everything he felt, all of the hate he had spent towards this man. "Worked it out? Worked it out how because abuse isn't working it out. You don't even realize the things you've done to this family, you hit your own wife, your child!"

"I taught you lessons! Lessons you needed to learn, that she needed to learn. As for you being my child, that will be the worst mistake I have ever made." The words stung Jason, burned his heart, but he couldn't let it show.

"I'm happy she left. Mom deserves so much more than you could ever give her. You are a sorry excuse for a husband and an even more pathetic father. And it took me too long to realize that. I made excuses for you. I told myself that tomorrow you would fix your shit and try, even if you weren't, that you would try to be a good father." Jason breathed sharply. "But you never did. And I was weak, but I'm not weak anymore. I will never make that mistake again. I'll never see you as my father again. And I am not your son." A tear slipped down his face, but he didn't move to wipe it. He stayed there; hands planted firmly on the table, watching as Brian turned from angry to concentrated, loathful. His face turned red, resembling a ripe tomato, and Jason thought that if smoke could come out of his ears, it would be.

"You ruined this family, Jason. You're going to hell." Jason cracked a smile, dry lips parting sinisterly.

"I'll meet you there. Fucker." Brian moved swiftly, stepping around the table and catching Jason by his throat. He slammed against a wall, photos of their broken family crashing to the ground.

"Not my son, huh? I'm glad about that; otherwise, it might be familicide." Jason's eyes widened as he realized what Brian's intentions were. "You can't meet me in hell, Jason, if I put you there first."

Jason wasn't sure what agony felt like, but if he had to guess, it wouldn't be far from what he felt next. Brian pulled him back, slamming his head onto the wall. Jason grunted, grabbing his hands and attempting to tear them from his throat where they were squeezing. He gasped for oxygen, feeling his head growing lighter. He wigged his head around, copying Scarlett and biting down on Brian's hands. He yelled, pulling away from him, which gave Jason just enough time to stomp down on his foot. Brian cried out in pain, holding his foot, while Jason coughed and spluttered.

I have no idea what I'm doing.

But that wasn't important; the important thing is to stay alive. *Stay alive and you won't die.* Once he felt like he could breathe again, Jason started through the house, entering the dining room, which led to the door. He reached for the knob, but before he could do so, strong arms yanked him backwards. A knee drove into Jason's stomach, and he grunted, doubling over. Brian grabbed his wrist, dragging him out onto the front porch. Jason struggled against his grip, but it wasn't of any use. When they exited the house, Jason found a moment of opportunity, hitting Brian in the throat with his free hand. Brian gasped, a choking sound emitting from him, and stumbled back, clutching his throat. Jason shoved him over, and that, paired with his momentum, sent Brian flying into a potted plant on the porch. It broke with a satisfying crash, dirt and shards of pottery scattering the concrete. Jason grabbed Brian's arms, hauling him up and against the wall. He wanted to corner him and make him feel like he had made Jason feel his whole life. But when he grabbed his father's shirt collar, hoisting him up like Brian had done to him hundreds of times, he couldn't bring himself to do it. This was what he got for trying to stand up for himself; he couldn't even inflict that same hurt on the one who did it first. He took a small step back, almost shamed at what he was going to do, when something hard jabbed him in the stomach again. Jason gasped, all the air fleeting his lungs. Brian grabbed the baseball bat off the porch, holding it sideways and using the length of the object to thrust Jason backwards. His head hit the concrete corner of the step, and stars filled his vision for a moment. Jason's vision went blurry, though he was sure that it was red on his hand when he felt the back of his head. Nausea crept up on him, and he wanted to throw up. His head felt like it was stuffed with cotton, but he sat up nonetheless, shoving his father down into the dirt of the pot once again.

"Fuck you, Jason." Brian spat, and Jason's leg erupted in pain. Sizzling, seething pain like he'd never felt before. He screamed, clutching his leg where a large shard of the pot now stuck out from deep in his thigh. Jason collapsed onto the porch, his leg unable to stand with the pain seeping through his every nerve. Blood streamed down it in crimson rivers, and Jason felt it sticky and warm on his fingers. He was seeing black spots in his vision now, like dozens of tiny seeds crowding around his line of sight. He felt like he was floating, his mind a million years outside his body. He used his arms, clawing at the dirt and concrete to get away from his soon -to-be murderer. Brian grabbed his ankles, dragging the raven-haired boy around to the side of the house. He dumped Jason in the dirt, next to the edge of their home, outside the line of vision of anyone who was to pass by right now. Jason tried to take notice of the little surroundings he could make out. His heart stopped when he noticed one thing. The bat from the porch, now encased in Brian's hands. The first blow was like someone throwing a large rock at you. It landed on his leg, and Jason groaned, crying out.

"I'm sorry it has to be this way, Jason, I really am." He swung again, the bat striking his ankle, which cracked loudly. He couldn't feel it anymore. Jason was so far gone that he was sure he wouldn't feel anything ever again. "But some lessons just can't be taught. And to those who can't learn 'em, well, the world would be better without them."

Whack. His ribs cracked, and Jason found it increasingly harder to breathe.

"Please. Dad." He croaked.

Another blow.

He felt the bruises blooming on his right and his arm could taste the blood in his own mouth. But now he wasn't in his own body. He was above it, watching down on himself as he was beaten to death, bruised and bloodied. It felt peaceful. And Jason could honestly feel acceptance in his heart. Longing, of course, for all the things he would be unable to do. His training, was all for nothing if a scholarship wasn't to be had. A wish that he'd made up with Beau before he left. And a feeling of lost love.

Scarlett. If he wouldn't live to go to college anyway, he could have at least had her. He could've loved her. *Whack*. He braced for the impact of the bat, but when it didn't come, he froze. Brian crumpled to the ground, red staining the top of his head. And a dark figure appeared from behind.

33

SCARLETT

Scarlett wasn't sure what she expected Jason's house to look like, but it certainly wasn't this. After the movie, she went back to her house to review for Spanish but noticed Jason's track bag still lying on her floor. It had been there ever since the party when he'd been over, and she hadn't even thought that he might need it back. She decided now would be as good a time as ever, and since her parents were out to dinner, she wouldn't have anyone to tell her otherwise.

She drove to his house, Frank Sinatra playing smoothly on her speaker. She loved the way his voice sounded, the way his lyrics managed to convey utter love and adoration. What she didn't say was how she'd heard him leaking out of Jason's ear buds and gave him a try. When she pulled into his driveway, she was surprised to find that his house didn't look anything like she thought it would. For all she'd overheard with Jason and Coach Allen at their last track meet, she assumed it would be a small, eerie shack, or a house very obviously home to some suspicious people, but it was none of that. In fact, Jason Everett's house looked about as normal as you could get. Green lush grass lined the front yard, surrounding a tan concrete path which led to a porch of the same material. The house itself was white, with a red roof and windows splayed around it.

Scarlett stepped out of her car, lugging the heavy bag over her shoulders.

What the hell is he putting in this thing?

She'd been tempted to snoop earlier but decided against it. He was her enemy, yet she still had morals. She started up the steps, and creepy nighttime darkness cast over the world. In the void, she noticed a few things. Things that would be normal if she only knew a little less about the Everett family, if she weren't so curious. A potted plant lay broken on the porch, dirt spilling out of the cracked pottery. The door was open a crack as well, barely at all, as if someone tried to shut it but didn't have the time to double-check. There was a baseball glove on the grass, but no bat or ball anywhere. The curtains on each window were flung open, revealing a clear line of vision into the house, which Scarlett found weird for nighttime. Usually, curtains were there to keep people from looking inside, not to be removed.

She glanced around the porch, dirty blonde hair tied up in a braid out of her eyes. She wore a blue hoodie with her track number embroidered on the back and a star on the sleeve. She'd gotten it from Milo as his parting gift, a reminder of her sport and passion, as well as a hint of him. The hoodie stretched out over a pair of white linen pants, the type of pants ladies in their sixties wear to the beach on cool mornings. On her feet were a pair of black Adidas, adding a quarter inch to her frame. She tucked a stray piece of hair behind her ear, which threatened to fall from her updo every five minutes. She wanted to knock on the door, wanted him to let her in, maybe even ask her to stay. It's not like she had parents who wanted her to be with them at the moment, so she really didn't have much to do. She raised her fist to the door, preparing to knock. Her eyes trailed down the door as she held her knuckles to the wood, unsure why she was so hesitant. Her brow creased in frustration, sweeping once more over the front yard to gather herself. Her breath hitched for a reason beyond herself. She recognized the feeling.

Name five things you can see, come on.

It was a trick her dad had taught her for when the world felt like too much —something to do to ground yourself. Scarlett wasn't sure why she needed to be grounded at the moment but she gave it a shot anyway .

"Baseball glove." She put down a finger. "Grass." Inhale, exhale. "Weird . . . broken pot." She turned, facing away from the door. "Gardening gloves." She said, eyes falling on a green glove tucked behind a bush in the corner of the yard. "And..." Her gaze flickered across the concrete steps. Scarlett felt her stomach drop. She reached her hand up to her mouth, gasping instinctively. There, on the concrete steps, and leading down the path in tiny droplets. "Blood." Suddenly, Scarlett didn't feel safe anymore. Every little thing was a threat, and a clue. She felt so out of place, like something was truly very wrong.

Her suspicions were confirmed when a pained groan rang in her ears. She held her breath, tiptoeing towards the source of the noise. It was around the side of the house. *If there's a serial killer back there, so help me.* She peered around the corner, heart hammering. Just enough to see—but not enough to be seen. What Scarlett saw, she would describe as much, much worse than a serial killer. Jason lay on the ground, completely covered in blood, dirt, and grass. Dirt from the plant. He was breathing, but his chest rose and fell unevenly, and it looked labored. She struggled to see the other figure, though through the darkness she could tell he was tall and bald. In his hands, he held a baseball bat, the one missing from the scene in the front yard. *No.* In a swift motion, this man swung the bat above his head and brought it crashing down on Jason's ribs. Jason flinched, curling in on himself and calling out in agony. Scarlett bit her cheek, drawing blood in her mouth to keep from screaming. She had to help, but that wouldn't be possible if she were caught herself.

She turned away from the gruesome scene, running back around the house to the front porch. She tried the door, and the crack in the opening allowed her to slip into the house. She wanted to look around more, to see what other strange signs existed in the Everett household, but that would have to happen later because right now Jason was dying. Or he could be dying. Maybe he was already dead. Bile rose in Scarlett's throat at the thought, but she forced it down, the acidic burn climbing back down her throat. She saw another open door, leading to a garage. Scarlett hesitantly stepped in, looking for something, anything she could use to help. Her eyes narrowed in on a golf club leaning against a tall cabinet. *Perfect.* She snatched it, fingering it, before going around the other side of the house. She emerged through the bushes; leaves stuck in her hair and branches scratching her arms. She made it to the clearing where Jason lay, now with a clear view of his attacker.

"Please. Dad," Jason begged, voice barely above a whisper. *Dad.* The bile rose again, but this time she couldn't force it down; she leaned over the bush, and vomited, as silently as she could, grateful that they lived in a noisy neighborhood. She wiped her mouth with her sleeve, readjusting her grip on the weapon. She moved swiftly, creeping behind the dark figure now identified as Jason's father. This is what he meant. He raised his hands above his head, poised to strike again. Scarlett felt a tug in her gut, a sense of protectiveness. She couldn't let him hurt Jason. But she couldn't get herself killed either. Scarlett froze for a moment, the adrenaline and fear for herself almost stopped her. She could go home. Call 911, get out of there and survive. She almost did, then the bat struck again, and Scarlett knew she didn't have time. *Fuck it.* Forgetting all about being stealthy, Scarlett stepped right behind Mr. Everett, raising her own makeshift baton and taking a deep breath in. *You can do this, Scarlett. Come on, Jason will not be having shark fin soup today*. She brought down her arms quickly, sending the golf club right down on Brian's head with as much force as she could gather. Jason's father didn't even have time to react before he fell to the ground, unconscious. She froze for a moment, then kicked the body for reassurance. Jason's father did not move.

Scarlett dropped her weapon, now tinted with blood and instantly dropped to her knees before Jason. Blood pooled around his leg, and Scarlett gagged when she caught sight of a deep wound in his thigh, oozing red. His ankle was bent at an odd angle, along with his shoulder, which seemed dislodged. There was blood around his head, too, which Scarlett concluded to be a concussion of some sort, at least, but she couldn't be sure. She really could use Marcus right now. The boy himself seemed far gone, his eyes glazed over and becoming more distant by the minute. His lips were parted slightly, once white, shining teeth now crimson.

"Jason, please look at me." She moved to his head, grabbing his face in her hands, and leaning him onto her lap. Jason's eyes flickered slightly, gaze slowly shifting to her.

"Scar." His voice was so quiet, Scarlett had to strain to hear him. And for once, the nickname just flew past her head.

"Hey, it's me. It's OK, you're OK." She stroked his hair with her fingers, locking the other hand his, staring into his onyx eyes.

"Fuck, I didn't think I'd ever see you again."

"I'm here. Right here." Jason blinked, like he was double checking that she really was.

"Your pants. I got blood on your pants," he said, glancing at her white linen flares. She smiled.

"It'll come out."

"Are . . . you sure? Blood . . . stains." He struggled to speak, needing to pause for breaths every few words. Scarlett laughed lightly, though her eyebrows were creased in concern, a tear rolling down her cheek.

"I'm not worried about that at all. And you shouldn't be either." Jason peered at her through half-open eyelids, reaching up with his good arm to wipe the tear from her face.

"Don't be sad. It doesn't hurt." He smiled, and Scarlett almost broke.

"Good. That's good." She said, running her thumb along his cheek. Jason's eyelids fluttered, and Scarlett could tell he was giving up. "Jason. Hey, Jason, you need to stay with me, OK?" she begged, shaking him lightly. Onyx irises opened for a second more, locking with her stormy gray ones.

"I'm sorry. Please don't be mad." More tears flowed down her cheeks now; Scarlett could taste their salt.

"I'm not mad, never mad. I just care about you, so you need to keep fighting. Can you do that for me?" she asked, smiling down at him.

"Anything . . . for you." He smiled, eyelids closing once more. His grip on her hand loosened, his body going limp in her hold.

"No. No, no, no. Jason!" She shook his healthy shoulder, tapping him on the cheek. "Stay awake, you need to stay awake, please!" He didn't move, breaths rising and falling unsteadily. Scarlett sobbed, breath hitching as she begged for this boy, who saved her life while pretending not to care, who unknowingly gave her first real dance, who threw a snake in the bushes for her, becoming drained of life before her eyes. She couldn't take it.

"Y-your scholarship! You need to get it, please. I need someone to beat me, right? You need to fight, *please, Jason*!" She fumbled with her phone, struggling to get a grip on the device with the sticky blood coating her fingers. "You have a best friend, Marcus. He loves you, Jason; he needs you." She logged into her contacts. "You have a track team, a bunch of kids who care about you, a-and who wants you to succeed." She dialed 9-1-1, and the tone rang. "You have me, Jason, you have me—and I *love you*!" The tone ended, and an older woman's voice rang on the line. "9-1-1, what's your emergency?"

The ambulance was cold, like death was present. Scarlett sat next to Jason in the back of the van, who was strapped down to a gurney. Three tall paramedics swarmed around him in the back of the vehicle, asking him questions and patching up what injuries they could before making it to the hospital. Jason didn't answer any of these questions; of course, his head was strapped in a neck brace, and dried tears were sticking to his unmoving face. Scarlett had never felt so scared, for him, for his life. But she was also scared of what she admitted. Something she would have only said had he been unable to hear her. That she loved him. Scarlett told herself it was just the adrenaline, just something she said in the moment when she wasn't sure if there would be any more moments with him. She interlocked fingers with his still hand, squeezing gently.

With the other hand, she called the one other person whom she knew would drop anything to help her.

"Hello? Dad?"

"Hey, Scar, what's up?" he asked, voice friendly and warm. So unaware. Scarlett felt so much relief in his voice, so much familiarity. She sniffled, wiping a tear from her cheek. "Honey, what's wrong?"

"It's Jason. From track, he um, he got in an accident, he's in trouble, Dad. I um— I found him, and we're in the ambulance right now," she cried, losing her composure.

"Which hospital are you going to?" he asked in a surprisingly calm tone.

"Ridgeway, I think. Dad, I didn't know what to do, it was so scary, he was just *lying* there!"

"Take a breath, Scarlett, I'm on my way. I'll meet you at the hospital, just be brave for me, alright?" Scarlett nodded, looking over the beaten boy strapped down in front of her. His eyes were shut, black curls framing his face, already painted with purple bruises. She wanted to cry harder, to feel everything, to let it out, but felt utterly disappointed when she could hardly feel anything now. She was shocked, still confused and disoriented from the scene in front of her at that moment, still wanting answers.

"I want you to ask the doctors where in the hospital they're taking him to. Can you do that?" Mr. Artega asked, his car engine starting up in the background.

"Yeah." Scarlett turned to one of the doctors, fervently wrapping bandages around Jason's head and disinfecting cuts on his leg. "Where is he going? So, my dad knows where to find me." The doctor looked up; he was blonde, though his hair was tied back with a scrub cap. He had icy blue eyes that made Scarlett slightly uncomfortable holding eye contact with.

"The ICU. Intensive Care Unit. But first, he'll need surgery for his leg, as well as a scan for any internal bleeding and head injuries," he said, voice deep and focused.

"D-did you hear that?" Scarlett asked, turning her head back to the phone.

"I heard. I'll be there soon, Scarlett, but until then, just stay with the doctors, and go where they tell you to go. I'll find you." At his last word, Jason flexed his fingers in Scarlett's hand lightly, as if the phrase had sharpened his senses.

Scarlett squeezed back, unsure if he was even able to feel it. To feel her. "I'm right here," she whispered. "I'll always be here. I refuse to leave you."

Then, the ambulance doors opened, and several paramedics rushed in, grabbing Jason out of the ambulance and wheeling him into the large hospital doors. "No, wait, let me stay with him!" she called, climbing out of the vehicle and rushing to his side.

"You can't be in the surgery; the waiting room is right over there." A female nurse instructed, grabbing Scarlett's shoulders and turning her towards the brightly lit room. Scarlett tugged and pulled out of her grasp, she couldn't leave his side, not when she'd just promised she'd be with him. Even if he hadn't heard it, a promise is a promise.

"Ma'am, please just step away from the gurney, you can't be in here." She reached for her again, but Scarlett's hands locked onto the iron frames of Jason's bed, walking right alongside it as he was wheeled through the large white halls.

"Just let me stay, please, I promised!" The nurse grabbed her again, holding her back as the paramedics took Jason away. Took her Jason away. She struggled against the woman's grip, but her arms were like vices.

"I'm sorry, honey, they'll take good care of him; you have people looking after him in there." She took her by the shoulders, leading her into the waiting room, and Scarlett was too broken, too disturbed to care. She couldn't protest anymore.

"But it won't be me looking after him. How do I know they're doing it right?" She looked the nurse in her eyes, pleading with her irises.

"I can give them special instructions if that would make it easier?" she asked, pushing Scarlett down into a chair lightly. Special instructions? To be honest, Scarlett really didn't think they would care to do anything 'special' for her other than shun her away from Jason. "Oh, um, yeah. Tell the doctors to keep it warm in there —he gets cold easily. And um he doesn't like needles. . . tell them that too." The woman nodded, smiling with her eyes. But it was pitiful. Pitiful and practiced, like everything in this place.

"One more thing. Tell him, tell him that I'm waiting for him when he gets out. So, he has to fight, OK? Tell him to stay alive for me." She felt her eyes burn, those eyes that were so tired of crying. Sick of feeling.

"I will. Now, please just wait here, and I'll send someone out when it's over."

"When it's over? You mean when the surgery is over?" The nurse squeezed her hand, smiling again with fake, rehearsed lips.

"Yes, when the surgery is over. Your friend is strong, but he needs you to be strong for him, too." The nurse flashed one last smile before hurrying back to the room, no doubt to smother another terrified family member or friend with invitations to the white-walled waiting room. Scarlett sat in the chair, remembering everything that happened—going over it again and again. If she'd just left earlier and gotten to him quicker maybe she would've been able to help him sooner. If she hadn't let him leave the theater, he never would've gone home in the first place. If she hadn't been so weird about him, so hateful towards him, maybe he would've opened up to her. She could've helped. She could have saved him. But she didn't. So, she sat in a room that smelled of antibiotics and sterilization products. And she cried, cried because she didn't know who she was anymore. Cried because someone she cared about was dying. Cried because she was too blind to see that she had cared about him earlier. And now Scarlett might never get to say it to him. And he might never know that she loves him.

34

SCARLETT

Nineteen hours.

That's how long it had been since Jason's surgery, and he still hadn't woken up. The doctors had concluded that Jason suffered a brain hemorrhage as a result of his trauma to the head. As well as a fractured wrist, dislocated shoulder, broken ankle, and a stab wound in his thigh. They were able to handle the head trauma, draining the blood and wrapping his head up like a mummy. Scarlett glanced at his other injuries. The white bandages covering his thigh, the hard cast around his ankle and wrist, and the sling attached to his shoulder to keep it in place. He was attached to various tubes, swirling and tangling around him, to various machines. An IV drip was inserted into his arm, and Scarlett cringed. She knew he'd hate that if he were awake or aware. Unfortunately, he was neither as he had been for far too long, Scarlett thought. Sensors were placed on his chest, monitoring his heart rate, blood pressure, and anything else doctors would need to know. Scarlett watched his heartbeat rise and fall in rhythmic pulses on the monitor screen. But for all the distractions in the room, all the tiny details she could think about in that moment, her sight inevitably drifted back to him.

Jason looked so helpless, so hurt. But at the same time, he looked so calm, like this wasn't a brush with death. Like he was just a little kid, taking a nap after school, or falling asleep during a movie night. If this were a movie, Scarlett would be begging whoever was watching to grab the remote and change channels. But it wasn't a movie, it was real. And the kind of thing you never would have assumed you'd go through happens, and it's something you can't expect, because it should never be expected.

Jason's heart monitor beeped frantically, the pulse rising with faster rhythms. "Jason," she whispered, clinging to his hand tighter.

He stirred slightly, fingertips brushing against hers. Scarlett watched partly in fascination, and partly in pure unfiltered relief as Jason's eyes slowly peeled open, drowsy and unfocused. Onyx orbs flittered around the room before shutting half closed again, struggling to remain awake.

"Hey, Jason," she repeated, leaning into his line of sight. His eyes met hers, though in them was not warmth or kindness. No, when he looked at her, there was only a sense of unrecognized confusion.

"Jason, please keep your eyes open—it's me, Scarlett. Scarlett Artega, do you remember me?" Jason stared at her, blinking slowly.

"Scar," he said, parting his dried lips. His voice was groggy and not entirely his own, which Scarlett blamed on the IV drip pumping painkillers and sedatives into Jason's body. Still, she visibly relaxed, exhaling deeply.

"It's me, how do you feel?" She reached for his face with her hand, stroking his cheek gently, lovingly.

"Can't really feel anything right now," he whispered, eyelids fluttering. "Wow."

"What? What's wrong, what hurts?"

"You're beautiful." He paused, staring at Scarlett like she was the sun and the stars. Like she was the universe. "Guess I can feel something." He smiled, and Scarlett was pleased to see his white teeth shining bright, not suppressed by crimson.

"Oh, save it, you're completely high right now." She said, though the butterflies in her stomach, which climbed up her throat, begged to hear more. Scarlett wanted to find out just what that gorgeous mouth had to say.

"I know I'm high. You really think I'd be able to say this if I wasn't?" Scarlett stilled, examining his body language.

"Say what?" She inhaled. It was odd seeing him like this still, even if he was awake. He exhaled a breathy laugh, nose crinkling in that way she adored. "Say what, Everett?"

"Say that I think you complete me, Scar. Say that I've thought so for months." He blinked slowly. "Say that it terrified me to think I could ever stand you, but now what scares me is the thought that I might have to live my life without you in it. Because that's completely *terrifying*." He laughed, eyes never leaving hers.

She was breathless, speechless, floating a million miles away, longing for that moment back. The moment when she realized it was mutual. When she realized he loved her, too. For the first time in her life, she thought that maybe— just maybe —she found something more permanent than college. That perhaps this was what it was about the whole time.

"Jason, do you, um . . . . remember anything from last night?" she asked, eager to change the subject. This was all too scary; these feelings, which she'd wanted to hear for months, sounded weird to her like it shouldn't be. Jason creased his brow with a calculating look on his face.

"Not much. Will you tell me?" Scarlett placed a hand over Jason's, her smile touching her gray eyes.

"When you're a little better." His eyelids drooped, medicine coursing through his veins. "And a little less drugged." Jason smiled, as his eyes fell shut, freckles illuminated by the lamp on his bedside.

"Always telling me what to do, Scar," he mumbled; probably unaware he was even speaking.

"I'm sorry, would you rather have me stop and you get into even more trouble?"

"No, don't stop. I like it," he said, fingers loosening in her grip once more. Though this time, there was no pain etched in his expression. Only a slight smile, the shadow of a dimple splayed across his face. Constellations of freckles dotting his nose. And the light flush of pink painted across his cheeks.

"Is he your boyfriend?"

Scarlett's head snapped from her gaze on Jason, falling onto a short, broad woman wearing scrubs and pushing a cart of medical supplies into the room.

"No. What?" she fumbled, anger lacing her tone. Who did this lady think she was to come in here and start assuming things?

"Slow down, honey, I meant no disrespect. You two just seem like those kids," she said, stalking over to the side of his bed.

"Those kids?" She smiled.

"There's always one lovesick couple here, and I like to know about them. Makes me believe in love more, reminds me of my youth." Scarlett scoffed, raising an eyebrow.

"Well, I'm glad it makes you happy, but he isn't my boyfriend. Just . . . a friend." He wasn't just a friend; he was more than a friend. So much more. But Scarlett was afraid that if she said those words out loud, they might actually come true. The nurse nodded her head towards Jason's loose hand, interlocking with Scarlett's.

"Friends, that's exactly what I think when I see that." She laughed, setting to work, changing his IV and checking Jason's temperature.

"You seem to have a lot to say, let's put a name to that attitude, shall we?" Scarlett retorted, rolling her eyes. She really was not in the mood, and it's not like this lady was sparing her any of her thoughts, so why should she?

"Abigail. My name is Abigail. I have been a nurse here for fifteen years, and I adore my job," she said in a sweet tone. Her body was burly and stocky, arms filling her sleeves, yet she didn't look overweight, just muscular. Her stature was intimidating, yet her voice was so sweet and kindly that you hardly noticed.

"OK, Abigail—who adores her job —how can I help you?" Scarlett said, not letting go of the feeling of her hand in Jason's.

"No, it's what I can do for you. You're close to the patient. I am the nurse." She smiled.

"I wouldn't say close. I know him." Scarlett argued, conflicting with herself.

"You know him well, it seems, or maybe I'm misjudging the hand holding and looks of affection. That seems 'close' to me," she explained, crossing her bulky arms. Abigail crossed her arms when Scarlett didn't reply. "Fine, so you're not close, don't tell me."

Scarlett sighed. "I don't know what we are. But I know he needed my help then, so subsequent ly I'm here now." Scarlett spared a glance back at the resting figure; eyebrows relaxed in sleep.

"Well, you're a good person, I know that much. Anyone who would do as brave a thing as you has a good heart." Scarlett smiled.

"So . . . you know?"

"Word travels fast, and once you talked to the paramedics, we got word of the situation. I'm sorry you had to go through that, but you were brave, and you saved that boy. What's your name again?" Abigail asked, pulling up a chair and parking next to her.

"Scarlett Artega. And it wasn't brave, it was human. Anyone with half a brain would do what I did," she explained.

"You'd be surprised how many people wouldn't. To some, it's second nature, but not always. Sometimes there isn't a hero nearby, and we must thank God that you were here to save this young man. Just because it was a high-adrenaline situation doesn't undermine how brave you were, Scarlett." Her words felt like honey, so unlike her structure. Scarlett blinked out the tears forming in her eyes, not sure why they were there in the first place. Probably, it was all just catching up to her. "Oh, sweetie," Abigail said, drawing her in for a hug.

The nickname only made her eyes wetter, a reminder of the annoying boy who would call her that. Now, all she wanted was to be on the track again, with Jason calling her 'Sweetie' and Scarlett flipping him off because of it. Scarlett hugged this random woman, so strong yet so kind and almost instantly felt better. She wondered if Abigail had this kind of effect on everyone.

"I just don't know what to do. This is the kind of thing you see in movies and stuff, not the kind of thing that happens." Abigail smiled sadly, her round, rosy cheeks rising.

"It's not in your nature to know what to do, and that's alright. We'll take it one step at a time, and together. Your job is just to be here with him. He needs to know that there's someone here who cares about him. You can be that person."

Scarlett thought about it, more nights spent in this asylum, with sterile everything and crisp blankets that provided little warmth. She would give anything to go home, but then she thought of him lying there, unsure of what even happened. She thought of his freckles and how his nose always scrunched up when he smiled. How his eyes looked in the sun, dark chocolate irises looked magnificent in the light. She thought about his laugh, the sound vibrating straight through her very soul. And immediately, the thought of staying in a hospital for a few more days seemed like a Christmas present if it meant she could provide Jason with some level of comfort. If she could help him.

"Yeah, I um, I can do that." Her eyes fell on him again, and her stomach tugged nauseatingly at the forest of machinery tangled around him. "He looks horrible. With all the tubes and patches." She shuddered, peeling her eyes away when Abigail turned her face gently.

"Don't think about them like that. These tubes and patches are helping him survive. They're making him stronger. See how sometimes it's not the image that needs to change, but your perception of it." Abigail smiled, and Scarlett noticed a small chip in one of her front teeth.

"I guess this image is a hell of a lot better than when I found him. That was . . . wow." Scarlett felt her bottom lip wobbling as flashes of the incident threatened to reappear.

"You're a senior, right? So, what's the plan for college? Any specific majors?" Abigail sat up straighter, fully attentive.

"Why are you changing the conversation? Can't handle a little bit of melancholy?" Abigail laughed, a sound that shook Scarlett to her core with its warmth.

"Baby, all there is in this hospital is melancholy. I figured I could do my part to bring a little joy into the place. As for the subject change, I think you need something to take your mind off your . . . acquaintance." *Acquaintance? That's not nearly accurate; he's much more than that.* She tensed. *Why does it matter if it's accurate? She's asking you a question, you idiot.*

"Sure, why not?" She breathed out a sharp exhale. "I don't really know, honestly. My whole life, my parents wanted me to run track like my brother, he's a whole scholarship athlete, an Olympics dreamer that whole shebang. So naturally, I must be a carbon copy of him for my parents to acknowledge I'm there." It wasn't common for her to share her past like this, but she didn't expect it to feel so good coming off her shoulders. The words flowing out of her like this were a rehearsed speech. "He runs; I run. He goes to Oregon State on scholarship . . . well, I'm still waiting on that. But so far that's the plan, with no idea of the future except for a fear of what it holds."

Abigail raised an eyebrow, crossing her legs like a therapist. Like someone who doesn't understand but wants to try. Scarlett could appreciate that. "Did you know I was supposed to be a software developer? By my parents' requests, of course."

"What? That's so different . . ."

"From where I ended up? Yeah, but what can I say? The heart wants what it wants." Scarlett frowned. *What the hell does my heart want?* Scarlett internally face-palmed.

She knew what it wanted. If only her brain could stop interfering, she would've given her heart to Jason a long time ago if she could just stop *thinking.*

"And how did they react to that?" Scarlett began picking her nails out of habit, flicking the fragments of keratin onto the floor.

"Disappointing at first, but proud as hell once I did it. It took them time to realize my dreams were really theirs, but after that . . . it gets a lot easier. I'll thank myself for making that choice for the rest of my life, or I'd be behind a computer screen all day instead of giving people a second chance at life." She laughed, but Scarlett found it anything but funny.

She was in awe. First, that she would have the courage to defy her parents like that, and second, that she lived through it with no regrets. Regrets were a constant worry, probably a result of being tied down. Now, she was afraid to fly, because there was always a chance her wings would fail her. And like Icarus, she would fall, she would fail. And her parents would be right all along. To be honest, that scared her more than anything —more than the snakes, and the planes.

"Point being, you only get one life. There are no do-overs. So, Scarlett, tell me—why the hell *would* you spend the one life you get, your life, pleasing other people? They have their own lives, don't let them take yours because they're greedy for more life than they were given." She took Scarlett's hand in hers.

"What do you love?" Scarlett felt her palm, her fingers thick, and gently held her own bonier ones.

"What do I love? I love track when it's not about scholarships. I love my friends, especially Meghan and Zoe. I love

Spanish, and my dog." She could continue, but Abigail put a hand up.

"Spanish? Tell me about that."

"Oh. What do you want to know?"

"I want to know as much as you want to tell me. I've been told I'm quite the listener." Scarlett smiled, resisting the urge to grab her hands back and pick at them some more.

"I've loved Spanish since eighth grade, I'm in IB Spanish right now. Something about it, the way it makes me feel. It's gentle and sharp at the same time. Like a rose, sweet but dangerous if you get too close. It's interesting to me how there are so many ways of saying everything. I mean, there are over twenty different Spanish dialects, and probably more that we just don't know yet. They all say the same thing, but it's the way they say it, the context around it and the sayings from their history that they combine it with that sets each one apart. It's fascinating. Completely fascinating." She breathed, heart quickening just from thinking about the language of love.

"Sounds to me like you found your thing. Scarlett, why do you care in the world about what your family wants from you when you have this passion? You could make a lot of good with this." Scarlett shrugged.

"Dunno, I want them to be proud of me. To think that I'm a success. I guess along the way I just realized that for that to happen, I had to sacrifice what I wanted for myself. To give them what they wanted. And for some reason, I was willing to do that." Scarlett's eyebrows creased as she spoke, her mind reeling. Why would she let them take her spark like that? To grab her life in their hands and mold it to their specifications like clay. Abigail seemed to think the same thing.

"Respectfully, I doubt I would get along with your parents. Any mother or father who needs their children to be the same as them to feel accomplished clearly has some serious issues." She laughed lightly to herself, waving at the air in dismissal. "I can't make this clear enough, it's your life, Scarlett, and as much as I'd love to watch you at the Olympics on my television one day, I'd be even happier knowing you're out there doing what fuels your heart, drives your fire. It's not your fault your parents' fires lost their coals." Spoken like the experienced.

It was hard to believe that it would really be worth it. That she could take this step in her life and to hell with her family's expectations. At the same time, however, it felt incredibly tempting. To live her life free from the thoughts of others would be living a life free from judgment. Free to do the things she'd always dreamed of and make an impact on the world that she wanted. Not her mother. Not Milo. What Scarlett wanted.

"You might be onto something, Abigail. You're pretty wise for someone with a dozen purple owls on their name tag." Abigail laughed, glancing at the plastic card over her chest, bedazzled with various stickers and drawings.

"It's you kids who make me wise. A lot of you are going through things I wouldn't have even thought about at your age. It makes me think. And —" she said, peeling an orange owl from her tag and sticking it on Scarlett's phone case. "—it makes me want to see you succeed. So do that for me, alright?" Abigail stood up, planting one last hug over Scarlett's frame, before gathering her things, checking over Jason once more and stepping out of the room. From down the hallway, Scarlett could hear a child squeal with joy upon the burly woman's entrance.

"Abigail, hi!" he exclaimed, laughter reverberating through the walls. Abigail greeted him; her voice was loud and so sweet.

And at that moment, Scarlett realized what it meant to love your job. To have an occupation that makes you want to get up in the morning, to want to see the change in what you do. She thought about track, the joy it brought her, but simultaneously the pain. She couldn't do that. No matter how much she wanted to make her parents happy, she couldn't live a life like that. Spending her days doing something she knew in her heart wasn't her calling. Some decisions are hard to make; they require pros and cons, careful consideration. After Abigail, this decision was one of the easiest Scarlett could make. She didn't know if her family would approve, if they would even tolerate it, but that didn't matter. Scarlett Artega refused to run at Oregon State—not when she was meant to soar.

35
JASON

He felt her before he saw her.

Jason's body ached, and while he felt less dull and groggy, the pain had only gotten worse as the medication wore off. His arms and shoulders were throbbing, and there was intense pressure in his thigh. Jason tried to open his eyes; aware he was awake but unable to physically do so. He could hardly move aside from finger movements.

Then, he felt something even more than the pain. Scarlett.

He could sense her fingers lingering tentatively over him, suspicions confirmed when a light hand brushed hair out of his face, gently holding his face in her hand. Jason felt elated at the touch, sparks dancing inside him. It was strange how one small touch could mean so much, especially when it shouldn't. He'd let her hold him forever, would rip his own heart out so Scarlett had a keepsake of him. Jason was so in deep now. But it was something about her delicate demeanor with sarcasm and attitude buried beneath that made Jason long for more. She was interesting, and Jason didn't quite get her. But oh, how he wanted to. Fingers brushed him again, this time moving from his face to his hair, where Scarlett began to play with the strands, curling them between her fingers. Jason wanted to melt. *Have my hair, have my heart, fuck, have me,*

Scarlett. Jason felt a tug on his head, and his hair was being divided into sections. Was she. . . braiding his hair?

Now Jason needed to open his eyes. He focused, drawing every ounce of his strength just to come out of his stupor and behold the goddess in front of him. His eyelashes flickered open, revealing the dirty blonde girl, dressed in a baggy hoodie, hair flowing slightly curled down her back. She was focused on his hair, not even looking at him, which was perfect for Jason, who found comfort in watching this girl when she didn't even know it. The candid image of Scarlett was even more beautiful because she wasn't trying. Wasn't putting on a show or switching up her personality to fit whatever friend she was with. She was just genuinely . . . her. Jason adored this version of her. He smiled at her, drinking in the moment while he could. Another tug jerked his head slightly, and Jason had to know what this ingeniously beautiful girl was doing.

"Are you braiding my hair?" His throat was drier than expected, making for an embarrassingly obvious voice crack. Scarlett jumped a bit, startled, then gained her composure with a smirk.

"What if I am? This place has nothing to do," she explained, making no effort to cease the patterns she weaved into his curls.

"Careful, keep touching me like that, and you might fall in love with me." Scarlett stilled, dropping his hair, but not meeting his gaze.

"You're quite arrogant, you know that?"

"It's not arrogance if it's not exaggerated. You're in love with me."

"You don't get to tell me what I am."

"That's not a no then."

Since when am I bold like this? Jason wondered this, yet simultaneously concluded that Scarlett made him do things he wouldn't usually do. He was like a puppet, and she was the puppeteer. Jason was utterly and completely under her control.

"It's not a no, you're right. But not a no isn't a yes." *Don't I know it.* "How's your head?" she asked, glancing at the bandages around his forehead.

"Fine, it's my leg that hurts." To Jason's surprise, Scarlet turned her attention towards his leg, looking over it like she was reading the fine print of a contract. Scarlett would be the type of person to read the fine print after all.

"I'll get Ab-the nurse; she can probably help. I —"

"Don't do a thing. I want you here, no one else."

"My dad's in the lobby right now, does that count?"

Jason's mouth fell open a little in shock. Her dad? Jason imagined her scared out of her mind and calling her dad, and while it wasn't funny, he laughed like a kid. His shoulders shook, which only increased the pain, yet he laughed anyway, because he couldn't cry. Scarlett looked in surprise for a moment before giving in and laughing too. Soon, they were just two teenagers with too much to carry, laughing because it was all they could do to keep the sadness at bay.

"I guess that doesn't count. But no nurse, she'll just stick a needle in me." Scarlett scoffed.

"You really should get over that, you know."

"Says the girl who all but cried over a snake. I think I'm allowed to be scared of needles, thanks," he retorted, earning him a smile from Scarlett. It was warm and genuine, and Jason decided he needed to make her smile like that more often.

"Can I ask you something? Why did you really stay? I mean, you could have just gotten me here and dipped, but you stayed." Jason voiced what he'd been wondering since the first time he saw her here. Scarlett sighed.

"There's not exactly anyone else here to look after you, is there? I needed to stay, or I wouldn't forgive myself if something happened and I wasn't there because I decided to go home. It wouldn't have been worth it." There was sadness in her eyes, reflected in her tone. "You don't understand, Jason, you were going to die. And no one was telling me anything about what was going on, so I stayed because when someone I care about is in trouble. I want answers, and I want to help," she confessed, probably brushing right over it. But it caught in Jason's throat like his Adam's apple. 'Someone I care about.'

"Not to ruin the moment, but you realize you just confessed to caring about me?" Jason jeered.

"I'm realizing." A flush crept up Scarlett's neck while Jason performed a happy dance with his arms, swaying in his bed. "Careful, you'll rip your stitches," Scarlett remarked.

"It would be worth it to see your face right now. Oh, and speaking of having nothing to do around here," he said, pointing to a backpack Scarlett had brought in the corner —the backpack was the reason she ever showed up in the first place.

"Check the front pocket." He winced, drawing his arm back, and Scarlett creased her brow in worry. "I'm fine, go check," he insisted. Scarlett walked over to the bag, carefully unzipping the front pouch. What she pulled out was nothing like she expected.

"My book! This has been missing like forever. Where did you find it?" she exclaimed, examining every inch of her copy of *If Cats Disappeared from the World*.

"About that, 'find' is a loose term. I borrowed it," he said sheepishly.

"Borrowed it? You mean you stole it." She narrowed her eyes at him, but Jason only smiled like the sun.

"I have read it a hundred times; I don't lie about my books. And I think you missed some key points, so I decided to enlighten you." He spoke calmly as if he were an angel of joy and not a boy who stole her favorite novel for the fun of it.

"Enlighten me how?" she asked before he even spoke. The pages of her book were lined with sticky notes, annotations, and phrases dotting the pages. Highlighted were some of her favorite lines along with an explanation of every scene. Jason dove deeper into this masterpiece than she ever would've thought. If Scarlett hadn't known better, she would've thought he lived in this book.

"I may have highlighted a few things. It's nothing." His finger twitched, as if missing her touch already. Jason felt possessive of her in a way he wasn't familiar with. Her gaze being turned towards a book rather than him made his heart pang with a jealous need for her. It was absolutely ridiculous. Who gets jealous of a book? A lingering glance? *I guess I do.*

"Annotating two hundred and two pages of writing is not 'nothing,'" Scarlett gaped, jaw on the floor.

"Like I said, nothing. Consider it a better gift than I got you at the aquarium, right?" She smirked.

"To be fair, if part of your gift was your advice, then it's safe to say that 'gift' saved me my dignity. And virginity, for that matter." Jason noticed her shrink back a little, like her flame sputtered a little at the thought of Beau. He hated to see her like that. So, he did what he did best. Change the subject.

"No one could take away your dignity, Scarlett, you have too much life for that," he said, and Jason meant it. "From the moment I saw you, I did hate you, but I hated how much you lived. How much of everything was about you. Like I was colorblind, and then I saw you, and the world was like a rainbow. No shitty guy can take that away from you." Scarlett flushed, smiling like the star that she is. A smile that made Jason's heart float.

"You have a way with words. But don't think I missed you changing the subject. Your present deserves to be appreciated, so allow me to do just that."

And just like that, Scarlett rose from where she crouched on the floor, leaving the book on Jason's nightstand. She perched up on his bed, drawing her legs over the fabric and pressing her hands onto the wall above his bed to steady herself. And then she kissed him. Her soft lips pressed against Jason's dried ones, exploring his mouth like a newly discovered cave. Jason opened his mouth slightly, allowing her tongue to creep in and discover him more. It was like a dance, perfectly choreographed. Jason couldn't think, couldn't breathe because whenever he thought of her, whenever he breathed, it was only the vanilla scent of the girl on top of him. She was everywhere, in everything. Jason reached up, running his fingers through her hair, falling deeper into the motion. His hands traveled down her shoulders, itching to grab onto her, to show her that he wanted to hold her forever and not let go. Scarlet pulled back, detaching their tingling lips. With a smirk on her face, she grabbed his hands from her shoulders and relocated them to her hips, pressing them into her curves deeply.

"That's better," she said.

"Scarlett, should we really be doing this? Enemies and all that?" Jason questioned, suddenly very aware of everything he was doing.

"I've been thinking about something, Jason. Loathing. Loving. The line between the two is undeniably thin, don't you agree?" All it took was that one sentence, and Jason was on his hands and knees, begging once again.

"Fuck. I agree with anything as long as it comes from you." They crashed into one another once again, hands in hair, fire sparking from their touch. Scarlett kissed with passion, though Jason could sense her caution. How she purposefully avoided his arm, shoulder, and thigh. How her stormy gray eyes met his onyx black ones every couple of seconds as if checking to make sure it was alright. If Scarlett could make out this explosively while half trying to spare his health, Jason wondered what she could do when he wasn't in the hospital. The monitor attached to his heart began beeping incessantly in response to Jason's pounding heart. He froze, red appearing on his cheeks. Scarlett only laughed, tilting her head back in an adorable manner.

"Nervous, roadkill?" She creased her brow, the freckle above her eye so clearly visible.

"I am a mess when it comes to you, Artega. Just accept that," he admitted, reaching up and planting a gentle kiss on her beauty mark. "I've always liked that freckle. It's like God's signature on you." She smiled, filling his heart.

"Less chatting. More kissing." Scarlett's hands grabbed the sides of his head, engulfing him entirely in her. Jason chuckled, reaching around her neck, grabbing the hood of her sweatshirt and draping it over her head, blocking her vision. She kept kissing, not even acknowledging the change.

"You can still kiss without seeing?" he asked, laughing.

"I once ran a 200-meter sprint with a bug stuck in my eye and still won. Don't doubt me," she mumbled, tracing his lips with hers.

"You can't doubt a genius. always prove you wrong." Scarlett flushed, resting her head on his chest. "That's another thing, since when can I call you 'Scar'? I'll admit I'm a little surprised you didn't elbow me just now." Jason cocked his head to one side, waiting for his answer.

"Since I decided I liked how it sounded coming from you."

"What does it sound like?"

"Like I'm a prize you're desperately trying to win. Like the sound of my name alone is worth all the Grammys in the world."

"Artist of the year sounds right for you, Scar. The masterpieces you can make with your mouth." He placed a finger on her bottom lip, and Scarlett kissed it lightly. "Your lips speak lyrics without any noise." He smiled, forgetting all about the pain in this moment.

"I'm flattered, Jason, truly," she said, batting her eyelashes. Scarlett hopped off Jason's bed, moving back to the chair she previously occupied. Jason grabbed her hand, opening it enough for him to slide his fingers in between hers.

"I wish you knew how long I've waited for this. How hard it was to pretend I wasn't." Jason breathed, stroking her knuckles with his thumb.

"For what moment?"

"Just being here with you. When I can see you with my eyes, can still taste you on my lips, and hear you in my ears. Everything about you overwhelms all my senses in a way I haven't known before. But now that I know it, I don't think I could live another way." He grabbed a strand of her hair, feeling its smooth texture.

"I've wanted you, Jason, for longer than I'd care to admit. Just not in this situation." She was right; the moment was golden, but the reason for that moment faded into rusted iron. And the truth of the matter was, Jason couldn't even remember all of it.

"Scar," he asked, locking his gaze on her.

"Mm?" Her eyes softened.

"I'm not high anymore."

Scarlett tensed, shoulders stiffening. "I would hope so, or kissing you would have been completely inappropriate." She smiled, but inside Scarlett knew what this meant. Jason wanted answers. Answers that Scarlett wasn't ready to give.

"Scarlett, please. I deserve to remember," Jason begged, and he could see Scarlett's heart break.

"No one deserves to remember this. Least of all you." Jason held her gaze and nodded. *It's ok.* He wanted to tell her. *You can't hurt me any more than he did.* Scarlett sighed.

"I don't know what happened before I found you, Jason, so I can only tell you what I saw." Her eyes grew wet, and Jason gave her hand a squeeze. "You had, um, blood and dirt all over you. I thought you were already dead, but then you moved. He hit you, Jason, your dad." Her voice cracked, but Jason was hardly paying attention anymore.

She began to explain how she found him and how she crept through his house to save him. The more she talked, the more Jason remembered. His mother was on the floor, begging her to leave. Brian promised to end Jason's life like he ended their family. He remembered fear, genuine terror like nothing else. And the peace that came when he realized there was nothing else he could do. By the time she'd finished, Jason's eyes were blurry with tears that he'd yet to shed.

"What are you thinking right now?" she whispered. Jason bowed his head, shaking it like that might rid him of the memories.

"I'm thinking I remember everything." His voice shook as much as his body did. Scarlett didn't say anything, didn't say 'I'm sorry' or 'you're so brave'. She knew better—knew that saying sorry didn't change anything. So, she didn't speak at all; instead, drawing closer, and taking Jason into her arms. His facade of unfeeling cracked like the ceramic pot. Jason cried, ugly, wet tears. He was sure he looked a mess, with messy hair and eyes that brimmed with red. Scarlett pulled him in tighter, wrapping her hands around his head and neck like she would protect him from whatever else was yet to come.

"I know, I know." She soothed, stroking his hair. He cried into her hoodie, no doubt soaking it with his tears, but Scarlett didn't move. She didn't shush him or tell him not to cry. Scarlett held and let him weep like a child into her arms because she knew if she wouldn't hold him, then no one else would.

"He was going to hurt her. I couldn't let him." Jason cried, barely audible. "Hurt who, Jason?"

"My mom. I didn't let him hurt her, so he hurt me." He cried hard, so ruggedly and broken. The sobs racked his body, and Jason hiccupped out his breath. He gave up, succumbing to the pain, allowing all the adrenaline to wear off and the fear of the situation wash over him like an acid beach. It reminded him of a movie he'd watched, *The Basketball Diaries*. He felt like Jim Caroll, crying like a lost little boy. It was all he could do. "He was going to kill me," Jason said. Over again, as every fragment of realization and torment and ache over the last eighteen years beat up on him. "He was going to kill me." He could faintly hear Scarlett sniffing, no doubt shedding tears of her own. Jason wished he could comfort her; he really did. But he couldn't anymore. For the first time in his life, he needed someone to just hold him. To love *him*. And in the warmth of Scarlett's arms, slowly the tears stopped, replaced by a comfortable silence. A feeling he hadn't felt in years. Unconditional, unfiltered love. He relaxed into Scarlett's hold, allowing himself to trust her enough to lower his guard.

She could be trusted. She could be trusted. She could be trusted.

He repeated this mantra as his episode of hysteria died down, replaced by exhaustion. His head throbbed, along with whatever other injuries Brian had inflicted on him. He could hear his heart in his head, pounding quickly, beating like a drum. But above all else, he could hear her, humming and whispering as she held Jason's head on her shoulder.

"I know, I love you, I know. I'm so sorry," she repeated, holding him like a mother holds their child with tender love. Jason fell asleep to the sound of her. Letting himself relax against one of the only people he knew he could trust. A trust that was formed less than a day ago, sure, but to Jason it still felt as strong and as valid as anyone else. Scarlett Artega was someone who loved him, someone who he could count on. That Jason knew to be true. On the cusp of sleep, he sensed a change in motion. Scarlett gently lifted his head from her shoulder, redirecting him to lie back on his bed. She tucked a piece of hair behind his ear, wiping away a tear from his face.

"No sad dreams, Jason." And he knew that no matter what, he wouldn't be able to have a nightmare. Not when Scarlett told him not to.

36

SCARLETT

He didn't tell her about the trial.

She didn't ask.

All Scarlett knew was that Brian was sentenced to twelve years in her local prison, and Jason would stay with his mother in a new apartment until he left for college. She saw Jason beforehand, mainly patched up apart from his braces, bandages, and scars. He wore Scarlett's favorite navy blue suit, with a light blue collared shirt underneath. His necklace was proudly displayed over the top, like it was the focal point of his outfit. The trial commenced two weeks after the initial attack, giving Jason time to heal and recover in the ICU. Jason didn't invite her to sit in, and Scarlett didn't blame him. She might've been the one who found him, but she was nothing more and doing that didn't entitle her to know everything about his life. She hoped, of course, that he would open up eventually, but now wasn't that time. Scarlett had to be alright with that.

Marcus had attended, as Scarlett predicted. When he visited just two days after that night, Marcus was a mess. It took both Jason and Scarlett an hour to calm him down, to convince him it wasn't his fault- that he couldn't have known.

"But I did know. I knew more than anyone else and still..." Marcus had lifted his eyes to Jason's, taking in the machinery. "Why didn't I notice? Why didn't you tell me it was this bad?" His voice cracked.

"You didn't notice because I was good at hiding it. Not noticing was sort of the point," he'd said. It was hard seeing him that way. To think that all along, he was going through something unimaginable while she was off picking arguments with him. To think that his best friend in the whole world couldn't save him, and that fact hurt Marcus badly. It was at that moment that Scarlett realized just how deep their bond went. He never left his side, leaving Scarlett to feel a little jealous. But when Scarlett knew how to make him smile and heal, Marcus knew how to make him laugh. The two went on for hours about anything and everything, from watching movies to Jason telling stories about Marcus's embarrassing childhood. And Marcus is steering clear of Jason's. He spent the rest of their time in the hospital with them, along with Scarlett's father, who'd joined not long after once the police reports and paperwork were finished like their own makeshift hospital family.

"He has a beautiful soul, but I think his heart might be a bit broken." He'd spoken. Good thing Scarlett specialized in repairing broken hearts —especially Jason's.

Scarlett sat on a bench outside the courtroom waiting for the finish. Marcus had texted her updates, like how long he'd be in jail for, and how Jason was holding up, though Scarlett wished she could be in there with him. She wouldn't be able to sit with him, but maybe just her presence . . . no. This was his life, and Scarlett was an intruder. Two large wooden doors swung open as a mass of people filed out of the room. First, it was just the viewers, followed by Jason and his mom. He led his mother by the arm, both looking shaken. Scarlett looked at Jason's mother and wondered how incredible this woman was, how much Jason loved her for him to sacrifice himself like that. She came forward to Scarlett, her kind eyes shining with pride. "Are you Scarlett?"

"I am." Not a second after the words left her mouth, she was wrapped up in a hug that could only come from a mother. And since the last time her own mother hugged her was before D.C., she drank in the feeling.

"Thank you for saving my son." The words hit hard. She knew it was true, but 'saved' seemed extreme.

"Of course, Mrs. Everett. But anyone would've done that, really." The woman shook her head.

"I didn't." She blinked, and a tear trailed down her face. "I'll never be able to say it enough, and while you may not understand, your mother would. You saved my life as much as Jason's. Thank you." She squeezed Scarlett's shoulders, then her own son's hand and left back through the crowd. Scarlett watched her go and felt Mrs. Everett's thankfulness wash through her.

"Hey, Scar," he said, voice hoarse.

Scarlett stood, planting her feet right before Jason's. She had to look up just to meet him in the eyes.

"Hey, roadkill." She opened her arms in a gesture, and Jason fell into them. His body melted, molded against hers. "It's over, Jason." She exhaled. "He's really gone now," she assured, running her fingers through his hair in a way she knew he liked.

He pulled out of the embrace, the tiniest hint of a smile on his freckled face. "I know. Is it weird that it kind of hurts? It shouldn't." Scarlett laughed bitterly.

"Why shouldn't it? He is still your father, Jason; you have the right to miss him. It doesn't make you a bad person to still want him." Jason looked up.

"But after everything I did, everything *he did*, missing him seems like the furthest thing in the world." He drew in a breath, dark eyes softening as Scarlett traced his jawline.

"Eighteen years, Jason. That's your whole life with him in it, and now he's not in it anymore. That must feel fucking *weird*. Don't feel ashamed for acknowledging that the person who's been there your whole life isn't in your life anymore," she whispered.

He just nodded, looking away like something else was on his mind. "So, what now?" Jason asked.

"What do you mean?"

"I mean, now that track is out of the picture. I hadn't thought about it until now, but that was my shot, Scarlett. I can't afford college without a scholarship. All my studying, the scholars' award, all for nothing?" His shoulders slumped, the weight of the situation crashing down on him.

"Not for nothing, you could still get a partial scholarship just for being a dedicated student. And you won't be hurt forever; they could still choose you for next year. You need to think positively." She smiled.

"You are by far the only positive thing in my life right now." Jason breathed on her neck, lips tickling her skin.

"Then think of me. It's not like you don't anyway, I see your glances." Jason chuckled, nose scrunching.

"You're very attentive. It looks good on you." His voice was deep, scratchy from days of bed rest and little conversation. He wanted to push on, to project all his worries about the future onto Scarlett, to confess every little thing that preoccupied his mind, though he had a feeling Scarlett would only scold him for thinking negatively. Who would have ever thought Scarlett Artega would care for his mental health?

"Enough stress about college, let's think about something else for a while. What are you doing for your birthday?" Scarlett asked. Technically, it had already passed during their long nights at the hospital, but Scarlett still wanted to celebrate.

"That's not exactly my biggest priority, but I'm not sure. Marcus offered to have us stay in Nevada for the weekend; his grandma lives there. Said he wants to give me the 'winter experience.'" Jason hummed, lighting up as he spoke. Scarlett creased her brow, and Jason smiled at the freckle above her eye.

"Nevada? I've never even seen the snow."

"Really? Never?" Scarlett shook her head. "Nope. I don't suppose you'd want me to tag along, would you?" She batted her eyelashes, in a way that made Jason reach over and plant a kiss on her forehead.

"What if I did want you to tag along?"

"Ask me then."

"Scarlett Artega," he said, placing his arms on her hips. "Would you do me the honor of coming to Nevada to celebrate my eighteenth birthday?" Jason smiled, revealing straight white teeth. Scarlett tapped her finger against her chin like she was deciding if he was worth her time or not. It was a teasing gesture that made Jason long for her all the more .

"I guess my schedule's free. After the championship, though," she pointed out. Right, finals.

"Does Coach know about this?" Scarlett asked, motioning to his crippled body.

"You didn't see him walk out? He was a little shaky the whole time, I mean, I'm sure anyone would be. But yes, he knows." Jason tucked a piece of hair behind her ear. "That doesn't mean I can't support you, though, does it?" Scarlett grinned, lighting up the dark courtroom hallway.

"You should make a sign."

"Already bought the poster board," Jason joked. Truly, he was completely bummed about missing. It had only been his dream for four years, and giving up something like that was far from easy, but Jason pushed on anyway because he knew this was important to Scarlett. It had been about him for long enough.

The day of the race came much faster than anticipated. Jason sat on the bleachers, crutches leaning up against the steel, and his hoodie was shrugged around his frame. He wore dark wash jeans and white Adidas, and he wore dark green face paint with smears across his face as a courtesy to New Wellis. Marcus sat next to him, and physically, he seemed fine. An injury like his so close to finals wasn't worth the risk, so he honorably sat the season out. That didn't stop him from attending every practice anyway, though. Coach Allen loved him, and so did the team, so it really wasn't much of a decision. Adam was at the end, joking with Marcus about something on his phone. He cracked a smile, laughing so loudly that Scarlett could hear it from where she was standing. Really, Adam should be warming up; his race was shortly after Scarlett's, but then again, when had Adam Hunt ever followed instructions step by step? It's not like Coach Allen would be pissed anyway, he had a soft spot for the blonde, though he didn't admit it.

Scarlett breathed in. It was a sunny day, with a definite chill in the air. Perfect for running. Jason spotted her warming up a bit away and caught her eye, blowing her an over dramatic kiss. Scarlett replied with a middle finger and a cocky smile. Disregarding the crude gesture, she smiled with a sincerity that only meant love. A shine in her eye, identical to adoration. She saw the three of them sitting in the bleachers —Jason, Adam, and Marcus. Scarlett couldn't help but laugh at him. Jason had actually brought a sign, which he displayed proudly above his head. It was a white poster with large green letters that read: *Life is a series of choices, and each choice leads us down a different path.* It might not make sense to others, but Scarlett recognized the quote from her favorite book immediately, and she understood what he was saying. She had control over whether she won or not. She could win this race and secure a scholarship or lose and let down the only people who really cared about her. She gave Jason a firm nod, then let her gaze travel further down the bleachers.

Her parents sat in the bottom row, with a bored expression on her mother's face, and an interested mask on her father's. At least he could pretend to be attentive, unlike the woman sitting beside him. 'It's not your fault your parents' fires lost their coals.' Abigail's voice rang in her mind. Before she could think, Scarlett's feet were taking her towards where her parents sat. As she walked, her confidence grew, her worries replaced by a sense of finality that she knew would only come once she'd done this.

"Shouldn't you be warming up, Scarlett?" Her mother asked, raising an eyebrow. Her brows creased together like her daughter's did. "I would hate for this interaction to be the reason you lose."

"It's alright, honey, she's warmed up enough. What's up, Scar?" Mr. Artega asked, grinning.

Scarlett's heart panged at his genuine interest in her, in her life. Mrs. Artega just rolled her eyes. *Just tell them, you'll only have the rest of your life to regret it.* Helpful, she thought. She took a deep breath in, relishing the moments before her life could change. Scarlett hoped she would remember the moments before disappointment engulfed her, or if that, too, would vanish with her shame.

"I need to talk to you about something. And I need you to listen to me." Her mother laughed, brushing her hair off her gray eyes.

"You act as if we're some terrible parents. Of course, I'll listen to you."

"I hope, because sometimes you say that, and end up twisting my words and —"

"Now you're wasting my time, please get on with it, dear." Scarlett fumed. It was always her time being wasted, never anyone else's. Always the world that revolved around her —the one true sun. Everyone else was just measly planets around it. And Scarlett was an asteroid in her life if anything. Her stomach ached, caused by the desire to get away from her mother. To stop being treated like an outlier. Fueled by the intense emotions swirling around her like a gust of wind in a storm, Scarlett took the leap.

"I just wanted you to know that this is the last race you will see me run track. So, I hope you enjoy it." Something was left in Scarlett's chest at the confession; she felt lighter than she'd ever felt before.

"Don't be ridiculous, what about your scholarship, what about Oregon?" Mrs. Artega cried.

"I'm not being ridiculous; I'm just realizing that what I want for myself isn't what you want for me. And last time I checked, this is my life, so I decided not to waste it on things not made for me, " she stated. As she spoke, the words became truer to herself.

"You're really going to let this girl give up everything she's worked for?" Her mother threw her hands up in the air, turning to her father. He had a solemn expression on his face, calculating what had just happened.

"I...I'm not sure. Scarlett, you've put so much into this. How do you know you won't regret this?" His voice was deep and calm. Scarlett admired his ability to keep his emotions in check.

"Honestly, I can't say that I won't. But right now, the thought of going to college for track and doing all this just because Milo did —just because it's what you want—is nauseating. It's not me, it's you all. And I'm sorry that maybe you didn't get to do some things when you were younger and you regret that, but I'm not going to let you project those regrets onto my perfectly good life!" For the first time, a small corner of her father's mouth upturned.

"Then I think there's not much we can do to stop you, can we? You always were the most stubborn." His eyes were sad, carrying with them the weight of his expectations and dreams for her. But his soul was happy, Scarlett could tell that much. She shook her head.

"No. This is something I've already decided." She grasped one of her father's hands and one of her mother's, who was scowling so hard, Scarlett thought her face might be stuck like that. "As for my scholarship, I wouldn't get that, you're right. But I did hear back from UCLA. I got in, you guys. And they're willing to give me a four thousand dollars per year scholarship. I know it's not what you wanted, it's not track, it's not Oregon State, but it's what I want. Part of me doesn't care what you think because I'm doing it anyway . But a large part of me, the part that's your daughter —"

She locked eyes with her mother, emphasizing every word, "wants your approval more than anything in the world." She finished, taking a sharp breath in. Her father was smiling, pride on his face. But her mother?

"Has everything I've done for you flown out the window? The money we've paid for private coaches, the time we've spent watching your progress, all meant nothing?" Pain flared in her chest.

"I know, I know. And I don't know how to get you to understand this, but this has never been my dream. Think —I mean, really think about it. Have I ever once asked for those private lessons, or the hours spent at the gym?" Her mother's look faltered for just a moment, reassessing everything she'd known to be true about her daughter. "Those were never my goals. They were Milo's. And you couldn't handle him leaving for college, so you took it out on me. You made me his clone, Mom. And I don't want to do it anymore. So, I'm sorry, I really am sorry if I'm disappointing you. I'm sorry if you won't look at me as your daughter again, but I can't live like this." Scarlett looked down, unable to look at her mother any longer. "I won't live like this. I'm done living as Milo's shadow. And I'm done running for you." She didn't waste time looking at her mother's shocked look. Didn't turn back when she yelled for her to come back, didn't watch as her father took her arm, leading her hysterical mother out of the meet. Scarlett locked her face, practicing the expression she'd known forever, and jogged to the starting lineup.

She was going to miss that little ref with the large megaphone. He stood on a step stool, raising the red amplifier to his lips.

"What'd they say?" Meghan asked, standing beside her on the line.

"Dad was fine. My mom was not." Meghan reached out a hand, rubbing her back comfortingly.

"I bet it's a relief, though, isn't it?" Scarlett breathed out a laugh, shaking off her hands.

"Like you could never imagine."

"Welcome to the 2024 track final. We have fierce competitors from Camden, New Wellis, and St. Coleman's today, and we have only the very best from all three schools. And only one person can win the girls 200-meter sprint for their school." He cleared his throat, wiping a bead of sweat forming on his brow.

"Lane 1, Veda Kalizan from St. Coleman's, lane 2, Kacey Tillman from Camden High, lane 3, Miley Yang from St. Coleman's, lane 4, Scarlett Artega from New Wellis, Lane 5, Meghan Truth from New Wellis, lane 6, Charlotte Williams from Camden High, and lane 8, Zoe Boyer from New Wellis." The short man bent over, placing a hand on his knee as he recovered from the use of breath. Meghan laughed silently at the little man, and Scarlett smiled. Her smile only grew when she saw Jason, laser-focused on her. 'Pretend there's a snake chasing you,' he mouthed. Scarlett tilted her head back and laughed. *Using my weaknesses to strengthen me. Nice going Everett.*

"Ladies, last call for line up." The ref shouted, so Scarlett sent Jason a last wink before readying her mindset. This really was it, now that her parents were in the loop. Her last race had to be her best one; there wasn't another way around it. She took Meghan's hand, giving it a squeeze which the brunette reciprocated.

"Ladies, on your marks." She set up her position, lining up her toe at the start.

"Get set."

She arched her back, butt sticking into the air. Scarlett didn't think she'd ever get comfortable doing that. The blare of the gun shot off in a second, and without even thinking, she launched forward, running like she'd never run before in her entire life. Scarlett wasn't sure what fueled this, but it was as if every muscle in her body was dunked in gasoline and lit on fire. She was a rocket. Scarlett passed Meghan, Kacey, Zoe, and Miley quickly, gaining speed. Charlotte and Veda were overtaken next, falling behind the flash of light that Scarlett had become. She felt invincible, indestructible. Scarlett poured her every thought into her running, her every emotion, trauma, goodbye, and hello. She took the pain from seeing Jason the way he was when she found him and added that into her pace. She took the cracks in her facade that Beau inflicted, the betrayal that she felt, and added that in, too. Each experience, each sense of hurt, only fueled her now. Everything else was a blur as she flew across the finish line, well ahead of her competitors.

"Scarlett Artega, with a 21.86, this is a new record for the girls 200-meter sprint, and a win for New Wellis in the championship tournament!" The audience erupted, and Scarlett felt someone grab her shoulders. Meghan beamed at her, having gotten third herself. Someone draped a gold medal around her neck, and she shook their hands out of instinct. Everything was solid, sudden, and overwhelming. Scarlett smiled, thanking her competition, and acting as she should, but inside, she was thinking about one thing.

"Scar!" he called, and she took off. Forgetting all about the aching in her body from her race, Scarlett tore back down the track, towards the voice. Jason was standing, leaning against the silver fence, reaching down for her. Scarlett laughed as she ran, moisture forming in her eyes. He was right there, so happy, so alive. She reached the bottom of the fence, jumping up and throwing herself into him.

"You did it, you did it, you did it," he repeated, hugging her with such fierceness, Scarlett thought she would suffocate. Gladly, for him, she would die a thousand times over, if only to see him like this again. "Scarlett Artega, you wonderful woman!" He laughed into the air, taking in the moment. Scarlett breathed him, realizing for the first time that she was genuinely happy. Her smile grew when Jason kissed the freckle above her eye.

"Wait, here." Scarlett lifted the medal from her neck, pulling it up over her head. She met Jason's eyes, offering him undivided eye contact as she lifted the award up and over Jason's own head.

"What? You won this, it's yours." His voice was convincing, telling Scarlett to take it back. His face told a different story. Jason looked over the medal, feeling the cool material in his fingers.

"Don't need it. I happen to have a prize worth much more than a high school medal." Reaching out, Scarlett grabbed the circle of metal from his fingers, pressing it back down onto his chest before he had the chance to remove it. "I don't care if it 's mine.' As long as you're mine, that's all I need." She felt his shaky exhale, and upon meeting his expression, the broad smile that spread across his face — moving his freckles, like she loved.

"I'm yours, Scarlett. I've been yours. Every time you crease your brow, I'm yours. Every time you look at me with those eyes like a storm, I'm yours. Scarlett, every time you breathe, I'm yours." Jason stroked her cheek, reveling in his confession. Scarlett made sure to exhale extra loudly, laughing a little as she did.

37
JASON

The world as a whole was confusing.

The trial was confusing, with accusations and confessions that he didn't know how to handle.

College was confusing, an uncertainty of ever having the university experience he'd dreamed of his whole life.

The only thing Jason seemed to understand was that he needed to have fun.

"Adam, get over here, we're leaving!" Marcus called, tossing him a can of beer. The blonde fumbled, dropping the container, which sprayed everywhere the second it touched the ground.

"Damn! Got any other, Marcus?" Adam batted his lashes, pleading incessantly.

Marcus rolled his eyes, smiling. "Last one, and don't soak my driveway again."

Jason watched as Adam proudly caught the second beer, cracking it open. Marcus had finally convinced him to venture to Nevada, after a long string of 'are you sure' and 'you need to live for once.' Despite his worries, Jason was undoubtedly excited about the outing. Himself, Adam, Marcus, Meghan, Scarlett, and Zoe piled into Adam's dad's

Chevrolet, with barely enough seats to hold them all. Scarlett was driving after many complaints from Adam.

"You're like Paris Geller," he said, flopping down in the backseat.

"If I die in a car crash, it's going to be at my own hand," Scarlett quoted, flashing Adam a cocky smile. Jason felt his heart pound, like it did whenever he had the chance to be this close to her. He sat in the passenger seat, enjoying a Snapple Peach rather than alcohol.

"How do you like being a passenger princess?" Scarlett whispered, the scent of vanilla drifting off her. Jason leaned closer, scrunching his nose.

"I'd be the passenger princess forever if it means you're my queen." He felt a sense of accomplishment when Scarlett flushed. It was like a little reward for his efforts. "Music, anyone?" Jason asked, answered by a chorus of shouts from the backseat. He reached for the stereo, blocked by a hand already resting on the device.

"Not so fast, roadkill. The driver always chooses," she announced, flicking through the playlists.

"Adam, what is this?" Scarlett laughed as she clicked on a playlist titled: *Adams Bangers*, composed of mostly Mitski and Boygenius.

Marcus laughed, leaning over the seat to take part in the actions. "Um, excuse me, don't judge, we're all allowed to have interests." Adam crossed his arms, sticking his nose up in superiority.

Scarlett raised her hands in surrender. "No judgment here, only admiration. Mitski is an icon." She scrolled through the other playlists, settling on a hype road trip mix.

Jason couldn't lie, Scarlett had good taste. Jason leaned his head against the window, watching the trees fly by as music blared. They took turns singing along the ride, almost like karaoke but with six teenagers who couldn't sing for shit. Jason quietly took out his phone, recording Marcus's rendition of Riptide by Vance Joy. He had the complete intention of using this as blackmail later, as payback for his Swan Lake fiasco from last month. Unfortunately, he wasn't half bad, making Jason wish he'd have chosen a harder song. Instead of gloating, he just focused his attention on her. Jason wanted to laugh. Scarlett wore a black long-sleeve shirt with lace on the collar and bottom.

"You aren't going to be cold in that?" He propped his face up on an elbow, blinking down at her.

"Should I have packed warmer?" she mumbled, eyebrows raising in curiosity.

"Should you have?" Marcus cracked up from the backseat, earning him a shove from Meghan.

"You can borrow some of my stuff. I brought some extra coats," she offered.

"Only because the last time you saw snow, I had to provide for you," Zoe pointed out Meghan rolled her eyes.

"I've learned from my mistakes." For all their bickering, they did get things done. Solving problems in less than thirty seconds. Jason was glad about that; he really didn't have the money to spend on a new jacket. If required, though, he knew it wouldn't be a decision at all before he was buying her the fluffiest, warmest coat he could find.

"Look!"

Jason peeled his eyes from his current read, *The Chain,* to find Scarlett positively bouncing up and down in her seat. She gawked at the powdery white substance covering everything like a winter village. It took Jason a second before he realized. *She's never seen snow before.* It was then that he decided to give her the best first snow day possible.

"The snow? Yeah, it's alright." He turned away to his window, laughing when Scarlett grabbed his sweater collar, tugging him back to her.

"It's beautiful, not alright! Look at this and tell me you don't think it's beautiful." Her gaze darted around the road, at the trees piled high with snow, the ground painted in a white blanket.

"It's beautiful. I just think there are some things even more magnificent." His eyes focused on her, smiling and so sweet.

"You're a flirt." She brushed off the compliment but blushed deeply.

It felt good to make her happy like this, but it was hard to make her only happy when he knew something that would make her ecstatic. The weight of his secret pressed against his chest like a weight. Eventually, Jason took over driving after much convincing from Scarlett.

"You're going to crash if you keep staring at the snow, just trust me," he'd said, and she cracked after he promised to go slow. As much as he hated driving on ice, it was worth it to see her glowing with joy, face pressed against the window as snowflakes flickered past the glass.

The drive was quick after that, distracted by the scenery, and of course, Scarlett. The car pulled into a wooden driveway, and Scarlett launched out of the vehicle the second it was parked. Jason smiled at her enthusiasm, stepping out of the car himself. The others piled out like a clown car, with Adam carrying Zoe out of the vehicle and to the porch.

"You are by far the most over dramatic person I've ever met," he grumbled.

"I can't get my UGGs wet!" she claimed, but Jason caught the wink she sent to Scarlett. Marcus helped Meghan into the cabin, where they were welcomed by an older woman in a green nightgown, curlers still in her graying hair. Adam and Zoe weren't far behind, the raven-haired girl clinging onto Adam's back like a koala.

"Damn, you're *strong*!" she cheered, pumping her arms into the air, while Adam struggled below.

"C'mon, let's go," Scarlett said from beside him, nudging Jason's arm. "You go on, I'll meet you."

"Important business to attend to?"

"Something like that. Go, really, I'll be right in."

He planted a gentle kiss on her forehead, ensuring his promise. Scarlett frowned, but obliged, trying not to slip as she padded across the snow to the front door. Jason took his phone out, looking over the email he'd been double-checking for days. It was weird, like Jason thought the material might vanish into thin air if he wasn't constantly checking it, but each time he opened the email, it was right there.

Dear Mr. Everett,

As you are aware, the recent events involving Mr. Brian Everett and Mrs. Jamie Everett, as well as the assault involving you, Mr. Jason Everett. Due to the charges filed against Mr. Brian Everett, as listed here. Child abuse, battery causing great bodily injury, domestic violence, and aggravated assault. You are eligible to compensation of $27000 paid by the State of California for all physical and emotional traumas received from this experience. You have also chosen to *press charges against Mr. Brian Everett for his felony and other charges, resulting in another $7000 deposit to yourself and Mrs. Jamie Everett as restitution. As a result of his actions, Mr. Brian Everett has been sentenced to twelve years in the county state prison, which will be served in their entirety at Salinas Valley State Prison unless otherwise informed. The jury provides their utmost apologies and condolences for your experience.*

Sincerely,

Jude Hendrix

California Victim Compensation Board

It wasn't much in the grand scheme of things, a total of $34000 for both him and his mother. Not much, but enough. The apartment his mother had rented was already paid for, meaning this money could be for him. For college. Florida University was roughly one hundred seventy thousand dollars for a four-year out-of-state student. Hell, even with compensation, it was still a stretch. But Jason had his job. He had funding, and with hopes, would have financial aid. They weren't poor, but they weren't rich enough to qualify. Jason smiled at his phone before tucking it away in his pocket and meeting the others inside.

Less than an hour later, the group changed into warmer clothes, Scarlett into a puffer jacket a little too long for her, and Jason into a black North Face puffer that hugged him firmly. Scarlett had her hair tied up into a curled ponytail, with two curled strands framing her face. Her nose was tinged pink from the cold, and Jason had the sudden urge to touch it. They found white ski pants for her to wear, matching her coat, so she positively looked like a snow bunny.

"You look like a polar bear," Jason remarked, tugging her close to him.

"Laugh all you want, at least I'm warm." She snuggled deeper into the clothes.

"You're forgetting, Scar, you're the only one that forgot warm clothes; the rest of us are plenty warm. But it's nice that you're thinking of us," he retorted, giving in and touching the tip of Scarlett's nose. She snorted, skipping off the second they reached a patch of snow in a clearing. It was like a dream, tall pine trees surrounding a perfect little patch of earth. Well, it was perfect. Now the neatly fallen snow was torn up, piles forming as Scarlett made a feeble attempt at a snow angel.

"No, not quite sweetie." Jason lay down next to her, feeling the cool snow even under his layers of clothes.

"You spread out your arms and legs and bring them up and down—like this." He raised his arms in the snow, bringing his legs together and apart at the same time. Scarlett tried again, getting the tempo completely wrong.

"Slower, you're making a snow *angel,* not a run over one." He smiled, reminiscent of the time she'd 'saved his life' outside of Safeway. Strange, it seemed she had a habit of saving his life. Scarlett just stuck her tongue out and tried again, this time doing a bit better.

"You guys look like an old couple," Meghan said, standing with a hand on her hip.

"Oh, let me live my life, Meg!" Scarlett said, laughing. There was snow in her hair, scattered around her dirty blonde ponytail as it fell.

"Meghan duck!" Scarlett shouted, but it was too late. A large ball of snow struck her shoulder, sending the brunette toppling into the snow.

"Ha!" Zoe shouted triumphantly.

Not a moment later, she herself was struck by a ball of snow thrown by Marcus. Jason could tell it was him because he threw it so gently, it didn't even shatter.

"Give it some arm, Marcus, like so." Adam quipped, winding up his arm like a slingshot before sending a snowball flying towards Jason, hitting him on the thigh.

"Ow!" He called out, gripping his leg. Adam went pale.

"Shit, man, I'm sorry I—" Jason whirled around, smashing his own snowball on the top of Adam's head.

"There you go, your crown, sir." Jason mock bowed, swearing his allegiance to the soaked boy.

"You're lucky I don't tackle people with broken bones, or you'd be a foot under the snow right now," he growled. Jason smirked, plopping a heap of snow onto his own head.

"There. *Even*." Adam cracked a smile as they continued frolicking in the snow like children. At other times, Jason might feel embarrassed playing around like this. But now, it seemed that was all he needed to cheer him up. That, and the view of his gorgeous. . . girlfriend? *Maybe girlfriend*, in the snow.

"Hey, follow me," Jason said, reaching his arm out to Scarlett. She sat up from her snow angel, white snowflakes covering the back of her head.

"Whisking me away somewhere?" She raised a brow.

"Only if you'll let me."

"You're allowed."

"Then hurry up, you're moving too slow."

Scarlett scoffed, feigning hurt. "Don't blame me, it's hard to walk in the snow." Jason realized that while he had snow boots, Scarlett was wearing only her sneakers, which must be soaked.

"Fine." He wrapped an arm around her legs and another around her back, lifting her like she weighed nothing.

"What the hell are you doing?" she exclaimed, wrapping her arms around his neck.

"Carrying you."

"Well, I can see that, but I mean, why?"

"You said it yourself, it's hard to walk in the snow. And I at least have real shoes."

"You have broken bones."

"I *had* broken bones. They're healing."

Scarlett scoffed, but Jason didn't put her down. He carried her to a clearing, through the trees, not too far from the others, but far enough. He set Scarlett down gently in the snow, loving how she landed on her eyelashes.

"Can I ask what we're doing here?" Jason leaned forward, kissing her freckle.

"Your eighteenth birthday party, we danced. Remember that?" he asked, his voice low. A tinge of red crept up Scarlett's cheeks, painting them an even brighter pink than what the cold did.

"How could I forget it? You wouldn't kiss me." She sounded embarrassed, like she regretted the whole night. Jason knew he did.

"You were drunk; I didn't want to take advantage of you." He brought his arm up over Scarlett's, leading her to spin. She did, hair twirling around her as she moved.

"If you haven't noticed, you're not drunk anymore. So, I figured a redo was in order." Jason brought Scarlett's hand to his lips, kissing it lightly. "Care to dance, Scar?"

"I was hoping you'd say that." She breathed, placing her hands on his shoulders, fingers lacing around his neck. Jason moved to place his hands on her shoulders, but remembered the hospital—Scarlett removing his hands and placing them where she wanted them. He lowered his grip to her hips, gripping her tightly. They swayed lightly, not moving Jason's foot too much. He'd wrapped a bag around the cast, but Scarlett told him he could never be too cautious. It fell into a sort of rhythm, with the two drawing closer with each passing breath. Scarlett leaned her head into the crook of Jason's neck, and Jason felt a sense of protectiveness over her. He tightened his grip on her ever so slightly. He had her now; he was not losing her.

"Hey. Jason, you're not wearing your AirPods. This is new for you." *Damn, she's so observant —this magnificent woman.*

"What if I said you're much more fun to listen to?" She looked taken aback.

"What?"

"I told you I would take them out once I found someone else worth listening to. If I could just make you laugh, it's more than every song ever composed just to hear it," Jason admitted, and it was true. He'd hardly even noticed he had stopped wearing them, but that made the realization that she was his music all the stronger.

"I'm glad I have that kind of effect on people."

"Wrong. You have that effect on me. They can have their music, and I can have you." He hugged her close, too afraid to let go. Too afraid to lose her.

"Scarlett I—"

"I have something to tell you," Scarlett said, eyes shining. "Sorry, you go first."

"No, you." Jason insisted, meeting her gray eyes. She sighed, looking like a goddess.

"I know what I'm gonna do. For college, I mean. No track."

"No track? Why?" Jason couldn't help but widen his eyes in surprise. Since when did she want to quit track? And since when did she know what to do with her life?

"It wasn't my dream; it was Milo's and my parents'. It just took me longer than I'd hoped to realize that. But not all bad, though, because now I have a plan." She smiled up at him, arms still wrapped around him like a blanket of vanilla.

"Tell me."

"I got into UC with a partial scholarship. I'm going to study Spanish, Jason. And then, be a professor someday. It took me long enough to realize that, but now that I know. I know that it's right if that makes any sense. It's my life, not theirs. A really smart person showed me that." Jason saw the spark in her eyes, the passion that flowed from her voice, and he knew it was right, too.

"Wow, I mean wow!" He lifted her up, spinning around in a circle. "You're going to do incredible things, Scarlett. Just one thing—promise me I'll be there to see them?" He needed to know, needed to have that finality, that Scarlett was his and no one else's.

"Is this your weird way of asking me to be your girlfriend?" She cocked her head, brows creasing.

"I thought it was cute."

"Everything you do is cute, Jason, and yes. Always yes." She kissed him fiercely, and Jason could taste the Strawberry

ChapStick on her lips. They pulled away, both flustered and greedy for more. But first, something else.

"Your turn. What were you gonna say?"

"First, what did your mom say?" Jason remembered the museum, when Scarlett's mother had flipped about her almost not qualifying. He saw that he had just read that message, and was glad Scarlett didn't want to read it. He had a feeling that if she wanted to, he wouldn't bring himself to hand her the phone.

"Pissed at first. Really pissed."

"She can't be that pissed if she let you come to Nevada." A small smile broke out on Scarlett's face.

"No. It took some time, but she came around. Turns out her mom made her run track, too. I played the generational trauma card." Jason let out a laugh.

"Only you, Scarlett, could use your mother's childhood to get what you want."

"I'm full of hidden talents." Scarlett shrugged. "Now tell me!" She tugged on his arm.

Jason inhaled, a slight smile parting his lips. "Read this."

He handed her his phone and pulled up the email. Scarlett read it, eyes darting across the page as she mumbled the letter's contents. When she finished, her jaw was on the floor. "Thirty-four thousand dollars, Jason?!" He nodded, unable to keep the smile at bay.

"Do you know what this means, Scar? With this, and my job. I don't need the scholarship. With financial aid, I can pay for FSU." He laughed at the whole thing. The most traumatic event of his life, yet somehow it yielded the one thing he wanted most in life. Jason saw the moment the realization hit her, as her whole being seemed to grow brighter.

"You can pay." She repeated. "You can pay, and you don't need a scholarship! Jason, this is, well, this—"

"It's everything I've wanted. Apart from you, of course, but we've just checked that one off, haven't we?" Scarlett laughed, high-pitched and genuine.

"Finally, for once, *for once,* I don't have to worry about working, or making sure the bills get in. Once I'm healed, I could even run again and not care if I win or not. I could come in last, Scarlett! And it wouldn't matter, I'm already accepted!"

"You never have to win again."

"I never have to win again."

"How about that? We did it, *damn.*" They settled into silence once more. Scarlett leaned against Jason as they danced slowly around the forest.

"Jason?" Jason hummed in response.

"Earlier, you said every breath you're mine. What about after that?" She didn't take her head off his shoulder, as if she was afraid letting go for one second would scare him off. After her last breath? Well, simple. Jason would go mad.

"I'll dance with you, like this, in heaven and the clouds forever." He kissed the top of her head, preserving the moment. She seemed to relax a little in his hold at the confirmation.

"I just don't want this time with you to be lost. Now that we have college plans and everything. . ." Jason understood what she meant. She was scared, scared of losing him, scared that these moments wouldn't last forever. His heart was clenched at the thought that she would worry even for a moment about him leaving, with college coming between them.

"Scarlett, listen to me. I will always have time for you. Always." He pulled back for an instant, tilted her chin up to face him. She flushed and looked away. Jason straightened.

"Hey! Hey—let me see you." She laughed breathily and faced him. He pulled her in closer, so that she might feel the rhythm of his heart just as it pounded at the hospital. Just as it had been pounding since she saw the darkness in Jason. Since she saw the no entry sign and decided to stay anyway .

"I will *always* have time for you." He kissed her neck, imagined her smile, and kissed it again. "And if I don't, I'll beg Horae herself on my hands and knees for more." He thought back to his history class and was suddenly glad that he'd remembered the Greek mythology unit.

Scarlett smiled slowly, and Jason had a vision of a sun slowly rising as it grew. " It's OK. I know you will." She melted into him again, and Jason felt whole.

It was uncertain, of course, but it was whole. He didn't know why, or how, but he knew it was enough. And sometimes, when things are good, you don't question them. Would a homeless man question a passerby handing them fifty dollars? No, they would take it and be grateful. So that's what Jason did.

He took it and resolved to live his life with as much grace and thankfulness as he could. Scarlett was worried no one would ever understand why she quit, but he knew that her brother and *mother* would never forgive her for throwing all that away. She imagined herself years from now, teaching her students the exact language that had motivated her academics for years. She figured they'd have questions, doubts. She always did. They would ask Scarlett why she gave up on running and why she never went to the Olympics after setting a record.

She would simply say, "It wasn't my dream. Just something I was good at, but that really wasn't enough after all."

She would continue with her lesson, and that was that. With Jason by her side, dancing with her slowly into their future, Scarlett truly doubted she'd mind the questions. And Jason could still run track once he healed, but he doubted he ever would. The action of the sport would forever hold memories of his father that Jason didn't want to think of ever again. But now, he didn't have to. Running could be a hobby, not an escape route. He would never have to run for money, or for a scholarship, or for his life ever again. Jason held Scarlett in his arms, any remaining throbbing in his leg instantly vanquished by the presence of this girl . He spun again, and again. He wanted her. For so long, he wanted her, and now she was here, now she *wanted* him. Scarlett Artega, queen of the track, now queen of his heart and everything Jason could offer—*would* offer, wanted him.

"I am never letting you go," he whispered into the crook of her neck.

"Bold of you to assume I'd ever let you," she said against his chest. Jason could feel the warmth of her breath through his many layers on his skin. He could feel the love that was Scarlett warming his own heart. It had been a while, he thought, since someone wanted to do that. He didn't care if anyone else ever would. She was all he needed. And right then, Jason knew why. He caught a piece of the sun. Bright, burning, and beautiful. He chuckled softly, thinking about their high school years. How much time could he have gotten back had they only gotten over their feud, fueled by dreams they never really had? It didn't matter. Not when he had the rest of his life to make up for it. And like the glowing being of warmth that was Scarlett, a truth that he despised then became the one truth that he held onto now. It was the reason he ran with her, and he always would. It was the reason he loved her. She knew him—like no one else ever had. Like no one else ever would. Only her.

ACKNOWLEDGMENTS

This is truly incredible. If you had told me a year ago that I would be a published author at fifteen, I probably would have laughed in your face.

I have so many people to thank—so many people who have helped me along this journey. Let's start!

My parents—Mom, you gave birth to me, so it's only right that you're first on this list. Your motivation and confidence in me ultimately shaped my dedication to writing this novel, and I am forever grateful.

Dad, I couldn't have done this without you. Every late night you spent helping me download files, every trip to B&N to gather information (and coffee)—each moment was an experience I will never forget.

My siblings! Peyton, Mason, Lucas, and Paola—you guys are so amazing, and I love you all so much more than I show it.

Mason and Lucas, you two have been by my side since birth, and I know that no matter what, I'll always have two sidekicks to back me up. Peyton, you've been my inspiration for so long, and while that was probably annoying at times, you've always meant the world to me. I hope I made you proud!

To my friends, I cannot name you all here (and am so blessed to have so many), but I'll just say AZAAZALEA for life!

My best friend Zoe Dyce—you are without a doubt one of the best humans I've ever met. These last ten years have been the best of my life, and I genuinely don't remember a time when you weren't in it (insert shark emoji and jellyfish emoji).

To my other book friends—Ella, I know I can always call you at 3:00 a.m. when the enemies finally become lovers. Josephine, I am so grateful fate brought us together. You're incredible!

To my editor, the wonderful Marinel Balde—thank you for bringing the dreams of a fifteen-year-old girl to life! You have sparked a career for me that will hopefully change the world one day!

English teachers! I love English teachers, and I've been blessed with some of the best! Melissa Randall, this is for you. I truly would not have begun writing without you—and perhaps without my eighth-grade speech I was mortified to deliver.

Some other people who I adore and motivated me along this journey—Sufjan Stevens, Lynn Painter, Chloe Walsh, Kailey Holbrook, Conan Gray, and so many others!

Finally, to my readers—it's still so wild to be able to say "my readers." The fact that I have any at all means everything. But if you're reading this, it means you fit that category and for that I thank you. Every line you read is a testament to my dream, which you've helped make a reality. I love you all!

Anyone else I could not fit in here—know that I love you and every one of you has a special place in my heart.

Also, a special shout-out to my dogs, for staying up all night with me while I wrote. They've seen me in the editing trenches.

See you soon!

Want to learn more about how
WHY THEY RUN
was created?

Go to:
<u>zoeywheelerbooks.com/dearfutureauthor</u>

or scan the QR code below for free
writing courses, tips, and tools!